NOV 26 2015
P9-DWI-703

POWERLESS

DISCARD

POWERLESS

TIM WASHBURN

PINNACLE BOOKS
Kensington Publishing Corp.
www.kensingtonbooks.com

PINNACLE BOOKS are published by

Kensington Publishing Corp.
119 West 40th Street
New York, NY 10018

Copyright © 2015 Tim Washburn

All rights reserved. No part of this book may be reproduced in any form or by any means without the prior written consent of the publisher, excepting brief quotes used in reviews.

If you purchased this book without a cover, you should be aware that this book is stolen property. It was reported as "unsold and destroyed" to the publisher, and neither the author nor the publisher has received any payment for this "stripped book."

All Kensington titles, imprints, and distributed lines are available at special quantity discounts for bulk purchases for sales promotions, premiums, fund-raising, educational, or institutional use. Special book excerpts or customized printings can also be created to fit specific needs. For details, write or phone the office of the Kensington sales manager: Kensington Publishing Corp., 119 West 40th Street, New York, NY 10018, attn: Sales Department; phone 1-800-221-2647.

This book is a work of fiction. Names, characters, businesses, organizations, places, events, and incidents either are the product of the author's imagination or are used fictitiously. Any resemblance to actual persons, living or dead, events, or locales is entirely coincidental.

PINNACLE BOOKS and the Pinnacle logo are Reg. U.S. Pat. & TM Off.

ISBN-13: 978-0-7860-3653-0
ISBN-10: 0-7860-3653-2

First printing: November 2015

10 9 8 7 6 5 4 3 2 1

Printed in the United States of America

First electronic edition: November 2015

ISBN-13: 978-0-7860-3654-7
ISBN-10: 0-7860-3654-0

To Gary Goldstein,
for believing,

and to Tonya,
for hitching your wagon to mine

ACKNOWLEDGMENTS

Thanks to Gary Goldstein for being willing to take a chance. My deepest gratitude to all those at Kensington who worked on *Powerless*, including Lou Malcangi, for the terrific cover design, and Arthur Maisel. Thanks to my agent, Jim Donovan, for his advice and guidance through the intricacies of the publishing business.

Although *Powerless* is my first published novel, there was much that came before. The one person other than my wife who's read everything I've written is Kristi Goodwin Self, M.D. Thanks, Kristi, for your comments and advice. Thanks also to Marcus and Pamela Whitt for perusing some of my earlier work.

I don't know who's more excited about the novel's release, me or my parents, Loren and Frances Washburn. *It's here, Mom!* Our children are the center of our universe. Thanks, Kelsey and husband, Andrew Snider, Nickolas, and Karley for brightening our world. Without you, life would be an empty shell. Thanks to Jack and Sue Cress for creating the woman who became my wife.

And finally–Tonya. You are a wonderful wife, a caring physician, a nurturing mother, who also happens to be my best friend. Your support has never wavered and I'm forever grateful. Thanks for being the love of my life and for journeying with me on this meandering path called life.

SEPTEMBER 29

CHAPTER 1

National Oceanic and Atmospheric Administration
Space Weather Prediction Center, Boulder, Colorado
Wednesday, September 29, 6:42 A.M.

The hushed darkness of the observation room is a breeding ground for sleep—especially for Daniel, this semester's intern. Tasked as the lone overnight worker, he is waging war against the heaviness of his eyelids during the final hour of his shift at the Space Weather Prediction Center. As his head droops to his chest a shrill noise pierces the silence so harshly he claps his hands over his ears.

Daniel rockets out of the chair as if being ejected from a flaming-out fighter jet and stumbles from one computer monitor to another in a frantic search for the alarm's source. With a shaky finger he thumbs his thick glasses farther up his nose as he races around the small room. This is the first time any type of warning has sounded during his two-month stay. His panic escalates. An alarm signaling . . . what? An asteroid on a collision course with Earth? The explosion of the sun? Or simply a minor malfunction?

His predecessor had briefly mentioned something about alarms but no further explanation had been offered. "Not a concern," he had been told. But now Daniel's concerned. His heart is pumping faster than a freight train going uphill. He comes to an abrupt halt in front of the computer attached to a direct feed from the Tucson observatory perched atop Kitt Peak.

The data scrolling across the screen looks more like ancient Greek to Daniel than some decipherable problem: a stream of numbers and words, most of them flashing red.

"This can't be good," he mutters as he fumbles with the keyboard in an attempt to silence the ear-piercing noise. His fingers gouge at the keys, trying every possible combination including the old standby: Control-Alt-Delete. No luck. Daniel is breathing fast and what began as a quiver is now a full-on shake as he glances up to see Dr. Kaylee Connor, one of the paid scientists, racing toward him.

"What the hell did you do, Daniel?" Kaylee shouts, hipping him away from the monitor.

"I didn't do a damn thing. It just went off." He leans in closer for another look at the screen. "What the hell is going on?"

Kaylee doesn't answer. Her gaze is focused on the data scrolling upward like a machine possessed. Her fingers punch a precise combination of computer keys, and the alarm stops. Daniel releases a long sigh. But then he notices the worry on Kaylee's face.

Without turning her gaze from the screen, Kaylee says, "Daniel, get Sam on the phone and tell him to get his ass over here, pronto."

"Are you going to tell me what's going on?"

"I don't know, damn it. Just get Sam on the phone." She glances up at Daniel. "Now!"

Daniel races to the nearest desk and grabs the handset

only to slam it down a moment later. "I don't know his number."

Kaylee shimmies her cell from the back pocket of her too-tight black jeans and tosses it across the room. "Sam's in my contact list."

While he places the call, Kaylee turns back to the monitor. "Not fucking possible," she whispers.

She glances up to see Daniel racing across the room, the cell phone extended like a relay-race baton. "Sam," he says, thrusting the cell into her hand.

She slaps the phone to her ear. "We have a serious situation."

"What's happened?" Dr. Samuel Blake, director of the Space Weather Prediction Center, says.

"A massive CME triggered an alarm." Her voice is laced with fear.

"How massive and when?"

"Off the scale. Our instruments recorded the ejection"—she glances at the clock on the wall—"about fifteen minutes ago. What do you want me to do?"

"I'll be there in five. Print out all the data and start calling everyone back into the office. No excuses. I want everybody on site and ready to go in thirty minutes."

Kaylee punches the off button on her phone and begins printing out all the material from the computer. Glancing up between tasks, she spots Daniel standing off to the side, a befuddled expression on his face. "Do something, Daniel. Start calling everyone and tell them to get their asses in here as fast as they can."

Daniel spins away.

"Wait! First, print out everything from ACE, concentrating on the last four hours."

"Is the coronal mass ejection headed this way?"

"We won't know anything until you print out the data. Now move your ass."

Daniel rushes to the workstation where the information from the Advanced Composition Explorer (ACE) satellite is viewed. His hands are shaking so severely he can hardly type. He logs on and begins to print out the data just as the computer screen winks out, as if the plug had been yanked from the wall. "Kaylee," he shouts across the room, "ACE is down."

She turns away from her workstation and moves to his side. "What do you mean 'down'?"

"The screen just went black."

"What's happening?" a deep voice booms across the room. They both glance up to see Samuel Blake, dressed in his usual khaki slacks and light blue shirt, striding in their direction. At six-two, he towers over both of them.

"ACE suddenly went off-line," Daniel says.

"I've told them a thousand times that satellite could die at any minute." Sam nudges Daniel away from the computer. "All those budget cuts are killing us."

"Why is this particular satellite so important?" Daniel says.

"Without that bird, we're blind." Sam's fingers race across the keyboard, holding down certain keys while punching others. When the screen doesn't respond, he slams his hand on the desk. He whirls the chair around and stands. "Kaylee, get on the horn to NASA. Find out what the hell is going on with the satellite." He makes a beeline toward his office down the hallway.

Daniel follows, tugging his jeans up with every step. "What about the telescopes? Will we be able to see the plasma clouds?"

"No. There won't be any visible indicators. It's just a seething mass of highly charged particles." Sam pauses at the doorway to his office. "If ACE is out of action we're blind. Without that data we won't know a damn thing."

Daniel turns away, but stops when Sam says, "Did you call everyone?"

"I'm in the process."

"Make sure they understand the urgency."

"Yes, sir." Daniel hesitates. "Dr. Blake, how long do you think before it hits here?"

Sam rakes his hand through his thinning hair. "Maybe twenty hours, if we're lucky. But it'll be a crapshoot without that satellite."

CHAPTER 2

Rural Oklahoma

Zeke jackknifes up in bed, gasping for breath as the horrifying images slowly fade from his mind. He leans up on his elbow to check the time. The glowing red numerals indicate it's either very late or very early. The air from the ceiling fan produces a rash of goose bumps across his sweat-drenched skin.

Zeke collapses back on the mattress and stares at the ever-circling ceiling fan, the blurring blades just visible in the faint moonlight leaking through the curtainless window. Next to the bed, Lexi whines. He reaches a hand down to comfort her. Her body is also trembling as he spiders his fingers through her curly black-and-white coat. It's as if she experienced the same dream. But do border collies have nightmares?

The dreams/nightmares aren't unusual, and though the frequency has diminished over time, their intensity hasn't. He wipes his other hand across his damp face while struggling to vanquish the remaining remnants of the dream. Tonight's episode is one of two recurring nightmares that crowd his unconscious thoughts. In this one the night is bitterly cold as he leans against the frigid metal interior of the rumbling Humvee as it travels along another of the treeless ridgelines that dot Afghanistan's northern border. He's not alone—four members of his squad are with him. With every nervous exhale their breath creates a thin fog within the confines of the lightly armored truck.

This movie in his mind almost always ends at the same moment: when the IED explodes beneath their vehicle and the screams of agony overwhelm the concussion of the explosion.

The second recurring nightmare is more recent, but no less terrifying.

The night sounds drift through the window. Coyotes howl in the distance, and the buzzing of what sounds like thousands of insects floats in on the faint breeze. Another night in rural Oklahoma. No honking horns or the laughter of people departing a bar or traffic noise, just the sounds of nature's nightlife. They wash over him until he fades into a restless sleep. A faint warmness on his cheek. He opens his eyes to see the sun hovering on the horizon, casting a slash of light on the far wall, turning a right angle where it meets the floor before spreading across the bed.

Zeke pushes the covers off and pads barefoot into the kitchen, cracking the back door so Lexi can escape to do her business. He throws on a pot of coffee.

He rubs his face with both hands, feeling as if he hadn't slept at all.

While the coffee brews, he shuffles across the hand-hewn wood floor and switches on the old thirteen-inch television. The ancient tubes warm and the grainy image of a newsreader on the set of the *Today* show fades onto the screen. Zeke turns back for a cup of coffee, half listening to the story playing behind him: "Residents in Alaska, Canada, and the northern portion of the U.S. were in for a treat during the night, with an unprecedented display of the aurora borealis. Scientists say the unusually high level of activity on the sun's surface will produce numerous solar flares, which will continue to light up the night skies. They emphasize, however, that there are no concerns about the sun's current volatility. That's good to hear. Matt, any unusual lights out on the plaza?"

He tunes out the rest of the chatter, and instead of letting Lexi in when she scratches at the door, Zeke joins her outside. He takes a seat in one of the four handmade chairs occupying the recently completed wooden deck. The attached house is a rustic one-bedroom, one-bathroom log cabin built from wood harvested from the eighty acres his parents inherited from Zeke's grandfather. Five of which acres his parents carved out for him when his life shattered for the second time.

The ringing of the old phone he salvaged from the barn interrupts his solitude. He pushes out of the Adirondack chair and hurries into the house. He already knows the identity of the caller. The only person who ever calls. He picks up on the fourth ring.

"Good morning, Mom."

"Zeke, would you like to join your father and me for breakfast?"

He sighs, struggling with their attempts to heal him. "Sure, Mom. Be right up."

He slips into the bedroom, pulls on a pair of well-worn jeans, and slides a flannel shirt carefully over his scarred shoulder. He walks through the kitchen and whistles for Lexi at the back door. It's only about a quarter mile of gravel road to his parents' home—far enough away for privacy yet still close enough if there's trouble. There hasn't been any since moving down, but today will prove different.

CHAPTER 3

NOAA Space Weather Prediction Center
Wednesday, September 29, 7:38 A.M.

All the scientists have trickled in and the control room is humming with a mix of concerned voices. Twenty people crammed into a room made for ten. Down the hall, Sam Blake sits in his office, the phone to his ear as he discusses the situation with other experts at NASA and the Air Force Weather headquarters at Offutt Air Force Base in Nebraska. Everyone is aware of the massive solar eruption as well as the pressing need to discover the ensuing path of the storm, but not one knows how the hell to go about it with the devastating loss of their eye in the sky.

Sam glances up at the knock on his door to see Kaylee leaning against the doorframe. Six years out of Cornell with a Ph.D. in space plasma physics, Kaylee just celebrated her thirty-first birthday. She is tall and lean. Her unnaturally dark black hair sports an asymmetrical cut streaked with purple highlights, and her pale skin is stained with tattoos. Today, she's dressed in skinny jeans that hug the contours of her long legs, and she's topped off with another of her vintage T-shirts, this one featuring

Led Zeppelin—a band that last toured when her parents were still romping around an elementary school playground. Despite the crisis, Sam smiles and waves her in.

Kaylee sits in a chair facing the desk and begins pumping her right leg up and down. Sam raises a finger in the air, answers one final question, and hangs up the phone. "What do you have?"

"NASA is clueless. According to their techies, ACE suddenly went dark. I mean, duh, you don't need to be an astronaut to uncover that little clue. But they've tried a reboot, a resend, and a dozen other re-somethings, all to no avail. They can't determine if the preliminary effects of the coronal mass ejection knocked it off-line or what."

Sam leans back in his chair, twirling his rectangular wire-rimmed glasses between his thumb and forefinger. "We are screwed."

"Tell me about it. What *are* we going to do, Sam?"

"I don't know. But we need to come up with some type of plan and do it quickly."

"How quick?"

Sam leans forward in his chair, resting his elbows on the cluttered desk. "No way to really know without that satellite. Remember studying the 1859 Carrington event?"

"Of course. The sizzling telegraph wires and the flash in the sky."

"And how long did it take for the telegraph wires to sizzle after the flash?"

Kaylee places a black-lacquered nail to her dark red lips. "Something like seventeen hours, wasn't it?"

"Correct. Seventeen hours and we're already an hour into this event. But I don't believe it will take that long for this storm to arrive."

"Why?"

"I'm not sure how much stock to put in their 1859

technology. Plus this ejection of plasma is much larger." Sam pauses, hoping for a rebuttal—for Kaylee to tell him he's crazy as a loon. But she doesn't. "Put another call in to NASA. I want a definitive explanation about the status of that satellite."

Kaylee stands and heads for the door only to pivot on her heel.

"How bad do you really think this storm could be, Sam?"

Sam returns the glasses to his face. "Bad, Kaylee. It could be catastrophic. Worse than a sky full of bombs, at least for anything depending on electricity."

Chapter 4

NOAA Space Weather Prediction Center
Wednesday, September 29, 8:01 A.M.

Sam shuffles into the solar observation room. His blue shirt is damp under the arms and a sheen of sweat glistens on his forehead.

"Sam, there have been several more CMEs in the last ten minutes," someone shouts.

"They'll be here fairly quickly, then," he mutters. He stands tall, squaring his shoulders. "Okay, listen up. I need everything you have assembled into a concise brief and I need it in the next fifteen minutes." He turns to Kaylee. "You're in charge of putting the data together." Sam turns and hurries back to his office.

The room explodes into a beehive of activity as everyone begins speaking at once. Kaylee stands in the center of the room and yells for quiet, then issues instructions. She flips open her laptop and begins typing, trying to organize the bits of shouted information into a workable timeline.

Back in his office, Sam picks up the phone and heaves

a heavy sigh as he punches in the phone number. *To hell with stepping on sensitive toes*, he thinks. He's chosen to bypass about ten layers of bureaucracy by calling direct to Dr. Debra Bailey, the under secretary of commerce for oceans and atmosphere and the director of NOAA.

"Director Bailey's office," the receptionist says.

"This is Dr. Samuel Blake at the Space Weather Prediction Agency. It's urgent I speak to the director right now."

"In regards to what?"

A gatekeeper with an attitude. Sam explains to the receptionist who he is as he doodles dirty words on a piece of scrap paper. The receptionist puts him on hold. His anger at the bloated government agency ratchets up another notch.

Finally, the phone is picked up on the other end. "Dr. Blake. What can I do for you?"

"We have a serious situation developing."

"How serious, and what exactly are you referring to?"

"A massive geomagnetic solar storm may be on a collision course with Earth."

"Might be? We don't know for sure? And when you say 'massive,' how massive?" Her voice is full of skepticism, and he can hear the shuffling of paper on her end.

"How about the total destruction of every electrical system north of the equator?"

The paper shuffling stops. "You can't be serious, Dr. Blake."

"I'm deadly serious. We need to begin a national mobilization to shut down power grids, and we need to ground all aircraft because of the potential loss of communications."

"Come now, Dr. Blake. You just said you didn't know if the storm would even hit here. You want me to ask the brass to cut off power to millions of people in addition to stranding travelers in some far-off destination based on a maybe?"

"I called"—he inhales a quick breath—"I called to request a videoconference so that I can explain the situation."

The director pauses, as if consulting her busy calendar. "How's tomorrow or the day after sound?"

Sam chuckles. "I was thinking sometime within the next fifteen or twenty minutes."

"What? Impossible. You know what a scheduling nightmare that would be. It will take most of the morning to even make contact with whomever needs to be contacted."

"We don't have most of the morning. There's no time to be worried about schedule snafus."

"When do you expect the storm to arrive?"

"Unknown. But my best estimation is between ten and seventeen hours."

A gasp on the other end of the line. "How bad could this storm be, Dr. Blake?"

"It might very well send a vast majority of the world into darkness for years, and maybe forever."

A long silence. He taps his foot, waiting for her to reply.

Finally she does. "We need to keep this under wraps until we can develop a response. I'll set up the videoconference within the hour. We need Homeland Security involved, as well as Energy and FEMA and the Joint Chiefs, and . . ." She ticks off several more organizations. "Did I leave anyone out?"

"Yes, you did. The President."

"I'll arrange it. You better be on top of all your facts and figures. I don't want to be the agency crying wolf."

"I think there are more important things to worry

about than saving face. I'll be in my office whenever you're ready, and please—every second counts." Sam slams the phone down and stands. He shoves his hands into his pockets and paces the small confines of his office, hoping they're not too late.

Chapter 5

The Marshall home, near Durant, Oklahoma

The screen door slaps shut behind Zeke as he and Lexi step through the back door of his parents' home. The house came with the property, and what began as a one-story wreck shedding shingles is now a three-bedroom rancher with gleaming stainless steel appliances arranged around the built-from-scratch kitchen. His mother's pride and joy. He finds her at the gas stove, an appliance large enough for a commercial kitchen. The aroma of sizzling bacon makes his empty stomach rumble. Zeke steps up and offers her a quick kiss on the cheek.

"Pour yourself a cup of coffee, Zeke," his mother says, reaching for a cup from the cupboard and handing it to him.

Barbara Marshall is taller than average at five foot eight, and her once-svelte figure has gotten less slender with age. A thickness has settled into her hips, but she's not overweight. Just a heaviness that seems to accumulate over a lifetime. Her mostly gray hair is pulled up in a ponytail and the apron wrapped around her jeans and sweatshirt is embroidered with KISS THE COOK across the front. Both of

Zeke's parents are closer to seventy than they would like to admit.

"You realize you don't need to cook for me."

"I know, but I was cooking breakfast anyway."

Zeke pours coffee and steps over to join his father at the scarred dining room table, one of the furniture holdovers from their early days—sentimental value, according to both parents. Zeke never asked what was sentimental about an old table, fearing the answer. His father has today's paper spread out before him.

"Anything interesting?" Zeke says.

"Is there ever?" His father folds the paper and tosses it onto one of the vacant chairs. Robert takes off the reading glasses, his sole concession to growing older. He is only an inch or two taller than his wife, but at six foot three their son towers over both. Zeke has the same broad shoulders and big hands as his father, but how he grew so tall is a mystery. His mother insists that most of the males in her family had been tall, so they chalk it up to genetics. "How are the tables coming?"

"Slowly. I may need your help sometime this week to mill a couple more walnut trees. I've just about gone through everything in the drying shed."

"How many orders do you have left to fill?"

"Three." When Zeke moved down here he helped his father, a retired civil engineer, put the finishing touches on a state-of-the-art woodshop, built—of course—to his father's precisely engineered plans.

"They all going to that designer in Dallas? Ruth's friend?"

"Yeah, she's created a good market for them. It's getting hard to keep up." To occupy his mind, Zeke started building tables—dining, end, and every other type. But these aren't just any tables. They're handcrafted and all the joinery is hand finished. They can't be found at IKEA; they reside only in some of the more expensive homes around Dallas.

"How much are you selling them for now?"

"More than I ever thought possible, Dad. Dining tables seating eight sell for ten grand."

His father whistles. "Damn, that's a lot of money."

Zeke senses his father's pride. Hell, he could give them away and his father would probably be happy, as long as Zeke had something to keep himself busy—busy enough so that the bad memories can't stake a claim to his sanity.

"Your sister called this morning and wanted to make sure we were coming for Thanksgiving," his mother says, sliding the steaming plates of scrambled eggs and bacon onto the table. Zeke's sister, Ruth, makes her home in Dallas with her husband and two children.

"On one condition," Zeke says between bites. "As long as Carl doesn't make me watch any more episodes of that doomsday-prepping show he's so fascinated with." He uses the distraction of their chuckling to slip a piece of bacon to Lexi, who's sitting patiently under the table in anticipation of a few stray crumbs.

"You know you promised to go and bring them home if something happened," his mother says.

"And I would, too, if something happened. But I think the odds are better of winning the lottery. I don't think we have much to worry about. Besides, Dad, you've stocked up on ten of everything, right?"

"No, eleven of everything. You can't be too prepared," he says, stone-faced.

Zeke sneaks another piece of bacon to Lexi before standing from the table. He gathers up the plates and carries them to the hammered-copper farmhouse sink his mother fell in love with at the kitchen showroom. "Mom,

I'm washing the dishes but I need to run out to the shop. Deal?"

"Okay, son, the dishes are all yours."

Outside, the portion of the cerulean sky visible through the tree canopy is devoid of clouds. The sunlight stabs through the leaves, creating a shimmering shade that sways with the breeze. Zeke passes the remainder of his mother's garden on the way to the workshop. The garden is a source of pride for her. Bright red peppers and a few late tomatoes hang limply, but everything else has already been harvested. After hours of online research she learned how to preserve what was harvested. The shelves in the garage sag under the weight of dozens of canned jars containing tomatoes and pickled okra, plus a large sack of dried beans that will probably end up being tossed out after a year or two.

As usual, Lexi matches her owner step for step until she spies a pair of squirrels spiraling around an old oak tree. She darts off with a bark, sending them scampering farther up the tree. Zeke crosses the threshold of the woodshop and flips on the lights. The interior illuminates as bright as a modern laboratory, with precise overhead lighting for each woodworking machine, as if they were on display in an art gallery. The woody aroma produces an instant calmness in Zeke. The different textures and colors of sawdust littering the floor create a natural, multicolored carpet. He sorts through the wood and counts out the number of walnut boards remaining and does a quick mental calculation to determine if he has enough to finish. Barely, but definitely not enough to start on another project.

He heads back to the house. When Zeke first moved here he was apprehensive about being so far from civilization. But he adapted quickly to a new way of living. No cell phone, only the one small television, and an ancient laptop, which he piggybacks onto his father's Wi-Fi connection on the rare occasion he needs to go online. Off the grid—almost. Robert and Barbara Marshall aren't so far off the grid, owning a television, a couple of cell phones, and two computers. The cell phones work better as paperweights most of the time because of the spotty coverage in this heavily wooded section of southeastern Oklahoma.

Zeke climbs the steps of the back porch and stops in his tracks. His parents are arguing, an uncommon occurrence. They stop when Zeke pulls the squeaky screen door open. His mother glances in his direction, a blush of pink on her cheeks. His father is staring at the honey oak tabletop as if memorizing the pattern of the wood grain. The sudden silence is uncomfortable, but in his gut Zeke knows what they were arguing about even though he heard very little of the hushed conversation. Him. Zeke squares his shoulders and holds his head just a tad higher as he walks to the sink.

"Son, you really don't need to wash the dishes," his mother says. "I'm quite capable of doing that."

"I know, Mom, but you cooked." Zeke rubs the soapy rag around the same plate three times as his mind spins. *Should I start a conversation about something I have no desire to talk about? No.* Moments later he places the last plate into the rack next to the sink and turns to face his parents. His father still won't meet his eyes.

"I called Ruth and told her we would be down for Thanksgiving," his mother says. "I told her what you said about Carl and his doomsday show, and she assured me he's no longer as fascinated by the end of the world. He's now engrossed with gold digging in Alaska."

"Maybe he and I can take a trip to Alaska and strike it rich," Zeke says.

"You'd have better luck digging worms in the garden. Now get out of my hair and go to work." His mother shoos him toward the door.

"Dad, you busy?"

"I'll be out in a minute, son."

Zeke reenters the shop and soon loses himself in the work. He grabs a board from the drying shed and fires up the planer to smooth its surface. The whirring blades emit a fountain of shavings as the spicy aroma of walnut fills the space. The noise of the machine cancels out all the others, including those within, until the lights suddenly flash off and the planer groans to a stop.

CHAPTER 6

The White House, Washington, D.C.
Wednesday, September 29, 8:11 A.M.

Presidential Chief of Staff Scott Alexander rushes through the corridors of the West Wing on his way to the Oval Office. The secretary of commerce has just briefed him on the possibility of an imminent geomagnetic storm, after word was passed up through the ranks of NOAA. With a secret love for all things science-related, Alexander is familiar with most of the studies dealing with the effects of space weather on Earth. After his brief meeting this morning, he took a moment to reread the results of the latest computer simulation. The report more closely resembles a script for a disaster movie rather than a scientific paper.

He arrives at the secretary's desk fronting the entrance to the Oval Office and stops for a minute to catch his breath and sort out his thoughts. He hitched his wagon to President Harris during his first run for office: a U.S. House seat left vacant after the incumbent was indicted on federal bribery charges. Paul Harris is a no-bullshit man, and the information Alexander is preparing to present could be a hard sell with the limited data available.

"Who's in with him?" he asks Barbara, the longtime presidential secretary. She's wearing a navy dress, refusing to wear slacks to work, and her short gray bob is, as it has been over the last twenty years, perfectly coiffed.

"The British ambassador, and they've been in there for some time. Do you want me to buzz the President?"

"Yes, please. And would you request the ambassador stay?"

Barbara raises her eyebrows. "You sure about that?"

"Yes, and please tell him what I have is urgent."

Barbara buzzes the office. "Sir, Mr. Alexander would like a brief word with both you and Ambassador Nelson," she says when the phone is answered. Scott overhears the President's portion of the conversation. Hears the surprise and the developing anger in the President's voice.

"Sir, he said it is very urgent." She listens, then replaces the phone. "Go right in, Mr. Alexander."

He takes a moment to straighten the lapels of his charcoal suit before pushing through the door to the Oval Office. A short, wiry man who always seems to be in motion, Alexander crosses from the hardwood floor onto the custom-made carpet and shakes the proffered hand of Ambassador Nelson. He takes a seat in one of the chairs flanking the two sofas occupying one side of the famous office.

President Harris stares at him. His famous smile is nowhere to be found. "What's this about?"

"I'm sorry for intruding, Mr. President. But we may have a developing emergency."

The President darts his eyes toward their guest.

"I think this also concerns Great Britain," Alexander says.

Ambassador Nelson scoots up to the edge of the sofa. "Don't tell me the damn Iranians are threatening nuclear destruction again."

GIBSONS AND DISTRICT
PUBLIC LIBRARY

"No, Mr. Ambassador, at least not that I know of."

The ambassador relaxes.

"It could be much worse." Scott pauses. "A little over three hours ago, the sun released a massive ejection of plasma that may be heading straight for Earth."

"May be?" the President says.

"Yes, sir. We seem to be having a satellite issue preventing the scientists from accurately predicting where it may hit. But—and this is more than speculation—if this plasma storm hits, the result could be devastating to most if not all of the countries north of the equator and possibly farther south."

President Harris clenches and unclenches his jaw. "Ambassador Nelson, would you please excuse us for a brief moment?"

The ambassador pushes his short, wide body up from the sofa and quickly exits the Oval Office.

The President stands. "What the hell, Scott? Was that necessary?"

"Mr. President, Paul, this goes beyond our borders. We need to begin preparations, and his country may be facing the same potential devastation."

President Harris paces to the windows. He's a big man—a former college offensive lineman who still looks as if he could suit up and play today. Except for the slight limp, the result of a nasty cut block that ruptured his ACL. He looks dapper, as always, in a dark navy suit, white shirt, and club tie. "Damn it, Scott, you just said you didn't even know if it's going to hit here. He's probably out there calling the prime minister."

"Paul, listen to me, please. We were briefed on this right after you took office. The effects might plunge both our countries into darkness for years. I wouldn't bring this situation to your attention if I didn't think it was serious. A videoconference is being organized in the Situation Room"—he glances at the heavy gold watch on his wrist—"within the next fifteen minutes. I think the ambassador should attend the conference so he'll be able to convey the seriousness of the matter to his country."

President Harris glares at him for a long moment before walking back to the sofa. He grabs the phone on the side table and instructs his secretary to send the ambassador back in.

Scott notices that, like almost every President, he's aged during the first three years of office. A man who loves to golf and spend time outdoors, the President now has the pallor of a desk jockey. His once-dark hair is now more gray than black and his patrician face displays many new wrinkles. *We've almost made it through the first term without any major catastrophes, and now that it's time to mount a campaign for a second term, he looks twenty years older.* Scott doesn't like what the office has done to his old friend.

Ambassador Nelson's face is a mask of concern when he reenters the Oval Office. "I just received a call from the prime minister, Mr. President. What Mr. Alexander said is correct. Our scientists are working in conjunction with those here in the States to get a better handle on the situation."

The President's grim smile betrays his growing concern. "I guess we have an appointment in the Situation Room."

Chapter 7

NOAA Space Weather Prediction Center
Wednesday, September 29, 9:11 A.M.

Doctor Samuel Blake sits in front of the stationary camera, his leg bouncing up and down as sweat pops on his forehead. He wipes it away. The videoconference, which includes the President of the United States, is way outside his normal realm. But the impending storm is forcing everyone out of their comfort zones. Sam runs his hands across the salt-and-pepper razor stubble sprouting from his chin as he stares at the dark eye of the camera lens. He's seated in the tiny conference room that doubles as a break room, and the aroma of burned coffee only adds to the sourness already churning in his gut. He glances out the window at the majestic Rocky Mountains, displayed in all their glory as the sun paints the ragged ridges in bright light. *How can things appear so serene?* he wonders.

He stands and shouts down the hall for Kaylee to join him, more for support than anything else. She signals her response with a brief wave as she continues to type on her laptop. He returns to his seat, removes a handkerchief from his back pocket, and polishes each lens of his glasses.

After replacing his glasses, he attaches the wireless microphone and places the small earpiece into his ear. The edges of the paper flutter as he reads through the brief one last time. Without warning, a tinny noise squeals through the earpiece. He reaches to yank out the earpiece but the noise dissipates, replaced by the sounds of human voices. He cocks his head, trying to listen. He doesn't have the luxury of a video feed displaying the other participants of the conference, just their voices transmitted via some satellite out in space. He hears someone say, "Five minutes," and he takes a few deep breaths to slow his heart rate.

A soft knock at the door. Kaylee enters the conference room, her face pinched with worry, and sits wearily in one of the chairs outside of camera range.

"There have been two substantial solar flares over the last five minutes from the same region of the sun," she says.

"What are the effects?"

"Some radio interference, and a small spike in a few of the electrical grids." Solar flares reach Earth almost instantaneously, while the floating plasma of the coronal mass ejections takes longer.

"This could get bad in a hurry, Kaylee." He looks at the clock, ticking forever onward. He reaches to his belt, double-checking that his microphone is turned on. "Kaylee, clip the other microphone on in case I need your help."

She reaches for the mike but struggles to attach it with trembling hands.

CHAPTER 8

The Marshall home

Zeke's father enters the shop just as all the lights wink out for the second time. Zeke yanks the hearing-protection headphones from his ears. "Second time that's happened, Dad."

"Power spike of some sort. Might even be a solar flare. Give it a minute, then try again."

Zeke shakes his head and stares at the board, smooth as a baby's butt on one side but raspy as steel wool on the other. "What makes you think it was a solar flare or whatever you said?"

"I don't. Could've been something else, but I know there's an increase in solar activity. And it happens more than you'd think." In addition to being a civil engineer, his father has a passionate interest in science. A real nerd, a designation he happily embraces.

"Why would it stop and restart?"

"It's like a circuit breaker in your house. A sudden spike will trigger the breaker, so you have to reset it. Same principle applies to the electric companies, but the breakers are much bigger with a different configuration, but the same general idea. Too much of a sustained overload and you could fry the transformers."

Some of that Zeke knew from his days in Afghanistan, where the electrical service had been as unreliable as a 1985 Yugo. But not for the soldiers, who had all the generating power needed, thanks to Uncle Sam. The lights flicker back on and Zeke reaches down and flips the planer's switch. His dad stands on the out-feed side as Zeke keeps the board straight until the machine's feeder pulls it into the blades.

Once the board is finished, he hits the kill switch with his knee. "So that's it? A little hiccup?"

"Hope so," his father says. "What do you want me to do?"

Zeke points to an almost-complete table on the other side of the workshop. "How about a delicate sanding on that table?"

"You got it." He walks to the workbench area and begins thumbing through the different grits of sandpaper arranged in an organizer. Zeke watches his father as he carefully removes a piece of sandpaper. As a teenager he chafed against that sternness, stiffness, or whatever it was, but now he admires his father for his decisiveness, his attention to detail. His hair is grayer and thinner, the creases on his forehead are a little deeper, but his mind appears to be as sharp as ever.

As Zeke turns away and carries the now-smooth board to the radial arm saw, the lights in the shop flicker again. He glances back at his father to find him staring at the light fixtures as if it's a problem with them. Not likely, with his careful electrical work, including precise voltages for each run of the wire.

"We have a backup generator, right?" Zeke says.

"Yes, it's tied into the propane tank. As long as we have propane, we'll have power. Shouldn't be a problem." He returns to sanding. Then he stops. "Could be a tree grounding out one of the high lines," he mutters.

"What's that, Dad?"

"Nothing, just talking to myself." Then, "When we first moved down here, the electrical service was spotty, but they built a new substation outside of town that was supposed to fix it. And it did. I hope it's not something else." There's a new note of concern in his voice.

CHAPTER 9

The White House Situation Room
Wednesday, September 29, 9:13 A.M.

President Harris steps into the Situation Room with Ambassador Nelson in tow. Every head in the room turns at their entrance and some people begin to stand, but the President waves them down. There are some raised eyebrows at the appearance of the British ambassador. Scott Alexander slips into the room behind them and takes a seat toward the rear. The President nods to the advisors arranged around the large conference table, pulls out the chair with a presidential seal embroidered on the back, and sits. Ambassador Nelson, half a foot shorter and about sixty pounds heavier than the President, takes the chair next to him.

The cold fluorescent lighting reflects off the polished wooden surface of the large table, which is surrounded by a dozen leather swivel chairs. Another thirty or so chairs are parked along the outer perimeter of the rectangular room, hugging the light-colored walls, which are dressed with a dark wood wainscoting along their bottom. There are large video displays mounted around the room, but the front wall is reserved for a much larger white screen lit by an overhead projector. Dark blue carpet runs from wall to wall, alleviating some of the coldness of the room.

"Who's on the videoconference?" the President says.

A staffer quickly hands him a typed sheet that details the names and their job titles, along with short bios. He scans down the list, passing over one bureaucrat after another until his eyes alight on the two Ph.D.s on the list. He scans their brief biographies. *Most of the others taking part in the videoconference will be just background noise—these two will have the answers*, the President thinks. He rereads the bios of Dr. Samuel Blake at the Space Weather Prediction Center and Dr. Sarah Garcia, an air force major at that agency's weather center.

"Thirty seconds, Mr. President," someone shouts over the murmur of voices, which die down. The large screen is divided into boxes showing the faces of the videoconference participants. The President scrutinizes the faces and focuses on trying to sort out who's who. Before he can ask, a name and a title appear under each box.

The boxes are arranged horizontally, with four frames per row, two rows stacked vertically. There are seven people on-screen: director of NASA, director of FEMA, secretary of commerce, and the under secretary of commerce in charge of NOAA, a scientist herself, but a couple of the others President Harris has never met. Joining him in the Situation Room are the other directors—Homeland Security, FBI, SECDEF, SECSTATE, and National Security, whose organization is tasked with running operations in the Sit Room. Of course the chairman of the Joint Chiefs is present in his dress uniform, his chest adorned with an array of colored ribbons. The President takes a moment to survey the faces of those surrounding him before turning his gaze to the screen. He realizes that the only people with real looks of concern are the two scientists.

"Good morning to all of you and thank you for joining

us," President Harris says. A few offer return greetings. "Dr. Blake, I understand you're the one who initiated this gathering. Will you please explain why?"

The small box representing Dr. Blake zooms full screen, the perspiration on his forehead evident as his face fills the wall. "Thank you, Mr. President. A little over"—he pauses to glance at something outside camera range—"three hours ago we were alerted to a massive coronal mass ejection from the surface of the sun. A CME, for those of you who don't know, is a storm seething with gas and charged plasma, full of energy particles embedded in a magnetic field." Sam pauses for a quick sip of water.

"Dr. Blake," says the President, "most of us have been briefed on solar storms, so why don't we get to the heart of the matter? Three questions need immediate answers. What makes this storm unusual? Why do you think the storm will hit here? And most important, if it does strike our planet, how long do we have?"

"This storm is different because of its size, sir. It's massive. The Advanced Composition Explorer satellite—ACE—that orbits about a million miles from the Earth between our planet and the sun, went dark almost two hours ago. It was the only tool we had to determine the storm's path, and unfortunately it was also the only tool we had available to determine the arrangement of our planet's magnetic fields. A crucial piece of information we need to determine the severity of the impact.

"So the arrival time is only an educated guess at this point. Some of my colleagues have suggested a time frame for CME arrival at Earth anywhere between one to three days. Several factors play a part in these guesstimates based on speed and size. But the only storm in recorded history of this magnitude occurred in 1859, and the effects of that storm were felt on Earth after only seventeen hours. That estimate was calculated using crude instrumentation, so I don't know how reliable or precise those observations were. This solar storm is larger than the Carrington event and I believe it will only accelerate as it advances, sometime in the next ten to fourteen hours."

"Take a break for a moment, Dr. Blake. Major Garcia, do you concur with Dr. Blake's assessment?"

The full-screen shot transitions to an attractive Hispanic woman in her midforties with dark eyes and dark, cropped-short hair. She's wearing her dress blues with gold oak leaves pinned to each shoulder epaulette. Sarah Garcia's face is just as serious as Blake's. "According to our instrument readings, Dr. Blake is correct about the massive size of the eruption. The only area where we differ is in the timing. Earth is already being pummeled by an array of solar flares, and I believe the time frame for arrival may be quicker than Dr. Blake indicated."

"Dr. Garcia, do you think this solar storm is on a path to hit Earth?" the President says.

"We don't know for certain, Mr. President. But as Dr. Blake has already suggested, the last information we received from the ACE satellite provides for a very strong possibility."

"Can we get both scientists on the screen at the same time?" President Harris asks of the crowded room. On command, both faces appear side by side.

"Dr. Blake, what could we be in for?" the President asks.

Sam arms the sweat from his brow. "The plasma storm could be devastating, Mr. President. Massive power grid failures, the loss of communication and navigation satellites . . . All the water and sewage treatment plants would go off-line, along with all public transportation that relies on the electrical grid. In addition, fuel will become scarce, and pipelines will no longer function. Basically, Mr. President, life as we know it would change drastically."

"A grim picture, Dr. Blake. Major Garcia, could it be as bad as Sam suggests?"

"I believe the worst you can imagine could occur, Mr. President. All flights need to be grounded soon, due to the potential loss of the navigation and communication satellites. We also need to switch off as many of the power grids as possible in hopes they could be restarted after the effects of the storm pass. But, sir, keep in mind this event will not only occur in the United States. This storm may have devastating consequences for every country north of the equator and possibly those countries farther south. Our systems, basically everything in our lives, are so reliant on electricity that the effects could be catastrophic. There's also the potential risk of meltdowns at nuclear power plants due to failed cooling systems."

Silence fills the room.

The President glances over at Ambassador Nelson. Most of the UK's electricity is produced by nuclear reactors. The ambassador stands, making apologies about having to step out to phone the prime minister. The President nods and returns his focus to the screen. As yet none of the other participants have spoken, until Director of Homeland Security Janice Baker chimes in.

"Mr. President, I believe they're overstating the effects of something which might not even occur."

"So, Janice, you want us to sit on our thumbs until the power goes out for however long?" The President's stern gaze is locked on the director's face.

"No, sir, but I think we should at least wait until we have confirmation this storm is even going to happen. Imagine the outcry if we order all flights grounded. That in itself will create a nationwide panic—"

"Mr. President," Dr. Blake says, "we cannot offer absolute confirmation due to the lack of available working instruments. But every moment we wait is critical. We don't know for certain shutting down the power grids will allow them to escape destruction, but it's our best option. We haven't experienced a solar storm of this magnitude since the advent of worldwide electricity. There are many unanswerable questions, but I would suggest, sir, that you call up the National Guard."

The chairman of the Joint Chiefs bristles. "Mr. President, most of our National Guard troops are deployed overseas."

President Harris makes no reply as he mulls over the implications of the coming storm.

Chapter 10

NOAA Space Weather Prediction Center
Wednesday, September 29, 9:42 A.M.

Sam slumps in his chair as the reedy voices continue to bicker over the small earphone in his ear. Kaylee, sitting near and listening in, puts her hand on his arm. The room feels as if the thermostat is set to max heat, and a stream of moisture slithers down his back.

"We're wasting time," he says to Kaylee.

"Give me a few minutes, Dr. Blake," the President says.

Sam blushes, not realizing his mike is still active. The nasal voice of the director of homeland security, who has the advantage of sitting next to the President, is the loudest.

"Sir, we need more definitive information," she says.

Sam covers the microphone with his hand. "Kaylee, run to the observation room and see what's happening. I need an update, anything I can use to convince these people. And please ask Daniel to bring me another bottle of water."

Kaylee removes the earpiece, unclips the microphone, and hurries from the room. Sam swivels his chair away from the camera and stares out the window as the arguing continues nearly seventeen hundred miles away. From what Sam can make of the conversation, the President seems to be leaning toward Janice Baker's assertion that more information is needed. A possibly fatal mistake. Kaylee returns and slides a pile of papers across the desk. Sam takes a moment to digest the latest information as Daniel slips in and places a bottle of water in front of him.

Sam says loudly into the mike, "Major Garcia, did you receive the latest update?"

"No, Sam, I don't have anything. What is it?" she says.

"Another large CME erupted almost five minutes ago."

"Is that one headed toward Earth, Dr. Blake?" President Harris says.

"Unknown, sir. But with these coronal ejections occurring more frequently we need to act now, Mr. President," Sam says, his voice laced with anger. "These other CMEs could arrive here much more quickly. Think of the first one as a snowplow clearing the road, sir. The following plasma storms will accelerate as they travel down the cleared path."

Janice Baker says, "But, Dr. Blake, you've said repeatedly you don't even know if they're heading toward us."

Sam addresses the President directly. "Sir, the first indications suggested they are. I wish to God I could say with one hundred percent certainty, but I can't. I will tell you this: I believe with ninety percent certainty they are racing toward Earth. Do we want to risk everything on a ten percent difference?"

Sam reaches for the water bottle as an eruption of voices fills his ear. Then the President's voice drowns out all others.

"Dr. Blake, Major Garcia, I'm going with your assumptions. I want a detailed plan to minimize the damage and I want it in thirty minutes. Get busy, people. Dr. Blake, do we have that long?"

Samuel Blake looks at the clock on the wall. "I hope so, Mr. President."

"I do, too," President Harris says before the audio connection goes dead in Sam's ear.

CHAPTER 11

The Marshall home

There have been no power surges during the past few minutes. Zeke puts the sandpaper aside and begins the process of creating another piece of usable walnut. As he turns for the drying shed, he finds his father staring at the subtle shading of the wooden top, a piece of fine-grit sandpaper dangling from his hand.

"Are you okay, Dad?"

His father turns away from the table, absently rubbing his left arm. "I'm fine, son. Guess I just spaced out for a moment." He stands and lays the sandpaper aside before walking stiffly in Zeke's direction. "I'm going to run back to the house."

"You feeling okay?"

His father brushes by him without a word. Zeke follows his progress through the shop and out into the sunshine. He appears to be walking with a slight limp.

Once his father is out of sight behind the ancient oak tree bulging onto the path from the shop to the house, Zeke grabs the walnut board and sights down the edge to check the crown. When gluing the boards edge to edge to form the table's larger top, it's important to alternate the crowns—the direction the grain of the wood is running—for stability. Zeke carries the piece of wood to the table saw to cut it to size. But before he can switch the saw on a scream pierces the quiet.

He pushes the board aside and races out of the shop. Rushing up the path, he finds his father crumpled on the ground with his mother kneeling over him. Zeke slides to his knees next to his parents. His father is unconscious. The dappled sunlight casts shadows across his father's ashen face.

"What happened?" Zeke says as he scoots a little closer.

"I don't know. I was looking out the kitchen window when I saw him just collapse." Zeke's heart breaks at the sight of tears streaming down her cheeks.

He reaches a hand out to his father's neck and is shocked by the coldness of his skin. His fingers fumble for a pulse: thready but persistent.

Zeke gets to his feet. "I'm going to call an ambulance." He runs toward the house, wishing, for the first time since he moved down here, that he had a cell phone.

CHAPTER 12

The White House Situation Room
Wednesday, September 29, 10:25 A.M.

President Harris returns to the Situation Room and sits wearily in one of the leather chairs. The director of the National Security Agency hurries into the room and takes the seat next to the President. He leans in to whisper to the President.

"What?" the President shouts.

All heads turn in his direction. "When?" he says in a softer tone. President Harris sags against the back of the chair as the NSA director finishes the conversation and pulls away.

The room is silent and the participants of the videoconference are frozen in place. The President jerks to his feet and places both palms on the table. "I was just informed—"

The NSA director leans over to put a hand on the President's arm. President Harris scowls and pulls his arm away.

"I think everyone in here has the necessary clearances, Charles."

"Not everyone," the NSA director says, nodding toward the front screen.

"Well, I just cleared them. The National Security Agency's satellite surveillance system is dead in the water."

A few surprised gasps.

"That means we have no way to track what our enemies are plotting. And God knows we don't lack for enemies. I want a detailed plan to further minimize the damage."

The President sits. "Dr. Blake, what the hell is going on? You do work for the Space Weather *Prediction* Center, don't you?"

Sam Blake meets the challenge head-on. "Yes, sir. I'm not going to argue semantics with you, Mr. President, but we are hindered by the lack of working instruments. I will tell you for certain that we are being hammered by solar flares stronger than any since the advent of electricity. These solar flares could play havoc—"

"Hold up, Sam," the President says before turning to the West Wing staffer who had materialized at his side. The young man, his suit coat buttoned and his red tie cinched tight to his throat, hands President Harris a single sheet of paper. The President puts on his reading glasses and quickly scans the contents as the room grows quiet. He lays the paper on the table, removes his reading glasses, and looks up at the monitor. "The good news continues. Most of Boston is without power. More solar flares, Sam?"

"Yes, and all this is a precursor to the much larger main storm. What's happening in Boston and what's already happened at the NSA is only the tip of the iceberg. The FAA is also reporting radio interference in the northern latitudes between ground stations and aircraft."

President Harris turns to the director of homeland security. "Janice, what's the plan?"

Janice Baker's hair looks like a bird's nest and the wrinkled white blouse she's wearing is decorated along the front with a coffee stain reminiscent of a Rorschach blot. Although her outward appearance is sometimes considered frumpy, she has a razor-sharp mind and the ability to adapt to rapid changes with concise, bold moves. She moves to the edge of her seat and rests her forearms on the table. "Sir, this is so far outside of our bailiwick. Tracking terrorists or stopping a terrorist threat we can do, sir, but dealing with a presumptive natural disaster is beyond our scope. That being said, working in conjunction with FEMA and the state leaders of various emergency management agencies, we have developed a response plan. I'll defer to Director Carter for an explanation of the specifics."

The President scowls. "Janice, your agency is going to be responsible for many of the actions that need to be taken. I don't want you taking a backseat."

She lowers her eyes. "I understand, Mr. President. We're ready to implement our portion of the plan."

The large screen fills with the face of Donald Carter, director of FEMA. A black man in his late fifties, he has the fleshy face and sagging chin of a lifelong government employee. He is well respected for his compassion and intelligence throughout the various FEMA agencies scattered around the country.

"Mr. President, we're in contact with a majority of the nation's power suppliers. We've asked them to reduce capacity to the bare minimum. They are reluctant to reduce supply below acceptable levels at the present time, but hope to phase down throughout the day. But, sir, they are expressing doubts about whether a switched-off grid is any less vulnerable." The director pauses for a sip of water.

"As for the airlines, we're asking them to ground all

future flights. They're not real happy, believing it to be a temporary problem."

"Mr. President," a voice says, interrupting. He glances up at the screen. "Was that you, Major Garcia?"

"Yes, sir. I believe all flights should be grounded now. Those that are in flight should be landed at the closest available airport."

The director of homeland security sits up erect in her chair. "We can't strand these passengers hundreds or thousands of miles from their destinations—"

"Director Baker," Major Garcia interrupts, "it's better to be stranded than splattered all over the ground because the pilot can't navigate or communicate."

President Harris holds up both hands. "Don, you've talked to some of the airline reps. What do you think?"

"They'll squeal like a stuck pig, sir. But Major Garcia might have a valid point."

The President mulls over the options. "Janice, tell your people to give the airlines a three-hour window. That'll allow most of the planes to reach their destination."

She nods and excuses herself from the table to make the call.

President Harris turns back to the screen. "Don, what other good news do you have?"

"Communications are going to be a major problem, sir. There is a high probability that a majority of the satellites are vulnerable, just as has already happened with the NSA. There may not be a bird left in orbit, sir.

"In conjunction with the National Emergency Management Association, we're trying to develop other lines of communication via high-frequency radio or some other type of system. I just completed a reread of the latest computer models of what might happen with such a large solar storm, and, sir, the outlook is dismal."

"'Dismal' doesn't accurately describe it, Don. Dr. Blake, Major Garcia—any way to narrow the timeline for arrival of the main storm?"

"It's just guesswork, sir," Major Garcia says, "but I do think the seventeen-hour scenario is too generous."

"What's your estimate?"

She blots the sweat from her face. "Ten, maybe twelve hours."

"Christ, a few hours to prepare for an event we have no conception of," the President mutters, but he's overheard by everyone. "Dr. Blake, you seem well versed on what the effects of the storm might be. Explain what might happen to our power grids."

Sam Blake's face fills the screen. "It's not what *might* happen, sir, it's what *will* happen. The geomagnetic storm will produce power spikes—enormous amperage—that will basically melt the transformers. The longer the length of the high-voltage lines, the more vulnerable we are. Unfortunately, our country has thousands and thousands of miles of high-voltage wire."

"Why can't we just replace the transformers and resume electrical service?"

"I'm not an expert on electrical power, Mr. President, but from the reading I've done, there may only be a few extra transformers in the whole country. We're talking huge, expensive, and complicated equipment. It takes anywhere from fifteen months or longer to manufacture just one. Not only that, but just transporting the massive devices is a long-term process. Increase that one to hundreds or even thousands, and it would take years to rebuild the electrical infrastructure."

The President turns his attention to the FEMA director. "Don, why don't the electrical companies maintain a supply of these transformers?"

"We'll need to ask them, sir, but I believe the issue is economics. As Dr. Blake said, these transformers are extremely expensive, and unfortunately our grid is so diverse most of the parts aren't interchangeable between systems."

"What if we force the power companies to switch off all power, at least until the worst of the storm passes?"

The secretary of commerce says, "Mr. President, even the loss of a few hours of electrical power would cause the loss of billions of dollars to our economy."

"If that's the toll for a few hours, Ed, what do you think the economic impact will be after a year or more without electricity?" the President snaps.

"Sir, if I may," Major Garcia says. "As Director Carter said, the electrical companies have already suggested a switched-off system may be no less vulnerable, but I would err on the side of caution and force them to hit the off switch. But I believe, regardless of the effects on the electrical grid, our primary focus should be activating the National Guard. We're looking at chaos on an unimaginable scale."

CHAPTER 13

Aura Hydroelectric Power Station
Sunndalsøra, Møre og Romsdal, Norway
Wednesday, September 29, 10:37 A.M.

Hard against the southern shore of the Sunndal fjord in northwest Norway lies one of the country's most advanced hydroelectric plants. A majority of Norway's power is generated by water, and most of the power plants are dug in along the coastline of the Norwegian Sea. Their distance from the more habitable southern portions of the country results in the need for long runs of high-voltage electrical lines to reach the more populous areas.

Engineers Lise Brekken and Baldor Amundsen are a couple of hours into their shift manning the minimalist control room of the massive power-generating plant when a flurry of alarms begins blaring. Lise, thirty-two, is a tall and athletic woman who has the Nordic features of her ancestors—well-defined facial structures with a square jaw, icy blue eyes, and long blond hair twisted into a ponytail. Her face tightens with concern.

"What the hell?" Baldor shouts over the noise. Lise glances at him and shrugs. She turns her focus to the keyboard in front of her, searching for the source of the alarms. Baldor, whose hairline only stopped receding when it ran out of real estate, picks up the phone to notify the plant director, then joins in the search on his own computer.

There had been an occasional alarm during their tenure, especially during periods of increased solar activity, but nothing like this.

They both glance up when their boss bursts through the door. Alrek Dahlmen, a short man who is nearly as tall as he is wide, hurries to where the two engineers are sitting and looks over their shoulders as the alarms continue.

"Shut it down," he shouts. "Shut everything down."

"But, sir, that will leave most of Oslo without power," Baldor says.

"Shut the damn thing down, or Oslo will be without power for the next year."

Lise and Baldor begin the process of shutting down the massive generators, but the three main generators stop suddenly of their own accord. The control room goes dark until the battery-powered emergency lighting flashes on. All of the computer screens flicker and go black as the alarms stop. The three of them stare at the dark monitors.

"What the hell happened?" Dahlmen says.

"We don't know. The instruments recorded several power spikes before the alarms started going berserk," Lise says.

Alrek, notorious for his disdain for women in the workplace, dismisses her comment and turns to Baldor. "Explain, please."

"I can't, sir. It's like Lise said. Everything was fine until it wasn't."

Dahlmen plants a fisted hand on his hip. "How severe were the power spikes?"

"On the edge of acceptable limits, but nothing we haven't seen before, sir."

Dahlmen turns to leave. "I want a full report, and I want it now," he shouts over his shoulder as he exits the control room.

Lise and Baldor stare at each other in the dimness of the dead control room.

"What the hell are we supposed to put in the report he demands?" Baldor says.

Lise sighs. "Better yet, how the hell are we going to produce a report? Every computer in the building is dead." Lise turns to Baldor. "How long do you think we'll be without power?"

CHAPTER 14

The Marshall home

Zeke slams the phone down and starts fumbling through the medicine cabinet above the stove. His hand lights on a bottle of aspirin and he yanks it from the cabinet as several other medications rain to the floor. He grabs a bottle of water from the refrigerator and hurries out the door, Lexi running alongside. The beauty of the day goes unnoticed this time as he runs down the path and kneels next to his mother.

"Has he said anything?" Zeke works to pry the cap off the aspirin bottle.

"He moaned a couple of times, but I don't think he's awake. What's wrong with him, Zeke?"

"I don't know. Has he had any health problems lately?" He finally gets the lid free and dumps three aspirin into his sweaty palm.

"No, but you know how your father is. I'm not sure he'd tell me if he was having any symptoms. He's so dadgum stubborn sometimes."

"Mom, open his mouth so I can slip some aspirin in."

She lifts her husband's head and pries his mouth open. Zeke slides the three aspirin inside. He gently places the water bottle to his father's mouth and dribbles enough water in to begin dissolving the pills.

"Why the aspirin, son?"

Zeke fiddles with the cap to the water bottle. Then he covers his mother's hand with his own and turns to face her. "Aspirin will help to thin his blood if he's had a stroke or a heart attack."

His mother moans and looks away. Zeke checks his father's pulse again, and it might be wishful thinking, but his pulse seems stronger. He wipes the sweat from his father's brow. In the distance, the sound of an approaching siren.

"Mom, stay with him. I'm gonna meet the ambulance." She glances up as he stands. "It's going to be okay, Mom."

Now if he only had the same reassurance for himself. The siren sounds closer as he reaches the middle of the gravel driveway. *Hurry, goddammit!*

The sun beats down as Zeke strains, searching for the ambulance. He is not a religious man, not after everything that he had witnessed, but he looks up at the cobalt blue sky and offers a brief, silent something to whomever or whatever might be listening. Then he sees the ambulance, a little more than a quarter mile away, and releases the breath he had unconsciously been holding.

He squats to wrap his arms around Lexi and rake his fingers through her thick, curly coat as tears wet her fur. She licks his face and he hugs her tighter. This is not the first time he's waited helplessly for the arrival of an ambulance. He stands as it turns into the drive and the siren dies in mid-whoop.

Two paramedics jump out, one male, one female. Both are young and athletic and they begin grabbing medical equipment from a side compartment of the ambulance.

Zeke steps up close. "We're going to need the stretcher."

The woman yanks open the back door and tugs the stretcher from the clamps on the floor.

"Can you explain what happened?" she says. Ramirez, according to the name tag pinned to her white uniform shirt. Petite and dark haired. She loads medical supplies onto the gurney.

"My mom saw him collapse as he was walking up the path in the backyard," Zeke says. "I checked his pulse—it's weak but it seemed to be regular. I also gave him three aspirin as soon as I could."

"You did good," she says. "Can you fill me in on his medical history as you lead the way?" Zeke grabs the front of the gurney and begins pulling it around the side of the house. He recites what little he knows of his father's health history.

The gurney bounces over several exposed tree roots as they round the house and make their way down the path. The other paramedic, a white guy named Dotson, according to his name tag, appears to spend all of his off time at the gym and seems content to allow his partner to ask all the questions. Zeke's mother stands to allow the man room to operate. He sinks to his knees and begins reaching for equipment from the bags with one hand while his other feels for a pulse at the neck. With a pair of heavy scissors, the man snips the length of Robert Marshall's T-shirt and begins attaching a series of leads to his chest.

Ramirez grabs a blood pressure cuff from one bag, whips the gray band around Robert's thin arm, and inflates the cuff. She one-hands a stethoscope into her ears and places the business end next to the cuff. A hiss of air escapes as she gradually deflates the blood pressure monitor. "Ninety over sixty," she says to her partner as she reaches for a bag of IV fluids.

Zeke can't tell from her tone if that's bad or good, but

he doesn't want to interrupt them to ask. She swabs his father's other arm with an astringent antiseptic and begins searching for a vein, finding one near his elbow after several flicks of her middle finger. She plunges the large needle into his arm and attaches the line from the IV bag, handing it up for Zeke to hold.

"Let's get him on the stretcher," Dotson says as his eyes focus on a monitor where a steady stream of green-lined peaks and valleys traces across the screen. Zeke hands the IV bag to his mother and kneels down to help the paramedics maneuver his father. He's somewhat surprised at how light his father is. He was never a large man, but Zeke never considered him fragile until his arms reach under his upper body. Together, he and Dotson lift him onto the gurney.

Ramirez pushes a lever with her foot and all three pull on the top rail of the stretcher. Zeke glances down and is surprised to discover his father's eyes open. He leans over and kisses his forehead. "You collapsed in the yard. You're on the way to the hospital."

It's hard to tell how much he understands, but he nods weakly. The three push the stretcher up the slight incline of the path and back around the house. Zeke looks back to see his mother shuffling up the trail, her head down and her shoulders stooped.

"C'mon, Mom," he says. "You ride with him in the ambulance and I'll grab the pickup and follow." She catches up to them as one of the paramedics swings the rear doors open.

CHAPTER 15

The White House Situation Room
Wednesday, September 29, 10:56 A.M.

President Harris is doing his best to block out the ongoing conversations while his mind spins through numerous scenarios—none of them good. *Cut off power to millions of people on a hunch? Force all planes to ground, stranding thousands of people hundreds of miles from their destination? Announce to the nation that our modern life is about to be thrust back to the Dark Ages?*

The President is stirred from his thoughts when several loud gasps replace the chatter. He glances up to see several hands pointed toward one of the television screens tucked into the front corner of the room. "What is it?" President Harris stands and works his way around the table toward the television. A large banner is superimposed on the bottom of the screen: "Fiery Crash in Seattle." "Oh my God," he mutters. "We need sound," he shouts to the room.

A switch, somewhere deep in the recesses of the Situation Room, is thrown and the voice of the CNN reporter floods the room. "Authorities say all radio communications were lost as one aircraft was landing and the other was taxiing onto the runway for takeoff. Both jets collided and instantly broke into flames. No word yet on which airlines or what flights or even the type of aircraft involved. Also, there has been no official word on the number of casualties, but I would think they would be numerous. This is Ron Bloom reporting live in Seattle. Now back to . . ."

The sound fades, leaving the conference room quiet as a tomb. President Harris paces the length of the room. He stops near the rear and pauses before turning to face his advisors. "I want all flights grounded this minute. I also want all power grids switched off within the next thirty minutes. Stop all trains, whether they are powered by the electrical grid or not. If we can't communicate with them we'll have a dozen more disasters on our hands. Have those in charge begin shutting down all nuclear facilities. Admiral Hickerson, activate the National Guard in every state. I don't care how much heat we take over this decision. We have to do what's best for the country. I want updates every thirty minutes. My staff will draft a statement and I will address the nation as soon as possible."

The President exits the Situation Room and everyone starts to talk at once. Scott Alexander is at the President's elbow as they walk toward the staircase leading to the first floor. "Mr. President . . . should we be concerned about the panic your address to the nation could cause?"

The President ignores the question as they make their way up the stairs and through the maze of hallways that make up the West Wing.

In the Oval Office the President collapses into the chair behind his desk. Alexander takes a seat in one of the flanking chairs. President Harris swivels to look at the sun streaming through the windows. It's a beautiful fall day in the nation's capital.

The President rakes his hands through his hair and

speaks without turning to face his old friend. "What the hell are we supposed to do, Scott?"

"We're doing everything that can possibly be done, sir." Alexander pauses as he tries to frame the words for his next statement. "We should think about moving you to the bunker."

The President swivels around in his chair. "I will do no such thing, Scott. And I don't want to hear another god-damn word about it."

"Yes, sir . . . but, Paul, we've been friends for most of our adult lives and I know how stubborn you can be. At the very minimum, we should start preparations for a move in that direction in the coming days."

President Harris gives Alexander a withering look. "We need to work on what I'm going to tell the nation, Scott. That's our focus right now. How the hell do I tell the people that life as they know it is going to disappear and the strongest nation on earth can't do a damn thing about it?"

Chapter 16

TransJet Flight 62, south of Newfoundland
Wednesday, September 29, 10:59 A.M.

TransJet Flight 62 is off the coast of southern Newfoundland destined for Paris after departing from Dallas. The Boeing 747-700 is on autopilot, cruising at 33,000 feet at a speed of 460 knots. Captain Steve Henderson has flown this route enough times to do it with his eyes closed. He turns to his copilot, and current lover, Cheryl Wilson. He removes his headset and motions for her to do the same.

"How about a romantic dinner in Paris?"

Cheryl rolls her eyes. "How many romantic dinners have we had in Paris? I'm more interested in a nice, private room-service dinner."

He frowns.

"In the nude?" she says.

He smiles. "I think I like that idea better."

Both in their midforties, they've been paired up in the cockpit for the last eight months. Each of them is recently divorced, he for the first time and she for the second. Both ex-spouses had voiced the same complaint—too much time away from home.

Without warning, an intense light flashes through the cockpit, momentarily blinding them. At the exact moment of the flash, the autopilot disengages and the aircraft decelerates. They both quickly clap on their headsets.

"What the hell was that?" the captain says as he wrestles with the controls, trying to maintain airspeed and altitude.

"I don't know."

He reaches over to toggle a series of switches. "Autopilot will not reengage."

Both scan the instruments searching for any indications of damage to the critical components of the plane. Cheryl toggles the radio button on the wheel to talk with Steve but finds dead air. Frustrated, she yanks off her headset. "What's wrong with the radio?"

He pulls his headset off. "I don't know, but the autopilot won't reset. The satellites can't seem to get a fix on our position."

"Could've been a solar flare. There's supposed to be increased solar activity, but I've never seen anything like that."

"Me, either. Think it had some effect on satellite tracking and communications?"

"It may have. Try the radio again."

He clamps the headset on and punches the radio button on the wheel. "Gander Center, TransJet Flight 62."

Static.

"Gander Center . . . TransJet Flight 62. Please acknowledge."

Gander Center is Newfoundland's air traffic control for all transcontinental flights flying the busy air corridor.

Steve pulls the mike away from his lips. "Cheryl, check to see if you have a cell signal."

"In the middle of the ocean?"

"Just check. We need some way to communicate."

She pulls her phone from the side pocket and lights the screen. "Nothing."

"What the hell is going on?" Steve stabs at the button on the radio, scanning through all available frequencies.

"Anything?"

Steve shakes his head and looks at his copilot. "We're screwed. We're flying blind in one of the busiest flight corridors in the world."

CHAPTER 17

NOAA Space Weather Prediction Center
Wednesday, September 29, 11:08 A.M.

Sam turns his chair to the window and stares at the sun-painted peaks of the Rocky Mountains. White patches from an early season snowfall glint in the midmorning sun.

Without turning in Kaylee's direction he says, "Where's your family?"

"New York."

"Manhattan?"

"Yeah. And my brother's at Stanford."

"Do you have any relatives living outside the city?" Sam's voice has taken on a soft tone.

"I have an aunt and uncle in Wisconsin. My mother's sister."

"You should probably call your parents and tell them to start making their way to Wisconsin, Kaylee. I don't think they want to be in New York City when the power goes out." He turns to face her. "Tell them what's happening, and tell them to hurry. I don't know if your brother will have time to fly to Wisconsin, but you need to call him, too."

"What about your family, Sam?"

"My ex-wife and two girls are in Southern California. A sister in Missouri. My sister should be okay where she is, but I'm going to call the ex and tell her to head up to the cabin her parents own in the mountains." He removes his glasses, rubbing the pinch points on his nose. "There's a well and a generator. At least I can tell them to stock up on gasoline. Once the fuel's exhausted, there's a mountain stream near the cabin."

"What are *we* going to do, Sam?"

He pulls out his wallet and thumbs through a stack of credit cards. He works the gold Amex from its slot and slides it across to Kaylee. "Have Daniel grab a couple of people and go shopping. Tell them to buy as many gas containers as they can and fill them to run the generator on-site. Tell him to purchase as much water and canned food items as he can. Spread the purchases around. Have them take the big panel truck parked out back."

"Worried about raising a few eyebrows?" Kaylee says.

"Maybe. The panic will start when the President delivers his address to the nation."

"When's that going to be?"

"Hopefully pretty quick. I don't think we have much time."

Kaylee takes the credit card and leaves the room.

Sam pulls his cell phone from his pocket and turns again to face the mountains. When he looks at the screen he's somewhat surprised to find he still has cell service. He scrolls through his contacts and winces at all the names. He stops on his ex-wife's name and punches the call link.

They divorced almost five years ago, and the reasons why still elude him. Grown apart was her excuse. His two children—Abby, now fifteen, and Gracie, thirteen—had the unfortunate experience of suffering through their parents' divorce. Over the years, both Teresa and Sam have mellowed enough to be civil to each other. The kids spend the summers with Sam, and one weekend a month he flies to Southern California.

"Hello, Sam," his ex-wife says in her raspy voice. Neither of them has remarried but the children recently told him their mother is now dating one man steadily.

"Hi, Teresa. I wish I were calling with better news . . ."

Chapter 18

The White House, the Oval Office
Wednesday, September 29, 11:42 A.M.

President Harris, his sleeves rolled up and his yellow tie loosened, sits behind his desk as a steady stream of advisors moves in and out of the Oval Office as if it had a revolving door. Everyone is attempting to carry on business as usual. Scott Alexander sits on one of the two muted-yellow sofas filling one side of the office, listening. Between guests, the President will sometimes ask his opinion, but otherwise he remains a spectator. He glances down at the thick sheaf of papers resting in his lap and riffles the pages with his thumb. *Enlil* is the name given to the latest computer simulation. Alexander has read the report from cover to cover—twice—coming away with the same impression each time: *we're in deep shit.*

He stands, tosses the report on the coffee table, and wanders around the room, trying to bleed off nervous energy. The President's chief speechwriter hurries into the room again, trying to craft the perfect statement without creating worldwide panic. *What's the point?* Alexander thinks as he stops near the window overlooking the Rose Garden. He turns away and continues prowling.

During a lull, Alexander approaches the desk and sits in one of the flanking chairs. President Harris glances up with a perturbed look on his face, "Nothing to do, Scott?"

"No, there's plenty to do, I guess, but I don't think strong-arming a senator over a piece of legislation is relevant now."

President Harris tosses his pen on the desk and leans back in his chair. "Listen, Scott, we don't know what the hell is going to happen, but we need to continue working. There's still going to be a government—even if we have to work by candlelight. Regardless of the doomsday prophets, this won't be the end of the world. Will it be hard? Damn right. Will people suffer? Yes, they will, but we can overcome, Scott. We have to—it's the only choice we have."

"I'm more concerned, sir, with the immediate effects of your address to the nation. How the hell are we going to control the reactions of the people? There will be looting, hoarding, and killing from the get-go."

"What are you suggesting, Scott? That we allow the people to remain blissfully unaware until the moment the storm hits? That's goddamn irresponsible."

Scott doesn't answer as the President stews over his statements. Then, in almost a whisper he says, "Maybe we should. What's to be gained by telling them in advance? A few gallons of gasoline? A few containers of water, which will go to the first ten or fifteen people in the store? Then what? We might be better off waiting until the playing field is level and no one has electricity."

The President stands and walks to the large windows.

Scott doesn't press the issue. While the President stews, he reads, again, the inscription woven into the perimeter of the custom-made carpet: *The welfare of each of us is dependent fundamentally upon the welfare of all of us,* a quote from Teddy Roosevelt.

President Harris turns from the windows and begins to

pace, the limp more evident. The silent reflection is interrupted when Janice Baker enters.

"I'm sorry for intruding, Mr. President, but I wanted to bring you the latest issue we're facing." She walks to the front of the desk as President Harris collapses onto his chair.

"What is it, Janice?"

"Sir, we issued the order to ground all flights but some of the transcontinental flights, especially those flying longer routes, never received word."

The President leans forward in his chair. "Are you saying we still have planes in the air with no way to communicate? Or to navigate?"

"Yes, sir. The FAA is trying to establish contact via high-frequency radio, but no one knows if it will work. If so, they'll try to land the planes at the closest available airport."

"Christ, I should have listened to Dr. Blake."

"Sir, most of these pilots could fly their routes blindfolded, they do it so often."

"They could when they had radios and navigation. Landing those planes could turn into a disaster in a heartbeat." He points toward the television screen, where continuing coverage of the collision at the Seattle airport plays in silence. "Hell, those planes were flying short hops and look what happened."

"Sir, they'll just have to—"

The intercom buzzes and the President punches the button. "Yes, Barbara?"

"Sir, Director Carter on line one."

The President puts the call on speakerphone. "Don, I'm with Janice and Scott. All right if I leave it on speaker?"

"That's fine, Mr. President. They probably need to know what's happening. And it's not good, sir. The New Orleans area has had three days of heavy rain. Enough rain that

Lake Pontchartrain and the Mississippi River are near their flood stage."

President Harris leans closer to the phone, resting his elbows on the desk. "Don't tell me all the new pumps the Corps of Engineers put in aren't keeping up with all that water."

"Well, that's the problem, sir. About half of them seized up when a power surge of some sort hit the system."

"What are you saying, Don? They don't have enough pumps?"

"No, sir. They're working like crazy to replace what they can, but . . ."

President Harris wipes his brow. "How bad is it going to get, Don?"

A pause on the other end of the line. "If it continues to rain, some parts of the city will experience Katrina-like devastation."

CHAPTER 19

Durant, Oklahoma

When the ambulance doors slam shut, Zeke darts back into the house to grab the keys to his father's pickup. After locking up, he steps outside and whistles for Lexi. She races around the side of the house as Zeke opens the door to the pickup. Lexi jumps aboard and he slides behind the wheel. The engine rumbles to life and he slams on the accelerator, leaving a trail of gravel and dust swirling behind them.

Zeke whips the pickup into the short driveway to his home and jumps from the cab. Lexi follows and enters the house when Zeke swings the door open. He tries to explain to her that he'll be back soon and gives her tummy a quick rub. He locks the door and hurries back to the pickup. After a quick U-turn he steers the truck onto the roadway. The two homes are located a couple of miles south of the main highway leading into Durant. Zeke white-knuckles the wheel as he steers around the larger potholes and shudders over the washboard sections where the asphalt and gravel have given way.

At the highway, he turns east and gooses the pickup up to seventy, hoping like hell a farmer on a tractor doesn't pull out in front of him. He focuses on his mother and the uncertainty of his father's health. The worry etched on her face as the ambulance doors closed gnaws on Zeke.

On the outskirts of town, he eases off the gas and slaps his thigh—Ruth needs to know what's happening. For the second time in one day he wishes he hadn't turned his back on technology. Zeke makes a left on Route 69 near downtown and drives toward the hospital.

Durant is a small town, home to a little over fifteen thousand people. But it's the hub of southeastern Oklahoma and home to the largest hospital in the region. He turns off at the hospital exit and slots the pickup in the first available parking spot. The lot is jammed with farm trucks of every size, many with hay spears pointing toward the heavens. Most are covered in a thick layer of gravel dust with slashes of red mud along the fenders. Zeke locks the truck and runs toward the emergency room entrance.

The automatic doors part and he follows the signs to the waiting room, where he finds his mother slumped in a chair. He takes a seat next to her and wraps an arm around her narrow shoulders.

"Do we know anything yet?" he whispers in her ear.

"No. They wheeled him into the emergency room as soon as we arrived." Her tears have ended, leaving a salty residue on her cheeks.

"Did he say anything in the ambulance?"

She shakes her head.

"Do you want me to call Ruth?" Zeke says.

"Not until we know something. The kids are in school and I don't want her thinking she needs to rush up here. I think it would be best if we had something more to tell her, don't you?"

"You're probably right." Zeke turns his gaze away from the hurt in her pale green eyes. They sit in silence.

The lights in the waiting room flicker and flash off, only to re-illuminate a moment later.

"That's strange," Zeke says.

"What's that, son?"

"The lights. When Dad and I were working in the shop the lights flickered on and off a couple of times. We thought the issue was isolated to our area—"

"Marshall family?" a tall black nurse says, using the heel of her tennis shoe to hold open the door. She's dressed in purple scrubs with a stethoscope hanging around her neck.

Zeke waves, then takes his mother by the elbow to help her up from the chair and leads her across the lobby.

"If you'll follow me, I'll take you back to the ICU," the nurse says.

They fall in behind her as she ushers them down the hall.

"What happened to my father?" Zeke asks.

"The doctor will explain, but I will tell you Mr. Marshall suffered a heart attack."

Barbara Marshall inhales an audible breath. Zeke slides his arm around her.

The hallway is lit with green-tinged fluorescent lights that reflect on the polished linoleum. As they shuffle past other patients' rooms, Zeke resists the urge to peek inside. The nurse stops at a door and ushers them into the room.

Zeke pulls up short, struggling to contain his shock at the number of tubes and wires snaking toward his father. His father is awake and smiles weakly. His mother shrugs off Zeke's arm and moves to his bedside.

Zeke turns to find another man in the room. Dark haired with dark skin, the man is in his midthirties, short and diminutive, with a white coat draped over his narrow shoulders. Zeke offers his hand.

"I'm Dr. Ahmed, and I'll be taking care of your father."

For the second time in as many minutes, Zeke works to conceal his surprise. In Afghanistan, and all through the desert, he met many Ahmeds. And most weren't pleasant encounters. The doctor's name, along with the familiar accent, puts Zeke on edge. "I'm Zeke Marshall and that's my mother, Barbara. Thanks for looking after my dad. Can you explain what happened?"

"Mr. Marshall has suffered a myocardial infarction, a heart attack. We are monitoring his heart through the use of an ECG machine, which measures the heart's electrical activity—"

"How bad was the heart attack?"

Anger flickers in the doctor's eyes. "I'm waiting for the blood work, which should be completed anytime. But, from looking at the ECG, I believe your father is a lucky man, having suffered a non–ST segment elevation myocardial infarction—"

"In English, please."

"I'm sorry, sir. May I continue?"

Zeke nods.

"As I was saying, not that any heart attack is good, mind you, but this type does less damage to the heart muscle."

"What could have caused the heart attack?" Zeke asks.

"A blockage in the arteries leading to the heart muscle. I administered a thrombolysis immediately upon his arrival to the emergency room. It is a clot-dissolving agent which helps restore blood flow and prevent further damage to the heart."

Zeke says, "So what's next? How do we treat the blockage?"

"Once your father is stabilized, I will send him for an arteriogram to discover how much blockage and in which coronary arteries. The doctors upstairs will be able to reduce the blockage using angioplasty and insertion of stents that will keep the arteries open."

"When are you scheduling the test?" Zeke says.

"Hopefully later this evening, if he has no more unusual ECG readings. I'll be back soon to check on your father while the nurses schedule the arteriogram." The doctor turns toward the door, then stops and turns back. "I understand you administered aspirin to your father at the scene."

Zeke nods.

"Probably saved his life," Ahmed says before exiting the room.

Zeke steps up to his father's bedside, not knowing how to express his feelings without it being awkward. "So much for all the jogging you used to do."

CHAPTER 20

TransJet Flight 62, south of Greenland
Wednesday, September 29, 11:45 A.M.

Captain Steve Henderson wipes the palm of his hand across his pant leg. Flight 62 is still some distance from landfall on the coast of Ireland. His copilot, Cheryl Wilson, is slowly dialing through the radio frequencies in search of a human voice. The loss of the autopilot has the captain glued to his instruments, trying to maintain a consistent speed and altitude. They're forced to navigate by compass and map, something neither has done since they were flying Cessna 172s back in high school.

"Holding altitude and speed are fine, Steve, but what are we going to do when we begin the landing process?" Wilson says.

The captain looks away from the instruments long enough to see the fear on her face. Cheryl Wilson looks younger than she is, with black hair streaked blond and cut in an even line just above the shoulders. "Pray, I guess. Other than that, we can only hope the home office is aware of our loss of radio contact and navigation abilities, and is working to establish communications with us on landfall."

"What if they can't?"

Henderson sighs. "You're killing me with all these questions, Cheryl. All I can do is drive the damn plane." He glances at the altimeter again. The air corridor they are flying is the main flight path for flights between Europe and the United States, often with jumbo jets within just a few thousand feet of one another. He turns back to his copilot. "Look, I'm sorry, babe. I'm a little stressed at the moment."

Cheryl says, "What if we detour north and put it down in Reykjavik?"

"What if every other plane in transit has the same idea? Without radio communications or any way to navigate, that would turn into a clusterfuck. I think our best course of action is to continue on to the UK and hope we can reestablish radio contact."

Cheryl turns away to stare out the windscreen.

"Listen, Cheryl, we need to work together on this."

Cheryl nods and reaches over the console to rub his shoulder. "Should we inform the flight attendants about the situation?"

"Hell no."

Cheryl yanks her hand back. "Why not? You don't think they have a right to know what's happening?"

"Not until *we* know what the hell's happening. The last thing we need is an airplane full of distressed passengers."

She shakes her head and looks away.

Steve turns back to the instruments, thinking: *the last thing we need is a lovers' quarrel in the cockpit of a plane flying blind.*

CHAPTER 21

The Oval Office
Wednesday, September 29, 11:55 A.M.

All thoughts of an address to the nation are put on hold as the President and his advisors work the phones in search of a solution to the impending disaster in New Orleans. The entry to the Oval Office is a revolving door with people streaming in and out, but no one has come up with a viable alternative. If it were just an electricity issue they could use generators to power the pumps, but the motors themselves are shot. In between calls, President Harris keeps a close eye on the television where the coverage of the collision at the Seattle airport continues.

The President hangs up the phone and looks over at his chief of staff. “This is just the beginning.”

Scott nods. “We’re doing everything that can be done.”

The President lowers his voice. “We’re fucked, Scott. Hell, we can’t even help one small area of the country. What’s going to happen when the entire nation is without power?”

“What are we going to do to stop it? We can’t. We’ll just have to do the best we can.”

One of the staffers turns up the volume on the television.

The CNN reporter is speaking. "Susan, we've learned that the two aircraft involved were 737-600s, each capable of carrying a hundred and thirty-two passengers along with five crewmembers. No word yet on the number of injured, and firefighters are still trying to contain the fires that continue to rage from spilled jet fuel. We've just received word that all flights are now grounded. No reason was given for the grounding, but one would think the disruption in radio communications, such as happened here, may be the overriding reason. I have called numerous sources but . . ."

Amy Whitworth, the chief speechwriter, hurries into the office and approaches the desk. Her blond hair is pulled up in a ponytail and most of her fingers are stained with blue ink. She slides a sheaf of papers across the desk. "Mr. President, this is the latest draft. But to be honest, sir, I don't know what to write that won't cause nationwide panic."

President Harris riffles the pages with his thumb. "It's impossible. That's why I'm thinking about not delivering a speech at all."

"But, sir, don't you think that would be irresponsible?"

The President waves a hand at the vacant chair. "Amy, have a seat for a minute."

She tucks her dress under her legs sits.

"How old are you? Twenty-eight? Twenty-nine?" the President asks.

"I'm twenty-nine, sir."

President Harris crosses his arms and leans back in his chair. "Let me ask you a what-if question. What would you do if I told you that the power was going to go out for months, maybe years?"

"Well, sir, I'd go get as much water and food as I could. Then, I'd go to the bank and withdraw all of my money. After that, I'd fill up my car with gas and get out of the city."

"Exactly. And your fellow three hundred million citizens will be trying to do the same thing."

Amy twirls a stray strand of hair around her finger. "But, sir, don't you think they have a right to know?"

"That's the ethical question I'm dealing with. Thank you for all of your work."

Amy takes that as her cue to leave. As she exits the office, the intercom on the desk buzzes. "Mr. President, Admiral Hickerson on line three."

The President hesitates, his hand hovering above the handset. "What do you think the grumpy old bastard wants?"

"Hell if I know," Alexander says, running his finger around the collar of his shirt to loosen it. At five-eight, he wears the same shirt size he wore in college.

Admiral Hickerson, the grandson of a famous World War II admiral, does not lack in ego. He tends to be somewhat disdainful of *political* presidents, believing they'll be around at most eight years, whereas he has devoted his life to his country. The President plucks up the handset.

"Mr. President," the deep voice says, "I'm getting a lot of blowback on activating the National Guard, sir."

"What kind of blowback, Admiral?"

"Well, sir, no one is privy to the information we possess and many are questioning the reasons for the activation."

"The reason, Admiral, is because I ordered it. Does there have to be more?"

"No, sir, I don't suppose there does. But what would you like them to do, sir?"

"Admiral, I don't care if they stand around scratching their asses. I want them ready to go when this shit storm hits."

CHAPTER 22

Durant

Some of the color has returned to Robert Marshall's cheeks. He lies in the hospital bed, an IV above his head dripping fluid into his body. His color isn't back to normal, but at least it's now a couple shades darker than the white sheets that surround him. He even feels well enough to carry on a conversation, which Zeke mostly ignores, as his mother and father speak in softened tones.

Zeke paces four steps forward before turning and pacing back along the windowed wall overlooking the corridor. The odors, the subdued lighting, the beeping of the equipment, the constant stream of nurses in and out of the room, the squeaky-clean floors—all a reminder of a time he would rather blot from his memory forever.

"Do you want me to call Ruth?" Zeke says.

His mother turns in his direction. "Why don't we wait until we have the results of the test, first."

"But I would want to know if I were her, Mom."

"I know, son, but she has to care for her fam—" The words die in her throat as her cheeks turn a deep crimson.

"You can say it, Mom. Family. It's been three years. I

know she has a family, but I still think she would want to know," Zeke says.

"Zeke, I'm sorry. I didn't mean to . . . I don't know what I was thinking."

"It's okay, Mom." Zeke steps toward the door and, without turning to look at his parents, says, "I'm going to walk for a few minutes."

He wanders down the hallway, with no specific place in mind, just to gain a little distance from his parents.

After the IED exploded beneath our Humvee chaos reigned inside. Through the smoky haze, the screams of my friends were loud enough to penetrate my near deafness from the explosion. The smell of cordite and singed flesh was overpowering. Someone, most likely the soldiers in the following vehicle, pried open the doors and the heavy smoke cleared. The bright beams of several flashlights washed over the interior and I knew immediately that two of my squad members were dead. There was blood everywhere.

Someone grabbed me by the arm and dragged me outside. Pain—all I felt was mind-numbing pain. Someone jabbed a needle into my arm and the morphine coursed through my body, taking the edge off. I must have passed out. My next memory was being loaded into a rescue helicopter. Above, the blades cut through the dark night.

I remained at the base hospital for two weeks. Shrapnel wounds covered my lower body, and my shoulder, which was hit with a large piece of flying debris, looked like hamburger. But I was alive. If I had been riding on the other side of the Humvee, I'd have been dead. At the start of the third week one of the doctors informed me I was being transferred to the VA hospital in Oklahoma City.

After arriving there, I struggled not only with the physical wounds but the emotional wounds—why did I survive and the others didn't? It was a question I couldn't answer until I met Amelia. With a head of red, curly hair and skin the color of porcelain, she had freckles sprinkled across the bridge of her beautiful nose. She was nearly as tall as I am, and I took every opportunity to peer into her green eyes as she led me by the elbow along the busy corridors. After four years of nursing, she had witnessed the tragedies of war firsthand, but she hadn't let the suffering consume her. Her cheery disposition was a welcome relief to every wounded soldier confined to the hospital.

From the first moment I saw her I knew she was the woman I wanted—to care for, to love like no other.

Every soldier in the hospital was in love with Amelia—hell, who wouldn't be? She was smart as a whip and, though not drop-dead gorgeous, attractive nonetheless. The red hair was often pulled back into a ponytail, revealing a face almost devoid of makeup.

I felt the envious stares of the other wounded soldiers as Amelia and I shared a meal at the two-top table tucked into the corner of the hospital cafeteria. I felt like the guy crowned prom king sharing lunch with her. The way she laughed, the way she cocked her head when she contemplated an answer to another of my endless questions, the way she brushed the strands of hair from her face—each little gesture was magnified in my mind.

"Can we go on a real date?" I blurted out during one of our meals.

"Zeke, if you haven't noticed, we're in a hospital. Besides, I make it a policy to not date my patients." She'd said it with a smile, but my heart was no less crushed.

"What about when I get out of the hospital?"

She paused for a long while. "Maybe."

CHAPTER 23

NOAA Space Weather Prediction Center
Wednesday, September 29, 12:09 P.M.

Samuel Blake is seated in his office reading through the latest data when Kaylee Connor taps on the door.

"Sam, we have reports of power outages in Alaska and Northern Canada as well as rolling blackouts all along the eastern seaboard."

"This storm is moving much faster than I thought possible."

"You think solar flares might be causing it or is this the leading edge of the geomagnetic storm?"

"I don't know. I would find it hard to believe that the CME is already here. I told the President we probably have another eight hours. And I thought that was a safe estimate. What does the latest data tell us?"

"That's just it, Sam. Not only is ACE dead, but as recently as five minutes ago, the Solar and Heliospheric Observatory was no longer broadcasting information."

Dr. Blake stands. "SOHO's dead?"

"We don't know. NASA is working to reestablish communication. They don't know if this is an anomaly or if the satellite is fried. My bet is that the satellite is toast."

"Damn." Sam thumbs his glasses farther up his nose. "I think the plasma storm could hit much sooner than we thought." He brushes past Kaylee, on a beeline back to the conference room. Kaylee follows.

Sam flips on the camera, clips on the microphone, and inserts the earpiece in his ear. "Can anyone hear me? Hello? This is an emergency. Is anybody listening?" He turns to Kaylee. "How does this thing work?"

"I think it has to go through the satellite for them to hear you."

"Well, we know that's not going to work." He yanks off the microphone and removes the earpiece. "See if you can get in touch with Major Garcia. Maybe she can work this up through the command, if I'm unsuccessful."

"What are you going to do?" Kaylee shouts after him.

"I'm going to try to contact the President." In his office, Sam scoots around his desk and sits. He taps the mouse to wake the computer but stares at the screen. Then he launches Google and types in a search phrase. When the results appear, he reaches for the phone and punches in the digits.

"Hello, you've reached the White House. All operators are currently . . ."

Chapter 24

Point Lepreau Nuclear Generating Station
Maces Bay, New Brunswick, Canada
Wednesday, September 29, 12:15 P.M.

On a point of land jutting into the Bay of Fundy, part of the Atlantic between New Brunswick, Canada, and Nova Scotia, sits Canada's only Atlantic coast nuclear reactor. Three years behind schedule and one billion dollars over budget on the latest refurbishment, the CANDU 6 reactor has just recently been restarted, generating 630 megawatts of electricity.

Pierre Gagnon, a slender man of French descent, and three other employees are manning the state-of-the-art control room that rivals even the most sophisticated control rooms at NASA headquarters. The front wall contains lights, dials, and gauges by the hundreds, all to prevent a nuclear mishap. Set away from the wall, taking up most of the middle portion of the room, is a large desk that contains the group data displays, or computers, which provide feedback from the nearly three thousand other sensors scattered throughout the plant. Gagnon is manning the main desk while swiping through cell phone pics of his recently born second son.

Without warning, the front wall lights up with warning lights and a siren sounds just before the power to the control room dies.

His cell clatters to the desk. His coworkers, who had been making progress notes at the main display, freeze in place when the lights extinguish. The automatic diesel generator kicks on to relight the control room. The backup generator powers only the control room so the nuclear plant can be safely shut down.

Although there are numerous built-in fail-safes to halt the fission of nuclear material during a power loss, the staff is drilled repeatedly on what to do when the plant loses electrical power. All four workers scurry about the room trying to put those lessons into play.

The monitors flicker back to life. "Power's out for the entire plant," Gagnon shouts.

"Did the control rods drop?" one of the other workers shouts over the noise.

"Negative on the control rods," Gagnon says. "They have not released." The control rods are suspended above the core by electromagnets and are designed to drop with the sudden loss of electricity. Constructed of materials such as hafnium and boron, the rods control the rate of fission.

"What about the injector system?" another worker asks.

"Waiting on computer reboot to know for sure, but why didn't the rods drop?" Gagnon says. Although they have drilled endlessly on these emergency measures, it's not the same when the real thing happens.

"Think the safety line on the rods is still in place from the refurbishment?" Antoine Cassel asks.

"Oh shit," Gagnon yells. "The gadolinium nitrate was not, repeat not, deployed. The injection system failed."

"What the hell is going on?" Cassel says. "All of those damn systems are supposed to kick in automatically."

His question goes unanswered as Gagnon grabs one of the numerous telephones and places the call that no employee wants to make. As soon as the phone is answered, Pierre says, "Sir, the reactor is still active without the cooling systems. We are facing the real probability of a core meltdown."

CHAPTER 25

TransJet Flight 62, near the coast of Scotland
Wednesday, September 29, 12:33 P.M.

Captain Steve Henderson wipes his brow. "Plot a course to London Heathrow."

"We're not going to Paris?" Copilot Cheryl Wilson asks.

"Hell no, we're not going to Paris. I'm not flying this plane over half of Europe with no navigation or communications."

Cheryl reaches for the book containing the maps of Europe as the captain uses his left hand to dial through the radio frequencies. "Glasgow Center, TransJet Flight 62 . . . come in." Nothing. He dials another frequency. "Glasgow Center, TransJet Flight 62, please acknowledge." He dials another and tries again. Not a peep.

"Check your cell phone again, Cheryl."

She reaches across the maps to extract her cell phone from the side pocket of the fuselage. "No service," she says as she tucks the phone under her leg.

"So much for room service in Paris," he mutters.

She glances at him. His mouth is clenched and his

broad shoulders are trembling from the constant strain. "We can do this, Steve. We need to use the same landing procedure we've used a hundred times."

"What happens if one pilot panics and doesn't follow protocol?"

"We're all professionals, Steve. I don't think we need to be concerned with someone panicking."

"I'm glad you're so self-assured." His size-fifteen shoes are working the pedals, battling a nasty crosswind.

"Come to a heading of one-two-zero," she says in her calmest voice.

"Turning to one-two-zero."

Cheryl traces their path on the map with a red manicured nail. "We're going to skirt Glasgow to the east, then turn south."

"Sounds like a plan. Keep an eye out the window for other traffic if you can. Please." Steve takes a deep breath before punching the button that triggers the cabin intercom system. "Folks, this is the captain speaking. We have been diverted to London."

The groans from the cabin can be heard through the closed and locked cockpit door. "I apologize for the inconvenience. We should be on the ground in London shortly, where ground personnel will assist you." He punches the cabin intercom off.

"You did good, Steve. Normal voice, no sense of panic."

"Thanks." The intercom light flashes and he hesitates before answering.

"Better explain to the flight attendants what's happening," Cheryl says.

He fingers the button and listens for a moment. "Lisa, come to the cockpit and I'll explain."

There's a single knock at the door a moment later.

Cheryl stands to unlock the cockpit door. Lisa Robbins has flown with Steve and Cheryl numerous times. She enters the cockpit as Cheryl retakes her seat.

"What's the deal, Steve?" she says.

He looks at her briefly. "We have no satellite navigation and no communications. Everything went dead just as we were passing the southern coast of Newfoundland."

Lisa takes a moment to digest the information. "What can I do to help?"

"Thanks, Lisa. Keep the passengers calm until we can put her on the ground. Tell them Paris is socked in with fog, or whatever else you can come up with."

"I can do that." Lisa exits the cockpit.

Cheryl relocks the door and returns to her maps. Making quick calculations on time and distance, she marks the time to the new compass heading. She pulls a binder from another side pocket of her seat and does a quick read of the landing procedures for London Heathrow. "Steve, we need to think about starting our descent."

Steve winces as he reaches for the throttles. "Where do we need to be?"

Cheryl glances at the altimeter. "Bleed off about six thousand."

He looks out the window for any glints of metal in the sun before slowly pulling back on the throttles. "Descending to twenty-seven thousand. Is the TCAS system on?"

"Yes, Captain," Cheryl says while she cranes her neck to survey the brilliant blue sky around them.

Steve eases off the throttles. "Now might be a good time to say a prayer."

Chapter 26

Durant

Zeke wanders into a vacant waiting room and collapses onto a chair.

I took Amelia's "maybe" response and ran with it. A week later, I gained my release from the hospital and found a run-down one-bedroom apartment near the hospital and signed a six-month lease. I could have cared less that the beige carpeting was stained or that the stove only had one working burner—proximity to Amelia was my only desire. Three days a week, I limped into the rehab office and worked with a therapist to regain my range of motion and had a lunch date with Amelia. Our lunches soon turned to dinners out, and I felt like the luckiest guy in the world when we spent the weekend at her place.

I found a good job, a career starter, and spent every moment of every day thinking about Amelia. Was I infatuated with her? You bet your ass I was. I was head over heels in love with that caring, understanding, brighten-my-world woman. The memories of war faded as our relationship deepened.

At the start of our fourth month of dating, I descended to bended knee. "Amelia, I love you more than life itself. Will you marry me?"

She clapped her hands to her mouth as tears drifted down her cheeks. "Yes, Zeke. Yes." She grabbed my hands and pulled me to my feet. We were both crying as she covered my face with kisses.

Amelia had been married once before, to her high school sweetheart, with a big, lavish wedding. The marriage lasted only two years, and another large wedding production wasn't on her bucket list. We agreed on a small civil ceremony with our very close friends and family members a month later.

After the ceremony we jetted off to the shimmering waters of the Caribbean for a week of sun. Laughter and lovemaking were constant staples of our week in paradise.

Two months later, we purchased our first home—a three-bedroom, single-story rancher in a neighborhood of other young couples. The house was older, built in the '50s, with brick along the bottom third topped out with siding painted a bright shade of blue we both laughed about. A project house in need of a little TLC.

One day a few months later, Amelia snuggled next to me on the sofa, her legs splayed across my lap, her tanned feet sporting the dark blue nail polish of a recent pedicure. She took my hand. "Zeke, I'm pregnant."

"You're what?"

"We're having a baby."

We were in the third trimester of Amelia's pregnancy when complications began to develop.

Claiming exhaustion one night, Amelia went to bed early, leaving me on the sofa, channel surfing on our new television. A horrible scream shattered the quiet. I raced into the bedroom to find my wife convulsing. "Amelia!" I screamed her name, unsure of what to do.

I sat gently on the bed and wrapped one of my arms around her thrashing body while I fumbled for my cell phone. With trembling fingers, I finally got the numbers 911 pressed.

"Hurry, goddammit!" I shouted.

The convulsions subsided after about twenty seconds and she slipped into unconsciousness.

"Amelia . . . Amelia . . . Amelia." I gently shook her but she didn't respond.

The rest of the evening was a haze of disbelief, pain, and worry as the ambulance arrived and the paramedics struggled to stabilize her. She was whisked out the front door, and I shuffled to the ambulance and climbed through the double doors. The paramedic was a flurry of activity as he started an IV and injected a variety of medicines into her body. I sat in a foggy haze, staring at the face of my unconscious wife.

"Eclampsia" is what the doctors told me. I didn't know what that meant. Amelia never regained consciousness and drifted off into a coma. One week later, she died, taking our unborn child with her.

Zeke turns away from those passing along the hospital corridor, wiping away the tears. He shuffles along the hall until his heavy breathing subsides and the tears have dried. He wipes his nose and makes his way back toward his father's room. He pauses before entering to allow the redness on his face to dissipate. When he steps inside, his mother stands up from the chair and wraps her arms around her son.

"It's really okay, Mom," he says in a hoarse whisper.

"This doesn't need to be a taboo subject. It's been three years. It's time to let all that go."

His mother's breath is warm on his chest. "I love you, Zeke. You've suffered more heartache than most people could ever endure." She takes a step back. "They're on the way to get your father for the heart cath."

"So soon?"

"They think he's stabilized enough and want to eliminate the blockage as soon as possible."

Zeke steps over to his father's bed and reaches for his hand. "You'll be fine, Dad. Hell, they do these procedures a dozen times a day."

"I know, son. I'm not worried." He pauses. "But . . . I want to tell you that I love you, son. I don't know if I've actually ever said those words to you, but now I have. I love you and I'm proud of the man you've become."

Damn, just when Zeke had the tears stopped. "I love you, too, Dad. You didn't need to voice the words for me to know that. Now quit being so damn sentimental—"

An unfamiliar nurse breezes into the room. "So, Mr. Marshall, you ready to get that ole ticker fixed?"

"Yeah, I am," Robert says. "But I wish they could just replace the batteries."

The nurse laughs as if she hadn't heard the same thing a dozen times. "This will be better than batteries," she says, pulling the bed toward the door. "We'll have that heart of yours pumping as good as the day you were born."

Before the bed clears the doorframe Zeke reaches out to give his father's hand one last squeeze.

The nurse glances over her shoulder. "If you two would like to wait in the waiting room, I'll let you know something as soon as I can."

* * *

Upstairs the nurses prep Robert Marshall for his cardiac catheterization. A sudden whirring noise sounds and the nurse leans over and begins to shave the groin area of his right leg. His body tenses.

The nurse stops. "Relax your leg, Mr. Marshall. No need to be embarrassed. I've seen just about everything there is to see." She has a singsong voice, an accent Robert can't place. Her round, dark face is creaseless, making it difficult to guess her age.

He relaxes slightly, but as the battery-powered shaver runs against the area near his testicles, his cheeks blush. The nurse clicks off the machine and swabs the shaved area with Betadine while another nurse starts an IV in his left arm.

"Okay, Mr. Marshall, we're going to wheel you into the cath room. You'll be given a mild sedative and the doctor will numb up your groin area before making a small incision. Then he'll thread the catheter up your femoral artery to your heart. Using a fluoroscope and a contrasting dye inserted through your IV, the doctor will be able to pinpoint the blockages. Then he'll place a metal stent into your coronary arteries to improve blood flow. Are you ready?"

"Do I have a choice?" he says.

The question goes unanswered as the nurse wheels him across the hall into a room where the lights are dimmed. They transfer him to another, firmer bed and wheel the empty gurney out of the room. Someone pushes a needle into the port on his IV line and he becomes sleepy, until he feels a sharp stick very near his manhood.

"Mr. Marshall, we're going to start the procedure." His groin goes numb, and he feels the pressure of the insertion, but no pain. He nods off as the catheter is slowly fed up his artery.

As the head of the catheter nears his heart, the room is plunged into darkness.

"Everyone freeze!" the doctor shouts. "I don't want to rip open a coronary artery because I can't see where the damn cath is."

They wait for the automatic generator to power on. The doctor holds his gloved hands a good distance from the device tickling the edges of Robert Marshall's heart.

"What happened?" A nurse says.

"Don't know, but it couldn't have happened at a worse time," the doctor says.

The darkness is profound, and the only disruption to the silence is Robert Marshall's steady breathing. After a few minutes, the lights come on, but they have to wait a few more moments for all the hardware to reboot.

Once they're up and functioning, the doctor shakes out his hands before grasping the device. "Let's get this over as quickly as possible."

Downstairs, Zeke and his mother are sitting in the waiting room when the lights go out. Zeke feels his mother's hand fumble for his.

"There should be a backup generator," he says.

"What about your father?"

"He'll be fine."

The lights flicker, then burn steady. The admissions people scurry around behind the counter, repowering the computer system as a steady stream of need-to-be-seen patients hovers around the counter.

Two ambulances approach, their lights sending waves of red and yellow pulses across the waiting room. Zeke stands and walks closer to the window to see what's happening. Another ambulance zooms by and all three screech to a stop at the emergency entrance. There's a flurry of activity as paramedics and nurses remove the injured. Three gurneys are wheeled through the automatic door of the ER. Zeke walks over to the admissions desk. "What happened?"

An older woman behind the counter answers. "Traffic accident. Apparently most of the traffic lights quit working. You'd think they'd have the sense to slow down if the light was out."

Zeke drifts away and returns to his seat.

"What's all the commotion?" his mother asks.

"Big traffic pileup. Something about the signal lights not working."

"That's odd."

Zeke glances at the overhead lights, a tickle of something creeping down his spine.

A nurse, dressed in purple scrubs, steps through a side door. "Marshall family?"

Zeke helps his mother from the chair and the nurse leads them into a small, private consultation room.

"The doctor will be in shortly," she says before disappearing behind a different door.

The two share a glance but don't speak. The doctor walks in and introduces himself. He sits wearily and hands across a couple of photographs of Robert's heart.

"Mr. Marshall is a lucky man," the doctor says. "We found eighty-five percent blockage on two coronary arteries, and ninety percent blockage on a third. I inserted three stents to reduce the blockage and improve blood flow. He should feel like a new man."

"When will he be able to go home?" Barbara says.

"We'll keep him overnight to make sure the incision site clots off." The doctor stands and shakes both of their hands before leaving.

"That's good, Mom. His heart attack could have been much worse," Zeke says. "If you'll hand me your cell phone I'll call Ruth to fill her in."

As they exit the small room Zeke powers up the phone. No service. He walks toward the window hoping to get a better signal. No luck. He walks toward his mother. "I can't get a signal on your cell. I'm going to try a landline phone if I can find one."

Zeke hands the phone back to his mother and strolls down the hall in search of a landline phone. He finds one tucked into a corner near the elevator. He punches in his sister's number and puts the phone to his ear—and hears nothing but the faint echo of his own breathing. He flicks the small white button where the handset rests and listens for a dial tone. Still nothing. He replaces the phone and steps over to the volunteer desk, manned by a pair of white-haired elderly ladies.

"Are you having phone issues?"

The one on the right offers him an apologetic smile. "Only if you're trying to make an outside call. It works for in-hospital numbers but for some reason we can't get to an outside line."

Zeke ponders this for a moment. "This happen when the power went out?"

"Why, yes, it did, come to think of it."

He taps the counter with his knuckle. "Okay. Thanks for your help." He returns to where his mother is sitting.

"I can't get the call to go through. Doesn't even ring."

"That's strange. I've never had any trouble getting through to her."

A different nurse appears in the waiting room and leads the Marshalls into the recovery room. Zeke's father is lying flat on the bed while a nurse applies pressure to the incision site. She's standing on her tiptoes, placing most of her weight on her outstretched hands. Robert Marshall grimaces under the pressure.

Zeke says, "I think your old ticker is ready for a marathon now." He turns to the nurse. "How long do you have to keep pressure on the wound?"

The nurse blows a stray strand of light blond hair from her face. "Just a few more minutes."

Zeke's mother approaches the bed and brushes her lips across those of her husband.

"You scared me to death," she whispers.

"It's not my fault I had a heart attack, Barb."

"How long have you been having chest pains?"

"I don't know. A month or two."

Barbara Marshall is on the verge of a scolding tirade when another nurse enters the room.

"Mr. Marshall, I know you were told that you would be with us overnight, but there's been a change of plans. The hospital is now running on reserve power and we need to discharge as many patients as possible. The generator is not large enough to power the entire hospital."

"I thought there were concerns about his incision site closing off," Zeke says.

"We're going to watch him over the next two hours and then release him to your care. Everything should be just fine," the nurse says as she turns to the door.

"What's up with the power?" Zeke asks.

"Don't know. The whole town is without power."

CHAPTER 27

TransJet Flight 62, approaching London Heathrow Airport
Wednesday, September 29, 2:51 P.M.

Copilot Cheryl Wilson is rereading landing procedures while keeping a very close eye on the plane's TCAS system. The Traffic Alert and Collision Avoidance System uses radar to locate the transponders of other aircraft in the area, provided the other plane has the same system installed. "I count six aircraft within range of TCAS."

Captain Steve Henderson wipes the sleeve of his shirt across his face. "Well, that's just fucking great. Are we clear of them?"

"Yes. Let's hope everyone follows the normal landing procedure. Take us down to twenty thousand."

"Descending to twenty thousand. How far are we from London?"

"About seventy miles. Maintain a heading of one-eight-zero. Are we going to maintain the normal rate of descent or do you want to steepen it?"

"Let's go with normal descent and pray everyone else is doing the same."

Cheryl quickly calculates their distance from the airport and writes the numbers down on the margins of the map. "Take us down to eighteen."

"Descending to eighteen thousand." He glances in Cheryl's direction. "This could get dicey. I want your eyes on the sky around us in case there's an aircraft out there with their transponder off."

She leans forward and scans the horizon before looking back to the TCAS system. "We're clear for now, but I have some bad news. Heavy cloud cover at about twelve thousand."

"The good news just keeps coming."

"You're doing fine, Steve. You should be nearing fifteen thousand."

Steve glances at the altimeter. "We're at fifteen."

"Good. Maintain your descent." Within a minute, the plane enters the heavy cloud cover and the cabin is shrouded in whiteness.

The TCAS screen turns amber as an audible alarm announces, "Traffic . . . traffic."

"What the hell am I supposed to do?" Steve shouts. "Pull up, turn, or descend?"

"Pull up! Pull up! There's a plane below us."

Steve pulls on the wheel and the nose of the large plane eases up.

"Throttle up!"

While pulling on the wheel, Steve jams the throttles forward as the warning continues—"Traffic, traffic."

Steve glances at the altitude indicator. "Where the hell is it?" The plane shudders and the light for engine four flashes red. "We're hit! Shut four down now!"

Cheryl scrambles to kill the number four engine by cutting off the fuel supply, then strains to look out the side window. "How bad is the damage?"

The audible warning from the TCAS system goes silent,

but a series of red lights on the instrument panel flashes repeatedly.

"Don't know." Steve's jaw is clenched as he struggles to maintain control. "She's a wobbly bitch. I don't know how much longer I can keep her in the air."

Cheryl puts a hand on his arm. "You're doing good, Steve."

Steve works the throttles, trying to balance engine thrust. "We have to get out of this cloud cover." He pushes the wheel forward and the nose of the plane tips forward.

"Easy, Steve. Level off a little."

"Find me another airport. We're not going to make London."

Cheryl quickly searches her map, trying to pinpoint their position. She scans the instruments, looking at the altimeter and compass heading then back to the maps.

"I found a small field near Northampton."

"How small?" Steve says as he uses every ounce of energy to control the plane. They're still socked in with clouds.

"The runway's about forty-one hundred feet. I don't know if we can make that."

"We're going to have to. We've burned off most of the fuel, so maybe. What's my heading?"

"Come to two-one-zero. By my calculations we're about five miles from the landing strip." She stares at the dense whiteness surrounding them.

At thirty-two hundred feet they break through the heavy cloud cover, and both exhale an audible breath.

"You see the runway?" Steve looks out the side window, and the damage to the outermost left wing becomes apparent. "The tip of the left wing is sheared off and she's yawing to the right. I need full flaps to bleed off some speed."

Cheryl pushes down the handle that controls flap settings. "Full flaps. Make your heading two-three-zero. We should be about four miles from Northampton." She points out the window. "I see the airport."

Steve follows her outstretched hand and centers his gaze on the long strip of concrete.

"This is going to be nearly impossible. See any other traffic?"

Cheryl sweeps the horizon. "No, it looks clear. Slow and steady, Steve. We're almost there." Her voice is reassuring, calm.

He banks the plane in a short, right turn, lining up on the runway as Cheryl deploys the landing gear. A nasty crosswind is playing havoc with his efforts to control the wounded jet. Steve's feet are pushing one way then the other, using the rudder to control the side-to-side drift. He eases back on the throttles. "Damn, that's a narrow son of a bitch." He struggles to keep the nose centered on the runway.

A computer voice in the cockpit says, "One hundred."

"It's wide enough," Cheryl says. "Sit her down, nice and easy, like every other time."

"Fifty . . . forty . . . thirty . . ."

The captain eases back on the throttles a little more and pulls up the nose.

"Twenty . . . ten . . ."

"C'mon, damn it." With a squeal, the tires make contact and the nose slowly lowers, touching down. He slams the throttles to the reverse thrust position and uses both feet to stand on the brakes. Sweat is pouring down his face as the jet shudders.

"Don't know if I can get her stopped." His legs are Jell-O as every item not tied down in the cockpit slams against the front bulkhead.

Steve glances out the window as the rushing scenery begins to slow. His legs are locked against the pedals. "Oh shit," he says when he glances back toward the front.

At the very end of the tarmac is a large excavator parked perpendicular to the runway, surrounded by piles of earth. The brakes howl in protest as he continues to stand on the pedals. Slowly, the giant plane loses speed.

Only a hundred feet of runway remain as the large excavator looms ever larger in the windshield. The plane jerks to a stop. Steve sucks a deep breath and hits the cut-off switches for the three remaining engines. He looks out the cockpit window to see a lone car approaching, lights flashing. He turns to look at the small cluster of industrial buildings, and for some reason the fact that all the buildings are dark registers on his subconscious.

Chapter 28

The Oval Office
Wednesday, September 29, 3:36 P.M.

Scott Alexander is keeping an eye on the breaking news playing on the television in the Oval Office. He triggers the remote and the volume increases as the mayor of New Orleans conducts a live press conference.

"Mr. President, I'm asking for your help now. Don't leave us stranded like your predecessor did during Katrina. We need immediate federal help. Half of the Ninth Ward is underwater and the water level is rising. Please, Mr. President, the time to act is now . . ."

The intercom buzzes. President Harris stabs the button.

"Director Carter is here, sir."

"Send him in please, Barb."

The President stands and meets the FEMA director mid-room and steers him to one of the sofas. Alexander kills the sound and tosses the remote on the side table before moving to one of the facing chairs.

President Harris points toward the television. "Anything we can do about New Orleans, Don?"

"We're doing everything we can, sir, but we're spread

thin. The Corps of Engineers is working like hell to replace the pumps, but that's like putting a Band-Aid on a bullet wound." Don pauses for a moment, then throws up his hands. "It may be time, sir, to write that area off. If we're truly going to be without electricity for months or years, New Orleans will become an uninhabitable swamp."

"Do what you can, Don, at least while we still have power. How's the rest of the country?"

"Nothing good, Mr. President. Most of Alaska is without power, as are portions of Canada and the higher elevations of Colorado. The Canadians are dealing with a potential meltdown at their Atlantic coast nuclear reactor. I put all state FEMA departments on urgent status and all available workers are en route to their designated areas. But I have to tell you, sir, I don't know how much urgency there will be without some indication of what is happening. Are you still planning on addressing the nation?"

President Harris glances at Scott before answering. "We're still debating the merits."

"But, Mr. President, we need to offer the people some type of warning. I haven't given specific instructions to the state agencies on what to prepare for, but I would like—"

The intercom buzzes again. The President punches the button, "Yes, Barb."

"Sir, there's a call which came through the White House switchboard from a Dr. Samuel Blake, claiming he needs to speak—"

"Put the call through, Barb." He waits for the phone call to be routed through, then punches the flashing button putting the call on speakerphone.

"Sam, what's the latest?"

"I've been trying to get a call through for the past hour, sir. I don't think we have eight hours."

"How long do you think?"

"I think it could happen at any moment, may already be happening. Our remaining instruments are indicating massive spikes in the Earth's magnetic field. The electrical interference is off the charts."

"What are you telling me, Sam? We're too late to do anything?"

"Maybe, Mr. President."

The President's shoulders sag. "Okay, Sam, I'll send out the word. Are you in a safe place?"

"I don't know, Mr. President. There may be no safe places when the power goes out."

Silence. Then the President says, "I'm going to do everything I can to make sure we have safe places, Sam. Take care." President Harris reaches over and disconnects the call.

"This is it?" Don asks.

President Harris nods. Then, in a toneless voice, says, "Make sure we have some way to communicate, Don. Tell your people to be ready for the worst, and tell them to stay out of harm's way as much as possible."

Carter stands from the sofa on shaky legs. "I will, Mr. President." He turns and shuffles out of the office.

President Harris turns to Alexander. "Scott, will you get Janice on the line, please? I guess our decision to notify the public is now moot."

"I will, Mr. President." His reply is a raspy whisper as he steps behind the desk and dials the phone. He murmurs a few words into the handset. "Line one, sir."

The President pauses before picking up the handset. "Scott, where's the First Lady?"

"Over at the Park Hyatt giving a speech to a group of college students."

"Call her detail and tell them to hustle her back to the White House."

"Yes, sir."

President Harris punches the button. "Janice, alert all of the law enforcement units across the country to be on emergency status. Explain what is going to happen and tell them to prepare for the worst. This country may be overrun by lawlessness. I also want you to order a national emergency alert."

"What's changed, Mr. President?" she says.

"According to Dr. Blake, it may already be happening. I don't know how much time we have, but do what you can."

"I will, sir." The phone goes dead in his hand.

President Harris pushes up from the sofa and shuffles over to the windows, muttering, "God have mercy on us all."

Chapter 29

Fairbanks, Alaska
Wednesday, September 29, 4:26 P.M.

Junior Hickman, a large, barrel-chested man, climbs into the bucket truck to make one final line connection before he and the crew break for lunch. With the temperature hovering around thirty-three degrees, he's working in a sleet-snow mix interspersed with a bone-chilling rain. He gives a thumbs-up to the other two men on the crew and, using a joystick attached to the bucket, begins his ascent toward the new high-voltage line they're building along Route 2, on the outskirts of Fairbanks.

Junior, a twenty-five-year veteran lineman for Alaska Power and Light, has experienced the extremes of Alaskan weather. The day-after-day cold that seeps into his bones during the winter months and the battles with swarms of mosquitoes during the summer. He extends the boom to near-maximum capacity to reach the lower wire. Because the HVDC—high-voltage, direct current—line is not yet energized he forgoes the elbow-length rubber gloves and doesn't bother with the rubber shields in the area he will be working. To finish this section of line, Junior needs to pigtail a bridge line between two wire terminations so the electrical current can travel from one section of line to another.

The cold, wet conditions make it difficult for Junior to get a firm grasp on the six-foot piece of heavy cable. He slips the wire over his shoulder and works on one end at a time. With a specially designed clamp he secures the first end. He jogs the joystick to position the bucket closer to the other end for the final connection. With his right hand, he reaches for the suspended cable to attach the other end of the pigtail. As his wrench meets the clamp's bolt the two fuse together. Almost instantaneously, Junior Hickman is vaporized by over one million volts as the unseen geomagnetic storm slams into Fairbanks.

The nonmetallic fiberglass bucket, specifically designed not to conduct current during electrical repair work, suffers no ill effects. However, the small joystick handle was not subjected to the same design specifications. The bucket is parked within a hair's distance from the power line, and the surge of electricity arcs to the handle and instantly melts the wiring. As the massive power surge searches for ground, the current races down the truck's boom, killing Junior's coworker, who had been leaning against the truck sipping a cup of coffee.

The third coworker, who had been standing some distance away, stares, his mouth agape, uncertain what he has witnessed. One immediate thought surges through his mind: those lines weren't due to be energized for another three months. He fumbles for his cell phone and, because his hands are shaking so violently, has to hold the phone with both hands to punch in 911 with his thumb. He puts the phone to his ear while his mind spins for a valid explanation. The phone is dead. He pulls it away and glances at the screen to see the words NO SERVICE in the upper left corner.

The worker, in his third month on the job, turns in a tight circle, not sure what to do. He steps toward his coworker on the ground. It's clear he's dead, or at least his chest is still, but there's no way in hell he's checking for a pulse. He kneels down, calling out the man's name, his voice rising an octave with each repeat.

A thought hits him—*the company radio.*

He jumps to his feet. His hand is within six inches of the damp, silver, elongated door handle when he jerks his hand back. He backs away and stumbles several steps before slumping to the damp ground.

Chapter 30

The Channel Tunnel (Chunnel), between Paris and London
Wednesday, September 29, 4:41 P.M.

Almost an hour into their two-and-a-half-hour trip from Paris to London, Abigail Edwards is struggling to control two wired, but tired, children. Zoe, five, and Ella, three, have already endured a long day. But their excitement to see their London cousins has them hyped to the max. After moving from London to Paris a little over a year ago, the once-inseparable cousins are meeting for a weeklong vacation. Both girls are sporting pigtails, which sway side to side with the gentle movement of the train.

The train zips along at nearly one hundred miles an hour, tethered to a twenty-five-thousand-volt cable running overhead. As it races through the southern tunnel toward London, the track gradually descends until it's two hundred feet under the English Channel.

Abigail leans her head back against the headrest as Ella and Zoe climb across her lap—again. The two coloring books she had brought along to entertain the girls lie discarded in the seat next to her. She's silently cursing her husband for having to cancel at the last minute to attend to some developing bank crisis.

Abigail tucks a stray strand of her blond hair behind her ear, then claps her hands. "Girls, for the umpteenth time, will you please sit down?" Her words have little effect.

They're fortunate that the last train to London is not overcrowded. The only person annoyed by the girls' behavior is their mother. Abigail digs through her purse and extracts her cell phone, hoping—praying—for a text message from her husband that the issue is resolved and he will be following in the morning. But there are no messages or missed calls.

She thumbs a quick message to him but before she can press send, the lights in the cabin flash out, plunging the train into absolute darkness. She screams for the girls. Gravity pulls her forward as the train rapidly decelerates. The battery-powered emergency lights click on, but as a source of light they're anemic. The train is still moving but is quickly bleeding off speed. She jumps from her chair in search of the girls.

She finds them in the row ahead, hunkered down against the floor. She grabs their hands and pulls them to their feet.

"Mommy, what's going on?" Zoe says.

"I don't know. I think the train lost power." She ushers them into their original seats as the train comes to a dead stop.

A man dressed in a grease-streaked blue uniform races down the aisle, a loud radio squawking at his belt.

"Are we stuck, Mommy?" Ella asks.

"No, honey, we're not stuck. We'll be under way soon." She thrusts one of the coloring books toward Ella. "Want to color Mommy a pretty picture?"

A few people near the front of the car stand and begin talking among themselves.

Abigail gets to her feet. "Zoe, will you help your sister color a pretty picture for me?"

Zoe purses her lips. "She doesn't color right."

"Will you show her the correct way to color?"

"I do, too, know how to color," Ella shouts.

Abigail rakes her fingers through her hair and lightly stomps her right foot. "Okay, both of you color your own page."

Another blue-uniformed man hurries through their car. Abigail watches him pass with a growing sense of alarm. "Girls, have you seen my phone?"

Neither answers, now engrossed in a coloring competition. Ella's tongue sticks out as she colors close to the edge of a line.

Abigail remembers having the phone just as the lights went out. She squats, searching the floor, but the dim lighting makes the task nearly impossible. She crabs sideways and finds it jammed against the leg of the seat two rows ahead. She picks it up and pushes a speed dial as she puts the phone to her ear. When nothing happens, she pulls the phone away and glances at the screen—*No Service*. She sighs and retakes her seat.

She glances forward to see more people up and about. Abigail finds it odd that no one has made an announcement concerning the current predicament.

"Girls, I'm going to stretch my legs. You two stay here."

She receives two nods.

Abigail walks toward the front of the car, eavesdropping on conversations along the way. She pauses near two elderly ladies seated together, listens for a moment, then leans down. "Excuse me, I didn't mean to listen in, but you mentioned something about the power going out?"

The two elderly ladies glance up and the one on the left smiles before answering. "I was on the phone with my hubby before the lights on the train went out. He said the power had just gone off at home. Then my phone lost the signal."

"Is your husband in Paris?"

"Oh no, deary, we're Londoners. Do you have any idea what's gong on?"

"No, I'm clueless, but you would think they would make some type of announcement."

The other lady says, "If we're without power they might not be able to use the intercom."

"I didn't think of that," Abigail says. "Thanks for your time and I apologize for intruding."

"Weren't no intrusion, deary," the first woman says.

Abigail makes her way back to her seat. Just as her butt hits the chair, a young, red-faced conductor barges through the door at the front of the car.

"Ladies and gentlemen, due to extenuating circumstances, we are asking all passengers to disembark the train and make your way toward London on foot."

An angry chorus of jeers drowns out his next few words. He holds up his hand to silence the crowd.

"It seems that power is out in Great Britain as well as northern Europe. Please take only those items that you can comfortably carry." The conductor rushes down the aisle, headed for the next car in line.

Abigail waves her hand to flag him down. "Excuse me, sir."

He stops.

Abigail says, "How far is it to London?"

The young man hesitates before answering. "About twelve miles, ma'am."

Chapter 31

Seattle, Washington
Wednesday, September 29, 4:43 P.M.

Mr. and Mrs. Herbert Washington, in town from Des Moines to visit their son, are first in line for the next available elevator—their first trip to the top of the Space Needle. They had argued all morning over whether to eat lunch at SkyCity Restaurant. Herb, a hardworking dairy farmer, insisted it would cost too damn much, but Arlene, his wife of forty-one years, nagged until he gave in.

His wife tiptoes up to whisper in his ear. "We need to live a little, damn it. Especially after the scare you gave me last summer with your heart attack." She reaches her fingers out and gives him a tickle in the ribs. "Loosen up, Herbie." The Seattle humidity is playing havoc on Arlene's hair after a cut, color, and perm back home. She runs her fingers through the off-shade auburn curls in a futile attempt to respring them.

Herb scowls, but he wilts, seeing the pleasure of something new in her eyes.

The elevator door opens and one of the workers shouts, "Step aboard for the next launch!"

"What the hell does she mean, 'launch'?" Herb says.

"That's just what they call their elevator rides."

"Well, I'm not launchin' nothin," Herb mutters as Arlene grabs his hand and pulls him aboard. They move toward the far wall as the crowd of people swells around them. The elevator is stacked six deep before the door finally closes. Almost four inches taller than anyone else on the elevator, Herbert doesn't feel as cramped as Arlene does. She's snuggled up closer to him than she had been on their wedding night.

When the doors close, the interior of the elevator is plunged into darkness. Herb reaches for the handrail, wondering where the hell the lights are. With a whir the elevator starts and within a few seconds the elevator is awash with daylight. Herb and Arlene are pressed tight against the glass as the Seattle skyline widens before them.

Twenty-six seconds into the forty-one-second ride the elevator jerks to a halt, forcing several riders off balance. But with no room to fall, they wobble like bowling pins. A collective groan erupts.

The overly cheerful Space Needle worker manning the elevator, Chrissy, according to her name tag, reassures everyone aboard that all is well. "Occasionally the elevator will stop due to intermittent electrical issues. We should be under way in a matter of seconds."

Herb, not a fan of heights, forces himself to take a series of deep breaths as Arlene provides support by squeezing his hand. In between breaths, he notices something strange. The monorail cars below are stopped midtrack. He slowly moves his gaze upward. The construction crane a couple of blocks away stands frozen in time, the metal beams lashed to its tether swaying in the breeze.

Herb leans down to whisper to his wife, "Arlene, something's not right."

"We'll be fine. That nice young lady says this occasionally happens."

"I'm not talking about that," Herb says. "It looks like the power is out all over Seattle."

Arlene, who had avoided looking out the window to keep a handle on her vertigo, turns to look. "The cars are moving."

"They're not running on electricity. Look at the signal lights. They're all dark. Do you see any lights on in any of those office buildings?"

Arlene looks from one side of the skyline to the other. She leans forward, cups her hands around her face, and scans again. She turns back to Herb, her eyes wide with fear. "What are we going to do?"

What was a low murmuring of voices increases in volume. Someone else has discovered Herb's secret. A tall, lanky kid, maybe college age, turns from the finger-smudged glass. "Do you guys have a backup generator?"

Flustered by the question, Chrissy, not much older than the questioner, answers, "I don't really know. We should be under way in a few more moments."

The lanky teenager points to the hazy skyline. "Dude, there's not a light on in any of those office buildings. The whole city is dark. We're not going anywhere."

Angry shouts follow his statement. Chrissy is barraged by one question after another. An elderly woman turns hysterical, screaming about her claustrophobia. Herb is getting a headache. He shouts above the din, "There has to be an emergency phone."

Chrissy, on the extreme outer limits of her capability, screams for everyone to shut up. The noise level lessens, but a few passengers are still muttering some unkind remarks. She turns back to the control panel in search of the hidden phone and finds it behind the panel marked: PHONE. She opens the panel and pulls the phone to her ear.

Silence. She fingers the cradle button repeatedly but the silence continues. Frustrated, she punches the fire bell and is rewarded with more silence. She hangs up the phone, replaces the panel, and places her forehead against the polished anodized aluminum interior.

"Well?" Herb asks.

Chrissy turns away from the wall. "The phone is dead."

The claustrophobic woman screams again. Herb pulls the cell phone from his pocket and he's not really surprised to find he has no service. Other hands begin reaching for other phones and it's not long before everyone discovers their lifelines have been severed.

CHAPTER 32

Upper West Side, New York, New York
Wednesday, September 29, 4:46 P.M.

After receiving an earlier call from Kaylee, their daughter working in Boulder, Greg and Lara Connor are on their way home from their second trip to the bodega over on Amsterdam Avenue. On the first trip they focused on nonperishable food items. The pickings were slim: three cans of Hormel chili—with beans; two cans of SpaghettiOs—though they left four on the shelf; several cans of Vienna sausages; six oblong containers of Spam; two large multipacks of ramen noodles—one chicken, one beef; three loaves of bread; and a box of PowerBars. They bypassed the cereal and chip aisle as well as anything refrigerated.

On this trip Greg is lugging two cases of bottled water, which ride precariously on his shoulder with a hand on top for stability. Lara is struggling to carry four one-gallon containers of the same. In Greg's other hand rides a twelve-pack of beer, their one luxury item. Lara had wanted to pick up a case of wine but Greg said they should opt for water on this trip and maybe get the wine later. Both had left their respective offices—Greg, a financial services manager, and Lara, a retired teacher who's now a receptionist for a local dentist—shortly after Kaylee's call to her mother.

"Let's stop at the bank on the corner," Greg says.

"Why?"

"I'm going to cash a check so we'll have ready cash."

"To buy what, exactly?"

"You never know."

They park the supplies near the entrance and Lara stands watch while Greg enters the bank. Before approaching the counter, he pauses to check their available balance with his smartphone. *How much to take out? All of it?* He settles on three thousand dollars and writes the check before passing it across the counter to the teller.

"How would you like your cash?" she says.

"Uh . . . good question," Greg says. He pauses to think it through. "Let's do ten hundreds and the rest in twenties."

The teller, who doesn't look old enough to be out of high school, arches her eyebrows and quickly counts out the money, snapping through the crisp bills effortlessly. The normal envelope used for cash back isn't large enough to hold the stack of twenties. She grabs a manila envelope from beneath the counter, slides the cash in, and hands it across the counter.

"Have a good day, sir," she says.

Greg turns for the door, but he pulls up short, wondering if he should offer some type of warning about the impending disaster. Instead, he pushes through the door and reloads the two cases of water onto his shoulder.

The sidewalks are teeming with people, and Greg and Lara receive several odd looks. The weather is warm and both are perspiring heavily under the unrelenting sun of a late-September heat wave. A slew of window air conditioners along the building fronts are churning to cool the humid air. Condensation drips down like a localized rainstorm.

They dodge cars along 69th Street and reach the other side. Greg lowers the water to the ground so that he can dig out the keys to the lobby of their building. Unlike some of the other apartment buildings in the neighborhood, theirs is not staffed with a doorman.

As Greg slots the key, he senses a shift, a subtle change he can't put his finger on. Then, a loud blaring of horns, the sharp squeal of rubber on pavement, and the sounds of a heavy impact draw their attention to the intersection of Columbus and West 72nd. Two cars had slammed into each other. Greg glances up at the signal light to see who was at fault, only to find it dark. Then it hits him—all of the air conditioners had stopped.

"Is this it?" Lara whispers.

"Maybe," Greg says as he twists the key and pushes open the lobby door.

"Well, is it?"

"I don't know, Lara. Maybe—probably. The sconces are out in the elevator lobby, so I'd say something's happened."

Before picking up the cased goods, Greg steps over to the elevator and punches the button. The glassy-eyed center remains dark. "Elevator's out."

Laura sighs. "Great."

Although both are in their midfifties and in relatively good shape, they are sucking air as they step onto the sixth-floor landing. Lara carefully sets her four jugs down next to the apartment door. But Greg is not so gentle as the two cases slide from his shoulder, sending water bottles skittering down the hallway. Lara gives him a scolding look, which he ignores while fishing for his keys again.

He unlocks the door and Lara breezes past. Greg scoots the four jugs of water inside, then goes in search of the missing water bottles. The corridor is dark, the only light coming from a small window at the end of the hall. Once he's corralled all the plastic bottles, he carries them into the apartment and drops them on the sofa.

"Greg, I was trying to call Kaylee to tell her we made it home but my cell phone is not working."

"You try the house phone?"

"It's dead, too."

"Shit. Did Kaylee say how long we'd be without electricity?"

"No one really knows. She mentioned it could be a week or longer. But on the grim side, she also mentioned several months, maybe years."

Greg shakes his head. "If it's more than a week we're royally screwed."

CHAPTER 33

NOAA Space Weather Prediction Center
Wednesday, September 29, 4:51 P.M.

With most of their scientific equipment now off-line, Drs. Blake and Connor have taken refuge in the conference room. A knock on the door sounds and Daniel, the intern, sticks his face around the partially open door. Sam waves him in and Daniel pulls out a chair and sits.

"Dr. Blake, how long you think we have before the storm hits?" he asks.

"Not long. I'd expect—"

The power to the Space Weather Prediction Center flashes off.

"I guess that answers my question," Daniel says. "Want me to see about starting the generator?"

Sam doesn't answer for a moment as he stares through the window at the rugged ridges running lengthwise up the mountain. "Just look out there. The sun is shining and the wind is waving the tall grass. You wouldn't know our world is about to be turned upside down." He turns to face Daniel. "Hold off on the generator until dark. There's not a damn thing we can do anyway."

"You have someplace to stay, Daniel?" Kaylee asks.

"I have a small one-bedroom near campus. I guess I can stay there until the power comes back on."

Sam takes off his glasses and rubs the bridge of his nose. "You need to find a better place to ride this out."

"Why? I have enough food to last for a while."

Kaylee sighs. "You don't understand, Daniel. We'll be without power for months. Maybe years."

Daniel sits in silence. Eventually, he finds his voice. "But . . . but . . . why? Can't the electric companies just swap out the broken pieces?"

"If only it were that simple," Sam says. "Do you have somewhere else you can go?"

"I guess I could go to my parents' home in Denver."

Sam leans forward in his chair and places his forearms on the table. "If you're going to your parents' house you need to leave right now." He pokes the table with his index finger. "Don't bother going back to your apartment. You need to get in your car and start driving this instant."

"What's the urgency?" Daniel says, befuddled.

"Because once people realize the power is not coming back on, they'll go nuts. There will be people trying to escape to somewhere else and it won't be long until the roads will be clogged with out-of-gas cars. You need to be on the road right now."

Daniel stands and shuffles toward the door. He stops and turns. "But I don't know if I have enough gas."

"Take a couple of the five-gallon containers you guys purchased this morning and put them in your car."

"But what about the generator?"

"Screw the generator," Sam says. He pushes out of his chair, steps toward Daniel, and puts a hand on his shoulder. "Once you're on the road, don't stop for anyone. It's only about an hour drive. You should be okay." He pats Daniel on the back. "Take care, Daniel. I guess you won't have to worry about writing that thesis for a while."

Gripped with uncertainty, Daniel stands awkwardly at the door. Kaylee steps around the table and wraps her arms around him.

"I know I've been hard on you. But you're going to be a damn good scientist." A tear rolls down her cheek.

Daniel steps away from the embrace, wiping away his own tears. He sniffles, then smiles. "Wow, Kaylee crying. Thought I'd never see that."

Kaylee punches him in the arm before quickly brushing the moisture from her face.

Daniel offers a small wave before disappearing through the door.

CHAPTER 34

Washington, D.C.
Wednesday, September 29, 4:59 P.M.

First Lady Katherine Harris is midway through her speech to the hundred or so college students when a Secret Service agent strides across the small stage and whispers in her ear.

Annoyed at the interruption, she questions the agent in an angry whisper. The agent nods and slinks away from the podium.

"Ladies and gentlemen, I apologize, but I've been summoned back to the White House." She glances up at the crowded room and smiles. "Even I can't ignore the President."

The room bursts into laughter. Out of the corner of her eye, she sees the agent stalking closer. She holds up her hand to stop him.

"The one thing I want you to take away from today's—"

The room plunges into darkness to a chorus of high-pitched screams. Hands grab for the First Lady and pull her through a rear door. A series of flashlights click on as her detail sweeps her down a back hallway and into the waiting Suburban. She slides across the smooth leather,

her personal secretary, usually only a step or two away, lost in the madness.

"Where's Sharon?" she says to Agent Davis, who crowds in next to her.

"Go!" he shouts to the driver before turning to face the First Lady. "She's in another vehicle."

The heavy truck jets down the alley, followed by another pair of large, black Suburbans. Lights flashing and sirens roaring, the driver hooks a right and guns the powerful engine. They scream two blocks before traffic gums up at Washington Circle.

Katherine Harris, staring through the bulletproof glass at the darkened buildings in the gray duskiness, says, "What's happening?"

"I don't know, ma'am." Agent Davis turns for a glimpse out the side window as dread tickles his spine. "It looks like the power is out all over the city." He turns back to the First Lady. "We weren't offered an explanation—only ordered to bring you home."

"Has there been some type of terrorist attack?"

"No. We wouldn't be going to the White House if this were a terrorist situation."

Katherine Harris doesn't ask the question that instantly pops into her mind. Instead she says, "How would my husband know the power was going to go out?"

Agent Davis ponders the question for a moment. "I honestly don't know."

"Seems rather strange, doesn't it?"

"Yes, ma'am, it does."

Due to stoplight failure, the three-car procession comes to a grinding halt halfway through the traffic circle. The driver slaps his palm on the steering wheel. The lights and sirens have no effect on cars with nowhere to go. He clicks off the siren. Closed in by trees on two sides, they're forced to wait. Slowly, the traffic begins to move forward. Two car lengths later they come to another halt. The First Lady glances out her window to see two agents now standing beside the armored vehicle. Their focus is directed away from the truck.

"This is a clusterfuck," Agent Davis mutters.

The line of cars moves another ten feet and the driver, spotting an opening, bumps over the curb and swerves around the trees. He shoots across the grass to Pennsylvania Avenue, five blocks from the White House. He retoggles the siren and steers the beast of a vehicle onto the sidewalk. But the press of humanity is too dense to drive through. People, used to the luxury of riding the Metro home, press forward with no way to evade the Suburban even if they so desired. The driver curses out loud and eases off the curb, forcing his way back onto the roadway. He reaches over to snap off the siren again.

Four agents now appear, taking up positions on both sides of the Suburban.

The First Lady turns to Agent Davis. "It would be faster if we walked." A big-boned woman who grew up on a farm in Oklahoma, Katherine Harris always has a ready smile. But her steadfast determination sometimes chafes those around her.

"Impossible. Your safety is paramount, and wading through these crowds is a security nightmare."

She waves to the window, where a steady stream of people shuffles past. "Why? These people only want to get home after a long day at work. They could care less who's walking along beside them."

"With all due respect, ma'am, we are not leaving the safety of this vehicle."

A flash of anger flares her cheeks crimson. "Agent Davis, if I remember correctly, you work for the President. Now, since I'm married to the man you work for, I'm getting out of this fucking truck and I'm going to walk fucking home. Got it?"

Agent Davis exhales a heavy sigh. He places the concealed microphone to his lips and issues a series of commands before pushing the heavy door open. He stands on the sidewalk and assists the First Lady of the United States from the truck. The other agents quickly form a perimeter around their charge, and like a moving rugby scrum, they walk toward the White House.

Chapter 35

Edmond, Oklahoma
Wednesday, September 29, 5:01 P.M.

Walter Williams, known as W-squared to his friends, groans as he stands up from kneeling in his newly created flower bed. The overhead sizzle of the power lines running to the electrical substation behind his house is the only annoyance of his otherwise peaceful afternoon.

"Damn city," he mumbles as he retrieves the garden hose from the back patio. Walter waged war against the city council over the location of the new electrical substation. The small section of land *was* city property but it had been vacant since the day he and his bride, Mary, moved into their new home over thirty years ago. Now his quiet time in the backyard is accompanied by what sounds like five hundred pounds of bacon being cooked in the world's largest skillet.

He cranks the water on and drags the hose toward the back fence. The store was having an end-of-season sale and Walter and Mary loaded up on half-priced plants. He planted several yews, both spreading and the more upright variety, along with the feature plant: a large Japanese maple with delicate, cascading limbs. The finishing touches, this afternoon, are the three flats of pansies he planted throughout the bed to provide color for the upcoming winter.

Walter splashes the water across the yellow, purple, blue, and white flowers. He nearly jumps out of his gardening clogs when a shower of sparks erupts thirty feet in the air behind the fence. He tiptoes to peer over the fence. Of the dozen or so transformers spread throughout the station, four or five are shooting large gouts of flame skyward. Once-attached wires hang limply from their metal stanchions.

He shakes his fist toward the sky and yells, "Hot damn! That'll teach those sumbitches."

Sirens sound in the distance, but Walter hopes they don't arrive until the whole damn thing has melted to the ground. He reaches down to retrieve the hose and discovers a feeble trickle of water. "Huh." He scans the length of the hose for kinks.

Another pop, then a much louder explosion. Walter races to the safety of the covered porch, dragging the hose behind him. He does a little happy dance and turns a full circle. A thin man with jutting hip bones, he closely resembles the Scarecrow dancing in *The Wizard of Oz*.

He crashes back to earth when Mary sticks her head out the patio door and says, "Walter, the power's out."

He glances at the hose lying on the ground and what was a trickle is now a drip. Edmond relies on water wells to provide a good portion of water to residents, a fact that Walter is just coming to grips with.

There's one last large sizzle as the electrical substation enters its death throes. A loud snap follows and he glances up to see the overhead cables whistling toward the ground. They slam onto the roof of his house with a clap of thunder. Years of accumulated dust on the overhanging porch roof drifts down to coat him.

Walter's mind spins. It took the city nearly sixteen months to complete construction of the new substation. After several moments of thought, Walter mutters, "Son of a bitch" as he slides the patio door open.

Chapter 36

Amarillo, Texas
Wednesday, September 29, 5:16 P.M.

Eleven-year-old Shelby Johnson latches on to her mother's hand and drags her toward the newest addition to Doug's Family Fun Park: Doug's Demon—the first loop roller coaster in the Texas Panhandle. The park unveiled the new ride to kick off the summer season but this is Shelby's first opportunity to take a spin. Her friends talked all summer about how freaking fun it was.

As they watch the coaster race through the upside-down portion of the ride, Shelby's mother is regretting her decision to bring her daughter to the park. Usually Shelby brings a friend to ride with, or at a minimum her older brother, but today is the last day the park will be open for the season. All of her friends had other commitments and Shelby's fourteen-year-old brother is no longer interested in riding with his little sister. As a divorced single mother, the job fell on Caitlyn's shoulders.

"I don't know, Shelby. I'm about to get sick just watchin' it."

"C'mon, Mom. Look how short the line is. It's two minutes of your life."

"But what happens if I get sick and puke everywhere?"

"Jeez, you're not going to get sick. See how fast it goes through the loop? You're only upside down for maybe two seconds."

Caitlyn crosses her arms and watches another cycle. Her stomach lurches when the coaster races down the steep incline and spirals around the rails.

"Please, Mom."

When her mother doesn't respond, Shelby sighs, crosses her arms, and turns away.

After a pause Caitlyn relents. "Okay. I'll ride it one time."

Shelby turns back to her mother, all smiles. She grabs her mother's hand and leads her through the back-and-forth maze until they reach the end of the line.

Caitlyn glances around and says, "Why is the line so short if this ride is all the rage?"

"Look around, Mom. There's hardly anyone at the park today."

Caitlyn's apprehension grows with each step closer to boarding Doug's Demon. After two more cycles, they're next in line. Shelby runs through the gate and heads for the first car.

"Shelby Johnson, you get back here. I'm not riding in the front."

Shelby hangs her head and retraces her steps, joining her mother in the third car back. Two older teenagers take the now-vacant first car. The coaster is made up of eight cars, each painted a bright candy-apple red with wisps of smoke airbrushed along the exterior.

A college-age worker sidles up to their car and secures the over-the-shoulder apparatus and tugs on it to make sure the connection is secure.

"Anybody ever fall out of this thing?" Caitlyn says.

"Not today," he replies with a crooked grin. He moves on to the next car.

"Don't worry, Mom. Madison rode it six times straight."

"I don't really care what Madison did."

Caitlyn watches as the smart-ass college kid picks up a handheld microphone and reminds everyone to keep their hands inside the car. He then punches a button and the coaster accelerates away from the platform. The cars connect to a chain with a loud clunk and they ascend.

"Oh God, oh God, oh God . . ." Caitlyn keeps up the litany until they reach the apex of the hill. Then she screams.

The coaster races downhill through a tight right turn before whipping into a left turn and descending into darkness. They bolt over a short hill, and her stomach lurches as the car dips down through another sharp curve. Clack, clack, clack—they're climbing again.

At the top of the next hill, just as they're teetering on the downfall, the flashing lights running the length of the track wink out. But Caitlyn takes no notice. The coaster accelerates in free fall, but as it nears the loop it begins slowing down, sparks shooting out beneath the wheels. Up the loop they go, but not with enough speed to make it all the way around.

The ride comes to a dead stop with Caitlyn and Shelby hanging upside down.

"Get me out of here!" Caitlyn shouts as she squirms in the harness now digging into her shoulder blades.

"Mom, hush."

"I knew I shouldn't have gotten on this damn thing."

"Mom!"

"Why aren't we moving, Shelby?"

"I don't know. It'll start back up in a minute," Shelby says with more bravado than she feels.

They hang upside for five minutes until the worker shows up beneath them. The lopsided grin has been erased from his face. "I'm sorry. We lost power. The coaster has a fail-safe. It automatically locks the brakes in the event of a power loss."

"Well, unlock the damn thing," Caitlyn shouts.

"I can't," the young man stammers. "I need electricity to unlock the brakes."

"How in the hell are you going to get us down?" Caitlyn shouts. Her face is nearly purple from the blood pooling in her head. She experiences a sharp pain, which robs her of breath.

"I called my boss on the radio. He's on his way over."

Other riders begin hurling insults at the young man, but Caitlyn remains eerily quiet.

"Mom," Shelby says, turning to look at her mother. "Mom?"

Her mother hangs listless. Shelby screams. Gulps in air and screams again, not knowing that her mother had been carrying within her a ticking time bomb in the form of an undiagnosed aneurysm.

CHAPTER 37

Houston, Texas
Wednesday, September 29, 5:21 P.M.

His hands covered with blood, Dr. Aaron Jackson asks one of the nurses to wipe the sweat from his brow. Eleven hours into a particularly difficult heart transplant, he takes the opportunity during the brief break to arch his back and stretch side to side. He adjusts the magnifying surgical loupes resting on his nose and plunges his hands back into the chest cavity of Mr. Joseph Hall, the lucky recipient of the new heart. Mr. Hall had waited eight long months teetering at death's door for a donor heart.

"Almost there, kids," he says to those in the room, his voice muffled by the surgical mask.

Dr. Jackson works out of the South Texas Transplant Center, and is performing his third heart transplant of the year. He is among the half a dozen surgeons crowded into the sterile room, where he continues to make the final plumbing connections. He works to connect the pulmonary artery. He carefully threads the polypropylene suture material through the patient's artery, then through the donor heart. With his forearm he readjusts the magnifying loupes and continues stitching. No larger than a human hair, the suture material is difficult to see with the naked eye, but the magnifying glasses lie heavy on his nose.

The huff of the ventilator and the whoosh of the cardiopulmonary bypass machine are the only noises other than the exhaled breaths of those in the room.

"Jen, can you reposition the light?" he says to one of the nurses.

She reaches a gloved hand up and pulls the intense lamp closer to where Dr. Jackson is stitching. He continues to stitch as the other physicians lean in to follow his progress. With a final flourish he ties off the suture and snips the end of the thread with a pair of surgical scissors.

"I think we've finished," he says, looking up to survey the hidden faces of the other surgeons. Each gives him a nod.

"Okay, people, have extra suture material ready as well as more surgical sponges in case he springs a leak."

He takes one final look, then says, "Switch off bypass." The whooshing stops and he begins to gently remove the clamps attached to the arteries leading to the new heart. As he unclips the final clamp, and before he can determine if the heart is pumping, the room descends into darkness.

"Oh shit," someone shouts.

"I need more light, stat!" Dr. Jackson shouts as he flicks on the feeble beam attached to his magnifying loupe.

"Christ, we've got a bleeder. Sutures!"

Three stories below, Chief of Maintenance Virgil Hunsaker reaches for his time card to clock out for the day when a shower of sparks erupts from the main electrical panel. The basement is submerged in sudden darkness. A white-hot flame erupts from the breaker box as he races toward the developing disaster. The acrid odor of burnt plastic fills the space as a smoky haze obscures the just-coming-to-life emergency lighting.

He yanks a fire extinguisher from the wall and shoots a spray of foam toward the fire. A door is yanked open across the room and one of his workers rushes in.

"See what's wrong with the generator," Virgil shouts to the man.

"How come it didn't switch on?" the worker says.

Virgil empties the extinguisher and the flames abate.

"Don't know. We got hit with a massive jolt of something. We've got to get that generator running right damn now."

Six months ago, the hospital had installed a new main line from the recently built electrical substation a block away.

With the sleeve of his uniform shirt he yanks the melted cover from the generator's transfer panel.

"Oh shit." The breakers in the panel are fused together.

"People are going to die if we can't figure out a way to bypass this goddamn panel," Virgil says.

He glances at his watch to determine how long the hospital has been without power, and winces.

"How about we run a cable directly from the generator and tap into the main line after the breaker box?" Virgil says.

"Might work," his young assistant says.

In the darkness, Dr. Jackson drops the first suture-loaded forceps to hit his palm. "I dropped it. Someone find me a goddamn light. More sutures." Another set of forceps hits his palm.

"I can't see a damn thing." His hand fumbles through Mr. Hall's chest cavity in search of the leak. "I've got more than one bleeder, but I can't see to suture them. Somebody call downstairs and tell them this man's life depends on the backup generator."

A nurse races to the phone and snatches up the handset. "The phones are dead, Doctor."

"Yeah, well, this man will be dead if we don't stop the bleeders and get this heart pumping in the next two minutes. Somebody stick their hand in here and start cardiac massage."

One of the other doctors leans over the table and begins squeezing the still heart.

"I cannot suture without more light. Find me a goddamn flashlight right now," Dr. Jackson says in a low, menacing voice.

There's a mad scramble to find a flashlight or anything that could be construed to be a light source. Someone produces a small penlight from one of the drawers and passes it forward to the attending nurse. She clicks it on and splashes the narrow beam into the chest cavity. A large pool of blood is forming around the new heart.

"Suction!" Dr. Jackson shouts.

"Doctor," one of the other nurses says timidly, "there is no suction."

Doctor Jackson howls out a scream of frustration.

Five minutes later, the hospital's backup generator powers on. Mr. Hall, the proud recipient of a new heart he had waited eight months to possess, is on the verge of bleeding out.

"Hang two units of AB positive," Dr. Jackson orders. "Charge paddles."

The nurse hands him the defibrillator's paired internal paddles. He waits for the physician delivering cardiac massage to clear his hands from the chest cavity before placing the paddles on either side of the new heart and triggering an electrical shock.

He pulls the paddles clear. “Suction, please. I need to be able to see the entire organ.” His voice has lost all urgency.

One of the nurses places a tube into Mr. Hall’s chest and suctions out the spilled lifeblood of their patient.

“Charge paddles.” He inserts the paddles and triggers another shock. No response. He dejectedly hands the small paddles to the nurse.

He exhales an exasperated sigh and says, “Time of death is 17:59.”

One Week After

Chapter 38

On the Mississippi River, New Orleans

Aboard the *Ragin Cajun*, a paddleboat plying the waters of the Mississippi River in New Orleans, the mayor of the city stands on the top deck observing the devastation enveloping her city. After ten days of nearly constant rain, the recently rebuilt system of levees, floodwalls, and pumps is overwhelmed by water. For fifteen billion dollars the city was supposed to be safe from flooding. But with parts of the Big Easy as much as seventeen feet below sea level, dealing with water intrusion is a constant battle. Of course the whole pumping system was built with the premise that there would always be electrical power to operate it. After the Corps of Engineers replaced the fried pumps, the generators ran for three days before they ran out of fuel. With Lake Pontchartrain and its 630 square miles of surface area on one side and the mighty Mississippi River cutting through the center of town, New Orleans has always been a disaster waiting to happen.

Her chief aide, Chad, lumbers up the narrow staircase and approaches. At sixty-two, Margaret Atwell retired from her job as vice president of a technology start-up to run for mayor of her hometown city. She won in a landslide against a former mayor recently released from prison, but now she'd give anything to turn the clock back.

"Madam Mayor," Chad says as he approaches, "we've received word that the 17th Street, Orleans Avenue, and London Avenue canals are flooding." On Chad's belt is a two-way radio attached to a clear earpiece inserted into his ear.

She takes of her glasses and rubs her nose. "God, can't we get any good news?"

Chad lowers his head and shuffles his feet.

"Send out evacuation orders to those parishes. Have we heard any more from the Corps of Engineers?"

"No, ma'am. Last I heard they were trying to get a fuel barge up the Mississippi."

"Unless it gets here in the next couple of hours, the entire city will be underwater."

"I'll see what I can find out."

"Thank you, Chad. Would you also get in touch with the local emergency services office for an estimate of the time needed to evacuate the city?"

"You want to evacuate all of New Orleans?"

"I certainly don't want to, but we may not be left with a choice." She walks over to the railing and Chad follows. "I'm not sure this city can recover again."

"But we always have."

She turns to face him. "According to scientists, the city is sinking as much as an inch a year. That, coupled with the rising sea levels, may spell the final doom for our city."

Chad takes a step closer to the mayor. "When did you turn into such a pessimist?"

Mayor Atwell looks down at the muddy water coursing under the boat. "I'm not a pessimist. I consider myself well-grounded in reality. But the harsh truth is that New Orleans may become an abandoned city soon to be reclaimed by the marshes. The insurers will raise hell about rebuilding the city only a few years after Katrina."

Chad pulls the radio from his belt and talks quietly into the handset. After a brief conversation he reattaches the radio. "According to emergency services, evacuating New Orleans takes about thirty hours."

Mayor Atwell kneads the back of her neck. "I don't think we have any choice. Contact the governor's office so they can issue the order to evacuate."

Chapter 39

The Marshall home

The doctor's predictions proved true—Robert Marshall *is* a new man, with more energy and vitality than he's exhibited in years. The power is still out after a week and the generator is running on fumes from the propane tank. Zeke and Lexi have taken up residence with his parents so the generator would have to power only the one water well.

Zeke, lazing in the spare bedroom, dog-ears the page of the well-read paperback and walks into the living room, where he finds his mother reading and his father holding the shortwave radio to his ear.

"Anything?" Zeke says. His father has been fiddling with the radio all week.

"I pick up occasional voices, but nothing steady. From what I can gather we were hit with some type of solar storm."

"Hear anything about how long we'll be without power?"

"I don't think anyone knows. But if I recall correctly from an article I read in *Popular Science*, it could be a good while. Months certainly, maybe a year or longer."

"What are we going to do for water when the propane tank runs dry?" Barb says, joining the conversation.

"I've got maybe five gallons of gasoline out in the shop. We'll have to rig up something for the generator but that'll keep it running for a few more days. After that, I guess we'll be hauling water from the creek."

"That water's not fit to drink," Barb says.

"We'll have to boil it before we can drink it. Don't know that we have many choices, my dear."

"Dad, I'm going to drive into town. I think it's worth the gas. Maybe I can find a few things to restock the pantry, or at least find out if there's somewhere to get more gasoline."

"I don't think you're going to find much, son. But knock yourself out."

"Zeke, we could use some more toilet paper if you come across any."

"I think toilet paper is the least of our worries," his father says.

"I'll look," Zeke says, giving his mother a wink. He opens the back door and whistles for Lexi. She creeps from beneath the old shade tree and takes a moment to stretch, leaning back on her haunches with her front feet fully extended in front of her.

"Take your time," he tells her. Once she's all limbered up she approaches the pickup, her tail wagging, and climbs into the cab.

Zeke slides behind the wheel of his father's pickup and double-checks the fuel gauge—half a tank. He slips the truck into gear and eases out onto the roadway. First time all week any of them have driven anywhere. The pickup is the only automobile on the road as he makes a right turn onto the highway. The first stop is the small convenience store/bait shop a short distance away.

As he draws near, he doesn't even tap the brakes, because the old broken-down store is boarded up as if anticipating a hurricane. Broken glass, near where the windows once were, is scattered all over the front drive. The lone fuel pump stands like a sentry in the dusty parking lot, its handle discarded on the ground. Despite his declining hopes, he decides to continue on toward Durant.

And finds more of the same. Boarded-up businesses and a street absent of human activity. He swings by the hospital and he's surprised to see the parking lot empty with the exception of a couple of random cars parked on the outer edges of the lot. He makes a detour and drives up closer to the hospital's entrance, where he discovers a chain threaded through the metal door handles secured with a heavy padlock. He gooses the gas and makes his way back to the main road. Lexi, sitting up in the seat, stares out the window, as if she can sense that all is not well with the world.

The eerie feeling is inescapable as he motors through what used to be a fairly busy place, but now more closely resembles a forgotten ghost town. The shiny newness of the plywood is the only indication of the recentness of the disaster.

Zeke drives a little farther down the road to the new Walmart and pulls up short, shocked at the chaos in the parking lot. Carts lie overturned, boxes are piled up everywhere, long-spoiled food litters the asphalt, and shattered glass from the large front windows winks in the sunlight. No plywood covering the double-wide entrances and exits—everything has already been carted away. Dejected, he makes a U-turn and heads toward home.

The brilliant sun streaming through the windshield forces him to slip on his Ray-Bans. A few cottony white clouds dot the sky, their shadows drifting across the black asphalt. A beautiful fall day. There is no traffic on the return trip, either, but he does pass several people walking alongside the roadway. Their grim facial expressions leave him unsettled.

As he nears the turnoff toward home, he spots two pickups making a right turn into one of the campgrounds bordering Lake Texoma. From this distance he can't tell whether they're families simply searching for shelter or something more sinister. His sudden trip to town has opened his mind to some very unpleasant thoughts. He experiences a growing sense of dread.

The road leading to the neighborhood homes is the same road that leads to the campground, only in the opposite direction. He bumps down the poorly maintained road for two miles and turns in to the gravel drive of his parents' house. He taps the brakes and brings the pickup to a stop, observing the surrounding area from a new perspective. The homes are far removed from the main road and they are shielded from view by an expanse of juniper trees along the north side of the drive. You'd have to be close to stumble upon them, a slight measure of security from would-be marauders. Nevertheless, he circles behind the house and parks the pickup in the barn. As he climbs from the cab, he does the one thing he hasn't done since moving down here—he locks the doors to the truck.

"Anything?" his mother says as he draws near.

Zeke shakes his head. "Nothing. The bait shop is boarded up and the Walmart looks like a war zone."

She holds the screen door open as he brushes past, Lexi following closely behind. His father is still in the living room, patiently twirling the knob of the shortwave receiver. To save batteries, he turns it on only a couple of times a day.

"You find anything, son?"

"Nope. You could shoot a cannon down Main Street and not hit a thing. It's eerie as hell out there, Dad."

Zeke pulls out one of the kitchen chairs and takes a

seat. When they remodeled, his mother insisted on an open-concept floor plan, so most of the main floor is one large room open to the kitchen.

His mother hovers nearby, her faced pinched with concern. "Do you think Ruth and Carl and the kids are all right?" She has asked the question a dozen times over the past week, always with the same answer—no one knows.

"How about I go down and get them?" Zeke offers for the eighth or ninth time.

"And I can go with him," his father says.

"You're not going anywhere, Robert." His mother pauses for a moment and, when she finally speaks, the answer is different. "Maybe you should, Zeke."

"I'm willing. What do you think, Dad? There's not enough gas for me to get all the way to Dallas and back home, but I've been thinking about it most of the week."

Robert Marshall scoots up to the edge of his seat. "How're you going to do it with no gasoline?"

"I'm going to trailer the three horses as far as I can while leaving me enough gas to make it back. I'll park the truck and trailer in a secluded area and ride the rest of the way while leading the other two horses."

His father raises his eyebrows. "How are you going to get five people back to the trailer with only three horses? Besides, when is the last time you've even ridden a horse?"

"Ruth and Carl can double up with the kids. Shouldn't be a problem. And the last time I was on a horse was in Afghanistan."

Chapter 40

The Oval Office

President Harris, looking as if he has aged a year in only a week's time, trudges through the doors of the Oval Office. Forgoing his usual suit and tie, he's dressed in a pair of khaki slacks and a sweatshirt with the Presidential seal embroidered on the chest. His shoulders sagging, Chief of Staff Scott Alexander follows behind, looking as beaten down as the President. The White House had burned through a tremendous amount of fuel in the last week using a diesel generator to provide power. Rooms were closed off and any unneeded appliances or computers were unplugged. The President and the First Lady had their essential items moved to the first floor to conserve energy, but the massive size of the White House still consumes too much power.

The President shuffles behind his desk and sits.

"Sir, we need to think about relocating," Alexander says softly as he drops into one of the chairs flanking the desk.

"Where to, Scott?"

"The bunker in Pennsylvania—"

"I'm not going to a damn bunker, Scott. How many times are we going to have this conversation?"

"Then let's go to Camp David. We have underground storage tanks where we could survive and function for the duration of this crisis. Plus, sir, anywhere away from here will be much safer."

The President swivels in his chair to stare out the stretch of windows. E Street is deserted, with both ends barricaded by National Guard troops. "I'm not going to slink out of town with my tail between my legs like some cur dog."

"Who's going to know? There is no television, no radio, and hell, they can't even print a newspaper without electricity. Listen to me, Paul, please. You're not safe here. There's looting all through the District and reports of numerous gangs of roving thugs—the lowest life-forms—who would like nothing better than to storm the one place that represents authority."

"Hell, Scott, half the army is barricaded around the White House. No way they would ever get within a half a mile of this place. Besides, what about those without any protection?" the President snaps back. "What kind of message would that send? Their President slipping away during the night?"

"With all due respect, sir, they aren't the President of the United States."

President Harris offers no response as he turns his gaze to the brilliant sunshine streaming through the bulletproof windows.

Their argument is interrupted when the intercom buzzes. President Harris swivels back to his desk and punches the button, "Yes, Barbara?"

"Sir, Admiral Hickerson is here."

He sighs. "Send him in."

Admiral Hickerson enters the office in his dress uniform and walks stiffly across the carpet. "Mr. President," he says by way of greeting. There is no warmness in his words.

President Harris waves to the remaining chair. "Admiral, have a seat."

He carefully sits, his shoulders erect, his bearing ever the military officer. The man's weight probably hasn't fluctuated more than five pounds during his thirty-year military career.

"Sir, I think we are reaching the point where we need to declare national martial law."

The President stares at him but the admiral doesn't shy away from the scrutiny.

"Why, Admiral? Are conditions deteriorating that quickly?"

"Yes, sir, they are. Unlike anything we could imagine. Some of our National Guard units are reporting casualties in the more densely populated areas. In addition, armories in Los Angeles, Philadelphia, and eastern New Jersey have been overrun, with God-knows-what weapons now on the street. I've had to beef up security at all facilities, leaving us awfully thin in manpower."

"Christ," the President mutters. "It's only been a week, Admiral."

"I understand, sir, but I believe it'll get much worse. People are desperate and that desperation will increase exponentially with each passing day. If we are going to have any chance of containing the violence we need to declare martial law."

President Harris takes a moment to digest the information, then turns his chair to face the windows. "Do you know, Admiral, that we, as a government, haven't declared national martial law since the Civil War?"

"I wasn't aware of that fact, sir. But if there was ever a time to do it again, that time is now."

"What about active-duty troops?"

"Most of our forces are overseas and we don't have the fuel to get them all home, much less their equipment. The training battalions scattered throughout the country are busy guarding their own bases. I believe it is imperative that we declare martial law, Mr. President."

"How am I to inform the public their country is now a military state?" the President says, turning to face the admiral. "Hell, I can't deliver any reliable messages to a majority of the people who depend on us to keep them safe."

"Unfortunately, sir, we can't notify the public. The only thing we can do is issue the order down the chain of command."

"So, basically, Admiral, you're asking for permission to turn our guns on our own people?" President Harris whispers.

"Nothing as dramatic as that, sir. But we do need to reestablish some sort of law enforcement. The vast majority of the people are kind and caring, willing to offer help when able to. It's the ones that take whatever they want who need to be held in check."

CHAPTER 41

The Connor home, Upper West Side

Lara Connor is draped in blankets as she peers out the window of their sixth-floor apartment on West 69th Street. Disgusted, she turns away. "I saw another group of those whatever-the-hell-they-are—thugs, I guess," she tells her husband, Greg.

He glances up from his book and nods, so that she knows he's heard her. Otherwise, she is bound to repeat the statement until he offers some form of acknowledgment. They haven't been out of each other's presence for a solid week, and the little irritations between them are magnified with each passing hour. Not to mention the strain of living without electricity and running water in a sixth-floor apartment in the most densely populated city in the country.

The early warning from their daughter, Kaylee, had given them enough time to stock up on water and food—at least enough to last them a bit longer than others—but not enough time to escape the city.

"What are we going to do, Greg?"

Greg sighs and folds the book over his knee. "We don't

know how long the power is going to be off, Lara. It could come back on tomorrow."

"Kaylee specifically said it might be a long time before the power comes back on. We can't stay here, Greg. What are we going to do when the weather turns cold or when we run out of food? Join those roving gangs of delinquents, taking whatever we find?" Her fear, frustration, and hopelessness masquerading as anger—again.

Greg dog-ears the page of his book and lays it on the end table. He pushes up from the deep recesses of his favorite chair and walks over to the window. They aren't blessed with sweeping views of the magnificent city—only their little corner near West 69th and Columbus Avenue. The nearly leafless trees provide a clearer picture of the busier of the two streets, but the only thing he can see are the cars parked pell-mell all around the building. The automobiles struggled for their last sip of gasoline and rest now, expired, in the middle of the now-useless street.

He stares out the window while absently rubbing the back of his neck. He turns and answers his wife's question. "Do you wanna try to make a break for Wisconsin? I'd like nothing better, but how the hell are we going to get there, Lara?"

She plants her hands on her hips. "We can drive the car as far as it will go . . ." She pauses. "Then I guess we walk." She immediately realizes how silly it sounds.

"Walk? Hell, Lara, we aren't mountain climbers or hikers or outdoorsy people. We live in an apartment in the middle of New York City. And how are we going to drive? Haven't you seen the street? We wouldn't even be able to get the car out of the parking garage." Greg pauses and takes a deep breath. "I'm sorry, Lara. I'm just fed up with the whole situation."

Lara turns away.

Greg places his hand on her shoulder. “How about we walk the thirty or so blocks down to the Lincoln Tunnel to see if we would even be able to walk across to New Jersey?”

“You want to go now?”

“Yes, we can walk down and back before it gets dark.”

“What about all those hooligans roaming around?”

“If we stay in the recesses along the street we should be okay.”

Lara tucks a strand of gray hair behind her ear. “I don’t know, Greg.”

“C’mon,” he says, walking toward the coat closet near the door. “We could use some fresh air.”

“Okay . . . I guess. But don’t we need a weapon of some sort?”

“If we get to the point where a weapon is needed, we’re already in deep shit.”

CHAPTER 42

The Sanders home, University Park, Dallas

Ruth Sanders stands in the nearly depleted pantry and throws her hands up. Dressed in a pair of running shorts and an old college T-shirt, with her shoulder-length dark hair tucked into a high ponytail, she grabs a couple of cans of SpaghettiOs. She blows away a layer of dust from the tops of the cans. She shakes the bread sack with her free hand and the faint rattle of bread crumbs only depresses her further. The peanut butter jar had been scraped clean yesterday, leaving a crude collection of odd canned goods that had lined the back of the pantry for months. She turns away before the tears can begin again.

Ruth had scrounged through the attic a couple of days ago in search of anything that might be of use and had stumbled across several cans of Sterno gel, left over from when they actually hosted parties in their home. She lights one now and slides it under the cookie-cooling rack she's using for a stove top. After wiping the tops of the cans, she pierces the first lid with a recently discovered hand can opener and rotates the handle. The aroma wafting up from the grave of the interior forces her to turn her head to keep from gagging. She opens the other can and unceremoniously dumps the contents into a small pan and gives it a quick stir while holding her breath. Ruth shuffles over to the kitchen window to check on her children playing in the backyard.

Noah and Emma are climbing and swinging on the new fort Carl had assembled a month or so ago. Her heart breaks over how thin they look after only a week. The two kids from next door have joined in on the fun. To watch them, you wouldn't know the world is swirling in turmoil. They lob a daily barrage of questions she has no answers for. Their biggest concern is when they might have to return to school.

The children adapted quickly to not having electricity or running water, much quicker than Ruth and Carl. If it weren't for the lack of normal comforts and the dwindling supply of food, not having the kids plopped in front of a television or computer would be refreshing. Until reality sets in.

Carl sneaks into the kitchen and wraps his arms around her, tenderly kissing the nape of her neck. At five feet seven inches tall, Ruth had gained ten pounds after Emma's birth despite almost daily trips to the gym. She's lost half that in a week.

"That looks yummy," he says, wrinkling his nose. "Smells even better."

"Beggars can't be choosers." They're working hard to maintain some normalcy.

She turns to face him, still wrapped in his arms. She reaches a hand down and rubs his stomach. "Your little paunch is disappearing. Hell of a diet plan, huh?"

Carl smacks her on the butt. "That's not a paunch." At six feet tall he's a shade over the two-hundred-pound mark. He has little time for the gym, working long hours as an architect on several buildings along the ever-expanding Dallas skyline.

Ruth slides a stray sliver of her dark hair over her ear and pushes out of his embrace, leaning against the kitchen counter. "Seriously, Carl, what are we going to do? Do you see any way we can make it to my parents' house?"

"I don't see how." He takes a step back. "There's maybe a quarter tank of gas in both cars, and after walking around a bit, the roads are jammed with stalled cars. I just don't see any way."

"We need to do something, Carl. We'll be out of food in a day or two." She pauses, then says, "Damn, I wish we had some way to get in touch with them. I know Zeke would come get us."

"Honey, they know where we are and if there's any way Zeke can make his way down here he will. We need to hold on until the power comes back on or he comes."

"What are we going to eat in the meantime?"

"Mrs. Chlouber down the street's a big gardener and she cans a bunch of her stuff. Maybe we can find something around here to barter with."

"Like what?"

"I don't know. Maybe I'll ask her if she needs anything. Or she might be willing to sell me some, since most of her family lives out of state." Carl slips out of the kitchen on his way to the front door.

"What's she going to buy?" Ruth says to her retreating husband.

Carl shrugs and steps out the front door.

Chapter 43

The Marshall home

Zeke stirs awake with the sun, the first rays painting an orange tinge to the slate-colored sky. His hand drifts down and he works his fingers through Lexi's curly fur as his brain processes his upcoming trip. *How can you make a detailed plan when you don't have all the details?*

The birds start their morning chatter, their singsong melodies drifting through the open window on the wings of a refreshing morning breeze. He turns to stare out the window, hoping for some spark of creativity, or if not a burst of creativity—a well-laid plan delivered to the windowsill through some type of divine intervention.

The sill remains empty, so he shrugs off the covers and pads into the kitchen on autopilot. His parents are still asleep, unusual because his mother is almost always the first one up. He shakes the coffee can and the last of their meager coffee supply rattles around near the bottom. He rations a small portion of the grounds into the coffee filter and uses a plastic bucket of water to fill the reservoir. He pushes the start button and nothing happens. He slaps his forehead and mutters, "Stupid."

He shuffles to the back door and Lexi escapes to do

her morning business. He returns to the coffeemaker and dumps the coffee grounds back into the can. To make coffee he would need to relight a fire. More trouble than it's worth. Instead, he grabs a couple of maps from the junk drawer in the utility room. The ink on the cover page is faded but the paper remains crisp from lack of use. Zeke pushes the table closer to the window and spreads the maps out. It takes him a moment to get oriented, not having used a real map in years.

He joins the two maps along the Oklahoma–Texas border and searches for the roads leading from Durant to Dallas. His finger traces along the red and blue lines, and he decides Route 75 south to Sherman is the best way. Trailer the horses to Sherman and saddle up the horses there for the trip into Dallas. He does a quick mental calculation of the distance and how much fuel remains in the pickup. Sherman is going to be as far as he can safely go and expect to return home, especially pulling a loaded horse trailer.

Which leaves him about sixty-five miles to trek on horseback. He could drive it in a little more than an hour, but by horse it'll take the better part of two days to get to his sister's house. The two-day timeline would mean pushing the horses fairly hard, but not nearly as hard as the return trip will be with four extra people. Two days down, probably three days to make it back to Sherman—and that's only if nothing goes wrong. Nearly a week. That much time sitting astraddle a horse has his ass already protesting.

The estimated length of time only works if everything goes perfectly. A week without electricity will have created some desperate people. Desperate for anything they can get their hands on, and three horses on the hoof will have some of them thinking.

Now that he's settled on a route, he grabs a pencil and

begins making a list of the items he'll need for the trip. At the top of the list is weapons, which he has in abundance. You don't go to war, see and do the things he did, and not immediately arm yourself when you get back to the real world. What human beings can do to one another during war is reason enough to load up on firepower. Most returning soldiers, used to being gunned up most of a twenty-four-hour day, arm themselves when they return home. Call it a crutch or a pacifier or whatever you want to call it, but the soldiers call it survival.

Number two on the list is food, for both him and the horses. He recalls seeing a couple of fifty-pound bags of oats in the barn, enough for the horses, but his options for food are much more limited. Not willing to take any of the meager stores away from his parents means he will be foraging for food along the way. Something he's done before and can do again.

The third and last thing on the list is water. He studies the maps and tries to pinpoint water sources about every five to ten miles between Sherman and Dallas. The area is lousy with small creeks and lakes, meaning water for the horses won't be much of an issue. But he hates like hell having to tempt dysentery fate by drinking the runoff from fertilized fields and lawns. He either needs to pack a bunch of water or find some way to purify what he finds.

Zeke glances from the map to see his mother shuffling into the kitchen, the robe he bought her last Christmas cinched tightly at her waist. Her hair appears grayer from the strain of his father's recent heart attack and the upending of normal life.

"Morning," he says. "Want me to start a fire for coffee?"

"Sounds good, son," she says, coming to a stop at the table. "What's all this?"

"I'm trying to plan the trip to Ruth's house," he says,

standing from the chair and making his way toward the fireplace. The nights haven't been cold enough to keep the fire going all night so they only light it to cook on during the day. He grabs a few pieces of week-old newspaper, the last of the stack, and shreds it into long strips. He stacks a few pieces of kindling on top of the paper and rakes a match across the rough surface of the brick.

"You're stopping in Sherman?" his mother says.

Zeke nods as he returns to the table. Using his finger as a pointer, he traces the route he plans to take.

"Why don't you drive a little farther so you won't need to ride the horses so far?"

"There're several cars off to the side of the road just in this little area. Think what the scene will be in a densely packed area like Dallas and the surrounding suburbs. Plus, I need to save enough gas to get back home."

His mother looks up with new worry on her face. "I don't know that I want you to go, Zeke. It could be dangerous. Maybe it's best to wait for the power to come back on . . ." The end of her statement trails off to almost a whisper.

"I can take care of myself, Mom, but I'm not sure I can say the same for Ruth and Carl. God only knows what's going on in Dallas. The standoff between the police and the lawbreakers is a wobbly teeter-totter on a *normal* day. We can hunt for wild game here. The only wild animals in Dallas are those walking around on two legs."

She winces. "That's exactly why I don't want you to go."

"I can promise you that what I might encounter won't be a fraction of what I faced in Afghanistan. I have to go, Mom."

Barbara Marshall turns away.

Zeke lowers his voice. "Emma and Noah will be much safer here."

At the mention of her grandchildren, Barbara turns to face her son. “Okay, Zeke. You win.” She wipes away a tear. “How long do you think the trip is going to take?”

“I figure less than a full week to get down and back.”

She walks toward the nearly depleted pantry. “When are you leaving?”

“Early in the morning. I want to be in Sherman just as the sun comes up. That way I can cover as much ground as possible during the daylight.”

“I’m going to put a few things together for you to take.”

“I’m not taking our food. I’ll forage along the way.”

“Zeke, I’m not sending you without food. I won’t hear of it. I’ll put something together and pack a first aid kit for you to take along.” She sticks her head back past the doorframe of the pantry to emphasize her point. It’s no use arguing with her.

Zeke folds up the maps and adds a log to the fire before walking down to his house to retrieve his cache of weapons.

CHAPTER 44

The Connor home

Lara and Greg Connor stand as still as statues in the lobby of their apartment building, well away from the large windows that front the street. As they stepped out of the stairwell they spotted a group of people passing, and from appearances, not nice people. They decided to delay their departure. The midmorning sun paints a slanted patch of brightness along the interior of the handsomely decorated lobby.

Greg inches closer to the window and cranes his neck in both directions before waving his wife forward.

"Are you sure this is a good idea?" Lara whispers.

"I think we'll be okay."

"I don't know, Greg." She wraps her arms around herself as Greg eases the door open a smidge.

"C'mon, I don't see anything," he whispers. He puts a tentative foot on the sidewalk and glances back to make sure Lara follows. Huddled together, they walk toward the corner of their building. This is the first time they had been outside all week. Greg raises his arms to let the cool breeze billow through his jacket while turning his face to the sun, relishing the warmness. He lowers his face and sweeps the street with his eyes.

By the time they reach the end of the block and glance south down Amsterdam Avenue, a rivulet of sweat has begun inching down Greg's back. The street is clogged with automobiles of every make and size. Several people are out and about, but they seem to be more focused on their own situation than another couple taking to the streets. Not wanting to draw unnecessary attention, Greg uses hand signals as he leads his wife across the exposed intersection to the safety of the next building.

A sudden, sharp tug of his shirttail forces him to stop.

"Greg, let's go back," Lara pleads in an urgent whisper.

He turns and grasps her by the elbow. "We need to see if the Lincoln Tunnel is open. If we can get to the Jersey side we can maybe find a way to get to Wisconsin."

"How are we going to get to Wisconsin, Greg? Walk?" Her voice is too loud.

He shushes her. "If we have to, yeah. You said it yourself, we can't stay here."

She moans. "Why don't we gather our things and go? Why do we need to walk all the way down and back just to see? Let's just go."

"Because I don't want to be out here with what little food and water we have without knowing if we can even get across the Hudson. Too risky."

"And this isn't?"

"Let's go a little farther. Maybe we can tell without having to walk all the way. Okay?" His voice is calm but fear lingers in his eyes.

She hesitates before nodding.

"Keep your eyes open and if you spot anything unusual, grab me, don't yell out." He turns and begins walking down Amsterdam, hugging the side of the building.

The area is eerie with no traffic noise or the shuffling of thousands of feet. The stores are all closed, with their overhead doors of woven metal lowered to keep people out, when on any day before the crisis they would be begging you to come in and shop. Slowly, they make their way another two blocks, but that rivulet of sweat has turned into a stream.

Greg glances in both directions at West 65th and waves his wife forward. They quick-step across the intersection and duck into one of the thousands of protective enclosures created by the scaffolding that appears all over New York where buildings are being renovated or repaired. Greg quickens his pace now that they are somewhat obscured from view, but comes to a sudden stop when a scream shatters the quiet. The breath is snatched from his lungs.

He whips his head around to see his wife standing with her hands to her face, staring at something in one of the building's alcoves. Greg turns and races to her side, hissing for her to be quiet. He stifles his own scream when he discovers the nude bodies of a man and a woman, similar in age to themselves, lying crumpled in a corner. Someone had stripped all of the clothing—every scrap of material—from the bodies. One immediate question hits Greg: *were they already dead before the clothing was stripped or were they killed for their clothing?*

Lara struggles to suppress the sudden urge to vomit. Greg wraps his arms around her and shuffles sideways to limit her view of the bodies.

"Let's just go home, Greg," she blubbers into his chest. "Please?"

"Okay, honey," is the only answer he can formulate. They begin retracing their steps, much more slowly than before, whispering to each other as they recross West 65th.

They make it all the way to their street before the silence is shattered again, this time by a shout.

"Hey, you!" Greg turns to see a group of seven or eight people only a block away.

"Run!" he shouts. He grabs Lara's hand and they race around the corner to their building. A furtive glance over his shoulder reveals that the gang is now running in their direction and gaining. Greg and Lara screech to a halt at the lobby door of their building as he fumbles in his pockets for the key.

"Hey! We ain't going to hurt you," someone shouts.

Greg steals another glance just as the group rounds the corner.

"Hurry, Greg!" Lara shouts.

His fingers fumble for the key in his pocket. He yanks it out and jabs for the door lock.

"Hey! We jus' wanna talk to you," someone says as laughter breaks out among them.

Greg's hands are trembling, and Lara is yanking on his free arm as he struggles to insert the key. He turns for another quick peek only to discover the group only a hundred yards away. He slots the key and twists. He and Lara burst through the doorway as Greg yanks his key free and inserts it into the interior side of the lock, throwing the bolt home just as the group of thugs reaches the large window.

The glass flexes with each blow of their fists as Lara and Greg race to the stairwell.

Chapter 45

The Sanders home

Carl swings the front door open and eases out onto the porch of their 1930s-era home. Built in the Queen Anne style, a long, deep porch occupies much of the front façade. He takes a moment to survey the street and finds nothing amiss. A few people are out and about, but no one he doesn't recognize. The neighbor across the street, Dusty, offers Carl a friendly wave and he returns the gesture. Dusty and his wife were in the midst of a raucous divorce before the power died. It was only a couple of days later that husband and wife were reunited on the front lawn, both forgiving past sins to face a different world together.

Carl descends to the walkway and hesitates for a moment at the intersection with the sidewalk to take another look around. Satisfied, he turns left and casually strolls along under the canopy of ancient oak trees lining the street. The dappled shade moves with the wind and an occasional leaf drifts down after having served its host. A small pile of leaves is bunched against the curb. The branches of the stately oaks spread outward nearly a hundred feet. But they come with a price that must be paid every fall, when most homeowners curse their existence.

Carl turns up the drive leading to Mrs. Chlouber's home, three doors down the street. Mrs. Chlouber is a widow who lives alone. Her three children are scattered across the country and her husband passed four years ago. She has lived in the same house since the late '70s and it's now more than she can care for, but she insists on staying.

Carl extends his finger to the doorbell before he can remember the bell won't work. He knocks softly on the door and puts his ear to it, listening for approaching footsteps. Silence. He peers through the side window, but the dim interior doesn't reveal any movement. He reaches over to the door and raps his knuckles again, this time a little harder as his gaze remains on the interior. Nothing. Not even Mr. Twiddle, her overweight tabby cat.

"Where the hell could she be?" he mutters as he steps away from the door. Carl walks past the garage door and springs the latch on the gate to the backyard. He takes another glance around before disappearing behind the wooden privacy fence. Feeling like an intruder, he slips along the brick façade and turns the rear corner to find the sliding patio door pushed open. He pulls up short and studies the area before going any farther.

His mind sorts through possibilities. *Maybe she's just airing the house out. But the screen on the door is open, too, leaving the home open to an invasion of the pesky mosquitoes that plague the area, not to mention an easy escape route for Mr. Twiddle. No way would she leave the door open and not close the screen, especially with the threat of West Nile virus.*

He approaches the open door with a knot forming in the pit of his stomach. "Mrs. Chlouber?" he says through the open doorway. "Sarah?" he says louder. No response.

He steps tentatively across the threshold. The light here in the back of the house is brighter than it had been at the front but it is still a grainy gloom. "Mrs. Chlouber?" His voice is tight, tense.

Carl steps farther into the room, a living area overlooking the backyard. He creeps toward the kitchen. An unseen menace has the hairs at the nape of his neck standing at attention. He slides up next to the entryway to the kitchen and sneaks a quick peek. "Sarah, are you in here?"

His gaze drifts around the kitchen. "Mrs. Chlo—"

The words die in his throat when he spots a pale leg extending beyond the kitchen island. Carl tamps down the sudden urge to run, and rounds the island to discover Sarah Chlouber lying on the floor. Her face is almost unrecognizable from the beating she had sustained. He kneels down to feel for a pulse, a futile effort given her eggplant-hued skin. He gets to his feet and stumbles backward, his brain swirling for a next move.

Could the killer still be in the house?

His throat constricts while his eyes flit around the kitchen, straining to hear the slightest sound. No movement, no sounds. Carl tiptoes toward the living room, sweeping his vision from one dark corner to the other.

His body thrumming with the sudden dump of adrenaline, Carl hurries back to the kitchen. He gives Mrs. Chlouber's body a wide berth as he makes his way to the pantry. The door squeals as he pushes it open and he pauses to listen while his heart rate races like a Thoroughbred heading down the stretch. Though the light is faint, there's enough to see that the pantry is empty.

Carl backs out and glances at the body again. *What to do? Can't call the police. Can't call any of her children. How are they going to know that their mother is dead?* It's a hopeless situation. He feels terrible about leaving Sarah Chlouber on the floor of her kitchen. As he makes his way back through the living room he quietly calls for Mr. Twiddle. But if the cat's in the house he's hidden.

Once through the patio door, Carl hurries around the side of the house and grabs for the gate. He stops, takes a deep breath, and peeks through the slats of the fence. *How would I explain sneaking away from a house with the owner dead inside?*

Carl eases the gate open only far enough for him to slip through and sighs with relief when he discovers the area absent of people. He hurries away from the house, but forces himself to slow down once on the sidewalk. He nearly jumps out of his skin when a cat darts out from the bushes and races away. It's Mr. Twiddle, but Carl doesn't have a prayer of catching the spooked cat. He'll send Ruth out later to see if she can round him up before he ends up on a dinner plate.

His thoughts turn from the cat to a more troubling issue: *Who killed Sarah Chlouber? And more to the point—is that person still around?*

CHAPTER 46

The Oval Office

Thick sheets of steel have been installed over the once-magnificent windows along the back wall of the Oval Office. Several shots had been fired at the windows during the night, and although the glass is bulletproof, the Secret Service had installed the steel panels immediately after. The cold metal makes the office feel more like a dungeon. President Harris shuffles into the darkened interior and walks to his desk, the immensity of the nation's problems weighing heavy on his mind.

The President sits and, out of habit, swivels his chair to look out the windows. "Goddammit," he says aloud.

The door swings open and the President turns to see who is entering without being announced. He groans inwardly when Chief of Staff Scott Alexander steps through. The two are involved in another running battle that has spanned two days.

"If that isn't proof of how unsafe this place is, then I don't know what is," Alexander says, pointing at the covered windows. He approaches the desk and takes a seat in one of the chairs, uninvited.

President Harris doesn't answer, shooting his aide—and friend—a nasty glare. "What's the latest from Admiral Hickerson since declaring martial law?"

"I spoke to him this morning. According to him, the military is getting a handle on the situation. Whatever that means."

The President turns his chair and stops in midswivel. "Are those metal panels really necessary?"

"The Secret Service seems to think so. Which only proves my point that—"

President Harris holds up his hand to silence Alexander. He begins riffling through the mounds of paper cluttering his desk. It seems pointless to press a legislative agenda when more than half the members of Congress are stranded God knows where.

"Mr. President, Paul, this is the last time I'm going to bring the issue up, but we need to at least move operations to Camp David." Alexander cringes, waiting for the expected outburst. But he's surprised when his friend pauses a moment to consider his statement. He pushes just a bit more. "The First Lady would certainly be more comfortable there."

President Harris pushes the papers aside and stands. He's gaunt from worry and his hollow cheeks are sporting a rash of black and gray stubble. He begins to pace the area where the windows once opened on the world, his hands fisted at his side.

"Okay, Scott. Let's move to Camp David. But we'll do it by motorcade instead of the big spectacle with the three helicopters."

"We can't go by car."

"Why the hell not?"

"Because every road leaving Washington is jammed

with stalled cars. We'd get maybe three blocks, and that's only because the Service had all those vehicles towed away."

"Why aren't we clearing, at minimum, one road?"

"Because it would take a hundred wreckers a month working twenty-four/seven to even make a dent in the problem. In addition, we don't have the fuel to run the wreckers. Besides, it's pointless anyway," Alexander says.

President Harris stops pacing. "What happened to all those National Guard tankers I ordered to be filled?"

"Maybe only a third of them were filled before the power went out."

"Where are those?"

"A majority of them are keeping hospital generators running. Unfortunately, most of them are probably down to the dregs."

"What's going to happen when that happens?"

"I don't think you want to know, Mr. President."

President Harris turns away and begins pacing the perimeter of the oval room. He stops and says, "One helicopter, and one only."

"One presidential helicopter," Alexander clarifies. "We're going to need several other choppers, or one making several trips to get most of the staff out to Camp David."

President Harris bristles with anger. "The whole damn country is going to know their President is bailing."

"Can't be helped, sir. And we're not bailing—just changing locations. As I pointed out earlier we have no working press. Our main focus is your safety."

"When?"

"Tomorrow night, after dark."

"So you were counting on me to cave?"

"No, sir, but I wanted to be prepared if I was successful in convincing you."

"Scott, you're a damn terrible liar."

"We've been friends for a long time." A wry grin forms as Alexander walks from the office.

CHAPTER 47

University Hospital, Baltimore, Maryland

Approximately forty miles from the White House, the medical staff at University Hospital is struggling to reduce the number of patients in the hospital. Not helping the situation is the constant stream of newly injured, who straggle into the hospital on an hourly basis. Dr. Iftikar Singh, a short, precisely groomed man who grew up in New Delhi, is waiting for the last of the medical staff to filter in for his hastily called meeting. Chosen by the staff to be medical director, he is now facing a multitude of life-and-death decisions.

After everyone is seated, he stands and approaches the lectern while looking out over the audience. The seats rise from front to back, with those on the rearmost row some thirty feet above the small floor space at the front of the room. Dr. Singh takes a deep breath before addressing his fellow doctors. "I have just been informed by military personnel that the hospital only has enough fuel to run the generators for approximately another twenty-four hours."

The room boils with angered shouting and cries of anguish. Dr. Singh gives them a moment to vent before continuing.

"It is not something we can control—"

He pauses as the shouting begins again. A slight accent from his native country of India is noticeable, but having been educated in American universities, his English is very good. It's the cultural differences that cause the most problems for him. In America, medicine is so advanced that many patients receive life-continuing care for injuries and illnesses that would mean a certain death sentence in his home country.

"Please be quiet," he says into the microphone. The noise level drops enough to continue. "As I was saying, it is out of our control. You need to begin weaning the patients off any medication they are receiving. We are closing the doors to any new patients." The room is silent enough for him to hear the worried breathing of those nearest him.

"What about the patients on vents and other mechanical devices?" someone says from the middle of the room.

He leans toward the microphone and says in a whisper, "They will die."

He glances up at those he had been working with for years. "All we can do is provide comfort to those families, and do the best by our patients. We are not alone. Most every hospital across the country is dealing with the same critical decisions we are now facing."

Another doctor says, "Can we still suture wounds, give pain medicine at least until the pharmacy is depleted?"

"The pharmacy is nearly depleted. We have not received a shipment of medication since the power went off over a week ago. We could make an office with daylight exposure available for those who would like to continue to treat the injured until all supplies are exhausted. But as a hospital we must close the doors."

Dr. Singh pauses again and sweeps his gaze around the room. "How many of you are still caring for patients?"

Almost every doctor's hand shoots up. He looks over

the papers resting in front of him—the latest numbers that were supplied to him only moments before the meeting.

"According to hospital records, we have over two hundred patients in various sections of the hospital. We need to prepare these patients for immediate discharge. This is a very harsh reality, but there are no other options. For those relying on mechanical devices to survive, we need to disconnect life support as soon as humanely possible so their loved ones are given a chance to say good-bye."

With nothing left to say and with no reassuring words to offer, Dr. Singh steps away from the microphone and joins his fellow medical staff as they come to grips with the looming tragedies.

CHAPTER 48

The Marshall home

"I wish I knew what the weather was going to do," Zeke says. He and his parents are sitting around the kitchen table, his mother again in her robe, and his father dressed in a pair of sweats and an old T-shirt. It's early, the sun still well below the horizon, as he packs the few remaining items he'll need for his trip. Shadows flicker on the wall as the light from three candles bathes a portion of the room in a warm, weak, yellow light. The surroundings resemble an old western movie, as they huddle around the table now laden with guns, saddlebags, and a bedroll.

"I have an *Old Farmer's Almanac*," his father says.

Zeke's not sure if it's said in jest or whether his father believed he was offering a useful suggestion. "I don't think that's going to give me the seven-day forecast, Dad. I'm trying to decide how many warm clothes to take."

Robert Marshall takes a sip of weak coffee, brewed with yesterday's grounds. "This time of year, I'd pack a coat and a rain slicker. It shouldn't get too cold, but you need to keep an eye on the horizon. If a cold front comes through it could trigger some thunderstorms." Robert leans forward and places his forearms on the table. "Are you sure you don't want me to go with you?"

"No, you need to stay here and take care of Mom. I left you a 12-gauge and a couple of boxes of shells in the garage. And you've got your deer rifle."

"I don't think there's anything to worry about."

"You never know, Dad. I saw some pretty shady-looking people heading down to the campsite at the lake. You need to be aware of what's happening around you," Zeke says, the soldier in him coming to the forefront, "and don't be afraid to use the damn shotgun."

His father arches his brow. "So you want me to shoot first and ask questions later?"

"I didn't say that, Dad. Just don't let anyone get up close to the house. A shotgun pointed at their midsection will deter most people. Look, I'm just sayin' to be on the lookout, okay?"

His father nods and Zeke turns away to focus on his task. He pats his hip to make sure the Glock G30 is still riding comfortably in the paddle holster. He counts out the number of .45 caliber rounds and stows them away in one of the saddlebags. Three boxes of fifty: one hundred and fifty rounds. Should be plenty.

He slides the Kimber 84L rifle, with a Kevlar–carbon fiber stock, into an old rifle scabbard scrounged from the barn. The bolt-action rifle holds five .270 Winchester cartridges—four in the clip and one hot. The Kimber is an extremely accurate weapon, but only if the shooter knows what he's doing. Zeke does. Anywhere within four hundred yards is in the kill zone. The rifle is not an aim-for-center-mass-and-pray-type weapon—the .270 rounds are meant for instant death.

His father watches while Zeke counts out the ammunition. "That's a lot of firepower you're packing, son."

"I don't have any idea what I'm going to run into. But

you can bet I'll damn sure be prepared." Zeke settles on an even one hundred rounds for the rifle and cinches down the saddlebag.

The last thing Zeke adds to his armory, other than a standard camp ax, is his SOG SEAL Pup combat knife. He slips the knife into a sheath attached to his Danner combat boots, compliments of Uncle Sam. Gunned up, he's ready for war. "I'd be happy if I don't have to use any of the weapons, Dad. But it's much better to have 'em than not."

Zeke throws the saddlebag over his shoulder and heads for the door, but he stops, snaps his fingers, and makes a detour into his temporary bedroom. He tosses the saddlebags on the bed and reaches into the nightstand drawer to retrieve a silver locket strung on a twenty-inch sterling silver chain. Zeke puts the cold metal to his lips, then slides the chain around his neck, tucking the locket beneath his shirt.

He scoops up the saddlebag and returns to the kitchen. "Dad, want to help me load up the horses?" Last night they moved the three horses into the corral so they wouldn't need to go hunting for them in the dark.

Robert pushes out of the chair like a young man again and follows Zeke toward the back door. He stops and turns to his wife. "Honey, you pack him some food?"

"I packed him a few things," Barbara says.

"Dad, I'm not taking your food."

He shushes Zeke with a wave. "Pack him most of what's left. I can hunt some game later this evening. Ruth, Carl, and the kids are going to be hungry when you get there."

His mother retrieves one of her cloth shopping bags from behind the pantry door and begins loading in more food. Zeke shakes his head, but he hadn't considered the fact that his sister and her family are most likely out of food.

Daybreak is still barely a notion as he switches on the headlamp and steps outside. He walks to the pickup and tosses the saddlebags into the backseat. Zeke had backed the trailer up to the loading ramp last night. The horses are restless after a night of confinement, but with Zeke working from behind, and his father leading with a bucket of sweet corn, they load on easily.

These aren't quarter horses or Arabians or Thoroughbreds—they're working horses. Although they haven't been ridden in some time, they appear eager to work. Zeke turns away from the horses and spots his mother struggling with the bag of bounty she had assembled. He walks over and grabs the bag, surprised at how heavy it is.

"Did you leave enough for you and Dad to eat?" he says.

"We'll be fine. Now shush about the food. Emma and Noah are going to be hungry."

Zeke walks back to the pickup and places the bag of food onto the backseat. He turns and offers his hand to his father, but Robert brushes past his outstretched arm and wraps him in a full embrace—the morning's first surprise. It's the first time in a long time and the hug feels awkward, but Zeke hugs back, and thankfully, the embrace is short-lived. His mother steps in for one last hug, but unlike with his father, they squeeze each other tightly. Zeke can feel the dampness from her tears as they gather on his chest.

"Be careful, Zeke," she whispers. Finally, she separates from the embrace and takes a short step back.

Zeke's working overtime not to spill a few tears of his own. After a deep breath, he kneels down and wraps his arms around Lexi. He desperately wants to take her with him, but he's afraid she would be too tempting a target for people who are near starving. After a kiss on her forehead, Zeke runs his fingers through her thick coat one last time before standing.

With a small wave, he walks around the other side of the truck, climbs in, and waves good-bye again as the engine coughs to life. He triggers the passenger window down. "I'll see you three in about a week."

Chapter 49

University Hospital

Dr. Iftikar Singh has been up all night assisting patients. Six patients were removed from their ventilators during the overnight hours and all died within minutes. His most difficult task lies before him. He shuffles down the bustling hallway with the enormity of the moment weighing heavy on his mind. Although he had asked the other doctors to remove their patients from any mechanical lifesaving devices as soon as possible, Dr. Singh chose to wait till the very end for his last patient.

He exhales a heavy breath, straightens his coat, and runs his hand across his face before entering Room 236. A young couple in their midtwenties are seated next to the bed containing their four-year-old daughter.

"Good morning," Dr. Singh says in a halfhearted mutter.

Both give small nods. Their faces are masked with agony and fear. Chelsea had been admitted two weeks ago with a severe case of influenza. Since that time, and despite an array of medical procedures, her small body has deteriorated. The flu attacked her still-young organs with deadly precision. Chelsea has been on a ventilator for a week and the machines used to measure her brain activity indicated the decline was spiraling beyond hope.

Singh spent most of last evening with Chelsea's parents as he carefully, and as humanely as possible, described what was occurring with the hospital's dwindling fuel supplies. Now, searching for words, he starts and stops, then when he can't assemble a meaningful explanation, he says, "It's time."

Chelsea's mother breaks into heavy sobs and she angrily stands from the chair. "How could you?" she screams.

Her husband pushes out of his chair, a steady stream of tears dripping from his face onto his massive chest. He wraps his wife in an embrace. "Shh," he whispers into her ear.

"Why? Why?" his wife screams while pounding her husband's chest.

Singh has no answers—no words to alleviate the grief. He steps up and wraps his arms around the young couple as they deal with the loss of their only child. Dr. Singh has witnessed these terrible situations rip a family apart, and he offers a silent prayer to whoever may be listening that this couple can somehow overcome and heal each other.

Singh steps away from the couple and shuffles toward the bed where the dark-haired, and once bright-eyed, Chelsea lies. The wheezing of the ventilator is loud, pumping air through her tiny lungs. He reaches down and grabs her small hand as the parents join him at her bedside.

The mother's sudden anger is now replaced by wracking sobs. "I love you, baby," she whispers as she bends down and tenderly kisses Chelsea's forehead.

The father, weeping uncontrollably, releases his wife long enough to offer Chelsea a kiss on the check. "I'll see you in heaven," he whispers.

Singh wipes the tears from his eyes as he walks to the panel that controls the device keeping Chelsea alive. With a wince he switches it to the off position. The sudden silence fills the room as the ventilator pumps one last time. The parents lie down beside their child as her body, searching for oxygen, gasps for the final time.

Dr. Singh silently slips out of the room and shambles down the hall, wiping his eyes and wondering how such an advanced medical system can be wiped out by something that they had all taken for granted.

Chapter 50

The Connor home

Lara and Greg Connor, hungover from stress, had barely slept at all in their ever-increasingly colder sixth-floor Manhattan apartment. Greg pushes the heavy covers aside and quickly dresses in a pair of sweats and a sweat-shirt. He slides his feet into his favorite pair of slippers and heads for the bathroom, where he pisses into a five-gallon bucket sitting next to the now-useless toilet. Every other day, he lugs the bucket down six flights of stairs to empty it into the gutter near the front of the building.

When Greg finishes, Lara scrambles from bed and squats over the bucket before hurriedly dressing in her warmest clothes. They walk down the hallway and into the living room, where Greg takes a seat in his favorite recliner. Lara wanders over to peer out the window over-looking 69th Street. After yesterday's horrifying afternoon outing, she had spent most of the day on the lookout for their pursuers. It's still too dark to see much of anything, so she steps into the kitchen.

"Want some water, Greg?"

"How much is left?"

She sighs. "A gallon, other than the case of bottled

water we're saving." They had decided to keep a case of the bottles in reserve for traveling purposes.

"I'm good for now." He stands from the chair and shuffles over to the window, willing the sun to rise.

Lara pours a couple of fingers of water into a cup and walks it into the living room. She sinks onto the couch and takes a tentative sip, as if drinking the finest brandy.

Greg turns from the window. "We need to make a plan."

"After what happened yesterday?"

"We have no choice, Lara. I spent most of the night trying to come up with a plan. Maybe we should band together with some of the neighbors and make a break for New Jersey. From there we could move inland until we find some type of shelter." Greg walks over to his recliner and sits. "Plus, we'd have access to water from the creeks and streams, and we could forage for food."

"Who are you going to ask? The Scotts have two young children and the Mitchells are so frail they would never make it. Besides, what do you know about foraging for food? You're an investment advisor, not some survivorman like on television."

Greg's face tightens with anger. "Would you rather curl up here and starve to death? Or die from dehydration? We've got to do something." His anger dissipates as quickly as it flared. "I know what happened yesterday is upsetting—I am scared, too, but we're at the end of our rope here. I'll go floor to floor to see if anyone wants to join us, if that's what it takes. And I bet the Scotts are in even worse shape, with four mouths to feed."

"What about those people that chased us yesterday? I bet there are a whole bunch just like them prowling all over the city."

"We're going north this time. Up to the George Washington Bridge. And we're going to go at night."

"Why at night? No telling what we'd stumble into in the dark. We won't be able to see a damn thing."

"Exactly. We just need to be smarter about what we're doing."

"When?" Lara says, now resigned to the fact they are out of options.

"As soon as possible. Tonight."

Lara swallows the last of her water and stands from the couch. "I'll start putting some things together while you go find someone to join us on our suicide mission." She disappears down the hallway to their bedroom.

"Don't pack much, Lara. Only the bare necessities, like what's left of our medicine and a change of clothes. Maybe a first aid kit," Greg says, aiming his voice down the hall. He pushes out of his recliner and shuffles toward the window again while his brain swirls.

Lara, on the way from the bedroom to the kitchen, stops when she sees her husband at the window. "I thought you were going to talk to the neighbors?"

Greg turns from the brightening sky. "The more I think about it, the less sure I am about inviting anyone else along. I think our chances are better with just the two of us. We'll be able to move faster and quieter. But I'll make the effort if you want me to."

"Whatever." Lara throws her hands up. "I'm fed up with the whole goddamn situation."

Chapter 51

NOAA Space Weather Prediction Center

Most of the scientists and support staff working at the Space Weather Prediction Center slowly trickled away over the first two days—back home to their families around the Boulder area. The only two left are Dr. Samuel Blake and Dr. Kaylee Connor, both of whom have no family in the area and feel no pressing need to return to their dark homes. But the generator has slurped through most of the stockpiled gasoline, forcing them to think about leaving.

The supplies Sam had purchased before the power died were divvied up equally among the workers, some taking the items home to share with family, but not without a few heated discussions among the staff. The kindness and camaraderie lasted until the shock wore off. Sam used his eroding authority to divide what remained and was relieved when the last of the workers hit the door.

Seated in the conference room, Sam is staring out the windows at the jagged peaks of the nearest mountains. The weather is unseasonably warm, but the ominous clouds on the horizon suggest the Indian summer is about to come to a screeching halt.

Kaylee enters the conference room after sneaking a smoke outside.

"How many you have left?"

"Four. I think I'll save them for a special occasion."

Sam smiles. "Is there a fireplace in your apartment?"

"No. What about your house?"

"Yeah, and I have a pretty good supply of firewood."

"Well, I guess the question of whose place—yours or mine—is answered."

Sam turns to look at Kaylee. Her hair hasn't been washed in a week and hangs in a limp mess, obscuring portions of her narrow face. Devoid of makeup, her face displays creases around her mouth that appear deeper and more defined. Dark bags line the bottom of her deep-set eyes. She's absently twirling a strand of her dark hair while gnawing on her bottom lip.

The dynamic between them is different. From boss and employee to something on a deeper level. At least in Sam's mind. His only hang-up is the age difference. That, and the fact he doesn't have a clue about Kaylee's thoughts on the matter.

"Gather what you can and we'll head out."

"What, about five miles to your house?" Kaylee says.

"Yeah, thereabouts. I would offer to drive but I'm afraid the roads will be impassible."

"The hike will do us good."

Sam glances once more through the window at the angry clouds and follows Kaylee from the room. "Grab all the water you can find and you better grab a coat."

She gives a little wave as she retreats down the hall.

It doesn't take long for them to gather their meager supplies, and both are ready to go only minutes later. They exit the building to a cool breeze blowing off the Front Range. Sam pauses to lock the door, and he and Kaylee stroll down the access road that leads up to the Space Weather Prediction Center. At the bottom of the hill they take a left on Broadway, the main thoroughfare bisecting Boulder.

Sam's home is located north of the Space Weather Prediction Center, where College Street dead-ends at the foothills.

Seeing all the abandoned cars, Sam says, "I'm glad we decided not to drive."

"Yeah, we wouldn't have gotten far. This is unbelievable. It looks like a scene from a disaster movie."

"I only wish it *had* been a movie. We better pick up the pace," he says, glancing up at the encroaching black clouds.

"I think you're right." They accelerate the pace, almost jogging, as they pass one closed business after another.

"Keep an eye out, Kaylee."

"For what? I don't see anything."

"For other people. We haven't been outside and we have no sense of the mood. But I assume it's not good. Let's keep the noise to a minimum. If you spot anything, wave your hand. It may be better to hit the back roads before we reach the downtown area."

Kaylee nods, her breathing labored from the hurried pace. Sam hooks a left on a residential street as the skies open up, drenching them in a cold rain. Within half a block the rain transitions to sleet. It feels as if they are being pelted by buckshot. He slows down enough for Kaylee to catch up.

"Damn . . . Sa . . . m," she stutters out, "can we . . . slow . . . down?" Kaylee is incapable of drawing a full breath.

Sam slows slightly. "We need to get out of this before we get hypothermia. Pull your jacket up around your neck to keep the ice from drifting down—"

An icy north wind arrives, whipping the remaining words from his mouth. Kaylee shivers, and the biting cold forces her to quicken her stride. Both are wearing the only coats they could find—Windbreakers that provide little resistance to the gale-force winds now pummeling their bodies.

Sam turns his head and shouts, "I told you those cigarettes weren't good for you."

Kaylee shoots him the finger. "How . . . much . . . further?"

"Just a little ways." He, too, is beginning to huff, his heavy breathing creating a continuous fog.

"What's . . . a . . . little . . . ways?"

"About six or seven blocks." Sam jogs across an intersection, now heading north. The sleet is falling in sheets, melting upon impact when meeting exposed skin. Despite having his collar turned up, meltwater trickles down his back. He glances back and sees the laces of Kaylee's Converse sneakers covered under a heavy glaze of ice. The cold wind is relentless in its pursuit, finding every available crevice.

"C'mon," Sam shouts above the wind. "Almost there."

Two more blocks and they make a left onto Sam's street. They veer off the roadway and Sam leads them through a shortcut between yards. He reaches the back door of his home and struggles to retrieve the keys from the frozen pocket of his khakis. Kaylee catches up as the door swings open.

"Get those wet clothes off."

Kaylee begins peeling the frozen layers from her body. Within seconds she's completely nude. She wraps her shivering arms around her midsection and glances over her shoulder to see Sam, his mouth agape.

She laughs at the absurdity of the situation. "Blanket, Sam?"

The question snaps him out of his reverie. "On the sofa," he replies as he struggles with his own frozen clothing, sneaking a peek at Kaylee's retreating backside.

Sam enters the house in his birthday suit and grabs one of the throws from the sofa, but not before Kaylee gets a glimpse of the entire package. He searches her face for a wince, a cringe, anything that might express displeasure.

"You have a nice body, for an old man," Kaylee says.

He blushes as he wraps a blanket around him. "Uh . . . well . . . I . . . think I'll start a fire."

Kaylee laughs.

CHAPTER 52

En route to Texas

The traveling is fairly easy, with only an occasional car stranded on the roadway. Until he crosses the Red River into Texas. As Zeke nears the outskirts of Denison, the number of abandoned cars creeps upward with every tick of the odometer. He exits the highway at an uncluttered off-ramp and pulls into the parking lot of an abandoned convenience store

He kills the engine to save fuel and grabs the map from the door pocket. It takes him a couple of revolutions to get the map oriented to his liking. A quick glance at the intersection reveals the road name and he quickly pinpoints his position. If he follows Farm to Market Road 120 west to 131 it's a straight shot south to Sherman. Zeke studies the map's scale and uses his index finger and thumb to gauge the distance. Eleven miles—a ten-minute pickup ride or a half a day by horse. Zeke votes pickup and restarts the engine.

As he pulls back on the road he slaps the wheel, knowing he's behind his self-imposed timeline. To make up some time, he gooses the truck up to sixty while searching for the road leading south. The truck crests a small hill and

Zeke slams on the brakes as the turnoff to 131 races past the window. He eases up on the brakes and curses under his breath, hoping like hell he hasn't injured any of the horses.

At the next intersection he coasts to a stop and inhales a deep breath. After a few moments, he makes a wide U-turn and backtracks toward 131 at a more reasonable pace. He brakes gently and steers right at his turn.

Lesson learned. He eases down the road, never going more than thirty-five. Very few houses dot the landscape, just acres of pastureland interspersed with recently planted fields of winter wheat. On the outskirts of Sherman, he can make out the downtown buildings, jammed together tight as teeth. He pulls over again for another glance at the map, hoping to avoid any area where people may be gathered. He finds a road two blocks to the west that skirts the downtown area.

He hooks a right at the next intersection and begins hunting for someplace to park the pickup and trailer. A place removed from passersby. Farther on, he spots an oilfield road that winds around through the trees, and makes the turn. The truck and trailer bump across the cattle guard and through the already open gate. Zeke steers along the gravel path a good distance, and before stopping glances over his shoulder to make certain the main road is out of sight.

He steps from the cab and does a quick walk around the area. Off to the left is an opening through a dense group of cedar trees hugging the far fence line. "Should fit," he mutters as he climbs back into the cab. With shrieking from the branches along the fenders, he pulls the trailer far enough into the trees to hide it from view. After one final glance at the gas gauge, the needle hovering just south of half a tank, he kills the engine and exits the cab. He begins unloading supplies, tying to sort out in his mind the best way to arrange things for easy loading onto the horses. Now the tricky part is getting the horses out of the trailer without any of them trying to make a break.

Zeke whispers softly to the horses as he walks the length of the trailer, hoping to calm them from the drive. He slides the trailer's gate open just wide enough to allow one horse out at a time. He clips the lead rope to the first horse through and does it two more times until all three are secured to the side of the trailer. Before leaving, he and his father had discussed the best way to lead the horses and which one would be best to ride. They settled on Murphy, the gelding, as the best horse for him to ride while leading the two mares, Tilly and Ruby.

His fingers dance across Murphy's soft muzzle as he uses the other hand to position the saddle blanket onto his back. The task of getting the saddle aboard takes two hands, but once it's in place he begins cinching down the girth strap, waiting for the horse to exhale before tying it off.

Zeke feeds the bit into Murphy's mouth and ties the reins to the trailer. Ruby and Tilly get blankets before he mounts the two wooden carriers he had fashioned back home. He ties those off and slips a halter over the necks of both mares.

He glances up at the sun, trying to gauge the time. Still morning, but much later than he had hoped. He loads the remaining gear onto the horses and double-checks that his rifle remained in the scabbard. Not wanting to carry the keys to the pickup with him, he slides them up under the rear wheel well and jams them into a hole in the frame.

He leads the horses away from the truck and sweeps

his hand across his hip to make sure the Glock is securely holstered. He grabs the mare's lead and mounts Murphy. After a slight heel tap to the ribs, Murphy whinnies and begins walking toward the road. He pulls the horses to a stop at the edge of the pasture and looks back to make sure the truck and trailer are out of sight and to mentally mark the location for the return trip. He turns forward to mark the entrance gate in reference to the road and a big elm tree shading the opposite side. Satisfied, he works the horses around the side of the cattle guard, picking their way through a collapsed portion of barbed wire fence. From the lack of animal droppings, it's obvious there haven't been any cattle grazing in here for a while.

Zeke loosens the reins to allow Murphy to set his own pace—a nice, steady walk. He glances over his shoulder to make sure the mares are comfortable at this pace. They're plodding along fine. With nothing left to do but ride he takes a moment to look the area over. The bright sunshine highlights the flat landscape, revealing a good number of recently plowed fields in anticipation of spring planting. A sudden realization begins to gnaw his gut—the months ahead are going to be much more difficult than he first thought. The next field over is sown with winter wheat, the green shoots just breaking the surface, and thoughts of fallow fields follow him for the next mile.

The midmorning sun is relentless, and even though he's not exerting much effort, a steady stream of sweat works its way down his back. He's glad he had remembered to bring along an old cowboy hat. With the intense heat, Zeke begins searching for water sources as they walk forward, holding to the centerline of the empty roadway.

With the immense fields taking up most of the land, the few houses are scattered a good distance from one another—maybe a half a mile to a mile between them. The first one they pass is set close to the road and Zeke's hand drifts to the gun on his hip as they pass. No one is out and about and the only things moving are a few head of cattle grazing up close to the house.

Two hours later the horses have worked up a lather, as the black asphalt pushes the temperatures up twenty degrees. He steers Murphy off into the grassy side area. The heat instantly lessens but the danger of the horses stumbling into a gopher hole, or over discarded items along the roadway, increases. They've made good time and he pulls the sweat-saturated map from his back pocket to check their location. As best he can figure, they've covered over seven miles. Much better than he thought, although once they're closer to Dallas the pace will slow dramatically.

The small creeks they've passed have been bone-dry. Water is Zeke's main focus now. In the distance he spots a windmill turning lazily in the stingy breeze. He's hopeful it's not an ornamental piece of iron and is actually pumping water into a stock tank. The one negative about the windmill is its proximity to a house. As they draw closer, Zeke discovers that the windmill is confined within a four-stranded barbed wire fence. He makes the decision that, regardless of the danger, the horses need water.

He dismounts Murphy at the head of the driveway and leads the horses toward the house. His gaze scans the surrounding area, his senses on high alert. When he is about fifty feet from the house, the front door opens and an older man steps onto the porch with a shotgun pointed in Zeke's direction. Zeke stops and pulls Murphy and the mares to a stop next to him.

"Whatcha want?" the man shouts. The man is dressed in a pair of dirty pants pitted with holes and a pair of black suspenders strung over a no-longer-white T-shirt. A floppy black hat in the semi-shape of a cowboy hat tops out the ensemble. If Zeke didn't know better, he'd think he was looking at a reincarnation of Wishbone from the old *Rawhide* series.

"I was wondering if I could water the horses."

"Step up a little closer so's I can see you," the man says, the shotgun never wavering more than two inches on either side of Zeke's chest.

Zeke emits a couple of clicks out of the side of his mouth and he and the horses ease up closer to the man. The old man lets them get within about ten feet of him before ordering them to stop.

"Who are ya an' where ya heading?"

"I'm Zeke Marshall, sir. We're from up around Durant on our way to Dallas to get my sister and her family."

The old man ponders the statement for a moment as if he were making a life-or-death decision, which he may well be. "Take them through that gate there," the old man says, pointing his gnarled finger at the gate across the yard.

"Thank you." Zeke leads the horses to the gate and swings it wide. The horses can smell the water now, and they're anxious for a drink. He glances over his shoulder to find the old man still on the porch, the shotgun tracking their progress. The horses are tugging and shaking their heads in an effort to get loose. He releases the reins and the three horses charge to the big stock tank and begin gulping the cool water. A hose runs from the pump and into the stock tank, which he removes. The cold water is like the sweetest nectar as he puts the hose to his mouth. He drinks his fill before refilling his nearly depleted canteen. Zeke turns back toward the old man, to find him holding his ground. But, a sign of progress—the shotgun is no longer pointed in their direction.

Once the horses have drunk their fill, Zeke leads them

away from the tank and closes the gate. He would like to spend a few minutes chatting with the old man but he doesn't seem to be in a real talkative mood. "Thank you for your hospitality," Zeke says.

"You're welcome. You best be careful out there, young 'un."

"I will. Thanks again." Zeke leads the horses back to the road and offers a wave as he remounts Murphy. The four of them continue their trek along the deserted roadway. He glances at the sun again, now high in the sky, and figures they have about four or five hours of daylight left before they need to start searching for somewhere to bed down for the night.

CHAPTER 53

University Hospital

The last of the living patients and their families are ushered through the outer doors of the hospital just as the generator heaves a last gasp. Twelve patients had died during the last six hours as their ventilators or other life-sustaining devices were switched off. The hospital had been the scene of enormous agony as the loved ones said good-bye to those who could no longer be sustained. More agony is in store for those patients who are dependent on dialysis, oxygen, insulin, and certain prescription drugs.

Dr. Iftikar Singh, running on only two hours' sleep over the last forty-eight, sags against a wall as the hospital's maintenance crew turns the locks on the outer doors. Most of the medical staff departed as the number of patients dwindled. A clinic had been established in one of the outer buildings and some of the medical staff is manning that, but only during daylight hours. The only medical supplies available, a few bottles of antibiotics and a handful of suture kits, were transferred from the hospital.

Doctor Singh turns from the entryway and, with the aid of a small drug rep flashlight left over from the days when drug companies could provide such items, shuffles down the hall to his office. After thirty years of practicing medicine, the last week proved to be the most difficult of his career. Trained as a cardiologist, Singh is small of stature, and the once-fitted white lab coat hangs loosely on his narrow frame.

He opens the outer door to his suite of offices and flips on the light switch, cursing in his native tongue when the darkness remains. The feeble yellow beam from the penlight arcs around the white walls of the outer office as he trudges through the door to his inner sanctum. An array of diplomas, certificates, and various other official-looking documents are pinned to the wall behind the desk. But he takes no notice as he collapses onto his leather chair. After a lifetime spent treating patients, he's now adrift. He leans back in his chair and clicks off the tiny flashlight.

He hasn't seen his family in almost three full days, and his mind now turns to them and the myriad of questions facing them. His exhaustion, coupled with the darkness, slows his spinning mind and his head falls to his chest as a thin line of drool escapes the corner of his mouth.

The sound of the crashing of glass startles him from sleep. He panics, disoriented. Another loud crash follows, and Dr. Singh scrambles for the now-remembered flashlight. The sound of heavy footfalls echoes down the hallway. He rakes his hand across the desk in search of the penlight and knocks it to the floor. As he scrambles around in search of the light, a high-pitched giggle sounds, sending a shiver of fear down his spine.

A crazy, drug-fueled giggle. A tweaker's giggle.

He abandons his search and scoots over to the door that separates his office from the receptionist's desk. The approaching footsteps are louder.

How long was I asleep? He peeks around the corner of

the door to find the outer hallway beyond the obscured glass a black hole. No hint of light from the exit door at the end of the hall. *Did I sleep that long? Has night fallen?*

Still on his hands and knees, he crawls closer to the outer door. Voices. Multiple voices. The heavy footsteps rattle the glass inset adorned with his name and title. Singh reaches up and carefully pushes the lock button.

A shout down the hall: "Check all the offices—there might be some samples."

Seconds later a heavy crash, then, "Hey, dude, you didn't have to kick it in," giggle, giggle. "It's fuckin' unlocked."

The office three doors down sounds as if it is being demolished. Singh eases away from the outer door as the surging adrenaline eliminates any residual sleepiness. He crawls back into the inner office and tucks himself under the desk. A bead of perspiration pops on his forehead as the domino effect of shattering doors grows ever closer. He pulls his cell phone from the coat pocket and lights the screen. No service. He uses the wash of light to search for anything he can use for a weapon. He peeks over the desk and grabs the letter opener resting in the pencil cup.

A boot slams into the outer door and he nearly knocks himself unconscious when his head strikes the underside of the desk. The first kick fails, but the second kick sends the outer door crashing into the Sheetrocked wall, uprooting the small doorstop screwed into the floor. A cone of light sweeps from side to side, then up and down.

"Ain't nothing in here," the giggler says.

A grunt is the only reply. The flashlight beam withdraws and Dr. Singh slowly releases the held breath. His back is on fire so he pushes his legs to relieve the pressure. *Where's security? I can't be the only person left in the hospital!*

The destruction continues: kick, bang, giggle—curses

when nothing is found, then on to the next office. He makes a snap decision to get out while they are occupied elsewhere. He scrambles from under the desk and tiptoes toward what's left of the outer door. He leans his head out for a peek. The hallway is empty. Singh takes a deep breath. Another crash, more giggles. He bolts down the hall to the left. Running full out, he glances back over his shoulder and gets clotheslined off his feet. He grunts when he hits the concrete floor, the breath snatched from his lungs.

A beam of light pierces his pupils. Singh raises a hand to shield his face.

"Where you goin' in such a hurry, pard?"

Only a faint outline of a very large man is visible behind the light.

"I asked you a question."

"Home," Singh says, still gasping for breath.

"Is that right? Home to the wifey?"

Singh nods.

"Ain't that cute? Goin' home to get a little pussy? That right?"

"Please, just let me go."

"Where you from? You talk funny."

"I live in Baltimore," Singh says as he scrambles up to his knees. He doesn't see the boot that crashes into his ribs.

"Don't you be gettin' smart with me. Now, where you from?"

Dr. Singh is back on the ground, his arms wrapped tightly around his midsection. "India."

"One of them fuckin' dot heads?" The man barks out a laugh. "You one of them fore-in doctors?"

Singh nods, grimacing with pain.

The man snarls. "Get your ass up and show me where the drugs are."

"There . . . are . . . no . . . more . . . drugs. We used . . . everything—"

"Bullshit!" the man roars, sending another boot into the side of Dr. Singh's thigh. "Get your ass up right damn now!"

Singh struggles back to his knees and uses the wall to push himself to his feet. The man leans in to Singh's face, the foul odor of the man's breath washing over him.

"Where's the fuckin' drugs?" A rancid spittle coats Dr. Singh's face.

Singh tries to take a deep breath. "I am sorry. We have no . . . remaining drugs. I would tell you where they are, but they do not exist. I will lead you to the pharmacy area where you . . . can look for yourself."

"Don't get fuckin' smart with me," the man says, raking the barrel of his gun across Singh's face. "Lead the way, Mr. Doctor."

Singh stumbles toward the continuing demolition. "The pharmacy is one hallway over."

"I'm followin' you, dot head. Just lead the way." They turn the corner, and one of the thugs turns to face them. His eyes are wild and a giggle escapes his mouth.

"Who's we got here?" Giggle.

Singh can tell with one glance at the man's black hole of a mouth he's dealing with some serious meth addicts.

"This here's the doctor goin' to lead us to the drugs."

"Yippeeee!" Giggle. Giggle.

"There are not any drugs," Dr. Singh mumbles.

The giggling man takes two steps and leans in. "This is a fuckin' hospital, right? Don't tell me there ain't no drugs."

Singh offers a shrug and is rewarded with a swift punch to his gut, followed by another maniacal giggle.

Giggler waves his arm forward. "After you, Doctor."

Still struggling to breathe, Singh weaves down the hall past two other men destroying one of the last remaining offices. He leads them to an intersection of halls. "There is the pharmacy," Singh says, pointing to a door containing a sliver of security glass with a keypad next to the knob.

Someone from behind launches a foot into Singh's midback, sending him careening off the adjacent wall.

"Open it!" his original capturer says.

"I cannot."

"Open the fuckin' door."

"There is no power to the keypad. I could not open the door even if I wished to."

Three of the four drugged-up thugs step forward and press him against the wall. The giggler waves a knife in Singh's face and says, "Open the door or I'm goin' to slide this here knife through your rib cage and cut your damn heart out."

Fear and frustration finally take their toll on Singh. "I cannot. And it does not matter because there are no drugs in there. The pharmacy is empty, you dipshit." He immediately wishes he could take those words back as a searing pain radiates from the center of his chest. He looks down to see the black handle of a knife protruding from his chest. *Punctured the heart*, is Dr. Singh's last thought before he slides down the wall and convulses one last time.

CHAPTER 54

The White House

The West Wing is a flurry of activity as staffers load up the necessary items to be transferred to Camp David. President Harris bypasses the dungeon, formerly known as the Oval Office, and walks into the Roosevelt Room across the hall. There are issues requiring his attention, but the chaos provides an opportunity for a quiet moment. He slumps onto the peach-colored sofa, willing his mind to relax. Above the fireplace Teddy Roosevelt watches, perched atop his horse, and the President wonders, briefly, how much easier this crisis would have been during Teddy's tenure—back before the world was tethered to an electrical umbilical cord.

The problems caused by the nationwide loss of power continue to mount, wearing not only on him but everyone within the government. And if those problems aren't bad enough, Iran is rattling its saber. Word spread up the chain of command that the Iranians are threatening to invade Iraq and Saudi Arabia, lusting after the oil-rich countries. In an ironic twist, Iran's spotty electrical grid was spared most of the devastating effects of the geomagnetic storm. The United States and other allied countries are handcuffed by the dire straits at home. Although troops are still deployed in Afghanistan and other bases throughout Europe and Japan, supporting them is nearly impossible.

"I'd like to nuke those bastards," the President mutters. He turns away from the Roosevelt portrait to see Admiral Hickerson stepping across the threshold.

"There you are," the admiral says. "I thought you would be in the Oval Office."

President Harris doesn't reply. He offers the standing-ever-erect chairman of the Joint Chiefs, a war hawk if one ever existed, a nasty look.

"What is it, Admiral?"

"Sir, we have confirmed reports that Iranian troops are massing at the Iraqi border. We've sent up some drones and they should be on station momentarily."

"What do you want me to do about it, Admiral?" The President stands and confronts the admiral. "What the hell can we do about it? Launch a nuclear strike? That's about the only alternative we have right now."

A somewhat surprised Admiral Hickerson takes a step back. "Well, no, sir. I just wanted to inform you of the situation."

"Well, consider me informed, Admiral. If you have a plan, let's hear it, but right now I'm focused on *this* country's recovery."

"Yes, sir." Admiral Hickerson snaps off a quick salute before pivoting on his heel and marching from the room.

President Harris paces toward the fireplace as Chief of Staff Scott Alexander enters the Roosevelt Room. "What did Admiral Hickerson say to piss you off?"

"What makes you think I'm pissed off?" the President snaps.

"I can just tell."

President Harris turns to his most trusted advisor. "The Iranians, that's what. And it's not Admiral Hickerson's fault. There's just something about him that chaps my ass sometimes."

"I think he has the exact same effect on a good number of people."

The President laughs. "I think you're right, Scott." President Harris turns serious. "What are we going do about Iran?"

"Nothing right now, sir. We're not in any position to offer our services to anyone. Let them do what they're going to do and then we'll deal with them when our country is back on solid footing."

"But, when is that going to be, Scott? If we let the Iranians proceed we may never get them out of Saudi Arabia, much less Iraq."

"Oh, we'll kick their ass all the way back to their shitty sandlot. You know it and I know it. We aren't using the damn oil now anyway. Let's focus on our own recovery."

"You're starting to sound like an isolationist, Scott."

"No, sir. Just a realist." Scott changes subjects. "We are leaving the White House as soon as it gets dark. Anything special you want me to—"

An ashen-faced Admiral Hickerson rushes into the room, a piece of paper fluttering in his hand.

"Mr. President, the Iranian troops are already in Iraq. Video from the drone feeds suggest they may be massing for an attack through Jordan and possibly into Israel."

"That just raised the stakes, Admiral. Gather whatever you can and we'll meet in the Situation Room."

"Yes, sir." Another brisk salute and another heel pivot, and the admiral disappears out of the room.

"We're fucked, Scott. Delay the Camp David move immediately."

CHAPTER 55

The Connor home

"I guess it's just us," Greg Connor says as he steps through the door of their apartment.

"What do you mean 'just us'? They're going to stay here with no heat and no water?" Lara Connor says.

"I guess so. I almost had the Scotts talked into leaving, but they felt traveling with their two young kids would be too difficult. They want to wait the crisis out, hoping the electricity will come back on."

"Did you tell them what Kaylee told us?"

"Yes, but I think it fell on deaf ears."

"What about the others?"

"About half wouldn't even open their doors. The rest weren't interested in leaving."

"Well, that's just fucking great." Lara spins away from her husband and returns to her perch at the window. "So, we're going out there alone?"

"We don't have any choice. As I said earlier, we'll be better off with only the two of us." Greg enters the kitchen and reaches for the last of the gallon of water. He's winded and thirsty from clumping up and down six flights of stairs. He pours only a half glass and chugs it in one gulp and returns the glass to the cupboard.

"I don't know, Greg," Lara says from across the room, fear leaking into her voice.

Greg crosses the space and sits on the window seat, facing his wife. She turns from the window and locks eyes with her husband. With a deep sigh she collapses into his arms, snuggling up against his chest.

"I know you're scared. I am, too. But we have to leave."

She nods, her tears wetting the front of his shirt. Greg holds her and gently rocks his body, trying to soothe not only his wife, but his own surging fear. Lara leans away and wipes at the tears, sniffling.

"Okay, Greg." She pushes out of her seat, still wiping her cheeks as she walks into the bedroom. Greg watches her retreat, a sudden longing stirring deep inside. He follows Lara into the bedroom and envelops her in a standing embrace.

"I love you, Lara," he says, leaning down to kiss her. Her body responds to the kiss—the fear, the uncertainty, the difficulties ahead, all fade away as they take turns removing each other's clothing and collapsing onto the unmade bed. Their lovemaking is tender at first, but morphs into a deeper intensity, more animal-like, as they release the built-up tension that has invaded their lives. Neither has showered or shaved in over a week, but none of that matters as they quicken their movements, each uttering breathless words as they reach climax. Spent, they slide under the covers for warmth, and await the coming darkness.

Greg stirs awake sometime later, the last of the sun's brightness fading, the clouds a pink and purple smudge on the on the orange horizon. He turns to stare at his still-sleeping wife, a mixture of emotions stirring his mind. After lightly kissing her forehead, he slips from beneath the covers and pads into the bathroom, relieving himself in the bucket. He puts on his clothing and grabs an extra pair of jeans and a shirt and folds them into the backpack Lara had already started packing.

Quietly, he exits the bedroom and walks to the kitchen, where he opens the junk drawer and begins pulling out items: two flashlights, extra batteries, scissors, a roll of duct tape, and a small knife. Meager supplies for a potentially dangerous overland trek. From another drawer he pulls out two of the largest chef's knives they own. One he puts on the counter with the other supplies, the other he slips under his belt.

"What else do we need?" he mutters as he stands back to take stock of the items he's already accumulated. The cell phones on the counter are useless, but he moves one to the pile along with a charger, in case the miraculous happens. Soft footsteps sound and he glances up to see his wife, still nude from their lovemaking.

"Thank you for that, Greg," she says softly as she steps across the room and wraps her arms around him.

Lara's a tall, slender woman, and Greg winces as he runs his hands along the ribs now pressing against her skin. Her once-lustrous hair cascades over her narrow shoulders in clumps.

He leans down and kisses her. "I think we both needed that." He sniffs the air. "You put on perfume?"

"Hey, if I can't take a shower, the least I can do is mask the odor." Her hot breath warms Greg's chest. She looks up into his face, a trace of fear in her eyes, but a much more contented, maybe resigned, look on her face.

He gives her bare ass a light tap. "You better put some clothes on before you catch a cold."

She releases him and turns back for the bedroom. Over her shoulder she says, "I think a cold would be the least of our problems."

He tries to lighten her suddenly serious mood. "Hey, have I told you lately how perfect your little ass is?"

She stops and turns, brushing away a stray strand of hair. "You used my two favorite words—little and perfect," she says with a smile before turning back for the bedroom.

Greg walks to the coat closet and retrieves their warmest coats and an additional shoulder bag for the items on the counter. It's not cold enough now to justify the heavy coats, but it will be soon. He also grabs a couple of lighter jackets they'll need now. "How the hell are we going to carry all of this stuff?" he mutters as he lays the items on the sofa.

Now dressed, Lara enters from the bedroom, the backpack slung over her shoulder. "I packed the toothbrushes and toothpaste."

"Good. Can't let our teeth go to seed. You pack what few meds we had left?"

She nods and places the backpack next to the coats. "I sure wish we had some type of weapon."

Greg points to the knife tucked in his belt.

"I meant something that shoots, Captain Hook . . . or maybe you're an older Johnny Depp. But your hair is a little shorter and a lot grayer."

"I don't have access to a Hollywood stylist at the moment." He pulls the knife from his belt and brandishes it like a sword. "As for weapon, this is it. Maybe we'll run across one out on the streets."

"That's what I'm afraid of, Greg. And most likely it'll be pointed in our direction."

"We'll just have to be careful, stay out of sight as best as we can," he says, walking to the counter and pushing the supplies off into the bag. "Ready?"

"No. But I guess that doesn't matter," Lara says, shrugging into her jacket.

They gather up their items and descend the six flights of stairs, pausing for a moment in the lobby. Lara puts her nose to the lobby window and swivels her head from left to right.

"See anything?" Greg says.

"Nothing, but it's too dark to see very far."

"Exactly," Greg says, pushing the lobby door open, Lara following closely behind.

Chapter 56

Texas

Off to the west a line of angry clouds is riding low on the horizon as Zeke repositions himself in the saddle, trying to spare at least one ass cheek. The wind had shifted to the north and now has a bite. He tugs his jacket from the saddlebag and tries to put it on while maintaining his grasp on the reins. He and the horses are weary from a full day of riding. Pulling on Murphy's reins, he brings the parade to a stop so he can slide on his jacket. He takes the map from his back pocket and spreads it across the saddle horn.

He glances at the approaching clouds before turning to the horizon in front of him. A small cluster of buildings is jammed up close to the road a good ways in the distance. The landscape is as flat as one of his tabletops, allowing him to see for miles. He figures the distance to the small community to be about five miles. He checks the map and finds that Celina, Texas, is the next town—about eight miles north of Frisco. Still too damn far from his sister's home. He clucks his tongue to get Murphy started as he begins scanning the sides of the road in search of shelter.

The wind increases and the first splatters of rain start

to fall. The next house up is a large home with an elaborate gated entrance, but they pass by. The home doesn't feel right to Zeke. But his options are dwindling with each step down the road. He spies a group of willows huddled up next to a dry creek and thinks about seeking shelter there, but the cold rain urges him forward.

As they turn a bend in the road Zeke spots an old farmhouse with a large barn set off to the side a little ways ahead. Most likely a family farm that had supported the same family for several generations, he thinks. Two large green tractors sit idle next to the home. The rain drips from the brim of his hat as he dismounts Murphy and leads the three horses up the gravel drive. The house is a one-level rancher dressed in white clapboards in need of a paint job. A low-slung roof hangs over a wide-plank wood-floor porch.

The heavy rain masks his approach, but he doesn't spot any flickering candles through the dusty windows. A faint odor of wood smoke hangs in the air. He ties Murphy's reins around a low limb of an old oak tree and unzips his jacket for easy access to the Glock. He slowly works his way toward the front door, hoping that if someone is watching from inside his movements won't be perceived as threatening. He steps onto the porch out of the rain and removes his hat, shaking the water off before knocking on the screen door.

No answer, so he steps over to the front window for a peek inside. No movement. But the darkened skies don't allow for much light to penetrate the interior. He reaches back over and gives the screen door a more determined knock. Nothing. Desperate for shelter, he walks back to the horses and unties Murphy's reins. He puts his foot in the stirrup and pauses before pulling himself back into the saddle. "Screw it," he mutters, removing his foot and grabbing up the reins again. He leads the horses toward a gate fronting a ramshackle barn in need of much more than paint. The tin roof is rusted through in spots and one corner sags several inches below the rest of the structure. But it promises some relief from the rain. As his hand reaches for the chain securing the gate someone shouts from behind him.

He whirls around to see a rifle barrel pointed in his direction. No shotgun this time, but a high-powered rifle held by an extraordinarily beautiful woman with wet hair plastered to her skull. A long, dark slicker shrouds her body and she has a determined grip on the rifle. Zeke reaches for the sky, Murphy's reins still in his hand.

"What the hell do you think you're doing?" the woman shouts over the rain.

"I was hoping to bed down in the barn for the night. I was going to ask permission but no one answered the door."

"So you were just going to make yourself at home?"

"Well . . ." He pauses, struggling for the right answer. "Yeah, I guess I was. At least, at home in the barn."

"Who are you?" she shouts. The rain is dripping from her beautiful face, but the rifle never wavers, tucked tight against her narrow shoulder.

"My name's Zeke Marshall. I'm on my way to bring my sister and her family back home to Oklahoma. They're in Dallas, and I expect they're in dire straits by now." His arms are weary from holding them skyward so he lowers them to his side and gives them a quick shake to get the blood back in his hands. She hasn't shot him yet, so he continues. "Ma'am, I mean you no harm. I was just looking for a dry place to bed down and feed the horses." He steps up to Murphy and puts his foot in the stirrup. "I'll move along," he says over his shoulder.

The rifle lowers and the woman takes several tentative

steps in his direction. She stops about twenty feet away. "Go ahead. But I want you gone by morning."

"Thank you, ma'am. I'll be out of here at first light."

He returns to the gate and leads the three horses through and closes it behind him. The woman stands in the downpour, watching his every step. He slides the large barn door open just wide enough to lead the horses inside. Musty-smelling, but dry. Stacked in the corner is a good supply of hay, while the other side of the barn is dedicated to an assortment of old machinery and other items collected from a lifetime of farming. He removes the saddle and blanket from Murphy's back and unloads the supplies from the two mares. After untying the horses from one another, he pours a generous pile of oats onto the hay-littered floor and all three hungrily eat.

Zeke digs through the saddlebag to find something for *him* to eat, his first meal of the day. He discovers two peanut butter sandwiches his mother had packed, as if she were packing his school lunch so long ago. He carries the sandwiches over to a corner of the barn and sits gently on one of the hay bales. His ass is sore from being in the saddle and the densely packed hay offers little comfort, but at least the bale is stationary. He wolfs down one of the sandwiches and follows it with a long drink from his canteen. The little remaining water sloshes near the bottom, and he realizes he needs to water the horses again and refill the canteen.

The second sandwich he eats at a more leisured pace as he looks over his surroundings. It's like stepping back in time, seeing some of the old tools arranged on the pegboard hanging above an old workbench. With sandwich in hand, he stretches the kinks from his back and strolls over. Most of the tools are much older than he is, and some he can't determine their use, but many he's familiar with. He saunters toward the barn door and slides it back far enough to peek at the house. The woman is gone, presumably back indoors out of the rain. He turns his head the other way and spots a stock tank full of water. An old-fashioned hand pump stands nearby. Not knowing if his stay in the barn allows him access to the other accommodations, he's going to have to take a chance and pray she doesn't shoot him from the sniper's perch he envisions in his mind.

Zeke walks back to the horses, clips a lead to each of their halters, and grabs his canteen. After zipping up his jacket, he eases the door open a little wider and glances back at the house before stepping out. The rain has lessened and the horses, thirsty from the coarseness of the oats, nearly send him tumbling in their haste to get to the water tank. After another glance over his shoulder to make sure a gun barrel isn't pointing in his direction, he walks to the old hand pump and pumps the handle. A clear stream of water jets from the end of the pump. Zeke refills his canteen and takes a long pull directly from the cold, clear stream, dislodging the peanut butter clinging to the roof of his mouth.

The horses finish drinking and take the opportunity to do their business, as three fresh piles of horseshit drop. He wonders whether his gun-toting host would like him to pick up after the horses. But how? It's not like you can bag it. Other droppings are scattered around, but he hasn't seen any other animals. He makes the decision to leave the horseshit where it landed and leads the horses back into the barn. It's now nearly dark, helped along by the dense cloud cover, but it's not too late. Zeke guesses the time is somewhere around six.

The aroma of a wood fire and what smells like cooking meat rides the wind through the cracks of the old barn, making his not-yet-full stomach rumble. He walks from one side of the barn to the other, looking through the gaps in search of the source. He finds a standard-sized door at the back of the barn and steps outside to see the gun-toting woman at the back of the house cooking over a smoky fire. She's probably a hundred yards away, so he snuggles up next to the barn and observes.

Her movements are precise as she stirs whatever's cooking. Zeke doesn't know if she's cooking for one or if there's a house full of people to feed. He didn't get the sense that a large number of people inhabited the house from his brief peek, but they could have been hiding. She's not yet looked in this direction and he's fairly certain that she couldn't see him even if she did. She pushes her wet hair out of her face as she returns inside.

Zeke takes advantage of her absence and sends a steamy stream of piss into the tall grass bunched up near the edge of the barn. The temperature, miserably hot in the afternoon, has dropped maybe twenty degrees, the dampness making it feel downright cool.

He returns inside to search through the dimness for a lantern or some other light source and comes up empty. Anything of use was probably transferred to the house days ago, he reasons. He steps back over to his stash and stretches out on the floor, using a bale of hay for a backstop. He digs into one of the saddlebags and retrieves one of the two paperbacks he had packed. This one is a Louis L'Amour western from his father's collection of books. He opens to the dog-eared page and has just enough light to make out the words. The reading helps to take his mind away from the miserable accommodations.

Eventually, the gloomy dusk gives way to full dark. He stows the book and starts thinking about tomorrow's journey. If all goes as planned he should be in the northern part of Dallas by sunset. That would put him at Ruth's house by midnight or early the next morning if he beds down one more night. Of course his planning is based on a steady pace with no interruptions—surely a fool's plan. His scheming is interrupted when a slash of light flares between the cracks of the old barn siding.

He tugs down the zipper of his jacket and checks to make sure his pistol is still riding in the holster. He makes no effort to stand and assumes his least threatening pose. The light slashes again and from the pattern he can tell that it is someone walking his way waving a flashlight. He turns toward the squeal of the barn door to see the woman enter. Her silhouette is all that is visible behind the bright beam. She slowly advances, holding something in her other hand. Zeke moves his hand to the butt of his semiautomatic. *Did she come to shoot him for his horses?*

She stops a good distance away. "Do you have something to eat?"

"I have a peanut butter sandwich if you would like it," he says.

"No, that's not what I meant. Would you like some food?"

"If it's what I smelled cooking earlier, yes."

She steps closer and he spots the murder weapon—a plate covered with foil. Beyond the light he sees that she has switched from lugging the big rifle to a pistol now riding high on her waist in an old leather holster.

She stretches to hand him the plate.

"I won't bite. I promise." He reaches out and takes the offered plate.

"It's venison. I got lucky and brought down a deer early this morning."

"It smells wonderful," he says, removing the foil wrapper. With the fork she provided he feeds the first bite into his mouth and savors the feel of the hot meat on his tongue.

He waves the fork in her direction. "Pull up a bale of hay and have a seat if you want."

She steps back and he thinks that maybe he's frightened her, but she takes a seat.

"I also brought a lantern so that you wouldn't injure yourself in the middle of the night." She pumps up the lantern, flicks a lighter, and gently pushes it in without melting the cloth mantles. Once the lantern flickers to life, she extinguishes the flashlight. Zeke takes a moment for his first up-close look at his host. Maybe midthirties, Zeke thinks. Her red hair is a tangle of springy curls and two dimples form on her cheeks when the smiles. She has a splash of freckles across her small, upturned nose. Her lips are full and her oval face is in proportion to her thin frame. Zeke wishes the light were bright enough to see the color of her eyes.

"What have you heard during your travels?"

"To tell you the truth, you're the first person that I've talked to other than an old man who let me water the horses earlier today. So I haven't heard much, but I know from my father's intermittent shortwave radio that most of North America is without power. Some type of geomagnetic storm."

"Did you hear anything about when it will be repaired?"

"No, I didn't. But I think it could be a long time before they have all the power back up and running. That's according to my dad, who's somewhat of a science nerd."

The first glimmer of a smile forms on her beautiful face.

"Have you heard anything?"

"No, I haven't ventured much past the main road." She changes the subject. "So you're on your way to retrieve your sister and her family in Dallas on horseback?"

Her use of the word *retrieve* implies that she isn't some poor dirt farmer. "Yeah, it's the only way I could think of. I drove to Sherman and left from there, hopefully leaving me enough gas to get back home. There are dead cars scattered all over the roadways. Dallas will be impassable."

She pauses for a moment and laces her fingers together. "Does your sister have children?"

"Yes, two. Emma, who's five, and Noah, who just turned seven."

"I think they'll be excited to see their uncle."

Zeke wants to press her with questions but holds back, hoping that she'll answer them without being asked.

"I have one girl, Aubrey, who's eleven."

He finishes everything on the plate and sets it aside. "I love that name." He wants desperately to ask where Aubrey is now or where Aubrey's father is, but he doesn't want to spook her.

"Thank you," she says as her eyes moisten. She leans her head forward and pinches the bridge of her nose. After a moment of silence she continues. "My father took her out to see my sister in California, just before whatever happened. I wanted them to spend some time together, bonding time, so I volunteered to stay and watch the farm while they went." A sob escapes, and her eyes are wet with tears. "Now, I don't know how they'll ever get back home."

"This can't last forever," he says softly, wishing he could wrap her in his arms.

"My husband and I are going through an ugly divorce, or were, before everything happened. I thought the trip would be good for her. I took her out of school for two weeks so that she could travel with my father . . ." Her sentence trails off with another sob.

"Where do you live?"

"Southlake, just west of Grapevine. What about your sister and her family?"

"They live in the University Park area."

She smiles as she wipes away the last of the tears. "I love that area with all the older, graceful homes."

"Yeah, it's a pretty area, but there's just too damn many people for me."

"Not a people person?" She pulls on a curl of red hair and wraps it around her index finger.

"Depends on the people." Zeke repositions his body to relieve the pressure on his backside. "You must be pretty handy with that rifle you were pointing at me earlier."

She blushes. "Just taking precautions. I grew up hunting with my father, so, yeah, I'm pretty good with it. Of course the deer around here are fed by most of the neighbors, so it wasn't like I had to go stalking after it. I felt bad shooting it, but the pantry is completely empty. I have most of the meat drying over the fire now. At least I'll have deer jerky for a while." The tears have stopped but an underlying sadness remains.

"I don't want you to take this the wrong way," Zeke says, "but are you here by yourself?"

She hesitates before answering, and he thinks he might have overstepped. "Yes."

"Do you need anything or need me to do anything before I leave in the morning? I can chop firewood or maybe hunt for more game before taking off."

"Thank you for offering." The relief is evident in her eyes. "But I think I'm okay for now."

She stands and picks up the plate. "Thanks for talking with me. I didn't know whether my voice still worked, it's been so long since I've talked to another human. Make yourself at home." She walks toward the door and flicks on the flashlight.

"Thank you. But you never told me your name."

She turns to face Zeke. "I didn't? It's Summer. Summer Peterson. I was born on June twenty-first, the first day of summer."

"Summer, I'm Zeke. Zeke Marshall. A pleasure to meet you."

"See you in the morning, Zeke." She steps through the doorway and pulls the door closed behind her. She's gone, but the memory of her lingers most of the night as he tosses and turns, searching for a comfortable position on the hard dirt floor.

Chapter 57

The home of Dr. Samuel Blake, Boulder, Colorado

Sam and Kaylee spent most of the day by the roaring fire in the living room of his modest home. The sleet turned to snow, and about eight inches is piled in the yard, deeper against the French doors to the back deck. A fairly large puddle of water rests on the tile beneath the clothes drying on the hearth. Sam has changed into a pair of old jeans and a sweater and offered clothing to Kaylee. She refused and remains naked and comfortable under the blanket.

"I have some canned soup that we can heat up on the fire," Sam says.

"That sounds yummy."

Sam stands and makes his way into the kitchen. Night is almost upon them, so he digs through the drawers in search of candles. The fire provides enough light for the living room, but the kitchen is in near darkness. He paws through one drawer after another and finally stumbles upon his cache of candles in the bottom drawer. He lights one and grabs a plate, letting the melting wax coat the bottom so that the candle will stand upright. He does this two more times until the kitchen is awash in a flickering yellow light.

He carries one of the candles into the pantry. "I have tomato, chicken noodle, and some French onion," he shouts over his shoulder.

"Chicken noodle," Kaylee says. Sam would prefer the tomato, but goes with the chicken noodle. He opens the cans with a hand-operated opener and dumps two cans of soup into a heavy pan. Without thinking, he opens the refrigerator door in search of heavy cream and is bowled over by the smell of rotten food. He quickly slams the door shut before the odor can permeate the whole downstairs area. "Damn," he mutters, trying to restrain his gagging.

"What's that smell?" Kaylee asks, wrinkling her nose. She's made her way to the kitchen, the blanket draped over her shoulders. A small gap in the front reveals some sort of Asian letters tattooed lengthwise along her side. Sam looks away, embarrassed. But just as quickly turns for another glance.

"The fridge." He hands her the pan of soup. "Put this close to the fire while I clean it out, please." When she reaches for the pan more of her front is revealed. One breast is exposed and a small silver hoop dangles from the nipple, winking in the candlelight.

She follows Sam's gaze but makes no attempt to pull the blanket together. She offers Sam a wink and carries the pan over to the fire.

Sam grabs a large black garbage bag and begins cleaning out the refrigerator while trying to hold his breath. He opens the freezer door and gags. Blood from the steak fillets he had purchased on his last trip to the grocery store has congealed with the Chunky Monkey ice cream. On the verge of vomiting, he slams the freezer door and carries the garbage bag outside. He decides the rest of the mess can wait till later.

"Sam?" Kaylee says when he reenters the kitchen.

"Yes?"

"I need to go to the bathroom. What should I do?"

"There should be enough water in the tank to flush at least once, so go ahead. But don't flush it yet. We'll use it as long as we can stand it. In the meantime, I'll fill up a bucket with snow to let it melt. We'll use that to refill the tank."

"Okay." She wanders down the hall with the blanket trailing behind her like a bridal train.

He watches her go, a sudden surge of desire flooding his brain and parts lower. He suppresses the urge and gives the soup a quick stir. Though he's still slightly nauseated from the disgusting mess in the fridge, the aroma of the soup rekindles his appetite. He and Kaylee had been eating ramen noodles and PowerBars for the last week while at the Space Weather Prediction Center. He returns to the kitchen and pulls out two bowls and spoons and gathers the last bit of crackers from the pantry. He experiences a slight twinge of worry at the lack of remaining food stores.

Kaylee returns from the bathroom, the blanket bunched over her shoulders. Sam gets an eyeful of her body stem to stern and tries to avert his gaze.

"Sam, don't be such a prude."

His cheeks flush.

She steps forward and grabs his hand. "We're both consenting adults put in an extreme situation. Now take off your clothes and join me under the blanket. A little pre-meal workout."

"But I'm old enough to be your father," Sam says.

"Who cares, Sam? You're only fifty-one, and I'm an

old soul. Jeez, it's not like you're on the way to the nursing home. I mean, really? It's just us, and I know you want me—hell you've been screwing me in your mind for the past week. And don't think I haven't been doing the same. Human nature, Sam." She sweeps the blanket from her shoulders, exposing her white, but toned, body. She pulls him toward the sofa.

Sam pulls off his clothes and he joins her under the blanket. Their lovemaking is primal, each with a need, and Sam enters her with little foreplay. Kaylee responds, pushing her tongue deeper into his mouth as Sam slowly rocks back and forth.

"Faster, Sam," Kaylee whispers urgently into his ear. Her legs are locked behind him, pulling him deeper into her body. Sam quickens his pace, pounding into her in a desperate need for release as Kaylee moans and grinds against him. She leans forward and takes his nipple in her mouth, clamping her teeth down before switching to the other. Sam shudders, and Kaylee bites harder on his nipple until he is spent.

"You didn't go," Sam says, pulling out and lying beside her.

"I will." Kaylee reaches her hand down and Sam peppers her with kisses until she climaxes.

"I'm sorry," Sam says.

"For what?"

"For not finishing," he says while stroking the back of his hand across her midsection. "It's been a while for me."

"It's all good now. That's all that matters." Kaylee releases a contented sigh and leans in and brushes her lips across his. "Besides, there's always next time."

Sam smiles.

"What does this say?" Sam asks, lightly brushing his fingers across the tattoo along her side.

"'Live like there is no tomorrow.' It's in Japanese. I guess that's appropriate now, don't you think?"

"I hope there's a tomorrow," Sam says. "I want more of this." He rubs his fingers across her mons pubis, eliciting another shudder from her body.

"I'm starving," Kaylee says. She sheds the blanket and takes the pan of soup from the coals, comfortable in her nakedness. Sam shrugs off the blanket and his shyness and follows her into the kitchen. Kaylee ladles equal portions into the bowls and they both sit nude at the breakfast bar. As they eat, the roaring fire adds to the warmth of their overheated bodies.

"What are we going to do, Sam?"

"Stay here as long as we can, I guess. Do you have any better ideas?"

"No, I don't. I just wish there was some way to reach my parents. I'm worried about them. I called to warn them, but I know they probably didn't have enough time to get out of the city."

"Are they pretty resourceful? I mean, can they make their way out of the city now?"

Kaylee ponders the question for a minute. "I don't know. Dad has always been handy around the house, but how that transfers to resourcefulness, I don't know. But I hope like hell it does."

CHAPTER 58

West 77th Street and Amsterdam Avenue
New York City

Greg and Lara Connor have covered eight blocks in their trek up Amsterdam Avenue. Both are surprised at the number of people out and about. Backpacks are slung over shoulders and a good number of children are lumbering along behind their parents. Greg steers Lara toward a small grove of trees next to a playground for a brief rest. It's dark as hell with only the moon for illumination.

A squeaking noise from the unused swings swaying in the cool breeze screeches in the night. The basketball court on the other side of the playground is empty. On any other usual night basketball players would be waiting for their opportunity to enter the game. Greg and Lara share a bottle of water while surveying the area. They're both dealing with lingering fear from their last outing. But the presence of other people offers some comfort.

They wait for a family of four to walk past. "Let's go," Greg whispers. "Stay as close to the building as you can."

They move away from the sparse cover of the nearly leafless trees and hug the side of the buildings as they continue north on Amsterdam. The once-crowded restaurants along the sidewalk are deserted, most of the glass façades shattered by looters. Pieces of tempered glass crunch under their feet as they continue along.

They pass 96th and then 108th without incident. Now in Morningside Heights, an upscale community bordering Columbia University, they relax a little and slow their progress. More people are out, many of them college students in search of entertainment. Knots of people are scattered around the campus and the faint sounds of someone strumming an acoustic guitar drift along the chilly breeze.

Still over fifty blocks from their destination, Greg and Lara slow their pace further to better blend in with the crowds. Laughter pierces the night, something the Connors haven't heard since the whole mess started. The resiliency of these young people offers a small boost to their spirits. Greg approaches one of the students.

"Has anyone tried crossing the bridge?" he says to a young man stumbling along the sidewalk. A fifth of whiskey dangles from his hand.

"You don't want to go to the bridge, man," he says in a slurred voice. The young man is now standing directly in front of Greg, and his breath is ninety proof.

"Why?"

"Because they're guarding it on the Jersey side. Apparently, they don't want to be overrun by a bunch of New Yorkers."

"So no way across?" a dejected Greg says.

"No, dude. Why do you want to go to Jersey anyway? This is the greatest city on earth." He laughs and takes another slug of whiskey. He holds the bottle out. "Hey, man, want a hit?"

"I'll pass. But thanks for the info."

"No prob, friend. Y'all stay safe." The young man continues his stumbling lurch down the sidewalk.

"What are we going to do, Greg?" Lara says, throwing her hands up in frustration.

"We're going to keep going."

"Why? You heard the guy. They won't let us cross."

Greg turns to face his wife and whispers, "Because we have no other choice, Lara. We have to keep going. Maybe we can find a way to get across."

"So, we're going to just saunter across the bridge and say 'pretty please' to a bunch of armed men?"

"Goddammit, I don't know, Lara." He takes a deep breath. "Do you have any better suggestions?"

She lowers her head in silence.

"Look, Lara"—he cradles her chin in his hand and lifts her head up until their eyes lock—"if we can't cross, we'll just keep going north into upstate New York. At least we'll be out of this crazy city. Maybe we can find a little cabin at one of the state parks."

"And what are we going to eat, Greg?"

He shrugs. "I don't have all the answers, Lara. Hell, I don't even know all the questions. But I can promise there'll be much less competition for food, water, and other necessities away from this city. Let's make it to the bridge tonight, and we'll see for ourselves. Maybe we can find some way across."

CHAPTER 59

Near West 120th Street and Amsterdam Avenue
New York City

Greg leads them away from Columbia University and they turn west on 120th Street, trying to avoid walking through the main part of Harlem at night. Harlem is not any less safe than the rest of Manhattan, at least during the day, but two people shuffling along the streets in the dark might be too tempting a target for any neighborhood. At Riverside, they discover streams of people heading north. They turn right and duck into an alcove fronting an ornate old church. They watch as the people pass—a mixture of young and old, some with children and some without. A good number of people are pedaling bicycles, swerving around those afoot.

Lara leans over and whispers in Greg's ear, "Are they all going to the George Washington Bridge?"

Her hot breath sends a shiver along his spine. "I guess so," Greg whispers back. "I don't see how those on the Jersey side can hold back a mass exodus."

"Guns and bullets, that's how. They only have to defend an area about a hundred feet across to choke off both levels of the bridge."

"But still, that's a lot of people. They can't shoot them all."

"No, they can't. But do you want a front-row spot in the charge across?"

"Hell no."

"Exactly. Should we fall in with them?"

Greg nods and leads Lara away from the church. Within a couple of blocks they pass the entrance to Grant's Tomb as they continue their trek northward. In typical New York City fashion, the conversation between marchers is limited, most trudging onward with their eyes forward, their faces displaying grim determination.

As the Connors break into the clear where Riverside transitions to an elevated roadway, they look down on another stream of people clogging the Henry Hudson Parkway. Moonlight shimmers on the Hudson and the distant Jersey shore is eerily dark. Greg leads them over to the concrete balustrade, where they pause to rest.

Lara points toward the river. "Look, Greg, there are people in the water. Maybe we could swim across the Hudson."

"When's the last time either of us went swimming? It's nearly a mile across and the currents are treacherous. A few of them might make it to the other side, but you and I don't stand a chance."

Lara sighs and sags against the barrier. In the distance the two towers of the suspension bridge are silhouetted against the darker sky. On any normal night, the old lady would be lit up like a Christmas tree—with lights running along the nearly mile-long suspension cables and the towers, which would have been illuminated like pieces of fine sculpture.

Lara and Greg push off the wall and weave through the stalled cars, continuing on. As they pass West 158th Street the quiet shatters. They come to a dead stop. Muzzle flashes flare on both ends of the bridge. And not just sporadic fire. A sustained barrage of gunfire erupts. Still some distance away, the sounds of the battle are delayed for a few seconds before echoing in the void. On the city side, whoever is fighting is about a third of the way across the nearly five-thousand-foot-long bridge. Those on the Jersey side are firing from a position much closer to their side of the river.

"Damn," Greg swears.

"This was a mistake."

"Maybe our side can push across. I can't tell if there's fighting on the lower deck of the bridge. You see anything?"

His question is answered before Lara can reply. Muzzle flashes light the enclosed lower portion of the bridge—yellow strobe lights in a sea of darkness. With horror, they watch as an automatic weapon of some sort shoots tracers across the span, lighting the night sky with tendrils of red. On the top level, a streak of intense white light flashes and something on their side of the bridge explodes, sending a hot orange fireball into the cold night air.

Greg slumps to the curb. Lara tosses the backpack to the ground and sits down next to him.

"I had no idea those type of weapons would be in play. That's military-grade stuff. Anybody within three hundred yards of that machine gun will be shredded."

"Maybe our side has some, too," Lara says.

"If they do, they aren't using them. I wonder how long the fight has gone on?"

"I bet within hours of the blackout. I just don't understand why they won't let us cross to their side."

"It's called survival, Lara. I understand their position. I don't agree with it, but I do understand it. Turn millions of people loose on the other side and every available resource, already in very short supply, will be decimated."

Lara sags against him and rests her head on his shoulder. "What are we going to do, Greg?"

"We need to find a place to bed down and, I guess, we wait to see if our side can get across the bridge."

"But for how long?"

"A week, maybe. If it doesn't happen by then, we'll need to continue upstate."

"And go where?"

Greg pauses before answering. "I don't know. But I do know that we won't survive if we stay in the city."

They rest for a few moments as the battle on the bridge rages. Numerous automatic weapons are now in use and more of the larger explosions light the night sky, like a Fourth of July fireworks show gone terribly wrong.

After sharing a bottle of water and a PowerBar, Greg stands and pulls Lara up. He glances at his wrist before realizing he had left his watch at home to make them less tempting targets. He glances at the sky, but having no knowledge of the stars or the constellations he doesn't have a clue what time it is. But it must be late because the steady stream of escapers has slowed to a trickle.

They trudge onward.

CHAPTER 60

The White House Situation Room

After several hours of briefings, arguments, and petty power plays, they are no closer to a consensus on what to do about Iran. In addition to the regular participants—secretary of defense, chairman of Joint Chiefs, NSA, CIA, and the rest of the alphabet soup—the Israeli ambassador has recently joined the group. Contact with his home country is spotty, other than through his embassy. They need to rely on him for responses from his government to their many questions.

Israel is in the same desperate situation as the United States. But the Israelis, ever prepared, are already working to restore power with several backup transformers they had stockpiled. Living in a country surrounded by hostile enemies on three sides tends to make them better prepared.

"Power should be restored to most of Jerusalem within the next two weeks," Ambassador Har-Even says.

"What about the air defenses?" Admiral Hickerson says.

"The missile batteries are a priority and they are being powered round the clock by generators. We have one fairly good intelligence source placed in the Iranian government, but we haven't been able to contact this person. But my government believes strongly that Iran is poised to attack." He pauses for a drink of water. "We are massing troops along the borders of Syria and Jordan, but the prime minister wants to unleash an immediate air attack on Iran."

President Harris rubs the back of his neck. "What assets are currently in the area, Admiral?"

"Carrier Strike Group One, the USS *Carl Vinson*, is just now sailing through the Strait of Gibraltar. They're still a couple of days from the coast of Israel. Carrier Strike Group Seven is in the Gulf of Aden, and Carrier Strike Group Nine is sailing just outside the Persian Gulf. But that's a fairly large area and they're spread thin, not to mention our trouble with resupply. I ordered the 7th Fleet out of Japan to make ready upon your command. Even if they sailed immediately it'll still take them the better part of a week to get there."

"I think whatever is going to happen will happen soon. Order them to sail at best possible speed, Admiral," President Harris orders.

Admiral Hickerson reaches for the phone on the table and gives the command to launch the 7th Fleet.

After the admiral hangs up the phone, President Harris says, "Admiral, how much firepower can we bring to bear?"

"Nearly two hundred aircraft and a good number of cruise missiles. Enough to pound the hell out of them, sir. But I don't know if it's enough to make them turn tail back home."

President Harris turns to the Israeli ambassador. "Is your country ready to go?"

"Yes, Mr. President. Our aircraft are fueled and are on standby. But the prime minister has some concerns about the possibility of an extended ground war. Are there any

American ground troops available that can be rushed to the battlefield?"

"No," Admiral Hickerson replies. "If all goes as planned there will be no need for boots on the ground."

President Harris drains his water glass. "Ambassador, we're relying on what troops you have for now. As Admiral Hickerson suggested, we can hope we bloody them enough to send them running home." The President takes a moment to survey the faces around the table before asking the million-dollar question. "Does Iran have nuclear capability? Yes or no?"

Silence.

"C'mon, people, I need an answer," President Harris says.

"I don't believe they do, Mr. President," the secretary of defense says.

"I hope like hell you're right, Martin. Ambassador Har-Even, what are your thoughts?"

"My country believes they are still several months away from developing a viable nuclear warhead, Mr. President. But they are sneaky bastards."

"Well said, Ambassador. So everyone agrees Iran does not have the ability to launch a nuke?" He turns to each person in the room. Each offers a nod of his or her head.

"What about our allies?" the President says.

Secretary of State Allison Moore leans forward in her chair. "Sir, the lack of communications is severely hampering our ability to contact them. But we are working to bring them all on board."

"That's your job, Allison. You need to build a consensus, and you need to do it yesterday. I don't want the damn Iranians to encroach another hundred miles while we dither around with politics." President Harris stands from the table. "Let's meet back here in one hour. Ambassador Har-Even, inform your country we will reach a decision within the next hour or so. Make damn sure they're ready. Janice, when you get a few moments I'd like to meet with you in the Oval Office."

"I'll be right up, Mr. President," the director of homeland security says.

President Harris exits the situation room, Scott Alexander following closely behind.

"You're going to start a shooting war with Iran now?" Alexander whispers a little too loudly.

President Harris stops on the stair landing and turns to face his old friend. "If we don't, Scott, we may never stop them. We need to teach those sons of bitches a lesson."

Alexander starts to interrupt, but the President raises his hand to stop him.

"I know we're in the shit here at home, Scott. Believe me, I know. But if we allow Iran to march into Israel without lifting a hand, we may never recover our place in the world. We may be down, but we're damn sure not out."

The President turns away and takes the stairs two at a time. He strides down the hallway and enters the Oval Office. "Scott, would you get Prime Minister Williams on the line?"

Scott moves over to the sofa and calls the White House switchboard. Normally, the President would pick up the phone and place the call directly through a scrambled satellite connection. But things are far from normal. All transcontinental calls are patched through a cable laid in the ocean over fifty years ago. "The prime minister is on line one, sir. But please remember the line is not secure."

President Harris picks up the handset. "Hello, Wells."

On the line is Wellington Williams, the British prime minster.

For the magnitude of the situation, the phone call is brief.

"So you're with us?" President Harris asks, pausing for the answer. "Great. I'll make sure our ambassador is at 10 Downing within the hour. We'll need to relay information through the embassy." Another pause, "Good luck to you, too."

The President hangs up and leans back in his chair.

"So they're on board?" Scott says.

"Yes. They're as tired of dealing with them as we are. Once we finalize the plan, we'll bring Ambassador Nelson up to speed and send him over to meet with the prime minister."

The intercom buzzes. "Mr. President, Mrs. Baker is here."

"Send her in."

Secretary of Homeland Security Janice Baker steps through the door of the Oval Office and stops dead in her tracks. "I like what you've done with the place. Did you hire a new decorator?"

President Harris waves at the thick steel panels covering the windows. "Nope. Same decorator but with a little help from the Secret Service. You don't like the modern industrial look?"

"If you're going for a modern dungeon design, you've nailed it. But it's a tad dark for my taste." All three laugh as Baker steps across the carpet and comes to a stop in front of the desk.

"Have a seat for a minute, Janice," the President says, waving to a chair flanking his desk. Alexander moseys over and takes the seat on the opposite side.

"Bring me up to speed on how martial law is working."

"Well, sir, it's somewhat better. Reports of looting are fewer, probably because everything worth looting is already gone. Not much you can do with a sixty-inch television. But we have another problem we're dealing with. The people in the larger cities are trying to migrate away from their homes. Unfortunately, they're meeting armed resistance from residents in the less-populated areas. New York City and Boston are hot spots, with intense fighting."

"Where's the National Guard?"

"They're trying to curtail the fighting, but field reports suggest some of the National Guard units have splintered. Especially in the New York–New Jersey area, where home turf is king. When it comes to food and family, priorities change. Might be something you need to address with Admiral Hickerson."

"Admiral Hickerson's plate is full at the moment. Every branch of the military is neck-deep in trying to develop a plan to kick the shit out of the Iranians. See if your agents can coordinate with local police and National Guard units to put a stop to the fighting."

"Yes, sir. We'll do our best, but we just don't have the manpower to police the whole country."

President Harris leans back in his chair. "What about local law enforcement in the smaller communities?"

"Most of them will side with their constituents. They live with those people, and most likely they're even more adamant about keeping the outsiders away. We can't count on them to be effective enforcers of the law."

"Maintain your focus on the urban areas, then. The other situation will need to take care of itself."

"Do you think we'll be successful in turning back the Iranians, sir?"

President Harris leans forward in his chair and plants his forearms on the desk. "We're going to kick their ass. That, you can take to the bank."

Chapter 61

Office of the Supreme Leader, Tehran, Iran

President Mahmoud Rafsanjani's usual white button-down shirt is damp with perspiration as he and Major General Ahmad Safani make their way down the hall to the supreme leader's office. It's sweltering in Iran, but the shirt dampness isn't due to the weather. The two men walk silently along the long hallway paved with antique Persian rugs. No chitchat or idle chatter fill the void, as each is consumed with his own thoughts. The medals pinned to the chest of General Safani's crisply pressed uniform tinkle in the silence. Some were earned, but most of the medals are merely window dressing. President Rafsanjani glances over at the noise and smirks.

They slow their pace and turn toward the guarded office. One of the clerics that flock around the offices of the supreme leader opens the door, allowing the two to enter without breaking stride. The office is sparsely furnished with a small desk fronted by two chairs for guests. The white, green, and red flag of the Islamic Republic of Iran hangs limply in the far corner. Staked to the wall over the grand ayatollah's shoulder is a photograph of his predecessor, the man who grabbed power after the Iranian Revolution in 1979.

The grim-faced ayatollah waves them toward the two chairs that are parked a foot lower than the one the supreme leader sits in. "Why are the troops stopping their advancement?"

"Imam, we are—"

The ayatollah silences President Rafsanjani with a curt wave. "I want to hear the general's excuse."

General Safani's throat jerks with a dry swallow. "We are trying to negotiate safe passage with the Syrians and the Jordanians, Dear Leader."

The supreme leader jumps up from his chair. "Negotiate? Why would we negotiate with those swine? I want the troops advancing this minute!"

"But, Dear Leader, that will leave our flanks exposed—"

"No excuses! I don't care!" A spray of spittle shoots across the desk, spotting the faces of his two guests. "They will not stop our progress. Is that understood?"

President Rafsanjani pulls his hands from beneath his legs and waves one in the air. "Dear Leader, I believe the general is making a good point. We may not be able to reach our objective if we spend our resources fighting the Syrians or Jordanians."

The ayatollah leans forward and slams the desk with fisted hands. "I do not care what the Syrians or Jordanians do. They are merely a nuisance. A nuisance we will crush. I'm ordering you to advance toward Israel."

General Safani studies a spot on the floor. "But what about the Americans?"

"The Americans are weak. The great Satan can no longer care for its own country. I don't want to hear another word about the Americans!" He's back to shouting now. "I want Israel taken by the end of the week or I will find someone else to run the army."

Both the president and the general offer nods of submission.

"Dismissed."

The two stand and turn without looking at the supreme leader. Like two frightened dogs, they slink out of the office.

CHAPTER 62

Near West 155th Street and Riverside Drive
New York City

Greg and Lara Connor are dead on their feet. It's deep into the night and what was a trickle of walkers is now down to only a pair here and there.

"Start looking for a place to bed down," Greg says. His voice is raspy and his mouth is full of cotton.

As they round the curve where Riverside Drive splits, a little less than a mile from the George Washington Bridge, they spot a number of tents staked out in the trees. Numerous campfires dot the landscape, most reduced now to glowing embers. A little farther along, they find campsites set up on both sides of the road, with the tents growing denser with every passing block. The scene is reminiscent of an old Civil War photo, but with newfangled equipment. The fighting on the bridge is now reduced to brief bouts of gunfire.

"Where the hell did a bunch of New Yorkers get tents?" Greg says in a whisper.

"I don't know. But more importantly, I don't care. I'm cold and I'm exhausted, Greg."

"Do you want to find some vacant ground where we can lie down?"

Lara's teeth are chattering when she answers. "What about somewhere inside?"

"I'm not opposed to finding an inside space. But where?"

Lara stares through the darkness. "There's a taller building just up the street. Let's try there."

Another two blocks brings them to the front of a multistory building. It's too dark to read the full name on the sign but Greg can see the words MEDICAL BUILDING along the bottom. They trudge along the front façade searching for a door. They find one near the midpoint of the building, but it's protected by a metal roll-down door. They walk to the edge of the building and turn into a small alcove, where they find a blue metal door already pried open.

"What do you think?" Greg whispers.

Lara brushes past and he follows behind. The darkness is complete. Greg fumbles through his pocket for the flashlight and covers the lens with his hand before flicking it on. They're in some type of mechanical room with most of the space taken up by large machinery. They walk forward with Greg sporadically switching the flashlight on and off. On the far side of the room they discover a stairwell and begin to climb, their weary footsteps echoing in the darkness.

On the third level they ease open the door. Greg leans in and sweeps the flashlight beam back and forth. He sees a cluster of closed doors arranged in a staggered pattern down a long corridor.

Greg leans back and whispers to his wife, "Looks like a lot of small offices. What d'ya think?"

She nudges him forward. "I think I'm exhausted," she

whispers. "Just find us someplace where we can lie down and stretch out."

With most of the flashlight beam obscured by his hand, Greg and Lara tiptoe down the hallway. The first room they open is empty but Lara wants to be farther away from the stairwell. Near the middle of the hall they turn the knob on the door to their right and peek in. Two large lumps are lying in the floor, with two smaller lumps lying next to them. Lara quietly closes the door while Greg opens the one on the left. Empty. They shuffle into the room and ease the heavy backpacks from their shoulders.

"I need to use the bathroom," Lara whispers.

"Why didn't you go outside?"

"Because I didn't need to go then."

Pointing his flashlight at the floor, he clicks it on. The carpeted office is small, with a desk and an uncomfortable-looking chair. Nothing they can use for a makeshift toilet.

"I guess you're going to have to go in the corner."

"Greg, I can't defecate in someone's office."

"Whoever occupied the office is no longer here. They could care less whether you take a shit in the corner."

Lara shoots him an angry glare. "There has to be a bathroom down the hall somewhere."

"A bathroom which no longer functions," Greg snaps.

"I don't care. There'll still be a toilet." Lara digs through her backpack and pulls out a roll of toilet paper.

Greg hands over the flashlight. "Knock yourself out."

Lara plants her fisted hands on her hips. "You have to come with me."

Greg sighs, then waves his arm forward. "After you, dear."

They creep down the lightless hallway toward the other end of the corridor. Greg doesn't need to switch on his light to know where the restrooms are located. They clap their hands over their mouths to keep from gagging at the stench leaking from two opposing doors near the elevator vestibule.

"You want to go in there?" Greg says in an incredulous whisper.

Lara shakes her head. "Let's just run outside real quick. Maybe there's another set of stairs we can use on this end."

They walk to the end of the hallway and find, as Lara predicted, another set of stairs.

"What about our backpacks?"

"They'll be fine. It won't take but just a minute."

Greg, feeling a sudden increase of bladder pressure, agrees. He eases the door to the stairs open and the putrid stench of human waste overwhelms them.

"I'm not walking through three stories of shit just to take a piss outside. This looks like a good spot to me."

Lara sighs and moves hesitantly toward a corner of the stairwell. Greg places the flashlight between door and jamb and unzips his jeans. Once finished, Greg retrieves the flashlight and they creep back toward their temporary quarters. As they near the door to the small office, Lara grabs his arm and yanks.

She leans forward to whisper in his ear, "There's someone in there."

Greg turns to his wife. "You sure that's where we left our stuff?"

Lara nods emphatically. "I remember. I swear I saw a flash of light just now." Both turn to stare at the window next to the door. "What are we going to do, Greg?"

He stares at the door, struggling to formulate a plan. He lowers his head and whispers in Lara's ear, "I'm going to get our stuff, that's what I'm going to do. You stay here." He creeps forward but Lara yanks him back.

"Where's our knife?" Her breath is hot, urgent.

Greg frowns and points toward the abandoned office.

"Let's just leave, Greg," she says in a pleading whisper. "Let them have our stuff."

"No. What's left of our food and water is in there, not to mention the money."

"We'll find more food and water. And the money's not worth having."

"Where are you going to find more food?"

Lara shrugs.

Greg snicks off the flashlight and they stand in the darkness. After a brief moment, he says, "Stay here."

A light moan escapes Lara's lips.

Greg eases up to the doorway, weighing his options. He opts for surprise. He clicks on the flashlight and hurls the door open.

"What the hell do—"

A gunshot obliterates the silence.

Lara flinches, then screams. She races forward screaming Greg's name. She rounds the doorway at a run and catches a brief glance of her husband on the floor before the gun barks again. A hot poker hits her in the chest. She spins and falls, searching the hazy darkness for her husband.

A moment later, a beam of light drills her in the eyes as someone kneels down beside her.

Greg?

"I'm really sorry but my kids are near starvin'."

Lara tries to talk but her mouth won't work. She rasps out, "We share," before a final searing pain turns her world dark.

Chapter 63

The White House Situation Room

President Harris walks into the Situation Room before his hour deadline has expired. Though it's very late in the evening, everyone is present with the exception of Admiral Hickerson.

"Where's the boss?" The President directs his question to a group of military aides hugging the far walls.

One snaps to attention. "He should be here momentarily, sir."

"At ease, soldier. We've got more important things to worry about than protocol." The man slumps against the wall as the President pulls out the chair at the head of the table and sits. Scott Alexander slips in and takes a seat next to his boss.

The President takes a moment to survey the weary faces around the table. What he sees is similar to how he himself feels—weary, strained, and wishing for somewhere other than here. But, he reflects, they are some of the best and brightest minds in the world and he's glad they are on his team.

"How's everyone holding up?" the President asks.

A few "goods" and "just fines"—the standard answers.

"I know that's not true," President Harris says. "I want to thank you for your service. We all have family that we're concerned about, but the only option is to work hard at improving the conditions. You don't hear it enough, but again, thank you, and please feel free to take whatever you need for your families. I have asked the kitchen staff to provide you a generous food basket to take home. I need everyone at their best, and I know some comfort provided to your loved ones will ease the burden."

The small speech lifts the mood of the room, and several people are nodding in support of the President. But the good mood evaporates when Admiral Hickerson arrives, bringing with him a reminder of why they're there.

"I'm sorry, Mr. President, I was on a call with CINCPAC trying to iron out some issues."

"Understandable, Admiral. Would you bring us up to date on the planning?"

"Would SECDEF like to begin?" the admiral says, looking across the table at Secretary of Defense Martin Wilson.

"Why don't you explain what's happening in theater, Admiral, then we'll expand the conversation," President Harris says.

"Well, sir, we have good news and bad. We will be able to strike Iranian troops quickly and with devastating firepower. But the main issue is the length of engagement. If it persists longer than forty-eight hours, then armament resupply is our main concern. My staff is putting together a list of supplies at bases in Europe and Japan, but it will take us some time to move those weapons to the battlefield. Support ships have a good supply of armaments, but they'll be depleted quickly during the opening hours of battle. We can only hope that the Israelis are sitting on a large stockpile that we can tap into."

President Harris turns to Ambassador Har-Even. "You guys have a large stockpile of weapons?"

"We will be able to offer some weapons, sir, but I'm not sure how well they'll integrate with the sophisticated weaponry your ships use. We do have a good number of Tomahawk cruise missiles, and some of these could be transferred to American naval vessels," Ambassador Har-Even says. "I've been instructed by the prime minister to offer you use of anything we have."

"Good, thank you, Ambassador. I'll leave the specifics to your country on how best to resupply our ships."

President Harris turns back to Admiral Hickerson. "Can we move some supplies from here?"

"We can, sir, and we will. I ordered a ramp-up in munitions supply, and they're being loaded as we speak and should be en route within the hour."

"Is that the most critical problem we're facing, Admiral?"

"That's one of them, sir. There are two other critical problems we're dealing with. The first is the lack of real-time satellite imagery of the battlefield. We'll need to rely on drones to be our eyes."

President Harris leans forward in his chair. "The Iranians are in the same boat, Admiral. With the sophistication of our weapon systems we should have an enormous advantage over them. What's the other issue?"

"That sophistication of our weapon systems, sir. Most everything in our arsenal relies on GPS for targeting. AWACS will be of some help on the battlefield, but there's a high probability for considerable collateral damage. Without those GPS satellites it'll be like shooting in the dark, sir."

"Do the best you can, Admiral. That's all we can expect under the circumstances." The President leans back in his chair and sweeps his gaze around the table. "Now, another matter we need to discuss: what can we expect from the Chinese?"

All eyes turn to Secretary of State Allison Moore. In her midfifties, Allison appears much younger, due mainly to her maniacal morning workouts at the White House gym. Never married, she has devoted her life to public service, serving in numerous positions within the State Department. Her not being married is a source of speculation among those within the Beltway, but those closest to her know that Allison is twelve years into a committed relationship with her partner, Jill, a professor of music at Georgetown.

"I need to defer to CIA Director Green for some of this, but from what my staff put together, China is in a position similar to ours—basically the entire country is without power. I spoke with Ambassador Chen during our brief break to get the latest.

"The Chinese are not happy with Iran's aggressiveness, especially at such a difficult time for most of the world. They are more concerned, at present, with their own domestic situation. Frankly, sir, I believe they will actually be pleased if we bloody Iran's nose. With the political mess in both Afghanistan and Pakistan, they're concerned Iran could spread its forces eastward toward their border."

President Harris kneads the back of his neck. "So are they willing to be a part of our response?"

"No, I don't believe they will, sir. They will be content with turning a blind eye to the whole situation."

"What about the Syrians and the Jordanians, Allison?"

"They're none too happy about having Iranian troops at their borders. But Syria is in such political upheaval it will be impossible to build any sort of consensus among the arguing factions. The whole country is a simmering cesspool. Jordan, on the other hand, may offer some resistance but their effectiveness is severely hampered by their own devastating lack of electrical power."

President Harris shrugs. "We're in the same boat, yet everyone looks to us to fix the world's problems,"

"Nature of the beast, sir. We at least have generators and a flotilla of naval ships. The Jordanians have nothing. They may never fully recover."

"Any chance diplomacy will force Iran to withdraw its troops?"

"No, sir, I don't believe there is. We tried to contact the Iranian ambassador but apparently he was recalled sometime yesterday. He disappeared in the night. The Iranians don't want to deal, sir—they want to wipe Israel from the world map."

The President turns to the CIA director. "Isaac, do you concur with Allison's assessment?"

"I do, sir. We've played the diplomacy card numerous times only to have the Iranians change the rules midgame."

President Harris nods, then turns his focus to Martin Wilson, secretary of defense. "What do you think, Martin?"

"Mr. President, we are ready to proceed with whichever direction you wish to go."

"That's a political nonanswer, Martin," the President says with a flash of anger. "Let me put it more succinctly—do you think we should launch an attack on the Iranian troops now in northern Iraq?"

The SECDEF expels a noisy exhale. "I think we have to, sir. Israel is one of our staunchest allies. If we let Iran walk into Jerusalem with no response from the United States, the rest of our allies will abandon ship before it even begins taking on water."

President Harris turns back to Admiral Hickerson. "How long before the action could commence?"

The admiral leans back in his chair and crosses his arms. "I would like to delay another twenty-four hours to allow Strike Group One to get on station. That will put three carriers in theater."

The President turns to the rest of his advisors. "Do we have twenty-four hours?"

"Maybe," the CIA director answers. "According to the latest intel, the Iranians are slowing their advancement. I assume they are trying to broker a deal with the Syrians and the Jordanians for safe passage. But I wouldn't push it any further past the twenty-four-hour time frame."

President Harris takes a deep breath. "Admiral, put everything into place. We are a go the instant Strike Group One is within striking distance."

Chapter 64

Texas

The sound of gunfire bolts Zeke upright from a dead sleep. He reaches for the Glock and panics when his hand finds air. His brain fights for clarity. Then he remembers taking the gun and the holster off sometime during the night after the grip had dug into his side one too many times. He scrambles around on all fours as the faint beginnings of daylight leak through the cracks of the old barn planking. His hand brushes across cold steel. He grabs the gun, reattaches the holster to his belt, and jumps to his feet. He grabs for his boots and, hopping one-legged in a tight circle, pulls on one, then the other.

There are no more gunshots, but he doesn't know if that's a good thing or a bad thing. *Maybe whoever is shooting hit their target with the first shot.* A sense of dread descends on him as he stalks toward the sliding door. He eases the door open a few inches and sneaks a peek outside. Nothing seems to be amiss—no armed mob assembled on the small patch of grass fronting the house. He slides the door open a little farther and pops his head out.

He spots a figure walking in the foggy haziness of first

light. He can't tell from this distance if the walker is Summer or someone sinister. The person is toting a gun, evident by the dark shape of the barrel silhouetted against the gray horizon. He or she is also carrying something else in the other hand. Shivering from the early-morning chill, he slips out of the barn and creeps closer, one hand resting on the butt of his gun. Hunched over to lessen his target profile, he gets within twenty yards when Summer turns toward him, a wild turkey dangling from her grasp.

"You scared the hell out of me," Zeke says.

She waves him forward. "Come warm up by the fire. Sorry about waking you, but a whole flock of wild turkeys were grazing at the edge of the field. Couldn't pass up the opportunity."

He reaches his hands toward the fire and rubs them together as he studies her. Her curly mop is gathered up in a ponytail this morning, allowing him an opportunity to study her in profile. Her nose and chin are aligned in a near straight line and her deep-set eyes have a slight upturn. No jewelry dangles from her ears, but Zeke spots a couple of holes in her lower lobe. She probably hasn't showered in over a week, or washed her hair, but she is no less stunning. Dressed in jeans with a rip on one knee and an oversized sweatshirt draped off one shoulder, she moves the coffeepot closer to the edge of the fire. "Coffee will be ready in a jiff."

The sun breaks on the horizon, lighting the surroundings in an amber glow.

"You've got quite the setup here," Zeke says. A fire pit resides not far from the back door and an old picnic table is set off to the side. "You always up this early?"

"I can't sleep late. Must be because I go to bed so early. Guess we're turning into the pioneers—sleeping in rhythm with the sun."

Zeke points at the turkey. "Want me to clean that?"

"I gutted it already. It'll keep until I can pluck the feathers. How did you sleep?"

"I slept, I think," he says with a smile. "Ground was a little hard and my body is sore from being in the saddle all day. I'm not sure my butt is up for another round."

She chuckles. "You could stay here and rest up for a day."

"You made yourself pretty clear yesterday you wanted me gone by first light."

"Yeah, but that was before we talked last night. How did I know you weren't a serial killer?"

"So you're satisfied now. How do you know I'm not an extraordinarily charming serial killer?"

She smiles and the laugh lines enhance her beauty. "So, not just charming but extraordinarily charming?"

Zeke shrugs and offers his own smile.

She pours two mugs of coffee and hands one to Zeke. "I like to think of myself as a good judge of character. Seriously, you're welcome to stay as long as you want."

Zeke's not sure how to take that, maybe because his mind is churning through all sorts of possibilities. This is the first time he's truly looked at another woman since the death of his wife. "I should probably scoot on down to Dallas and grab my sister and her family." His response elicits the smallest of frowns, confusing him further. "I would like to stop by on the way back through, if that's okay."

"Absolutely. I'll bag a couple more turkeys in the next day or so to feed your family."

"You don't need to do that."

"I know I don't. But I want to." She drifts away from the subject. "I'd offer sugar and cream, but I have neither."

"Black is perfect. I'm going to put some more feed out for the horses," he says, turning for the barn.

"Wait. I'll walk with you."

They walk to the barn, not touching, but close enough to do so.

"Give them some of the hay in the barn, too," she says, glancing up at Zeke.

His heart skips a beat. "Thanks, I will. I wasn't sure if the hay was included in the accommodations."

Summer looks away and blushes before turning to punch his arm. "I couldn't invite a killer into the house."

"I'm glad you didn't. No telling who might be out and about. Better to be safe than sorry." He pushes the barn door to the stops and leaves it open, allowing enough light to see what he's doing.

He watches as Summer steps over to Ruby and runs her hands across her flank, whispering softly. It's obvious she's been around horses before. He grabs the sack of oats and pours a couple of neat piles for the horses, then scatters some fresh hay around for them to munch on. He turns to Summer. "How long are you planning to stay here?"

"I don't know. I don't have any place to go back to. We put our home up for sale when I filed for divorce. Aubrey and I were still living in the house, but I have no desire to go back. I feel like I need to stay here just in case Aubrey and my father make their way home."

Zeke has no desire to burst her bubble and offers no response. He grabs up his canteen and takes a long swallow, trying to frame the next question in the best possible light. He works on screwing the lid back on. "Any chance of a reconciliation between you and your husband?"

"Uh . . . no. We've been separated for over a year and a half. I held out some hope we might get back together, for Aubrey's sake if nothing else. But the longer I was estranged from him, the more I came to dislike the man. What about you? Married?"

"No . . . yes . . . I . . . was—" Zeke stops, not sure he

wants to break the scab of an old wound. His hand drifts toward the locket around his neck but he pulls it back. "I was married. My wife died during her first pregnancy."

She covers her mouth with her hands. "Oh my God. I'm so sorry."

"It's been over three years. Long enough that I should put the whole issue behind me."

Summer takes a step closer toward him but pulls up short. "I'm sorry for your loss."

"Thank you." He rakes his hand across his face. He can tell she's on the verge of asking more. "All right if I leave the door open so the horses can get to the water?"

"Of course. Let the horses roam for a while. Let's go back to the house and I'll fix some of the leftover venison."

They exit the barn and the chatter on the return trip is somewhat subdued. Zeke reaches for her arm and pulls her to a stop. "What happened was three years ago. You'd think I'd be over it by now."

He releases her arm, but instead of turning away Summer threads her arm through his. "I can't imagine how horrible that was for you. That's not something you can put behind you very easily. Time heals all wounds, they say, but they never specify how much time. You're a good man, Zeke Marshall."

Back at the fire, Summer pours more coffee for them before disappearing into the house. Zeke carries his coffee over to the picnic table and takes a seat. But he doesn't sit long. The hard wood sends a direct signal from his butt to his brain. Instead he makes his way over to the fire, contemplating how he's going to sit in the saddle for another long day.

She returns from inside with a heavy cast-iron skillet. He reaches out to relieve her of the burden and their hands touch, sending a pleasant jolt tingling up his arm.

The sensation felt exactly like a static shock, that little pop, and from her expression he can see she felt something, too. Unnerved, he sets the heavy pan on a nice bed of glowing coals while she returns to the house.

He takes advantage of her leaving and sneaks around the side of the house to relieve himself. As he returns around the corner she catches him.

"Bathroom?"

"How'd you guess? I kind of miss the sound of a flushing toilet."

"Try being a girl. You've got it easy."

She puts some meat into the pan and the sizzle and aroma make his stomach rumble. "I hope the meat's not spoiled. I kept it down in the cellar overnight."

He bends down to take a quick sniff. "I think we're safe, but we should cook it little longer just in case."

She nods and pours herself more coffee. They make small talk until the venison is cooked through. Summer loads up two plates and hands one to Zeke. Between bites, he looks toward the barn and sees the horses wander out and make their way to the water tank. After drinking their fill they leisurely graze on the few patches of still-green grass. *I should be miles down the road by now.* But the fire and the food are good reasons for the delay. Or so he tells himself.

The coffeepot soon runs dry, leaving Zeke without a ready excuse to hang around any longer. He takes his and Summer's empty plates and washes them both in a tub of water sitting by the picnic table. Using a rag, he wipes the heavy cast-iron pan clean, and with nothing left to do, reluctantly turns for the barn.

"I'm coming," Summer says, falling in step beside him. Inside the barn he saddles Murphy and puts the wooden carriers on both mares and secures their leads to one another. He leads the horses out into the bright sunlight, but pauses before putting his foot in the stirrup.

He turns to Summer. "Thank you for everything."

"You're very welcome."

They've arrived at an awkward moment. Zeke desperately wants to wrap his arms around her, but instead he pulls himself up and screams out a groan when his ass hits the saddle.

Summer bursts out laughing. "A couple of days until you're back?" she says, shielding her eyes from the sunlight.

"If you don't mind us stopping."

"I'll be angry if you don't."

He gives Murphy a little tap with his heels and the gelding leads them away from the barn and onto the gravel drive. After a wave, he and the horses take to the deserted ribbon of asphalt while his brain cartwheels through a confusing number of emotions.

Three hours of riding brings them to the outskirts of Frisco. From his position atop Murphy he can see where the Dallas North Tollway begins off to the west. But it no longer resembles a major highway—the road more closely resembles an overcrowded mall parking lot two days before Christmas. The trailer doors on the big rigs are flung open and the foul odor of decay drifts on the breeze. Zeke doesn't know if the stench is related to spoiled food or something worse.

The road he's traveling, 289 south, cuts through the heart of Frisco, Texas. Their progress slows as he walks the horses around more abandoned vehicles. Neighborhoods dot the landscape and Zeke loosens the Glock, but leaves it holstered. Up ahead he spots a group of people walking along the side of the road. He reaches down and slides the Kimber rifle out a few inches for easier access.

Zeke steers Murphy toward the opposite yellow line as they near the group. He relaxes slightly when he discovers the group to be five teenage girls, none older than about sixteen. He waves in passing and one or two of the girls shout for a ride while the others giggle.

He clears downtown Frisco with no further encounters. The weather is not blistering hot, but it is hot enough to be uncomfortable. Murphy is lathered around the edges of the saddle blanket and Zeke's shirt clings to his back. He pulls the map from his pocket and checks their progress, trying to determine how much farther to the outskirts of Dallas proper. Best as he can tell they're about twenty-five miles north of his sister's house. He glances up at the sun and estimates the time—past midmorning—closer to noon than ten. If he pushes the horses a little harder they might reach Ruth's house sometime well after nightfall. That would spare them from having to find another place to bed down for the night. He turns in the saddle to check on Ruby and Tilly and they appear to be holding up well. Murphy's the one he's worried about. He decides to play it by ear and not overburden the horses.

As they slog along, Zeke begins searching for a water source somewhere up ahead. A few more people are out and about, but well off the main road. No threats are pinging his radar. The road weaves back through a commercial area and he passes an Olive Garden, a Red Lobster, and an Outback Steakhouse. What once were windows or doors are now plastered with heavy plywood tagged with graffiti. It's bizarre seeing all the businesses that only a short time ago would have been getting ready to serve an overindulgent meal. Now they're abandoned, left to crumble in place.

The next block offers two shuttered banks and, for a brief moment, he thinks about money. Or, in his case, the lack thereof. Most everything will be based on barter for the near future. His thoughts turn to the fabulously wealthy people who inhabit portions of Dallas, including those who have purchased one of his hand-built tables. No food to buy, no trips to the mall, nothing on which to spend their vast sums of money. The playing field is leveled—socioeconomic barriers thrust aside.

The next block is more of the same, with all types of shuttered retail establishments, including a Home Depot and a Best Buy. Sunlight glints off something the next block down, near the entrance to another restaurant. The horses surge that way and he tugs gently on the reins to slow Murphy. The glint turns out to be a small pond with a fountain at its center. The mermaid's mouth is dry and crusty but plenty of water remains. He slides off Murphy as the three horses eagerly begin to drink. A few colorful fish are swimming around the bottom, but the horses pay them no mind. Zeke wonders how long it will be before those fish end up on a spike of wood over a fire.

Being out of the saddle brings brief relief to his sore behind. He arches his back and wiggles his hips to loosen up, then takes off his cowboy hat and mops his brow. As the horses drink, he seeks refuge under an overgrown holly bush for a little relief from the interminable sun. Once the horses have drunk their fill, Zeke takes a sip of water from his canteen. He's running low on water but there's no way in hell he's drinking from the pond. With reluctance, he remounts Murphy and steers him back on the road as his eyes continually scan for threats.

Chapter 65

The White House Situation Room

President Harris makes his way back to the Sit Room around four in the afternoon, slightly ahead of the twenty-four-hour delay that Admiral Hickerson had requested. His blue button-down shirt is open at the collar and the shirtsleeves are folded up nearly to his elbows. Under direct orders from his wife, they had enjoyed a long, private lunch and an escape upstairs to the residence for an afternoon tryst. As he waits for others to arrive, he exhales a contented sigh, thinking how lucky he is to have Katherine Harris in his life. She is far more than a wife. She is an equal partner in the marriage, a sounding board full of creative ideas, a wonderful mother to their daughter, and an enduring opti—

The President is stirred from his reverie when a steady stream of haggard military personnel trudges into the room. He reaches forward to pour himself a cup of coffee and calls the meeting to order. All the regulars are in attendance, a veritable who's who of the nation's top brass, with their aides lined up along the outer wall. Most of the military aides are dressed in shirtsleeves and their ties are loosened. Except for Admiral Hickerson, who is wearing a somewhat rumpled full dress uniform with the tunic buttoned up to his throat. All the requisite stars are attached to shoulder boards and buttoned in place.

President Harris takes a tentative sip of his hot coffee. "Admiral, what's the status?"

The admiral clears his throat, and when he speaks his voice is raspy. "We're ready to go, sir. We hit a small snag in getting enough drone pilots on location because of the satellite issues. We'll rely on the Common Data Link for field communications but we won't be able to view real-time video feeds here in the Situation Room. Strike Group One is in range and all ships and carriers are ready for battle-station alert upon your order."

"What about the Israelis?"

"They're champing at the bit, sir," Admiral Hickerson says.

Israeli Ambassador Har-Even had been invited to this afternoon's briefing but is not yet present.

"Are the Iranians offering air support to their troops?"

"Yes, sir. But they only have a couple of hundred aircraft available to them. A majority of their fighters are at least a decade old, and many much older. They're sloppy with their maintenance program, which leads me to believe the number of flyable aircraft could be much lower. Nevertheless, a good portion of their aircraft will be destroyed within the first hour of battle."

The President places his coffee cup on the table. "Will we be able to listen in on real-time radio communications?"

"Some, sir, but not all. For the first time since World War II, we'll need to rely on commanders in the field to make the important decisions. I trust them to do so, sir. They know their mission and I'm more than willing to put the nation's safety in their hands."

"I am, too, Admiral, but that doesn't mean we are out of the loop."

"No, sir, you're correct. There will be some issues, but I believe we can make it work."

President Harris turns from Admiral Hickerson and addresses the secretary of state. "Allison, any of our overtures to Iran had any effect?"

"No, sir. We tried to reach out to them, but they haven't even acknowledged our requests."

"Fuck 'em, then," the President mutters, but loud enough to be heard by the entire room. "Pardon my French. Frankly, I'm tired of the constant stream of horseshit that spews out of Tehran." President Harris glances up to see nods from most of his advisors. "What about the Jordanians?"

"They've been receptive, sir. They're not happy about the Iranians massing at the border. We can rely on them to inflict some damage, but how much is an unknown."

President Harris turns his focus to Secretary of Defense Martin Wilson. "Martin, how much damage can the Jordanians cause?"

"Skirmishes along the flanks of the Iranian troops. More of a pestering presence than anything else, but enough to force the Iranians to direct some attention their way."

President Harris offers a nod and inhales a deep breath. "So are we a go?" He turns to each advisor around the table and receives nods of acceptance. The mood is somber, but tense.

"Thank you for your support." The President turns back to Admiral Hickerson. "How is the operation going to unfold?"

"It's a fluid situation, Mr. President, but the Israelis are going to start the show by launching an aerial attack. That will allow our ships to pinpoint the Iranian radar sites along with their antiaircraft batteries. Our first salvo will be Tomahawk cruise missiles to eliminate those threats and then we launch our own aerial attack."

The President takes a moment to digest the information before turning to CIA Director Isaac Green. "Isaac, what will the Iranian response be?"

"Well, sir, hopefully we'll hit so fast and so hard they'll have no choice but to haul ass back home." His comment elicits a few chuckles. "In all honesty, sir, we don't know how committed they are to this path. We don't have any reliable assets in Tehran. We don't know if they're simply taking advantage of an opportunity, or if they are committed to the destruction of Israel, as they have asserted many times."

The President steeples his hands beneath his chin. "Should we direct some of our assets toward Tehran?"

No one jumps to answer.

Eventually, Secretary of State Allison Moore takes the plunge. "Sir, I think we should focus our forces on the advancing troops for the moment and see what type of reaction we receive from the Iranian leaders. The situation with Islamists all across the Middle East and Northern Africa is on the precipice of exploding. The last thing we want to do is incite them further by a direct attack on Tehran."

"All right, we'll hold off on attacking Tehran." He raises one finger in the air. "But I want to make damn certain you all know that option is still on the table." President Harris folds his arms across his chest and exhales a sigh. "Admiral, we are a go. Hit them with everything we've got."

Chapter 66

The Sanders home

The earlier discovery of Sarah Chlouber's body has shaken Ruth and Carl to their cores. The children are no longer allowed outdoors and the family is barricaded in their no-electricity, no-running-water home. With strict rationing, they've made three days' worth of food stretch much longer.

Ruth steps inside from the garage, pours three fingers of water into four coffee cups, and hands one to her husband.

Carl drains his and places the cup back on the counter. "How much is left?"

Ruth shoves a stray strand of her dark hair behind her ear. "Six bottles." She sags against the kitchen counter.

Carl steps over and wraps his arms around his wife. "The water wouldn't have lasted this long if you hadn't stocked up for Noah's soccer season."

Ruth wipes away a tear. "Why didn't I buy more?"

"So you're a fortune-teller? No one could have predicted what happened. Who thinks about buying a hundred cases of water? Nobody. You buy one and when that's empty you run to the corner store and buy another."

Ruth shrugs out of his embrace. "Kids, come get your water," she shouts down the hall as she shuffles out of the kitchen.

The kids wander in for their cup of water.

Carl leans against the breakfast bar. "Anybody want to work the puzzle again?" The family has worked and reworked the thousand-piece puzzle so many times the edges are frayed.

Noah and Emma groan and shake their heads. "I think some of the pieces got lost," Emma says.

"That'll make it more of a challenge."

Noah sets his cup in the sink. "No, Dad, that makes it impossible. Who wants to work on a puzzle where half the pieces are missing? Besides, I'm reading."

"Whatcha reading?"

"Hunger Games."

"Again? How many times have you read the series?"

"I dunno. But it's not like I can run to the library and grab something new."

Carl ruffles his son's hair. "I guess you've got a point there, kiddo."

All four are reading to pass the time. Books that had once been banished to the attic are now being recycled downstairs, but there is only so much sitting and reading a family of four can do. The bicycles parked in the closed garage are begging to be ridden.

Emma grabs her father's hand. "Dad, can I go over to Grace's house?"

The mangled face of Ruth Chlouber flashes in Carl's mind. "I don't know, sweetheart."

She tugs on her father's arm. "Please? She's just down the street. Pleeeassse?"

"I don't think so."

Emma lowers her head and stares at the tiled floor. Another piece of Carl's heart flakes away. "You know what, let me talk to Mom for a minute." *How do you explain to a five-year-old that a killer may be prowling the neighborhood without scaring the hell out of her?*

Carl finds Ruth sitting in the window seat, staring out the bay window. It's a frequent hangout for her since learning of Sarah Chlouber's death. Carl walks over and sits next to her.

"Emma wants to go down to Grace's house."

Ruth turns toward her husband. "How do we know her parents weren't involved in Sarah's death? Absolutely not."

Carl's anger and frustration bubble to the surface. "We're all going a little stir-crazy, but sitting in front of the window on constant lookout for a killer isn't normal, Ruth. We've known Grace's parents since the girls were born. Do you actually think they could be involved in Mrs. Chlouber's murder?"

"Desperate times mean desperate people, Carl."

"We can't stay cooped up in this house suspecting our neighbors of murder. Especially people we've known for years."

"How do you know there aren't other dead bodies? We're safer with all of us together."

"I don't. And you don't, either." Carl slumps against the wall. "Honey, we'll drive ourselves batshit crazy thinking about this." Carl reaches over and kneads Ruth's shoulder. "I think it will do Emma some good to spend some time with Grace."

Ruth closes her eyes in resignation. "Will you at least walk her down there and back?"

"Of course. I'll be back shortly."

Ruth stands from her vigil at the window and moves over to the sofa. The interior is dim even in the middle of the day because the front of the home faces north. The sun's rays, low in the autumn sky, don't penetrate much beyond the windows. She picks up the book she was reading, riffles through the pages, and puts it back down. Ruth pushes out of the sofa and returns to the window seat.

That's where Carl finds her upon his return. He sits on the cushioned window seat and leans against the wall.

"What are we going to do, Carl?" she whispers to her husband.

"I don't know. What are the chances Zeke is on his way here?"

"Pretty good, I think, knowing Zeke. The overriding question is *when*. We can't survive here for more than another day or two. We need to come up with some type of game plan, but I don't have a clue where to begin."

"We have nowhere else to go, Ruth. Leaving would be senseless. I'll get up early in the morning, around daybreak, and see if I can at least find some water."

Ruth turns to face her husband. "And where are you going to find this water?"

"There are vending machines fronting businesses are all along Lovers Lane road. Hell, I bet I could find a bunch of them inside the high school."

"What makes you think they haven't already been raided? Besides, how are you going to get inside?"

"I own a hammer and a crowbar. We need water, Ruth, and I don't care how I get it. Our family comes first."

"What happens to our family if you get arrested for breaking and entering?"

Carl sighs. "I'm not going to get arrested. When's the last time you've even seen a cop?" He pauses for a moment, thinking. "I dunno, maybe going when it's dark is a better alternative."

Ruth shakes her head. "Who knows what you could run into out there in the darkness?"

"I still have the pistol I bought from Zeke."

"How long has it been since you shot the thing, Carl? Not only would I be concerned about you running into a bunch of thugs, now there's added worry about you shooting yourself in the dark."

"How much water do we have left, Ruth?"

"I told you. Six bottles."

"There you go. We need water. I can handle the gun. All you have to do is point and pull the damn trigger. How hard can that be?"

"Can you shoot it accurately if someone is chasing you? It's all fine and dandy sitting here in a locked house, but you don't know what's out there," she says, pointing to the outdoors through the big bay window.

"So what do you want me to do?" Carl takes his wife's hands in his. "I've given you the options and you want to select none of the above, but that's not an option. We can't survive without water."

"What happens if you run into trouble? You won't be able to call and tell me. Or call for help if you need to."

Carl leans forward and brushes his lips against hers. "Nothing's going to happen."

"Mom! I'm hungry," Noah shouts from his room down the hall.

"Will you swipe some candy bars, too?"

Carl leans over and kisses her forehead "Almond Joy still your favorite?"

Ruth nods, a small smile pushing up the corners of her mouth. "When are you going to go?"

"Let's give it a couple of hours." He stands and pulls her up. "Now get in the kitchen and whip us up some of your magic."

She slaps him on the butt. "It'll have to be magic because there's only a can or two of stuff left to eat."

"That's what I love about you—always thinking of the positive," he says as she brushes past.

Carl grabs a flashlight from the kitchen drawer and steps through the connecting door to the garage. Ruth's two-year-old Lexus SUV, in desperate need of a car wash, is parked next to his almost-new BMW sedan. Now just two expensive hunks of metal taking up space. As he steps around the cars, he wonders what'll happen when the monthly payments aren't made. Then he stops in his tracks, wondering the same about the house. "I guess they can come and get them if they want them," he mutters as he continues to his workbench. Tools lie scattered across the plywood surface peppered with oil rings and paint stains. On the wall is a pegboard with screwdrivers, pliers, and a couple of different hammers held on by small metal hooks. He grabs one of the hammers, a couple of different screwdrivers, and a pair of pliers. From one of the drawers he withdraws a small pry bar and a utility knife and piles it all into one of those canvas carryall bags that are all the rage at the big-box home improvement stores.

Carl carries the bag back into the house and places it on the kitchen counter before heading upstairs to the master bedroom. He kneels down by his side of the bed and pulls out the small gun safe Ruth had insisted on when he bought the gun from Zeke. He enters the combination and lifts the lid on a Smith & Wesson model 1911—a .45 caliber pistol with a stainless steel frame and slide, dressed with crosshatched walnut grips. Zeke had assured him the larger round would stop most anything on two feet but the only thing Carl has killed with it are a few paper targets. Recalling Zeke's words, he suppresses a sudden surge of trepidation. Next to the pistol rest two additional magazines, which his brother-in-law had thrown in on the deal.

Carl takes the gun from the safe and tucks it into the back of his waistband. He slides the extra two mags in his front pocket and, when he stands, his too-loose jeans fall to his ankles. He laughs as he pulls the jeans up and notches his belt tighter. He removes the heavy magazines from his front pockets and puts them into the pockets of a light-weight jacket from his closet. Before descending the stairs he checks himself in the large mirror and readjusts things until only a slight budge is visible.

"Your bowl of soup is on the counter," Ruth says when he reenters the kitchen.

"Divide it between the kids. I'm not hungry anyway."

"You need to eat, too, Carl," Ruth says between spoonfuls of watery broth.

Carl grabs the bag of tools. "I'll find something while I'm out." The news he is venturing out perks up the ears of his children.

Emma, back from Grace's, claps her small hands together. "Daddy, can you pick up some chicken nuggets from McDonald's?"

Carl cringes. "I don't think they're open now, sweetheart."

Noah says, "Where are you going, Dad?"

"Just to run an errand, son."

"Can I go?"

"Not this time, little buddy."

Ruth stands from the table and sidles up next to Carl, whispering, "You're leaving now? I thought you were going to wait a couple of hours."

Carl steers them toward the living room, talking in a low voice. "I was, but it's dark enough now, I think. It's still light enough that I won't need the flashlight for a while."

Carl turns for the front door but Ruth steps around in front of him and tiptoes up to kiss him on the lips. “Be careful, Carl,” she whispers.

“I will. Lock the door behind me.”

“How long are you going to be gone?”

“Two or three hours probably. I’m not coming home empty-handed.” Carl slips out into the growing darkness.

CHAPTER 67

U.S. Navy Strike Group One
Off the coast of Egypt, Mediterranean Sea

Seaman Chase Oliver takes one last drag of his cigarette before flipping the butt over the rail of the USS *Bunker Hill*, a Ticonderoga-class guided-missile cruiser support ship for the carrier USS *Carl Vinson*. He turns to one of his fellow sailors, who has a cigarette dangling from the corner of his mouth. "Why the hell are they rousting us out of bed at three thirty in the morning? For a damn drill?"

"I dunno, cuz. It's the navy—I just go where they tell me, when they tell me," Seaman Diaz says.

"But the fucking middle of the night?"

"C'mon, Ollie, you were probably in your bunk jacking—"

Another loud siren sounds.

"Here comes the pretend missile launch," Seaman Oliver shouts as they work their way closer to the aft superstructure—standard operating procedure for missile launch.

The giant ship shudders and a yellow flame lights the night sky. "What the hell?" Seaman Oliver shouts to his friend.

"Well, cuz, don't appear to be no drill," Diaz shouts back.

Against standard operating procedure, they drift to the rail so that they can get a better view of the three-thousand-pound Tomahawk missiles exploding upward from the bow of the ship. One after another, the TERCOM radar guidance–equipped missiles launch from their vertical launching system. The smoke from their turbofan engines washes across the deck of the ship, temporarily reducing visibility.

"Look." Diaz points out to sea where other ships in their armada are launching the deadly cruise missiles. At over a million dollars a pop, it's not long before fifty million dollars in weapons are streaking through the sky.

"Who the hell we bombing?" Oliver shouts.

"Hell if I know. But whoever it is, I'm sure glad that I'm not on the other end of this shit."

The ship contains a mix of 122 missiles, and within minutes 20 Tomahawks have blasted from the deck of the USS *Bunker Hill*. The night sky is lit with missile after missile racing off to their targets. Shortly after missile launch, the aircraft carrier USS *Carl Vinson* begins launching her aircraft.

The F/A-18s streak into the sky as the smell of burned jet fuel envelops Strike Group One. There's a continuous stream of aircraft being hurtled into the sky by the ship's steam-powered catapult system.

"Look at those planes, Diaz," Seaman Oliver shouts. "They are loaded down with ordnance. Somebody is getting their ass kicked."

"Who do you think it is, cuz?" Diaz asks.

"Hell if I know."

CHAPTER 68

Office of the Supreme Leader

President Rafsanjani stares at the sun cresting above the mountain peaks east of Tehran as he slumps in the rear seat of his chauffeured limousine. After a quick two-hour nap and a much-needed shower at home, he's been summoned back to the supreme leader's office.

Unfortunately, the president had chosen the worst possible two-hour window for sneaking in a nap. While he had been resting, Iranian troops along the front line in Iraq had been decimated by attack after attack from the Americans and Israelis. He turns from the serenity of the mountains and glances again at the piece of paper containing the projected death toll. He rakes a single hand across his face as the long black car pulls into the heavily fortified entrance to the ayatollah's office. The car is halted and mirrors are run under both sides of the car. A soldier with a death grip on his Tondar MPT-9 submachine gun orders the windows down.

President Rafsanjani scoots forward in the seat as another guard appears on his side of the car. After a heated exchange between the president and the soldier, the gate is lifted and the car eases farther into the complex. Although a cold front had come in sometime during the night, offering a respite from the untenable heat, a bead of sweat forms on his brow when he steps out of the car. He mops his brow upon entering and comes face-to-face with a very grim General Safani, who gives him the tiniest of nods.

President Rafsanjani leans forward to whisper into the general's ear, "What happened, Ahmad?"

The general glances around at the large number of security forces and steers President Rafsanjani toward a quiet corner. "What happened, Mr. President, is the sleeping bear has reawakened. The Americans and the Israelis unleashed a highly coordinated attack on our troops. Most of our command and control units were destroyed in the first few minutes and most all of our airplanes lie burning in the desert."

The president grabs the general by the elbow. "What are you going to tell the ayatollah?"

"I'm not going to tell him anything," General Safani hisses. "That's your job. You and the supreme leader cooked up this foolish mission against my repeated protests."

President Rafsanjani leans back and tugs on the lapels of his suit coat. "You are in command, General. This disaster falls on your shoulders for such poor planning."

Safani turns away in disgust and, accompanied by two of his most trusted aides, shuffles down the hallway to the supreme leader's office as if trudging toward the gallows. He glances back to see that President Rafsanjani is hurrying to catch up, no doubt eager to tell his side of the story first.

As before, a cleric is on hand to open the door. General Safani pauses before entering and turns to his most trusted aide. He reaches into his freshly pressed tunic and removes a standard white envelope. "Make sure my family gets this if something happens to me," he whispers while handing the envelope to his aide.

Shocked at the implication, it takes a moment for the man to regain his composure before reaching a hand out to accept the envelope. The general turns away, runs a finger around the inside collar of his uniform, and squares his shoulders as President Rafsanjani brushes past.

The supreme leader is in a flurry of agitation as General Safani approaches the desk. The president is already seated in front of the desk, his head bowed as if he were a child being scolded.

"Tell me what happened, General," the ayatollah says through clenched teeth. The general begins detailing the circumstances of the predawn battle until the supreme leader slams his hand on his desk.

"Enough excuses, General. You should have foreseen this attack. Where are our intelligence assets?"

"I tried to warn you about the—"

The ayatollah unleashes another verbal tirade. He jumps to his feet and paces the area behind the desk. His face is a deep crimson and the veins at his temples throb with every accelerated heartbeat.

General Safani, who hadn't been offered a seat, stands and takes the withering assault as President Rafsanjani looks on. After a few moments the supreme leader collapses into his chair, having spent all the venom he could muster.

The respite doesn't last as he lurches to his feet again. "Send more troops. Send every able-bodied man to the front lines. I will not lose this battle."

"But, sir, most of our command structure is—"

"General, you are relieved of duty. I am placing you under house arrest," the ayatollah says in a low, menacing voice. He turns his attention to President Rafsanjani.

"You are a coward. If it weren't so easy for me to dangle your strings you would rot in a jail cell."

The president hangs his head, his eyes focused on the intricate pattern of the priceless Persian rug beneath his chair.

"Put another general in charge. I don't care who it is, but their success or failure will be a direct reflection on you. Keep that in mind as you make your selection."

He waves his hand. "Get out. The next time I summon you here, Mr. President"—he emphasizes the title—"could well be your last trip if you have not destroyed the Jews."

President Rafsanjani meekly stands from his chair and joins General Safani in leaving the office. Moving through the doorway, a pair of neckless uniformed Revolutionary Guards peels the general away, one at each elbow, as the president takes the long walk back to his car alone.

Chapter 69

Dallas, Texas

The last rays of the sun are hovering on the edge of the horizon and the temperature is maybe ten degrees cooler as Zeke ventures through one of the seamier areas he's ridden through. An outcropping of apartment buildings is butted up to the underside of the LBJ Freeway, occupying both sides of Preston Road. The fake, faded yellow stucco is flaking off most of the apartment buildings and the surrounding ground is hard-packed earth with tufts of weeds poking up at odd intervals. Window screens hang askew and the parking lot is littered with cars that look like they haven't been driven in years. A few huddled groups of people linger around the front doors of several apartments.

Zeke pulls on the reins to bring Murphy to a stop a good distance away and scans the area in the dying light. No obvious threats, but he loosens the Glock nonetheless. He takes advantage of the stoppage to study the map before the light fades. By his estimation it's about six miles to Ruth's house—a couple of hours of riding, three at the most, and they will be in her neighborhood. He tucks the map into one of the saddlebags and gives a little nudge with his heels to get Murphy going again. He swivels in the saddle to check on Ruby and Tilly. Both mares are trudging along but their shaggy heads are hanging a little closer to the ground.

He turns back to the front and catches sight of movement in the distance. The number of cars along this stretch of road is light compared to some of the other streets, but ample hiding space is available. He delivers another light kick to Murphy's ribs and the pace picks up. Zeke scans the grayness for more movement. His senses are now on high alert. The hairs are standing at the nape of his neck and the gloom is suddenly swirling with unseen menace.

More movement on the left side. He reaches his hand to the holster and pulls out the Glock, slowly bringing the gun around front. Now shielded behind the saddle horn, the pistol is grasped firmly in his hand. He doesn't need to look to know a round is chambered. Zeke always carries hot. As the horses approach a car parked parallel to the road, he slows Murphy to concentrate on the foreground.

About ten yards away from an old beater Malibu parked crossways in the street, four heads suddenly pop up in the clear. Zeke pulls on the reins and the small caravan comes to a dead stop. The four young men slink around the front of the dead car.

"I like your horses," one of them says. They're late teens, maybe early twenties, full of themselves by the way they walk. All four are smiling.

"Thanks," Zeke says, shifting in the saddle to allow more freedom of movement.

All of them are armed, their guns tucked in their waistbands, gangster style. Zeke sweeps his vision from one to the other, taking in their heavily tatted arms, their mangy hair, their leering looks of toughness. A quick glance to the side reveals a group of people edging closer. Not good.

"I'd like to have 'em," the one in front says.

The leader, Zeke decides, because he occupies the center. "They're good horses, but they're not for sale," Zeke says, his gaze boring in on the tough in front. They're bunched up in a group instead of being spread out, a tactical error on their part. He sorts out the order—his progression if he needs to fire. His one concern is how Murphy will react if he fires his weapon from the saddle.

"I ain't saying I'm going to buy 'em." The other three laugh.

Zeke glances to the right to track the progress of the other group. Closer. No time.

"Look, I don't want any trouble. I'd like to be on my way."

"Hear that, fellas? He don't want no trouble." With a large toothy smile the leader glances at his buddies.

Zeke sighs and grabs another handful of rein. "Let's all go on about our business."

"Or what?" the leader says.

"You best move along because you're not getting the goddamn horses."

The leader's smile turns to a frown as he reaches for the gun at his waist. Without hesitation, and with no remorse, Zeke raises his pistol and fires a single round from the Glock, punching a small hole in the man's forehead. He collapses to the ground as if his strings had been suddenly cut. Murphy bucks and stomps but Zeke wrestles for control and immediately switches his focus to the other three. The one on the right reaches for his gun but it hasn't even cleared his waistband when Zeke's second bullet punches a hole in almost the exact same spot as his friend's.

Off to his right, hands are grabbing for weapons. Zeke

buries his heels into Murphy's side and the horse, skittish from the noise and the scent of blood in the air, breaks into a full gallop, plowing through the other two men. He glances back to make sure the mares are keeping up. Other gunshots bark in the night. Zeke leans forward and hugs Murphy's neck, hoping like hell none of the bullets hit the horses.

Four blocks later, Zeke pulls gently on the reins to slow their progress. Murphy slows to a walk and Zeke removes a full mag from his pocket and reloads the Glock. He holsters the gun, hoping like hell he won't need to pull it out again. He stops the horses and climbs down from the saddle. He looks back to make sure there is no pursuit and spends a few moments checking the health of the three horses. No obvious blood. He whispers to the horses as he runs his hands across their lathered shoulders. Murphy is quivering and he spends a little more time stroking his soft muzzle and talking in a low, soothing voice. Once the horses are calmed, he climbs back aboard and loosens the reins so Murphy can set his own pace.

His own nerves are rattled from the gunplay. He inhales a series of deep breaths, but he doesn't dwell on the outcome. Those guys made a choice. Unfortunately, they made the wrong one. He scans for other threats as he vanquishes what happened from his mind. Army training.

He can't make out the street sign at the next intersection because full dark has descended on the lightless city. As they draw closer he sees the wording on the sign: WALNUT HILL LANE. From his recollection they are about two miles from Ruth's house. The day's hard riding and the sudden adrenaline dump leave Zeke with a stress hangover, and he slumps in the saddle.

They plug along until he starts noticing familiar sights—places he's visited. Restaurants where their family's eaten. His spirits lift as he focuses on the street signs. They pass

Hanover, Purdue, and Stanford and he steers Murphy left onto Amherst Avenue. Ruth's house is in the middle of the block but he can't yet see it. Damn, he wants off this horse. He wills Murphy to go faster until they are abreast the home Carl and his sister had spent a full year remodeling. He climbs wearily from the saddle and leads the three horses into the front yard, tying off Murphy's reins on the front porch railing.

Zeke limps up the steps and knocks on the front door. No answer. He knocks again and peers through the side window to see candles flickering in the darkness. Zeke has no idea what time it is. He knocks again and is rewarded by approaching footfalls.

His sister's voice drifts through the closed door. "Who is it?"

"It's me, sis," he says, suddenly overcome with emotion.

She throws the front door open, lunges through the storm door and into his arms. "Oh, Zeke," she moans into his chest. "I knew you'd come."

Zeke looks up to see two small heads peeking around the wall of the living room.

"Uncle Zeke," they shout in unison, charging across the empty space. They spill out onto the front porch and surround their mother and uncle, hugging Zeke's waist, his legs, any part of his body that they can reach. He breaks from the embrace and takes a step back. They've lost weight. Emma and Noah are skin and bones. His heart stutters.

"Where's Carl?" he says.

Ruth shakes her head as fresh tears begin. "He went to find water. But he's been gone for over five hours."

Zeke wipes the tears from her cheeks with his dirty thumb. "I'll go find him, sis. Give me a minute to get situated."

Ruth nods and gives her brother another hug.

Zeke kneels and embraces his niece and nephew and peppers their gaunt faces with kisses. "How do you like it with no Internet?"

"It sucks, Uncle Zeke," Noah says.

"Oh yeah? Your mother and I didn't have Internet until we got to be old," he says, giving each another kiss. He stands and walks back to the horses, which they spot for the first time. They race down the steps and run to Murphy, raking their little hands across his soft nose.

"Why are you riding Grandpa's horses?" Emma says as she moves from Murphy to Ruby.

"Had to, baby girl. I didn't have enough gas to make it down here and get you back to Grandma's and Grandpa's." He unties the saddlebag on Ruby's back and hands it to Ruth. "From Mom. You guys eat all you want. I'm going to put the mares in the backyard."

He unclips the lead attached to Murphy and leads the two mares to the side gate while Ruth and the kids return inside, the saddlebags containing the food grasped firmly in his sister's thin hand. After he removes the packs, he pours each horse a good portion of oats and takes another healthy portion around to Murphy, still tied up in the front yard. He's going to need to find them some water in a bit. While Murphy crunches on the oats, Zeke retreats indoors and finds his sister, niece, and nephew around the kitchen table with the bounty from the saddlebags spilled out in front of them. Noah has a mouthful of peanut butter and crackers while Emma munches a peanut butter and jelly sandwich.

"Eat, Ruth," he says, stepping closer.

"I will, but let them eat first."

"There's plenty, I promise. I have a big portion of deer jerky, too."

Ruth hesitates before picking up one of the sandwiches. She delicately unwraps it and takes a bite.

Zeke waits for her to swallow. "Where's the closest creek?"

"There's a creek across the next street that runs through the country club," she says, struggling with all her willpower not to inhale the food.

"I'm going to lead the horses down for a drink." He turns toward the door.

"Zeke." He turns to face her and she mouths a silent "thank you."

Zeke nods and disappears back into the darkness.

Chapter 70

The White House Situation Room

Due to the divergence of time zones, the President and all of his advisors are arranged around the large conference table in the Sit Room deep into the night. Admiral Hickerson and Defense Secretary Martin Wilson are shuttling between the Pentagon and the White House via helicopter. When at the Pentagon both are in nearly constant contact with the President and other advisors through the use of videoconferencing. The Sit Room has a direct line to the offices in the Pentagon.

"Admiral, what is the Iranian response?" President Harris says to the picture projected on the front screen.

"Sir, we aren't able to accurately determine their response. According to reports from the field we decimated their command structure, knocked out a majority of their air defense systems, and obliterated their feeble air force. Their troops are no longer pressing forward, but they also are not retreating."

"Any battlefield intelligence suggesting what they might do?"

"We've intercepted some of their radio chatter with the

help of AWACS aircraft on station, but nothing which gives us an insight into their thinking."

"What's the next phase, Admiral?"

"Israel is about to launch another air sortie, and we will follow close behind with our own aircraft. We're also continually pounding them with both ship- and sub-launched Tomahawk cruise missiles. Israel is also massing its troops along their eastern border, but they, like we, are hoping to avoid any type of ground war."

"How are we on supplies?" President Harris asks.

"So far, so good, sir. We have transferred a number of missiles to Strike Group One from the Israeli's stockpile of weapons. The rest of the fleet is well supplied, at least for another twenty-four hours, sir."

The President leans forward in his chair. "Is this going to be over in twenty-four hours?"

"Unknown, sir, but I hope so. I wish we had some intel out of Tehran that would provide an insight into their thinking."

"We're working on it, Admiral. Director Green will be in touch to update the situation shortly. Keep me posted, Admiral."

"I will, sir," Admiral Hickerson says before the screen at the front of the room transitions to black.

The President turns his attention to CIA Director Isaac Green. "Isaac, we need intel and we need it yesterday. Do we have any assets in Iran?"

"No, but the Israelis do. Unfortunately, the only source of contact is via satellite phone. Maybe"—the CIA director pauses for a moment, racking his brain—"we could assemble a joint team of agents to send into Iran through Afghanistan. There are a few CIA agents still in country. Let me talk to the Israeli ambassador, sir. We'll come up with something, hopefully within the next few hours."

"Good, Isaac. Allison, any luck contacting Iranian leadership?"

The secretary of state shakes her head as she replies, "Nothing, sir. Not a hello, thank-you, or kiss my ass, sir." Her reply elicits a few chuckles from the exhausted group around the table.

An ashen-faced national security aide rushes into the room, stops at the President's elbow, and leans in to whisper something in his ear. President Harris holds up his hand to stop him. "Tell everyone here—we're all in this together."

The aide, who looks like he's only a couple of years removed from graduate school, clears his throat before speaking. "Mr. President, one of the AWACS planes reported a massive launch of some type of missile on the outskirts of Tehran."

Gasps from those around the table.

"Heading?" the President barks.

"Unknown, sir."

He turns his anger upon his advisors. "All of you assured me Iran was incapable of launching a nuclear warhead. What the hell just blasted off? I want to know, and I want to know right goddamn now."

Advisors grab for phones as the President orders a reconnection with Admiral Hickerson and SECDEF Martin.

"Yes, Mr. President?" Admiral Hickerson says when the camera in front of him kicks on.

"Admiral, a large missile or some large something was launched from the outskirts of Tehran."

Admiral Hickerson's face transitions from astonishment to concern in the blink of an eye. "I'm on it, Mr. President."

"Wait!" President Harris shouts. "We have anything in our arsenal that can shoot the damn thing down?"

"Yes, we do, sir, but it comes down to a matter of trajectory. We need time for our systems to acquire the target, time we may not have." Admiral Hickerson pushes out of his chair and disappears from the frame.

"Goddammit, I want answers, people."

Chief of Staff Scott Alexander, who had taken a seat at the back of the room, carries his chair to the table and sits. He leans sideways and whispers in the President's ear. "Take a deep breath, Paul. We'll figure it out."

President Harris takes a long look at Alexander, then nods.

"Mr. President, we don't know exactly what launched. It may not be a nuclear warhead," one of the military aides says.

"Well, it's sure as hell wasn't a giant pop-bottle rocket," the President snaps. "I need concrete answers, son. Do we have any way to track the whatever-the-hell-it-is?"

"Only what we can pick up through ship radar on site or possibly from the AWACS aircraft. But their radars are configured more for a look-down scenario, not for tracing atmospheric flight," the director of the CIA answers.

President Harris throws his hands up in the air. "What the hell am I supposed to do?"

Alexander reaches out to put a hand on the arm of the President.

The CIA director says, "We need more info, sir."

"There isn't any more info, Isaac. What's the flight time to Israel?"

One of the aides at the back of the room clears his throat and says, "Minutes, sir—at best."

CHAPTER 71

Dallas

Zeke waters the horses in a creek bordered by multimillion-dollar homes that look out over the rolling fairways of the Dallas Country Club two blocks away. He can't actually see the fairways or the houses, because of the dark, but he has seen them before. Upon his return, he parks all three horses in the backyard. He strips the saddle and blanket from Murphy's back, his ass protesting too much about another round in the saddle. He'll walk on his search for Carl. He pulls the Kimber rifle from its scabbard and lugs it, along with the saddlebag of ammunition, into the house.

The first item of business is to replace the two missing bullets from the magazine out of the Glock. Task completed, he stuffs the reloaded mag, along with extra rifle ammunition, into his jacket pocket. He glances up to see Ruth watching him work with the weapons. It's their only real bone of contention. Ruth would prefer a world without deadly weapons. Zeke ignores her look of annoyance. "Which way did he go?"

She steps closer so the conversation can't be overheard by the children in the next room. "He was going to try and get in the high school, thinking the vending machines would have some water."

"The school right around the corner?"

"Yes. Highland Park High School."

"Was he going to try anywhere else?"

"I don't know, Zeke. He mentioned something about stores all along Lovers Lane, but nothing specifically." She glances back over her shoulder at the children sitting around the table. "What do you think happened?"

"I don't know, Ruth, but I'm going to find him." He triple-checks one jacket pocket for the extra ammunition, then the other to make sure the small flashlight he brought is still there. At the last minute he decides to leave the rifle behind. If there's gunplay it will be in close quarters.

"Be careful, Zeke."

"I will. I'll be back as soon as I can."

His sister follows him to the front door.

"What if he's injured? He took the gun he bought off you."

Zeke doesn't know if that was an accusation. "I'll find him, sis." He slips out into the now colder, and if possible, darker night, the Glock riding comfortably on his hip.

He makes his way down the block and hangs a left, crossing over Lovers Lane for the second time in the last fifteen minutes. On the other side he pauses for a few moments, listening to the silence. Nothing. No cars rumbling along the road, no humans out in the dark—dead quiet. He works his way toward the tall, dark structures silhouetted against the starry sky. The high school is large, and he sneaks between two of the buildings and comes face-to-face with what appears to be a baseball field. He scours the area for movement before continuing on.

The next building he approaches is big, and being close to the athletic fields, he assumes this must be the gym. He creeps up to the doors and discovers all the security glass punched out. He snakes his hand through the broken window and pushes on the bar that opens the door.

Slowly, he pulls the door open and steps inside. He halts for a moment to listen again. Silence. He moves farther into the building, enveloped in total darkness. He fishes the flashlight from his pocket and covers the lens with his hand before turning it on. He was right. It is the gym. The wide counter of the concession stand is covered by some type of roll-down metal door. He flashes the light to the side and spots the entryway to the concession area kicked open. He advances for a closer look, his hand hovering just above the pistol's handle. He takes a quick peek around the doorjamb and pans the flashlight around the interior. Empty.

He flicks the beam down the hall to get his bearings before switching it off. The doors to the gym's interior are about ten steps away. He clicks off the light and moves forward. Not having heard even a wisp of noise, he's fairly certain no one is hiding inside but he needs to clear the room before moving on.

He steps inside the door, his footsteps echoing in the cavernous space. He shoves aside his caution and flicks on the flashlight. "Hell, Carl could be bleeding out somewhere while I'm dicking around in here," he mutters. Zeke increases his pace and clears the two locker rooms. He shines the flashlight around the bleachers before exiting the gym. He kills the flashlight before stepping outside.

He eases along the exterior of the gym and comes to a long, rectangular, open area, the ghostly imprint of a goalpost silhouetted against the night sky. He glances around the field but sees nothing and hears even less.

The next building has glass starting about midway up the wall and he can tell at first glance it's a classroom. He walks to the back of the building, searching for a door. He finds it completely off its hinges, lying haphazardly across the lower portion of the doorway. He stretches one long leg over to clear the hazard, then the other. He pauses to listen. Silence. His head on a swivel, Zeke creeps down the long hallway.

CHAPTER 72

The White House Situation Room

The same NSA aide who had delivered the news of the missile launch rushes into the room and takes the same position next to the President. He starts to lean in but stops when remembering the earlier rebuff. He stands stiffly. "Mr. President, the missile exploded while still in Iranian airspace."

Audible sighs drift across the room.

"Was it a nuke?" President Harris asks.

"Unknown at this time, sir. From the size of the blast, if it was a nuclear device it did not detonate, sir."

The President slumps in his chair. "Thank you."

The aide takes his cue and disappears into the background.

"Thoughts, people?" the President says.

Everyone begins talking at once and Chief of Staff Alexander waves his hand to silence the excited voices.

CIA Director Isaac Green is the first to speak. "Does it matter, Mr. President, whether that was a nuke or not?"

"Go on, Isaac."

All eyes in the room are now focused on Isaac Green.

"Well, sir, they have launched what appeared to be a ballistic missile with hostile intent. What I mean to say, sir, is that they at least have the capability to launch. And although this launch was a failure, their capability to launch will be used again."

"What exactly are you suggesting?" Secretary of State Allison Moore says.

"What I'm suggesting, Allison, is to remove the head of the beast. Target the supreme leader and the president of Iran."

"Are you nuts, Isaac? Did you not listen to my earlier comments about igniting a worldwide Muslim uprising?"

Alexander leans forward and props his elbows on the table. "Are they not already causing havoc all over the Middle East and Northern Africa? How much more damage can they do? Hell, right now might be the best time ever to strike."

SECSTATE tosses her pen on the table and sits back in her chair. "You're both off your rocker."

"I think they have a valid point, Allison," the President says. "The Israelis are highly motivated to put an end to the constant threat that Iran presents for them."

"But, sir, what if the next group of leaders is even worse?" She grabs up the discarded pen. "Isn't it better to know your enemies well enough to judge their thinking?"

"You may be right, Allison. But this opportunity may not present itself again." The President turns to Director Green. "Isaac, get with the Israelis and develop a plan, then we'll decide the issue. Right now we need to be focused on getting them the hell out of Iraq, Syria, and Jordan."

"Sir, you don't think taking out their leaders will eliminate their will to fight? Those troops are fighting because the ayatollah ordered them to fight."

"I can't believe I'm sitting here discussing the assassination of a head of state," the secretary of state fumes.

"We're not assassinating anyone, Allison. At least not yet, anyway. I want a plan and I want it in the next two hours."

CHAPTER 73

Dallas

All of the classroom doors are open and what little light exists outside is enough to proceed without the flashlight. Zeke creeps down the hallway, only taking a moment with each classroom. He can't see into the darkest corners but his ears are attuned for the slightest noise. So far he's heard zip. He thinks about shouting out for Carl but doesn't yet want to make his presence known. He's weary from being in the saddle all day and all this lurking around has his every last nerve frayed.

He moves down the next hallway, clearing the rooms fairly quickly but the building seems to be never ending. He follows the dim tile pattern in the floor; making a left then a right, and now he's so confused in the darkness he doesn't have an inkling of where he is. At the next hallway intersection he makes a left and comes upon a large open area. Enough ambient outside light leaks through the panel of glass doors that he can make out a sign mounted up high on the wall declaring the room to his right the principal's office. Working his way around the perimeter he clicks on the flashlight and shines the yellow light into the offices. Nothing.

It's been a long time since Zeke attended high school, but he's betting school designs haven't changed much over the years. The people in them, yes, but most follow the same basic layout, which means the cafeteria should be close. And where there's a cafeteria there will be vending machines. He ducks down another hallway and walks quietly, searching for the cafeteria. It needs to be a large space in order to have fed all the students in a timely manner. He steps across the hall and glances through a door to see a big, empty room. He stops and pivots a three-sixty, searching for the faint outline of a vending machine.

"Carl," he whispers. "Carl." He pauses to see if his whispers receive a response. A moan. He clicks on the flashlight and sweeps the beam around the area. The light falls on a man curled up in a fetal position next to a threesome of now-empty vending machines. He steps over and kneels down next to the man. "Carl?"

The man moans in response and Zeke puts his hand on the man's shoulder only to have him try to scurry away.

"Carl, it's me, Zeke," he says, no longer whispering. He leans down as close to Carl's face as he can. Carl's jaw is hanging at an odd angle and dried blood coats his face in a heavy mask. "Carl . . . Carl . . ."

Finally he responds, trying to move his head in Zeke's direction.

"What happened?"

"Some ugs acked me." His jaw is not functioning enough to form the words.

"Can you stand?"

"Dunno. I ry."

Zeke grasps him under the arms and gently lifts as Carl shouts out in agony. He gets Carl on his feet and turns him around.

"Anything broken besides your jaw?"

"Don hink so," he stutters out. "My somach," he says, drawing one of his arms tight to his body.

Zeke's anger boils over at the sight of his injured brother-in-law. "How many were there?"

Carl holds up his five fingers.

"Five?"

Carl nods.

"How long ago?"

"Dunno, mus have passed ou."

"What type of weapons were they carrying?"

"Aseall bas."

"I'm going to take you home, Carl. Can you walk?"

"I hink so."

Zeke drapes one of Carl's arms over his left shoulder, leaving his right side open so he can get to the Glock in a hurry. He sweeps the flashlight from wall to wall, trying to piece together how to get back to the place he entered. To hell with it. He leads Carl to the front and hips his way through the first set of doors. They stumble across the small vestibule and crash into the final set of doors, shuffle-stepping out into the cool evening air. Zeke hadn't realized he had been sweating as much as he had been and the westerly breeze chills his damp body.

"What happened to your gun?" Zeke asks, the question just now coming to him.

"Ook it."

Damn, now he has to worry about someone around here toting the gun. He eases Carl down the steps to the sidewalk and pauses for a moment to listen. The only audible noise is Carl's labored breathing. They crab to the left and go around the outside of the school. Progress is slow. Zeke is mostly dragging Carl along, trying hard not to put any more pressure on Carl's damaged midsection.

They shuffle along the school's flank like two drunks

heading home from the bar. The journey is slow and Carl's moans are a magnet for trouble in the otherwise still night. They pause between buildings for Carl to catch his breath. His breathing is ragged and Zeke begins to wonder if his injuries are more severe than he first thought.

Zeke helps Carl to the curb while he continues to scan for threats. Not only are there a group of thugs running around with baseball bats, now there's a gun in play. The night seems brighter, but it could be an illusion after having spent the last hour in near-total darkness. After resting for a few moments, Zeke helps Carl to his feet and they trudge toward home.

As they pass what looks like a softball field, the sound of laughter pierces the silence. They come to a dead stop as a flash of uncontrolled anger floods Zeke's system. Another burst of giggles and Zeke pinpoints the source. They're concealed behind the concrete wall of what appears to be a dugout.

"That them?" Zeke whispers.

"Yeah."

"Think you can sit here on the curb for a moment?"

Carl nods and Zeke gently lowers him down. He makes his way over to the softball field and cuts through an opening in the fence just past first base. Slowly, Zeke follows along the fence until he's about ten feet from the front of the dugout. He pulls the Glock and glides up to the dugout opening. After a deep breath he swivels into the opening, the gun up and ready to fire.

The young men are seated on the long wooden bench at the far end of the dugout. They are so engrossed in what they're doing they don't notice that certain death is standing only a few feet away. Zeke steps closer. Their faces are awash in the spillover of a flashlight. The peach fuzz on their faces suggests they're young—maybe high school age. They're huddled together, intently focused on something. Zeke moves closer. A flash of metal in the wash of light. Carl's gun.

"That gun belongs to me," Zeke says.

They whirl around as if jolted with a cattle prod. Two shriek, one screams, but the boy in the middle, the one holding the gun, remains calm.

"What are you talking about, man?" the one holding the gun says.

"I want that gun." Zeke's voice is low, menacing.

"I found this gun," the boy says. There's now a slight tremor in his voice.

With his pistol pointed center mass on the gun holder, Zeke moves closer. A quick glance at the ground reveals a heap of wooden baseball bats.

"No, you took the gun, and I'm taking it back. I can shoot you and take the gun from your dead body, or you could just hand it to me."

The other boys are putting some distance between themselves and the boy holding the gun. Zeke really doesn't want to have to put a bullet in the young man in front of him, but he's not leaving without the gun.

"Give it to him, Richie," one of the boys urges.

Richie looks up at Zeke with a smirk.

Zeke moves closer, now only about five feet from boy and gun. "Richie, hand me the gun. Whether you live or die doesn't matter to me. But your death might upset your parents."

Richie reaches the gun forward and for a moment Zeke thinks he's going to fire, but the pistol dangles loosely from his finger. "Take it."

Zeke steps up, his gun never wavering from its arc between Richie and the other boys. He retrieves the gun from Richie's outstretched hand, turns its grip forward, and delivers a vicious blow to the side of the young man's face. Not hard enough to break his jaw, but hard enough to make him think twice about beating another human being. Richie slumps down on the hardwood bench, moaning in pain.

Zeke turns to the rest of the group. "If I see any of you out again, it's shoot first and ask questions later. Got it?"

Nods from everyone but Richie. Zeke reholsters his weapon and tucks Carl's gun into the back of his pants before disappearing around the side of the dugout. He helps Carl to his feet, and twenty minutes later Zeke lugs him up the steps to his home. Ruth swings the door wide before he can knock. Her face transitions from anticipation to horror.

"Carl! Oh my God, what happened?"

"He had a run-in with a group of delinquents."

Ruth slides under Carl's other arm, and together they get him into the house.

"I knew this was going to happen. I told him—"

"Ruth," Zeke says loudly, "not now. He's in desperate need of medical attention. Do you know anyone who could help him?"

"The kids' pediatrician lives down the street."

"Go get him. And hurry."

Ruth yanks a jacket from the coat closet and races out of the house.

The children stand and stare at their injured father lying on the sofa.

"Noah, find a washcloth and wet it with a bottle of water from my pack," Zeke says. "Emma, you help him."

Once Carl is situated, Zeke follows the children into the kitchen and walks into the bare pantry. All the food is gone, but on the top shelf he finds what remains of Carl's stash. He reaches for the red-wax-topped bottle and pulls it down. About two fingers of bourbon remains. Zeke grabs two glasses from the cupboard and returns to the living room. He divides the amber liquid between the two glasses and hands one to Carl.

"Drink. It'll help with the pain."

Carl's hand is shaking too much for him to get the glass to his lips, so Zeke leans over and dribbles some of the bourbon into his mouth. Carl works hard to swallow with his broken jaw. Zeke pours a little more, and continues until the glass is empty. Carl collapses against the back of the sofa, his entire body beginning to tremble.

Not good. Zeke knows from his battlefield days that Carl is on the verge of going into shock.

Emma and Noah return with the wet washcloth and Zeke gently wipes the matted blood from Carl's face.

"Is Daddy hurt bad, Uncle Zeke?" Noah says.

How to answer? "Yeah, he is, Noah, but your mommy went to get a doctor to fix him up."

CHAPTER 74

The White House Situation Room

President Harris walks into the Sit Room after a short nap and a quick shower. The fresh white button-down and slacks feel good, and they smell much better than the clothing he had been wearing for a full twenty-four hours. He glances around and notices several others had taken the opportunity to freshen up a bit, but everyone, him included, is running on fumes.

"I want an update on what's happening on the front lines before we discuss the other situation." He pulls his usual chair from beneath the table and sits. "Someone please get the DOD and the admiral on-screen."

They had switched off the battlefield radio chatter sometime ago because the thing only created more confusion.

Within moments the two appear, side by side, in one of the many conference rooms within the Pentagon. It's obvious from their fatigued appearance they didn't have the luxury of a nap and shower.

"Admiral, what's the status of the Iranian advance?"

"Sir, the Jordanians stepped up. They launched heavy artillery on the northern flank and peppered the Iranian forces with small-arms fire. That's about everything in their arsenal but it is having some effect. As of now, the Iranian troops are slowing their advance but they are not making any attempt to halt their progress.

"We along with the Israelis are continuing to pound the front with everything available to us, both aircraft-delivered and ship-based weapons. Frankly, sir, I don't know how much more punishment they can take. Their entire battlefield command and control units are emasculated."

"Admiral, you and Secretary Wilson are working with the CIA on a plan to target the Iranian leadership, correct?"

"Yes, sir," they answer in unison.

"What are your thoughts?" the President says.

Neither speaks for a brief moment, each waiting for the other to begin. President Harris solves the dilemma. "Martin, go ahead."

Secretary of State Allison Moore leans forward in her chair.

"Sir, the Israelis are demanding they be allowed to take action against the leaders of Iran. I believe, whether we give our blessings or not, they will launch an attack. I have to say, sir, that I tend to agree with them."

Secretary Moore scoots to the very edge of her chair. "C'mon, Martin. Have you and the admiral really thought this through?"

"Yes, we did, Madam Secretary. I think the positive consequences outweigh the negative by a large margin. This opportunity may not present itself again."

Secretary Moore exhales a sigh and collapses back into her chair. "I guess I'm going to have little say in this."

"Allison, there's a time for diplomacy and there are other times when diplomacy simply won't work. The Iranians don't want a political solution. They want to exert their newfound authority in the region. We can't allow that to happen."

The secretary of state throws her hands up and sinks deeper into her chair.

President Harris turns back to the screen. "Admiral Hickerson, walk me through the plan."

"The Israelis will take the lead, sir, using two of our bunker-buster bombs. We will refuel their aircraft over Iraqi airspace, but our main role will be suppressing any antiaircraft fire once they reach the border with Iran. Tehran is well guarded by a variety of antiair capabilities, including the latest version of ground-to-air missiles. But with an overflight of our own aircraft, we'll knock out their radars and most of the missiles. The Iranian air force is decimated, so we're not expecting any type of air response."

"Is there enough intelligence to confirm the whereabouts of the ayatollah and the Iranian president?"

"I've been assured by the Israelis they know the precise locations, sir. Somehow, they've made contact with their asset in Tehran."

"Martin, did we learn anything about whether the launched missile contained a nuclear warhead?" President Harris says.

"We don't know, sir, and may never know. The remains of the rocket fell to earth within the confines of the Iranian borders, so I don't see any way we'll be able to get a look at it," Secretary of Defense Wilson says.

The President leans forward. "What does your gut tell you, Martin?"

"I believe it is highly probable the bird was carrying a nuclear warhead. Otherwise, why would they launch it? We can only hope they shot their wad with the first shot."

"Thanks, Martin. I agree with you. I don't see them launching a ballistic missile with just a conventional warhead attached." President Harris pauses to take a sip of his coffee. "Admiral, why don't we launch cruise missiles?"

"Tehran is out of our range, sir. We thought for a brief moment about using drones, but that's dicey, sir, with all their antiaircraft capabilities."

President Harris takes another sip of coffee. "How long before the attack could begin?"

"The Israelis are ready, and our air support is ready. All we need, sir, is the go from you."

President Harris leans back in his chair and picks a point on the far wall to focus on. Everyone in the room sits in anticipation. After a few moments, he rocks forward and his gaze returns to the screen on the far wall, "Okay, Admiral. The mission is a go. Martin, will you contact our other allies and inform them of my decision?"

"I will, Mr. President," the SECDEF answers.

"Admiral, a couple of words before you go."

"Yes, Mr. President?"

"Don't miss."

CHAPTER 75

Office of the Supreme Leader

Ayatollah Rahameneiei is making preparations for *dhuhr salat* (the noon prayer) unaware that four Israeli F-15 Silent Eagle aircraft are streaking across the Iranian sky to deliver their payload right into his front room.

He begins his chanting, a mixture of whisper and song, before kneeling on the rug he has owned for most of his life. His old knees pop and grind until they meet the carpet. He leans forward with his forearms touching the ground and continues to chant in his native tongue. As the spiritual leader of his country there is much to pray for.

Before he can finish, a shriek of crashing metal sounds somewhere outside the office door, and he stumbles into a standing position only to be disintegrated when the GBU-28 bunker buster explodes.

Across the way, President Rafsanjani slept through the noon prayer. He was exhausted after his all-nighter in the control center of the Revolutionary Guards watching the progress of the Iranian army under the leadership of a new general. He startles awake when the five-thousand-pound laser-guided bomb crashes through the ceiling outside his bedroom. Hungover with sleep, he can't comprehend what it is, and before his mind can paint a mental picture, the massive explosion obliterates him and his home, along with the other structures built on his compound. The homes that had windows within a mile of his place no longer do, the concussive wave of the blast radiating out until it diminishes to just the faintest wisp of wind.

General Safani, under house arrest in his home a couple of miles away, knows immediately what the explosions are and who had been targeted. He offers a small prayer for their souls before a smile forms on his face.

Chapter 76

The Sanders home

Ruth bursts through the front door with a thin, balding man in his midforties following behind. He's dressed in jeans, sneakers, and a sweatshirt, and has a large black bag in his hand. Not the old-fashioned fold-over doctor's bag, but something similar to the bag Zeke had seen the paramedics retrieve from their ambulance when his father had his heart attack. The doctor calls the children by name before kneeling next to Carl, who is now lying sideways on the sofa.

Despite Carl's appearance the doctor remains calm. He asks Carl to lie on his back and the doctor begins gently probing the chest and stomach area, ignoring his broken jaw to search for more serious internal injuries. Carl moans when the doctor discovers a broken rib, then another.

"There doesn't seem to be any internal bleeding," Dr. Lewis says. "However, he has at least two broken ribs."

Ruth stands next to Zeke, wringing her hands. He slips his arm around her frail shoulders. The children have drifted to the other side of the living room, but still within sight of the doctor as he works on their father.

Satisfied no blood is present in the abdomen, or at least as satisfied as possible without the benefit of a CT scan, Dr. Lewis turns his attention to Carl's jaw. He works his fingers across the left side of Carl's face, using his touch to determine where the fracture is. He turns to his bag of supplies and withdraws a syringe and a small vial of medicine.

"Carl, I'm going to give you a shot of Demerol, a painkiller, so I can set your jaw. Without having access to an X-ray, I can't be certain the jaw is not fragmented. But it feels solid." He glances over his shoulder at Ruth. "How much does he weigh?"

Ruth stutters out her best guess. "Maybe one-ninety? Is that close, Carl?"

Carl moans and nods.

Dr. Lewis draws the liquid into the syringe. "I need to put this in the deep muscles of your butt because I don't want to risk a subcutaneous injection. Ruth, would you mind unfastening his pants and pulling them down enough to expose his bottom?"

Ruth, relieved to have something to do, walks around the sofa and slips her hands to Carl's belt. With some light back-and-forth tugging she exposes his butt enough for Dr. Lewis to sink the needle.

"Carl, I'm going to give the medicine a moment or two to take effect. What I'm going to do is called a closed reduction—basically I'm going to reposition the jaw back to its normal, functioning position. A surgeon would perform what's called a maxillomandibular fixation, where he would surgically place pins into bone and wire your mouth shut. But it's no longer a normal world, and I don't have any way of fixating the jaw, so we will need to develop some sort of sling which will immobilize the jaw while it heals."

At this point Carl's breathing has slowed considerably. The doctor reaches out and manipulates the broken jaw, repositioning it so that it no longer hangs askew. Holding Carl's jaw closed, Dr. Lewis glances up at Ruth. "Would you grab a clean T-shirt so we can make a sling?"

Ruth hurries down the hall and quickly returns with the requested item and hands it across.

"Ruth, hold his jaw closed for a moment, please," Dr. Lewis says.

Ruth complies and the doctor removes a pair of scissors from his bag and quickly cuts through the material, discarding the sleeve and neck portions. He folds the remaining material in half and leans forward to put the sling under Carl's chin before tying it off on top of his head.

"He needs to wear this sling continuously for the next four to six weeks. He will be restricted to a liquid diet. Normally I would suggest protein shakes, but any type of broth, or water with any type of ground-up protein is fine."

Doctor Lewis reaches into his bag and retrieves another vial. "Ruth, is he allergic to penicillin?"

"No. Well, at least not that I know of."

"My supply of antibiotics is limited. All I have is just some old-fashioned penicillin. But it should provide enough coverage to prevent infection." He pulls on the plunger and the milky white liquid fills the body of the syringe. Choosing a spot on the other side of Carl's still-exposed butt, he plunges the needle deep and slowly depresses the plunger.

"What about his broken ribs?" Ruth asks.

"Not much can be done for those. You can wrap his chest tightly to reduce the discomfort, but they'll need to heal on their own time schedule, maybe six weeks before they're no longer unbearable."

Carl has passed into dreamland as Dr. Lewis carefully

disposes of the used needles and syringes before standing. He slips the heavy bag over his shoulder.

"How can I ever thank you, Gary?" Ruth says.

Dr. Lewis waves his hand. "Don't worry, Ruth. These are trying times and we need to do these kinds of things for one another if we are to survive."

Zeke follows the doctor to the door. "Doc, can I have a quick word?" They step out on the porch and Zeke introduces himself.

"How long before he can ride a horse?" You would have thought Zeke had asked how long before Carl can blast off to the moon.

"I'm sorry?" a befuddled Dr. Lewis says.

Zeke explains the situation.

Dr. Lewis brushes his hands across the razor stubble on his cheeks. "It'll depend on his tolerance for pain. But I would allow him at least a week to recuperate before even attempting."

Zeke's disappointed with the answer. "Thanks, Doc. Is there anything I can do to repay you?"

"No need," he says, turning for the steps down to the sidewalk. He pauses and turns back. "Are you the Zeke Marshall who builds those fabulous tables?"

Zeke's turn for a surprise. "Yeah, that's me. Or at least was when we still had electricity. How did you know I made tables?"

"Because we own one, or did. One of the most beautiful tables I had ever seen, but I was none too pleased with the wife when I found out how much it had cost. Unfortunately, we had to chop the table up for firewood."

Zeke's face sags with regret, but an inspiration strikes him. "Tell you what, Doc, when the power comes back on, I'm building you and your wife another table free of charge. I've been saving this beautiful, figured walnut for a special purpose, and I think I just found a use for it."

"Terrific. I would like that very much. Once I recuperated from the sticker shock, I came to appreciate your craftsmanship."

"We have a deal, Doc. Thanks again."

"You're welcome, and I look forward to having another one of your tables grace our dining room." He turns down the sidewalk and disappears into the darkness.

Chapter 77

The White House Situation Room

Everyone is reassembled in the Sit Room after a four-hour break. President Harris used his time to have breakfast with his wife. No tryst was involved, but it was pleasant nonetheless, even with the ongoing mission weighing heavy on his mind. He glances over at the SECSTATE and can tell from her demeanor that she is still bristling with resentment. President Harris leans forward and drums his fingers on the table. "Can we get the admiral and Secretary Wilson on-screen?"

It takes a moment for the two to appear on-screen. "Admiral, were we successful?"

"I believe we were, sir. Video from the Israeli gun cameras shows massive damage to both areas where the ayatollah and the president of Iran were believed to be. We're intercepting radio chatter out of Tehran, hoping for confirmation. It may be a while, sir, before we know for certain."

Someone steps into the frame and hands the secretary of defense a piece of paper.

"Sir, if I may interrupt," the SECDEF says.

"Go ahead, Martin."

"I've just received a cable from the commander aboard Strike Group One. They report the Iranian troops are now in full retreat."

Those in the Situation Room cheer.

"Hopefully, that answers our question, Admiral," the President says over the din.

"It's a good sign we were successful. How would you like to handle the retreat, sir?"

"Allow them an unfettered retreat. Let them go home to their families," President Harris says, "but maintain position of the three strike groups."

"Will do, sir. Congratulations."

"The congratulations go to you and our troops along with the Israelis, Admiral."

The large screen fades to black. "Allison, what can we expect out of Iran? Who do you think is going to try to fill the void?"

Allison shuffles through the mass of paper in front of her. "My bet is General Safani, sir, at least on an interim basis until they can sort out who the next supreme leader is going to be."

"You don't think the progressives in Iran have enough power to shoot down the possibility of another religious zealot ruling with an iron fist?" President Harris says.

"Unknown, sir. That was my point before we assassinated the current leadership." She takes a deep breath. "Sorry, sir, that was out of line."

"It's all right, Allison. Do you see any way the Iranians will move toward a more democratic process?"

"Anything's possible, Mr. President. I think that should be our thrust going forward."

"I agree. Isaac, any chance we can take advantage of the confusion to get a look at their nuclear program?"

"Interesting point, sir," replies the director of the CIA. "I believe it's damn well worth a try."

"I do, too. Work with the Israelis and make it happen."

"I'm on it, sir," the director says as he pushes away from the table.

President Harris leans back and inhales a deep breath. "Let's move on to another matter. I would like an update on the progress to restore electricity. Can we get Donald Carter on-screen?"

From his office in the Federal Emergency Management Agency at 500 C Street, an obviously weary Director Carter appears on the screen.

"Don, how's the progress on power restoration?" President Harris says.

"Slow, sir. Extremely slow. We aren't able to find a manufacturer who has the capacity to build new transformers. Our agency has located what few are stockpiled, but transporting them is another issue altogether. Truck transportation is a no go, so we're exploring rail options. But we still need to get the transformers to the railhead somehow. We're talking of items that weigh in excess of four hundred thousand pounds and a normal railway car can't haul them. Frankly, sir, the whole thing is a logistical nightmare of epic proportions."

The President's face glimmers with faint hope. "How many spare transformers did you discover?"

"We found five, sir. But they will only interface with the grids along the West Coast, which leaves a large majority of the country still in the dark."

The look of hope on the President's face transitions to anger. "Is no one in the United States capable of making these damn things?"

"Maybe two or three companies, sir. A majority of our transformers have been imported from overseas, mainly from South Korea."

"Can't the U.S. manufacturers ramp up production?"

"It's a catch-22, sir. They need electrical power to run

the plants and that doesn't exist. The three main plants are located in the southeastern United States where there are no available spare transformers."

"Can we not supply them with military-grade generators to get their plants up and running?"

"Most of the military's largest generators are deployed to Afghanistan, Mr. President. We did find several in the states and we're working hard to get them on location, but even then, they'll only be able to supply enough electricity to operate a small portion of those plants."

"Is there nothing else we can do?"

"We're working every angle we can, sir. It's just going to take time," Director Carter says.

"How much time, Don?"

"Two or three years is the most likely scenario."

The President sighs. "This is priority one, Don. I want every available asset our country has devoted to building or acquiring new transformers."

"We're doing everything we can, sir."

Silence fills the room as the image of the director of FEMA fades from the screen.

"Allison, what's the status of the South Koreans?" President Harris says to the secretary of state.

"About the same as ours, sir. They upgraded their electrical grid over the last two decades, using our system as a model. Most likely any transformers they are able to build will be for their own use."

"So every man for himself?" His question doesn't elicit an answer.

Chapter 78

The home of Dr. Samuel Blake

Drs. Samuel Blake and Kaylee Connor have exhausted most of the food supply in Sam's home. Now they're hungry, but not a desperate hunger—yet. Kaylee, unaware her parents lie murdered in an abandoned medical building in New York City, is in an unusually good mood, considering the circumstances. She's sitting on the sofa thumbing through an old copy of *Astronomy* when Sam returns to the living room carrying a rifle. He's dressed in camouflage coveralls and a camouflage hat.

She looks up and laughs. "Let me guess. Elmer Fudd?"

"Not rabbit hunting. I'm going to bag us a deer." He props the rifle against the wall and takes a seat on the sofa. He works his fingers through his long, bushy beard.

"You look more like a swami. I don't think I knew you were a deer hunter. Or any kind of hunter, for that matter."

"Does that change your perception of me?"

She puts a chipped black nail to her lip. "I'm not a big fan of killing animals, but I have to say you're rockin' that camo look."

"I'm not really much of a hunter. I haven't been hunting in twenty years—probably the last time that rifle was fired."

Kaylee rests a hand on his thigh. "I thought we were living off the fruits of love."

Sam covers her hand with his. "I don't think love is going to fill our stomachs. It fills everything else I need—oh God, does it—but as someone once said: we can't live on love alone." Their playful silliness is a welcome relief from the drudgery.

"Do you have any bullets for that thing?"

"I think so. Somewhere in the garage. Or used to be. Might take me a while to find them."

"I'm going with you."

"To the garage?"

"No, I'm going hunting with you."

"I thought you just said you didn't approve of hunting animals?"

"I don't for those people who hunt just for sport. But if we're on the verge of starving to death, I can make an exception."

"You get dressed while I go find the ammunition."

Kaylee jumps off the couch to dress like they were going out on a date in town as Sam steps out the door and into the cold garage. It's large enough to hold three cars, but currently holds none. He and Kaylee had abandoned both of their cars at the Space Weather Prediction Center. The shelving against the far wall is stacked with reminders of a past life: an electric leaf blower, a trickle charger for car batteries, a drill and a power sander, and a couple of space heaters.

Sam walks over to the cabinets above his workbench and clicks on the headlamp he had retrieved from the kitchen. He begins pawing through drawers in search of the 30-30 cartridges he remembers seeing at some point over the last five years. He climbs on top of the workbench and searches through a couple of wall cabinets and finds them at the very back of a cabinet filled with yard chemicals. The box, oily from some spilled chemical, disintegrates in his hand, scattering bullets across the garage floor. He climbs down and scoops a handful of the dull brass and stuffs them in his pocket.

He reenters the house to find Kaylee in the kitchen, dressed in one of his old coats and a pair of old ski pants. The pants are about seven inches too long and her hands are buried somewhere in the sleeves of the coat.

"You look like a scarecrow. I'm glad we're going where we won't be seen."

Kaylee pirouettes with her arms wide. "Don't like the new look?" She stops and plants a hand on her hip. "Did you find the bullets?"

"Yeah, I did. Ready for hunting?"

"Aren't you missing your checkered hat, Mr. Fudd?"

Sam slaps her on the ass as he passes. "C'mon, silly wabbit."

He pulls on his heavy coat and leads them out the side entrance of his home. Most of the snow has melted under the bright sun, but there are still patches of white remaining in the deeper shadows. Sam's house sits at the base of a tall hill, the Front Range to the Rocky Mountains that stretch three thousand miles across two countries. Both are sucking air not long after starting up the hill. They're soon shedding jackets as they labor upward at a fifteen-degree angle. Sam's base layer is saturated with sweat, and he glances over to see Kaylee suffering the same fate.

"How . . . much . . . further?" Kaylee says.

"Don't know. First time I've been up here." He gives Kaylee a smile and she replies with a scowl. They're silent the remainder of the way until topping the hill many minutes later.

"Break?" Kaylee says, collapsing onto the surface of a large boulder. Sam walks over to join her.

Kaylee brushes the damp hair from her face. "Is Bambi going to come to us or how does this work?"

Sam squints up at the sun. "This late in the day, we need to find a water hole and catch them coming in." He scans their surroundings. "There's a creek down there. Probably be the best spot to hole up. The good news is it's all downhill to the creek."

"I hear a *but* coming."

"Well, it's uphill on the way back. And, hopefully, we'll be loaded down with deer meat."

"Great," Kaylee says. She pushes off the rock and begins walking across the ridge and Sam hurries to catch up. Instead of going straight down the backside of the large hill, they wind their way down, walking across the face then back, slowly descending to the small valley.

"Try not to make any noise," Sam whispers to her as he draws up close. He grabs a clump of grass and tosses it up into the breeze. "We need to be downwind of them, but I have no idea which direction they'll be coming from."

"What if we stay here?" Kaylee whispers. "The wind is in our faces and we can watch both sides of the stream from here. Can you shoot that far?"

"I think so. That's a good idea. I knew I would make a hunter out of you."

She punches him in the arm. They work their way a little lower until they come to a rock outcropping where they take up position. Sam grabs a water bottle from his coat pocket and offers the water to her first. She guzzles a little more than half and hands the rest back to him.

"It's so beautiful out here," Kaylee whispers.

"It is, isn't it? We should hike up here more."

Kaylee gives him an angry glare. "I didn't necessarily

say it had to be this exact spot, Sam. We can see almost the same thing from your back deck. A lot easier than climbing that damn hill again."

He smiles. "It'll probably be a while before the deer trickle in."

They lie down beside each other faceup, staring at the cottony clouds racing across the blue sky.

"How do you think this is going to end up?" Sam says while still staring at the sky.

"You mean me and you, or the world in general?"

"Both, I guess."

"It ends how it ends, Sam. I know you're a planner, that you like to have a plan for what happens in the next hour, the next day, and so on and so on. But it's not that way anymore. We don't know what's going to happen. As for you and me, our relationship continues until it ends."

"Can you really look at the world that way?"

"Sure. Remember what the tattoo along my side says? 'Live like there's no tomorrow'? That's more true now than ever." She turns to face Sam. "I love spending time with you, Sam. Hell, the sex is fantastic, but how can we plan for tomorrow if we can't conceive what tomorrow will be?"

"You're philosophical to still be relatively young. I thought wisdom came with age."

"Don't get hung up on the age thing, Sam. And quit trying to plan out your life. Let's just take it a day at a time."

Sam turns to meet her gaze. "I don't know if I can overcome my anal side." He turns back to the sky.

"We'll work on it."

The next few moments neither speaks, each enjoying the panoramic view.

Kaylee rises up to shimmy out of the ski pants. She's

now down to a pair of Sam's old gym shorts and a T-shirt. "Why did I wear these things anyway?"

"You'll be glad you have them when the sun goes down." Their lids grow heavy from the warmth of the sun and, with their bodies tired from exertion, they doze for a while.

Sometime later, the sun is lower in the sky when Kaylee awakens and leans over to kiss Sam. "Hey, sleepyhead, are the deer going to announce themselves or should we be on the lookout?"

Sam stirs awake, smiling. "Seen anything?"

"No, I fell asleep, too," Kaylee whispers. They switch positions and rotate over onto their stomachs, allowing them a 180-degree view of the small stream.

"Movement on the left," Kaylee whispers.

Sam levers a shell into the chamber and sights down the rifle. A doe and two fawns break from the cover of the trees. Kaylee covers her ears, bracing for the shot. But Sam lowers the weapon unfired.

"I can't do it," he whispers. "I can't orphan those two babies."

Kaylee leans in and kisses his cheek. The doe and two fawns walk to the small creek and drink their fill before moving on, presumably to bed down for the night. Sam continues to scan the area around the creek but grows discouraged as the light begins to fade.

Kaylee reaches over and taps his arm, pointing to the right with her other hand. A big buck comes sauntering in from the other side of the creek.

"What happens if that's the daddy?" Sam whispers.

"He's done his job, then. Besides, I'm hungry."

Sam lines up the sights, leading the buck and trying to account for the downward angle of his shooting position. He takes a deep breath and squeezes the trigger. The hammer snaps down on a misfire. The big buck perks his ears up and Sam hurriedly ejects the dud and levers in a new round. Sight. Breath. Squeeze the trigger. He flinches when the rifle roars in his hand. The buck races away.

"Damn it," Kaylee shouts, jumping to her feet as if she were going to chase him down on foot.

"I hit him. I know I did. Let's go look." They race down the hill and jump across the small stream.

"Look," he says, pointing at a trail of blood. "I knew I hit it."

"Where the hell did it go, then?"

"Sometimes they'll bound away if it's not a killing shot. But I think I hit him close enough to the heart that he can't get far." They follow the trail of blood into a patch of thorns and find the deer lying on its side, snorting in pain. Sam calmly cocks the rifle, works through the brush toward the front, and fires a round through the head.

"How the hell are we going to get this thing home?"

"I'm going to butcher it here and then we'll take all we can carry. Whatever we leave won't be here in the morning, so we need to get all we can."

Sam draws a knife from the scabbard at his belt and spends the next two hours butchering the deer while Kaylee watches from afar. With nightfall the temperature drops twenty degrees but the work keeps him warm. Kaylee, on the other hand, is back in her ski pants and coat but is still shivering.

"Gather some wood and I'll build us a fire," Sam says.

Kaylee disappears downstream and soon comes stumbling back, her arms loaded with deadfall branches. Sam lays his knife aside and forms a small fire ring out of rock and lays in some kindling. He strikes the lighter, the one he remembered to bring only at the last minute, and uses a clump of dead leaves to get the kindling to ignite.

Sam returns to the deer and strips out one of the loins. Once the fire is going, he spears the meat with a stick and, using two small Y-shaped branches, centers the meat over the fire. The smell of the cooking venison ratchets up their hunger.

Sam returns to butchering the rest of the deer while the meat sizzles over the fire. He strips off as much of the hide as he can and uses it to bundle the remaining cuts of deer meat. He twists the hide at both ends, creating a pair of handles. The weather has turned colder still and their breath steams in a vaporous fog. He removes the tenderloin from the fire and uses a boulder for a cutting board as he quickly slices the meat into equal portions. Kaylee hops from foot to foot until he finishes. They moan with pleasure as the warm, tender venison fills their empty stomachs.

Kaylee wipes a dribble of juice from her chin. "Why don't we stay here by the fire tonight? It'll give the meat a chance to freeze."

"Can't. The smell probably has every bear in two counties headed this way."

Kaylee whirls around, searching the darkness.

CHAPTER 79

The Rocky Mountain foothills, Boulder

Their labored breathing sounds like an approaching freight train as Sam and Kaylee climb the hill on the return journey. Although it's cold, both are drenched with sweat. Sam calls a halt and windmills his arms to loosen them up while Kaylee collapses to the ground and moans.

"Hey, Boy Scout, why didn't we bring a wagon or something to haul the meat back?"

"One, I don't have a wagon. And two, pulling a wagon over this terrain would be nearly impossible. You'd be cussing the damn thing before we got ten feet."

Kaylee laughs. "You're probably right. How long you think this meat will last us?"

Sam pulls the last of their water bottles from his pack. "A month or two if we can salt it or get lucky and keep it frozen. We'll have to play it by ear." He takes a small swig before passing the bottle to Kaylee.

Kaylee groans. "So we're going to have to do this again?"

"That depends on the power situation. But if it's as bad as we surmised, we'll have many of these trips to look forward to."

Another groan from Kaylee. She takes a final small drink from the bottle and passes the remainder back to Sam. He drains it and stuffs the dead soldier back into his pack.

"Let's move out."

Kaylee stands and salutes. "Yes, sir." They each grab one side of the deer hide and shuffle on.

"Let's shoot over to Pine Needle Road. Make the going a little easier."

"I'm all over easy," Kaylee says.

Sam steers them a little south and within ten minutes they're walking easier on smooth asphalt. He turns to Kaylee and smiles. "Now we could use that wagon."

"I got your wagon."

After two more brief rest stops they come to the clearing at the back of Sam's house. The waning moon provides enough illumination to keep them from tripping over the field of stray boulders as they hump the remaining three hundred yards. They drop the load of deer meat on the deck and sag to the steps.

Snowflakes float from the sky, melting upon contact with their overheated bodies.

"I guess we made it just in time," Sam says.

"We were lucky. We should probably be a little more observant about the weather conditions in the future. Wouldn't want to be caught out there in a big snowstorm."

The rate of snowfall increases. "You're right. We got so used to hearing the five-day forecast on the tube we just took the weather for granted."

"You need to bone up on your Boy Scout skills, Dr. Blake."

"I know enough to teach you a thing or two, Dr. Connor."

They laugh as they stare upward, the snowflakes caressing their faces.

The click-clack of a shotgun round being chambered shatters the quiet.

"Who's there?" Sam says.

No answer. Kaylee scoots a little closer to Sam and whispers out the side of her mouth, "Where's the rifle?"

"Deck," Sam whispers.

Exhausted and sore, he experiences a flash of intense anger. "Either shoot us or show yourself, you gutless bastard."

A shuffle of feet, then the click of a flashlight. A bright cone of white light momentarily blinds Sam and Kaylee. Sam raises his hand to shield the light from his eyes. "Who's there?"

"It's me, Doc."

"George?"

"Who's George?" Kaylee whispers. Sam shushes her with the wave of his hand.

"What's going on, George?" Sam strains his vision to see beyond the light. "Why do you have a shotgun pointed at us?"

The light pans to the ground. Kaylee takes advantage of the distraction to slink up to the top step and roll over onto the deck. She crabs in the dark, in a desperate search for the rifle.

"George, would you mind lowering the shotgun?"

"Can't, Doc."

"Just tell mc what's going on."

George walks a little closer, and in the wash of the flashlight, Sam notices he's limping. He's pushing his midseventies, but Sam can't recall ever seeing him limp.

"Are you hurt?"

"A little. But Janey is suffering from some type of infection. I need that meat, Sam. The protein will be a boost to her system."

"I'd be glad to share some of the venison with you."

George pans the flashlight back up, blinding Sam again. "Where'd your girlfriend go?"

The snick of a rifle bolt sliding home. "I'm right here, asshole. Drop the shotgun."

George takes a step closer, the shotgun barrel pointing directly at Sam's chest. "Sam, we can't survive without that food. We're in a desperate state. Madam, would you please place the rifle on the ground? I don't want to hurt my friend, but desperate people do desperate things."

"Then consider me desperate," Kaylee says in a menacing voice. She steps down to the second step, the rifle tucked tight to her shoulder.

Sam holds up both hands in opposing directions. "Both of you put your guns down. We can work this out."

Kaylee takes another step down. "George, you kill him, then I kill you. Then your wife will starve to death. Is that bloody heap of meat worth three lives?"

No more than six feet now separates the two guns. Killing range for a blind man.

Sam works to keep his voice calm. "George, you're a professor of history. You know as well as I that we must depend on one another during times of crisis. How many times have you emphasized that fact to your students when discussing some of the greatest calamities in our nation's past?"

The shotgun barrel lowers ever so slowly.

"Kaylee, lower your weapon, please."

"Not until he does, Sam. He might have been a professor but he's out of his fucking mind right about now."

Sam says in a gentle voice, "George, you can take as much meat as you need. We can always go hunt for more." He turns to glance at Kaylee in the wash of the light. The rifle is unwavering in her grasp.

A moan of despair escapes from George as the shotgun barrel swivels toward the ground. Kaylee takes two steps and puts the barrel of the rifle to his temple.

Sam lurches to his feet and pushes the barrel away before wrapping an arm around George's narrow shoulders. "Kaylee, take the shotgun and put that damn rifle away."

Sam leads George over to one of the steps leading to the deck and helps him down. He glances back to see Kaylee with the shotgun in one hand, but the rifle is riding against her hip, still pointed in George's direction. He steps in front of George, placing himself between the two sudden adversaries.

"Kaylee, would you mind getting a bag from the kitchen?"

"You're going to give up the meat we busted our asses hauling back here?"

Sam turns and fists his hands, ready to lash out. But her trembling arms and false bravado force a pause. "Please?"

As though reacting to a hypnotist snapping his fingers, Kaylee's posture relaxes and she exhales a deep breath. She retreats inside as Sam sits next to George, who's now sobbing.

Sam wraps an arm around his stooped shoulders. "Do you have any antibiotics at home?"

George swipes at a tear and shakes his head.

"I have some, but I can't give you all of it. You understand, right?"

George nods. "Anything would be a help." He rakes both of his knobby hands across his cheeks. "Listen, Sam, I don't—"

Sam puts his hand on George's forearm. "You were right. We are in desperate times. But if we can work together we might just survive."

Kaylee returns with a black garbage bag. Sam unfurls it and loads in a good portion of the venison before handing the bag to George. “Hold on—I’ll find some antibiotics.” Sam disappears inside, leaving the two would-be killers alone.

“I’m very sorry for my actions,” George says, looking at his feet.

“All you had to do was ask. Sam is such a softy he’d have probably given you the whole damn deer.”

George chuckles, then sticks out his hand. “I hope you can forgive me.”

Kaylee shakes hands. “You’re already forgiven. I’m not the type to hold grudges.”

Sam returns with a small box of Augmentin. “This is a five-day supply. Hopefully it will be enough to get Janey over the hump.”

George pushes to his feet, takes the offered drugs, and reaches for the bag of venison. “I’m so very sorry.”

“Do you want your shotgun back?” Sam says.

“Why don’t you hang on to it for a while.”

George retrieves his flashlight and lugs the heavy bag around the corner of the house. Kaylee and Sam drag the remaining meat into the garage and slide the door home. Sam begins stripping the bloody clothes from his body. Kaylee stands aside, watching him strip down to nothing, but his days of feeling uncomfortable in front of her have come to an end. Kaylee glances down to see her own clothes covered in blood. She strips down to her panties and bra and each takes turns washing up in a bucket of cold meltwater.

“I think I see some blood on your bra and panties,” Sam says.

Kaylee looks down, shrugs her shoulders, and strips off the last remaining garments. They walk quickly into the house and climb under the large overfilled comforter draped over the sofa.

Sam takes Kaylee's still-trembling hand in his. "Would you have really shot George?"

"Two weeks ago—not on your life. But today, you bet your ass."

CHAPTER 80

En route to Oklahoma

A full week has passed since Carl's encounter, and Zeke's finally making preparations to leave. Unfortunately, he forgot to bring saddles for the two mares and had spent most of the week trying to fashion something out of the cargo carriers he had built for the trip down. With a sufficient number of blankets, he's made riding passable, though not extremely comfortable for Ruth, Carl, and the kids.

The food his mother had packed was depleted within a couple of days and Zeke had scoured the urban landscape for any type of food. They've dined on squirrel and rabbit, supplemented with a goose he snared off the lake at the country club down the road. All of it cooked on Carl's state-of-the-art gas grill that Zeke had to gut so he could build a wood fire. Noah and Emma didn't much care for the squirrel or the rabbit, but they feasted on the goose meat.

A smudge of orange is just appearing on the horizon as Ruth uses her key to lock the front door of their home. They stand as a group on the front lawn and stare at their home, as if posing for a painting, while Zeke tamps down his impatience to be under way. Finally, after Ruth wipes the tears from her eyes, they all walk over to where Zeke's waiting, the reins of the three horses in his hand.

"Carl, I'm going to put Noah on with me until we see how well you tolerate the movement of the horse. Ruth, you and Emma are going to ride Ruby, and Carl, you're riding Tilly."

Zeke couldn't find anything in their garage to make any stirrups that wouldn't irritate the hell out of the horses so he's lashed a step stool to Murphy's back for later down the road. Right now, he uses a five-gallon bucket from the garage for Carl and Ruth to use for mounting the horses. Ruth stands on the bucket and throws her leg over Ruby's back and Zeke hands Emma up to her. He moves the bucket to Tilly and helps Carl into the makeshift saddle. Noah uses one of the saddle stirrups, and with Zeke's help, gets situated aboard Murphy, sitting in front of his uncle.

Ruth is comfortable on a horse, but he's not sure about Carl. "You want me to clip a lead to your horse, Carl, or can you handle her?"

"I'll be fine," he mutters through his closed mouth.

"Tell me if you change your mind." Zeke gently nudges Murphy forward and they fall in behind him. Zeke silently repeats the word *patience* as they trudge slowly up the street. He glances back frequently to make sure his party is keeping up and to see if Carl has passed out from the pain. They're troupers and they make better progress than he had hoped for. Along the way they stop for frequent breaks, to give everyone a chance to stretch their legs and to give the horses a breather. Ruth and her family hadn't ventured beyond their neighborhood during the crisis and they're astounded at the number of cars and trucks abandoned in the middle of the road.

Sometime later they close in on the place where Zeke

had shot two people. He calls a halt to resituate everyone. Noah moves over with his father, leaving Zeke free to operate. He doesn't tell them what had happened but they can sense his tenseness. He rakes his hand across his hip and loosens the Glock.

"Carl, you think you can manage if we have to run the horses a little?"

He nods and wraps one of his arms around Noah in front of him.

Ruth's face is pinched with concern. "What's wrong, Zeke?"

"Nothing. But I want to be prepared."

Zeke remounts and tells everyone to stay close. He scans from one side of the road to the other. As they near the car parked parallel to the road, he's relieved to see someone has retrieved the bodies. Dark stains form amoebas in the asphalt and Zeke's eyes are glued to the apartment complex. It's the middle of the day and he sees only one other person up and about. They pass unmolested and Zeke wiggles his shoulders to loosen the tension.

By the time they reach Beltline Road the sun is riding low in the sky. Zeke had been hoping to reach Summer's house before dark, but his hope fades with the light. Everyone, horses included, is exhausted. As they cross Beltline Road, he spots a golf course off to the east with a small stream running through the middle. He steers Murphy in that direction and turns in the saddle to make sure the rest are following. The area around the golf course is heavily wooded, he assumes to keep out prying eyes. *What could possibly go on during a round of golf that would concern the members enough to spend a fortune planting trees around the entire perimeter?* It made no sense to him, but he's cursing them as he searches for a way in. Maybe that's why, he reasons—to keep the unprivileged out. He finds a cut into the trees and he pushes Murphy in that direction. It's a service entrance of some sort blocked by a single iron-bar gate. There's just enough space on one side to squeeze the horses through.

He dismounts and signals the others to do the same. He puts a finger to his lips and ties Murphy's reins to the gate and steps a little deeper into the shadows to reconnoiter the area. There's a house fairly close, but he doesn't see any activity. Across the once-manicured fairway he spies a thicket of trees next to the small creek. Perfect. Houses line the golf course on both sides and he takes a moment to watch for movement.

Not seeing anyone out and about, he retraces his steps and unties the reins, then whispers to the others, "There's a house close on the right, but I didn't see anyone. But houses are all along the golf course. I'm going to lead us as far in as possible to put some distance between those houses and us. Take it nice and slow and be as quiet as you can."

He leads Murphy across the overgrown fairway and into the thicket of oak trees and persimmon bushes. He picks a spot equidistant to the surrounding homes and waits for the rest of the crew to catch up. They relieve the horses of their burdens and Zeke leads them down to the creek to drink. Once the horses have drunk their fill, he strings a rope between a pair of trees and clips the horses' leads to them, freeing them to munch on the still-green grass.

The night is nearly full dark by the time he's finished the chores.

"Uncle Zeke, can we start a fire?" Noah says, shivering.

"We better not, little buddy. Too many houses around." Zeke unfurls a blanket and wraps it around Noah's shoulders.

Ruth and the kids appear to be holding up well but Carl looks absolutely miserable. "How you holding up, Carl?"

"Fine" is his curt answer, but Zeke can tell he's in pain. They had been putting some of the deer jerky into a pot of water and heating it up to make a broth for Carl to drink through his straw, but without a fire there will be no broth tonight. He grabs his canteen and gives it a shake.

"I'm going for water."

"Where are you going to get water?" Ruth says.

"You know Dad. He's always good for something unusual," Zeke says.

His statement puts a smile on his sister's weary face.

"He had some water purification tablets tucked away. I have no idea where he got them, or when, but they're pretty damn handy right now."

"I miss Mom and Dad."

"We're going to see them in a day or two," he says before slipping down to the creek.

He dips his hand in the water and takes a sniff. With their constant need to fertilize their fairways and greens, golf courses are some of the heaviest polluters of waterways. *Don't want the members to be dissatisfied with a lack of lush grass*, Zeke thinks as he dribbles some of the water into his mouth. He walks a little ways away and tugs up a plug of grass. He discovers that most of the course is in Bermuda grass, which means the last application of fertilizer had probably been a couple of months ago. He dumps a few of the tablets into the canteen and returns to the small creek to fill it.

Back at camp, Zeke hands the canteen to Carl first. He pulls the straw from his pocket and pops it in and takes a long drink. Zeke shakes out four ibuprofen tablets from the first aid kit and hands them to Carl. He has to feed them into his mouth one at a time to keep his jaw from moving. When he's finished he passes the canteen to Emma for her to drink, then on down the line until it's his turn. The canteen is nearly empty by the time it returns to him. He pops some more purification tablets inside and returns to the creek for a refill.

By the time Zeke returns to camp, Carl is curled up in a blanket, dead asleep. "All right, guys, we have deer jerky for dinner."

After a few groans they all take a hunk of meat and begin chewing. It's not long after their makeshift dinner before everyone falls asleep. Zeke pulls the Kimber from the scabbard and wraps up in one of the blankets. It takes him a while to doze off, but the steady rhythm of the horses munching on grass is enough to send him over the edge.

Zeke is up before daybreak preparing the horses for another day on the trail. He freezes when he spots one of the homeowners walking her dog along the cart trails. But she passes without even glancing in their direction. He's glad the dog hadn't caught the scent of the horses, but the woman's appearance creates a sense of urgency. He kneels next to Ruth, both children snuggled up on either side of her, and gently stirs them awake. Zeke lets Carl sleep for just a bit longer, hoping the extra time will speed his recovery. While Ruth and the children take care of their morning business, he takes the canteen down to the creek to refill it.

When they're close to departing he wakes Carl up. A majority of the swelling has retreated, but Carl's jaw is a mixture of purple and yellow hues. It hurts to look at him. Carl steps behind one of the trees to relieve himself and they mount up. Zeke leads them off the golf course and back to Preston Road, where they turn back north, that much closer to home in Oklahoma.

After several rest stops, they make it to Summer's home sometime around midafternoon. Zeke dismounts, hands the reins to Ruth, and steps up on the porch while removing his hat. She must have heard his footfalls, because the door swings wide.

"Zeke," she shouts as she lunges into his arms. He wraps his arms around her, somewhat surprised by the greeting.

"I didn't think you were coming back," she says, taking a step back.

"We had some difficulties. Okay if we bed down in the barn?"

"No."

Zeke is momentarily stunned by her response. "I thought we agreed—"

She puts her hand to his mouth. "You're not staying in the barn." She looks past his shoulder. "C'mon in."

Chapter 81

The Oval Office

President Harris is at his desk when Chief of Staff Scott Alexander enters the Oval Office. "It's been a pretty good week, considering," Alexander says as he sits in the chair flanking the historic desk.

"Yeah, the old 'Other than that, Mrs. Lincoln, how was the play?' phrase pretty much sums up the week."

"Hey, the Iranian troops are heading home—that's something."

"I suppose you're right, Scott. But there's a hell of a lot more stuff to deal with. What did the South Koreans say?"

"They want about half of next year's total budget to ship the transformers to us."

"Those bastards." President Harris throws his pen on the desk and stands. "After all we've done for that fucking two-bit country?" President Harris begins pacing. "How about we pull every last American troop from their country? Did you ask them that?"

"No, I didn't," Alexander says, watching the President's furious march from one side of the room to the other.

President Harris stops and turns. "How much aid did we give them last year?"

"Offhand, I'd estimate about a billion dollars."

"Well, that stops right this damn minute. If they want to play hardball I'll shut them down before they even get started. I won't let another damn Hyundai or Kia roll off a ship. I'll strangle their damn economy."

"Paul, slow down before you stroke out."

The President stops and shoots Alexander an angry glare before stalking back to his desk.

Alexander waits for the President to sit. "They're just trying to get the most for their product. A product we're in desperate need of. And they know exactly how desperate we are."

"What happened to helping your fellow man? Are the South Koreans immune?"

"Not necessarily. The manufacturer is not a state-owned entity. It's a private business."

"Bullshit, Scott. The South Korean government has their hand in all those businesses. They're just using that for an excuse. Hell, they could take over the whole damn plant based on a national security need. I know how the bastards work." The President stands again and paces another lap around the office.

Scott gives him time to sort through the possibilities. Although President Harris can be a hothead when provoked, he's better known for his well-thought-out reasoning.

"Scott, would you please get President Choi on the phone?"

"You don't want to handle this through the State Department?"

"Hell no. It'll take six months for them to even connect on the phone. I want to talk to him man-to-man."

"Are you sure, sir?"

President Harris stops pacing and turns to face his chief of staff, "I'm sure, Scott."

"Okay, sir," Alexander says as he walks to the phone near the two sofas across the room. He instructs the President's secretary to place a call to the president of South Korea.

"I suppose you don't want an interpreter," Scott says.

"No. He got his master's and Ph.D. from Cambridge. He probably speaks better English than I do."

It takes longer than usual to place the call. Finally, the intercom buzzes. "Sir, President Choi on line one."

President Harris walks to one of the sofas and takes a seat, grabbing the handset on the way down. "Good day, Mr. President, thank you for taking my call."

Scott takes a seat on the opposing couch. He can hear only one side of the conversation, but he cringes during some of the more heated portions of the phone call.

After several minutes, President Harris plays his ultimatum. "Mr. President, I'm thinking of embargoing all future South Korean exports to the U.S."

Scott can overhear the raised voice of South Korea's president from where he's sitting. The President glances over at his chief of staff and raises his eyebrows as the verbal tirade on the other end continues.

President Harris listens, then says, "What was the last portion, President Choi?"

More babble over the phone. When the South Korean president finishes, President Harris says, "Sounds reasonable." More chatter on the other end. "I believe that's reasonable." More chatter. "Thank you, President Choi, for your empathy."

The President glances up and gets an eye roll from Alexander.

"Thank you. I'll talk to you soon."

President Harris replaces the handset.

"Well?" Alexander says.

President Harris smiles. "They'll have four of the largest transformers on a ship within a week."

"That's all?"

"No, there's more. They will ship four of the behemoths a month until our electrical grid has been restored."

"I'll be damned," Scott says. "What did you promise them?"

"Nothing. You were sitting right there listening to my half of the conversation. Did you hear me promise them anything?"

"So he caved at the threatened embargo?"

"Of course. Their country would return back to the rice paddy days if American markets were closed to their products." President Harris walks over to one of the bookshelves and pulls a lever. The bottom portion swings open to reveal a well-stocked bar. "Now, I'd say we've had a decent week. What'll you have, Scott?"

Chapter 82

The Peterson home

Ruth takes an immediate liking to Summer. Zeke doesn't know if it is because of Summer's reaction to his return, or simply a woman thing. Ruth has been by his side through all of the devastation and he knows she has a very tender spot in her heart for her big brother. Whatever the reason, he feels—hell—he doesn't know how he feels. Happy, maybe. For the first time in a long while Zeke feels some type of connection with a woman. Or the situation might be more complex. Maybe he misunderstood the look on Summer's face when she opened the door. He's starting to get a headache from all the thinking.

He leads the horses over to the barn to occupy his mind. He unsaddles Murphy and removes the makeshift saddles from the mares before ripping open a bale of hay. Zeke steps outside to the old hand pump to rinse the golf course residue from the canteen. He refills the canteen, then ducks his head under the chilly stream to wash the road grime from his face.

When he returns to the house he tells Ruth about the water pump and she immediately takes the children out to wash them up. Zeke hands the full canteen to Carl and he eagerly slurps the water through his straw.

"Are the turkeys still around?" he says to Summer, who is standing in the kitchen. Zeke walks closer to her, and she wraps her arms around him from the side.

"I'm glad you came back," she whispers.

His heart is hammering as if he had crossed the finish line of a marathon. "Me, too," he says, glancing down into her green eyes.

She tiptoes up and brushes her lips across his for the first time, sending his heart perilously close to redline. "The turkeys are still around, or they were yesterday. They should be out and about around sundown. I just hope they're not too skittish, having lost a member or two of thoir flock."

"I guess I'll just have to be extra sneaky." Zeke lowers his head for another, longer kiss but the spell is broken when Carl enters the kitchen.

"Orry." Carl smiles sheepishly, or as much of a smile as he can muster with a broken jaw. "Zee, any more jery?"

"You bet. I forgot you didn't get anything for dinner last night. I'll put a pot of broth on for you."

Carl waves over his shoulder as he slinks out of the kitchen.

"What happened to him?" Summer whispers, leaning into him again.

"He went looking for water and ran into some young boys with baseball bats. Broke his jaw and busted a couple of his ribs. But he's tough. He's been a trouper through all the travel."

Summer turns and pulls a pan from the cupboard as Zeke's brain cartwheels with emotion. His hand trembles slightly as he pours water into the pan and adds several strips of the jerky before carrying it outside to the fire.

The laughter of the children splashing in the cold water drifts on the breeze. Zeke turns in that direction and catches sight of his sister naked from the waist up. He turns away, feeling the blush in his cheeks. Even though Ruth is his sister, he hasn't seen that much of a woman in a very long time.

He moves the jerky around in the pan with an old wooden spoon as his eyes search the field for any sign of the turkeys. Off in the distance he hears an old tom gobble, and his mouth starts to water. While the broth simmers, he slips back into the house.

"Summer, where's the shotgun?"

"Behind the front door. Did you see the turkeys?"

"No, but I heard them." Zeke retrieves the gun and cracks open the breach to make sure a shell is seated. "How many shells?"

"There should be five in there. If you don't bring us a turkey with five shots, you may be sleeping in the barn after all."

Zeke smiles. "I don't think I'll be sleeping in the barn." He quietly makes his way out the door, easing the screen shut so he won't spook the soon-to-be dinner. He slides through the barbed wire fence and stalks across the pasture, pausing every few seconds to listen. He works his way to a small ridge where the land falls away to a small stock pond in the distance. At the peak, he squats down and peers over the ridge. About a dozen turkeys are picking at the acorns under a large oak tree about a hundred yards away. Too far to do any damage with the 12-gauge. Slowly, and as low to the ground as possible, he creeps closer. Turkeys are blessed with incredible eyesight, able to pick up the slightest movement.

He drops to a crawl and after ten minutes of crawling on his stomach through the tall grass he's within shotgun range. He eases the barrel through the waving grass and sights in on the closest birds. The shotgun explodes and the bird drops to the ground as the others start racing away. Zeke jumps to his feet and quickly jacks another shell into the chamber. He sights down the barrel at the fleeing turkeys and squeezes the trigger. Another bird drops. He jacks another shell, but the turkeys have raced out of sight, taking cover in the thick underbrush along the tree line.

He scoops up the two dead birds and begins field dressing them. With two quick slashes of his knife, he reaches in and pulls the entrails out. The warm blood coats his hand, making his grip slippery. He grabs the two birds by their feet and snags the shotgun from the ground.

Summer meets him at the fence and he hands off the shotgun. "No barn for me," he says as he parts the barbed wire and climbs through.

Summer smiles. "I was just providing a little incentive."

His knees weaken at the thought.

Noah and Emma are waiting for him in the backyard. Emma walks up close and stares at the birds in his hand. "What're those, Uncle Zeke?"

"Turkeys. Like what we have at Thanksgiving."

His comment confuses her. "Aren't they s'posed to be white?"

"These are wild turkeys. But they'll taste better than those white ones, I promise. Do you and Noah want to help pull the feathers off?"

She shrugs and puts one small foot atop the other. "I dunno. Are they dead?"

"Well . . . yeah, they are. C'mon, I'll show you how." The children follow their uncle toward the fire.

Summer returns from the kitchen with a large pot and hands it to Zeke. He carries it to the well and fills the pot with water and returns it to the fire. When the water is warm enough, almost boiling, he quickly dunks each turkey to help loosen the feathers. Ruth steps outside and he can tell she's none too happy about Noah and Emma getting dirty again after she had already cleaned them up.

"C'mon, sis. We could use your help."

"Yeah, Mommy, come over," Emma says, already covered with feathers.

Ruth walks over and begins plucking at the feathers. It's not long before all three are giggling and feathers are swirling in the breeze.

Zeke steps away and wipes the feathers from his shirt. "If you guys have this under control, I'm going to wash up."

"Go, Zeke, we've got this handled," Ruth says.

As he's passing the back door Summer reaches out to hand him a bar of soap.

Zeke stops and puts his hands on his hips. "What are you suggesting?"

"Nothing, sir." She giggles as he grabs the soap.

Zeke ducks into the barn and strips down to his boxers. At the pump, he fills a bucket with water. Though the water is freezing cold, it feels good to put some soap on his body after nearly two weeks. He soaks the rag that Ruth had used and carries it into the barn to wash his more private areas and pulls on a pair of jeans and a shirt he's worn only a couple of times. After slipping into his boots he grabs the only luxury items he packed for the trip—a toothbrush and toothpaste. When he finishes washing the road grime from his mouth, he rinses out his filthy clothes and hangs them on a rusty nail in the barn to dry.

From the barn he watches the scene up at the house. Ruth and the kids are laughing as Summer works around the fire. He fingers the locket around his neck, struck momentarily with remorse. He sighs and tucks the enclosed picture of Amelia back under his shirt. By the time Zeke returns to the house, the birds are plucked and Summer is sliding two heavy sticks through each one to hang over the fire.

Ruth blows a feather from her face. "Does Uncle Zeke want to take his adorable niece and nephew back to the well?"

He stammers for a moment, looking at his boots.

"I'm kidding, Zeke. Did you leave the soap down there?"

"Yeah, right at the base of the pump."

As she walks by, she leans in and gives her brother a peck on the cheek. "You smell clean, Zeke. Summer's going to like the new you," she whispers in his ear. She pats him on the butt like he'd just scored a touchdown, then leads the kids back to the well.

The aroma of cooking turkey lures Carl out of the house. "Amn a mells ood," he mumbles. "Ere's Ru?"

Zeke nods toward the barn. Carl walks down to join his family and he's soon down to his boxers, splashing water on the kids. After a short time all four trudge toward the house, shivering.

Summer giggles at the sight. "There's a couple of clean towels in the bathroom. Help yourself." She turns to Zeke. "I think I'll wash up before dinner, too."

Zeke tends the fire, burning through reserves of self-control to not sneak a peek of Summer washing up. He mindlessly stirs the coals and pokes the breast of one of the turkeys to check for doneness. Summer returns, her curly hair dripping water onto her T-shirt.

"I'm going to dry off and set the table."

"Your hair always this curly?" he says for something to say.

Summer holds the screen open and looks back over her shoulder with a playful smile lighting her face. "You don't have a straight-hair fetish, do you?"

"No, ma'am. I'm kinda partial to curly."

"That's good." Summer steps through the door and the screen slaps shut behind her.

A short while later Zeke removes the turkeys from the fire and carries them into the house. Summer and Ruth had set the table with real plates and real cutlery. He slides the turkeys off their spikes and onto a platter. As he carries the platter to the table he tries hard not to stare at Summer, who is dressed in a red, sleeveless dress that hits about midthigh. Ruth is wearing a similar dress, but in navy blue.

Zeke places the turkeys in the center of the table. "I'm sorry, ladies, for not packing a tie. I must say, it's nice to have two beautiful women at the table."

Noah makes a gagging sound and everyone laughs. Summer leans across the table to light the candles and Zeke steals a glimpse of her well-toned thighs only to get caught by his sister. She wags her finger and smiles.

Darkness descends on the plains as the wicks flicker to life, creating a homey scene, complete with shadows dancing along the far wall. Ruth does the honors of carving up the turkeys and she fills everyone's plate, including Carl's. He feeds small pieces of the turkey into his closed mouth, savoring every small, succulent piece. He can't chew but he does move it around in his mouth with his tongue. Emma and Noah dig into the tender breast meat and eat until they can eat no more. Ruth and Summer eat more slowly, savoring every bite. Zeke tries to eat slowly, but his fork is in constant motion between his mouth and the plate.

When everyone has eaten their fill, Zeke strips the remaining meat from the bones and grabs a wire rack to put over the fire. He arranges the turkey meat on the rack so that the fire can evaporate the moisture. Back inside, he places the carcasses into a large pot, empties his canteen over them, and puts the pot on the fire to simmer all night. A broth for Carl's breakfast, with enough to last the rest of the trip.

Ruth clears the table and the kids carry the dishes outside to the wash bucket by the picnic table.

"Leave 'em, kids. We'll wash them up in the morning," Zeke says.

He follows them back into the house, and Summer carries the candles into the living room, where they all collapse into the chairs around the fireplace. The weather has been unseasonably warm, but a chill arrived with the dark. Zeke mounds up some kindling and puts a match to it.

Emma crawls into Ruth's lap and within minutes she's fast asleep. Noah makes it just a bit longer. Ruth and Zeke carry them back to the spare bedroom and tuck them in.

Not much later, Ruth and Carl make their exit, picking the second bedroom next to the children. That leaves one bedroom for two people who don't know each other very well.

"I'll take the couch," Zeke says, sliding over to it. Summer surprises him when she stands from her chair and lies down beside him, propping her head on his chest.

"How are you holding up?" Zeke whispers.

"I miss Aubrey every minute of every day. But I know she's okay with my father and sister." She sniffles and swipes away a lone tear. "I couldn't have chosen two better people to look after my little girl."

Zeke wraps his arm around her. "This can't last forever. I'm sure there are people all over the world experiencing the same thing—a loved one far from home. They'll come home just as soon as they can."

"I know . . . I know. I've told myself the exact thing a thousand times. But that doesn't make the situation any easier."

He wraps one of her hair curls around his finger. "I know it doesn't. I wish that we would all wake up in the morning with the power back on and everything functioning like it has for every other day of our lives." Zeke spiders his fingers through her hair. "Aubrey will come home."

They lie side by side, staring at the fire. After a few moments, Summer stands and reaches for his hand. No words are spoken and no questions are asked as she leads him into her bedroom.

Chapter 83

The Peterson home

Zeke bolts up in bed. Summer reaches her arm out to comfort him. But it isn't a nightmare that wakes him this time.

"I heard something," Zeke whispers. For a moment he's disoriented in his new surroundings.

"I didn't hear anything," Summer whispers back.

The windows are cracked open and a chill has invaded the space. He slides from beneath the covers and pads toward the window. Months in Afghanistan had trained him to be aware of abnormal noises in the night. He slips on his jeans and shirt. In the darkness he fumbles for the hard polymer handgrip of the Glock. Not wanting to risk a flashlight, he searches the floor with his hands. In their haste to remove clothing, Zeke, usually a stickler for proper handling of weapons, can't recall where he placed the gun.

"Where did I put my pistol?" he whispers to Summer.

"Check the nightstand."

One of the horses trumpets a nervous whinny.

"Somebody's after the horses," Zeke says in an urgent

whisper. He yanks the nightstand drawer from off its tracks and the heavy gun clumps to the hardwood floor. He snaps up the pistol and tucks it into his waistband. In two quick strides he's digging through his jacket for the extra magazine and a tactical flashlight that mounts to the bottom rail of the gun.

Summer jumps naked from bed and quickly dresses. "I'll cover you with the rifle."

"Fine, but do it from the house. I don't know how many there are or what the hell they're up to."

Zeke gently raises the window to the stops. Afraid the front and back doors are being watched, he slides through the window and drops to his feet. He creeps toward the front of the house and peeks around the corner, but his visual range is limited to about ten feet. His senses, not as razor sharp as they had once been, but still sharp enough, suggest no one is present. There are none of the telltale signs: no rustle of fabric or the impatient shuffling of feet. The gate hinges to the barn squeal in the night. Zeke ducks low and races to the opposite corner toward the back of the house.

In the anemic wash of the moon, he makes out the silhouette of the three horses being led through the gate by two people. The darkness prevents him from guessing their ages, their sex, and even their size—just two forms leading away *his* horses.

His body surges with anger as he takes the Glock from his waist and seats the flashlight. He stands to his full six foot three and steps around the corner.

He makes it to within ten yards of the horse thieves before they notice that a gun barrel is tracking their escape. Zeke triggers the powerful flashlight and points it directly at their faces. The two men are in their early twenties and, from their appearance, they hadn't bothered to bathe or shave even when the power was on. Both are big and broad, nearly as tall as Zeke, and each is carrying about forty pounds of extra weight. The one on the left has a shotgun riding on his shoulder. Zeke pans the flashlight down and discovers guns tucked into the waistbands of their ragged jeans.

Zeke stalks closer, the Glock held at shoulder height and locked in a two-hand grip. "Let the leads hit the ground and step away from the horses."

The one holding the ropes releases them from his grasp, but neither makes a move to step away. Zeke wants to shoot them where they stand, but the safety of the horses is paramount. With his pistol never wavering, he steps over and gathers up the ropes. With a cluck of his tongue, he leads Murphy and the mares away from the men. There's not much he can do with the horses one-handed, but he quickly wraps the ropes around a fence post.

He takes three steps forward, the pistol fanning a small arc between the two men, the cone of light from the flash-light blinding them with each swing. "I want that shotgun on the ground."

The young punk shrugs and bends down to toss the shotgun on the ground. Something about the shrug seems out of place to Zeke. *These guys haven't said a word and they are nonchalant for having a gun aimed at their heads.*

A niggle of worry tickles the nape of his neck. "Now, using two fingers, I want you to very carefully remove those pistols and toss them over the fence."

Neither man moves.

Zeke takes another step forward. "You can remove your guns or die with them stuck in your pants. The choice is yours, but either way is fine with me."

The men make no move to disarm. Zeke fires a single shot and the man on the left slaps a hand to his ear. Blood seeps between his fingers as the man howls in pain. The smell of cordite hangs in the still, cold air. The horses stomp and thrash until the ropes come free, but they scamper through the open gate and race back to the safety of the barn.

Zeke waits for the man to stop wailing. "I'm usually not one to give warning. The next shot will drill into the center of your forehead. The hollow-point slugs will mushroom on impact and a good portion of the back of your head will disintegrate."

The man to his left moans as they begin to slowly reach for their pistols. "Now, I want you to grab them by the barrels and—"

A high-pitched scream erupts in the darkness. "Uncle Zeke!"

Zeke's stomach plummets and his blood runs cold. But the ingrained army training assumes command. He doesn't whirl at the voice and his gun hand never wavers from the two would-be horse thieves. Both are still holding the butts of their weapons with two fingers.

"Emma, are you okay?" Zeke shouts, berating himself for not checking the surrounding area more closely.

"Uncle Zeke . . ."—her voice is trembling—"there's a strange man here."

A new voice shouts out, "Earl, you and Bobby bring whoever you got on in here. And I don't want any more shootin'. You dumb asses will have half the county headed this way."

"Everything's going to be all right, Emma," Zeke shouts.

The man on the right laughs. "You got that right, cowboy."

A searing anger wells up from the depths of his core. The heartache of the last few years—the loss of his fellow squad members, the agonizing months of recuperation, and the staggering deaths of his wife and unborn child—solidifies into a fiery rage. Zeke explodes forward. He knocks the gun from the man's grip and rams the barrel of his pistol under the man's chin. Without hesitation Zeke pulls the trigger. He whirls toward the other man, who's fumbling to get a firm grip on his pistol. The Glock barks again and the man collapses to the ground.

Ten seconds, maybe fifteen. Zeke sucks in a lungful of air before stalking toward the rear of the house.

"Hey, boys, what's going on out there?" The man's voice is deep and raspy but contains no hint of fear. Zeke's fairly certain the man is older than the other two, not that it matters one whit whether he lives or dies.

With a clock counting down in his head, Zeke races up to the side of the house and takes a quick glimpse around the corner. The dying fire, coupled with the faint moonlight, illuminates enough of the scene for him to see Ruth and Carl along with Emma and Noah bunched together near the fire pit.

Summer is nowhere in sight.

A large, burly man stands at the rear of the group, a shotgun braced against his shoulder. Too close for Zeke to risk a shot. A mixture of fear and cold has Emma and Noah shivering as they stand next to their parents.

The man bellows, "Boys, somebody answer me." His request is met with silence.

Now or never. Zeke tucks his pistol behind his back and steps into the clear. "I'm sorry to say that Earl and Bobby are indisposed."

The shotgun swings his way. He exhales a sigh of relief and slowly approaches the group, meandering farther to the right to draw the shotgun farther from his family.

"Who are you and what did you do to my sons?" The man's finger caresses the trigger as Zeke stalks closer.

"Who I am doesn't matter." Zeke continues his slow pace forward, doing his best to tamp down the rage coursing through his body.

He comes to a stop ten feet from the man. At this range the shotgun would rip through his body from shoulders to ass. "Now, the way I see things is you can die where you stand or, choice two, you can gather up your sorry-ass sons and go back to the hole you crawled out of."

The man tenses. "You sorry mother—"

His head explodes in a red mist as the rifle shot echoes in the darkness. Zeke is moving before the body hits the ground.

A cry of despair and the sound of the rifle clattering to the floor escape from the house.

Zeke thrusts his pistol into Carl's hand. "There might be more. Keep an eye out."

Zeke jerks the screen door open and hurries down the hallway. He turns into the first bedroom and finds Summer sitting on the floor with her back to the wall, her head buried in her hands. Zeke sinks to his knees and takes her in his arms.

"It's not like shooting an animal," she blubbers into his chest.

"No, it's not," he says in a gentle voice. "But you did what you had to do."

She wipes at her tears and pushes him away. Anger flashes on her face. "You intentionally provoked that man."

Zeke drops to his butt and leans his back against the wall. "Maybe I did . . . but I"—he pauses and rubs his hands across his face—"I've seen more than my share of bad men. Men who spend their lives terrorizing others. Men who only take and never give. That man lying in the yard was that type of man."

Summer whirls to face him. "How could you know that?"

"I know from a lifetime of reading people." Zeke expels a heavy breath and reaches for her hand. "If we had simply disarmed him and his sons and sent him on their way they'd come back. Tomorrow, next week, maybe next month, but make no mistake, they would have returned. Life is difficult enough without having to look over your shoulder wondering if every odd noise is an announcement of their reappearance."

Summer turns away. "Did you kill those men trying to steal the horses?"

"Yes."

A cold silence. Zeke rests his head against the wall.

The screen door squeaks open and slaps shut a moment later. Murmuring voices drift down the hall. Zeke drags his legs under him and starts to stand. Summer reaches for his hand and pulls him back down. She rests her head on his shoulder and entwines her fingers with his.

CHAPTER 84

The Oval Office

First Lady Katherine Harris threads her way around the bustling West Wing and enters the Oval Office through the side door connected to the study. Her husband, dressed in a black knit shirt from Congressional Country Club, is hunched over his desk but he glances up as the heels of her boots strike the hardwood floor.

"Surprise," she says. Her trips to the Oval Office are few and far between. Most of their discussions take place in the privacy of their bedroom. But with the upheaval and the fact that they've taken up residence in the Roosevelt Room across the hall, their private time has been compromised.

He tosses the pen on the desk and pushes out of his chair. They meet halfway across the office and wrap their arms around each other.

"Have I told you recently how good your ass looks in a pair of jeans?"

"Not recently, no." She is dressed in jeans tucked into a pair of knee-high boots with a soft cotton red sweater filling out her ensemble. Her face is absent of makeup. With no cameras around, the staff of the White House has stretched casual Friday to include most every other day of the week.

He takes her elbow and steers her toward the opposing sofas. President Harris sits and she cozies up next to him.

"When are we leaving for Camp David?"

"Tomorrow night. We have to slink out of town under the cover of darkness." There's lingering bitterness in his voice.

Katherine scoots up to the edge of the sofa and turns to face her husband. "Paul, I know we've had numerous discussions on the topic, but I want you to send someone to retrieve Juliette and David."

"I thought we decided not to intervene."

"Lord knows our daughter is strong willed, but I can't stop worrying about her. And I love our son-in-law to death, but I don't know how resourceful he is."

"Not being able to put together a bookcase from IKEA doesn't mean he's not handy."

"David is about as handy as a toadstool."

They both chuckle.

The President grasps one of his wife's hands. "What happens if they've left their condo? They could be anywhere in Southern California."

"Where would they go?" Katherine asks. "I could maybe see them camping along the beach, but I have a feeling they haven't gone too far astray. Call it mother's instinct."

President Harris stands and begins pacing, his hand on his chin. "It could take weeks to find them."

"I don't care. I want our only child here with us."

"What if they refuse to come?"

"For all of her independence, I'm betting a week without running water and minimal food has changed her outlook."

The President stops pacing and turns to face his wife. "Your instincts are well honed."

"Why do you say that?"

"Because I have a small squad of soldiers from the California National Guard keeping an eye on them. Juliette and David are camped in a park down the block from their condo building."

"Why didn't you tell me?"

"One, I know they're fine. And two, I wanted to see how long your resolve held."

"Damn it, Paul. Just because you're the President doesn't give you the right to withhold family secrets from me." She stands from the sofa and walks to her husband. "Are you going to bring them home?"

"There are some logistics to work out. And there are some political issues we need to overcome. I don't want to be accused of using scarce resources for personal matters."

Katherine's cheeks turn red. "I don't give a damn about politics. I want—" Her tirade is interrupted by a soft knock on the door to the study. They both turn in that direction.

Chief of Staff Scott Alexander steps into the room. The First Lady takes three angry steps in his direction and raises her finger to his chest. "Out, right this damn minute, Scott."

A voice behind the door speaks. "Wow, Mom, glad to see you haven't lost your spunk." Her daughter walks into the room, followed closely by her husband.

Katherine turns to her husband. "Asshole."

Those in the room erupt with laughter.

CHAPTER 85

The Peterson home

A night disrupted by gunfire and death ended with the most passionate lovemaking Zeke had ever experienced. He stirs awake before the sun breaks on the horizon. One more grim job weighs on his mind. He slides from beneath the covers and slips on his clothes and carries his boots in hand as he tiptoes from the room. He eases open the door to the second bedroom and pads across the floor to stir Carl awake. While Carl dresses, Zeke pulls on his boots and steps outside to stir the coals in the fire pit.

He avoids looking at the dead man lying in the yard.

After adding a couple of logs to the fire, he pours water into the coffeepot and sets it next to the coals to warm. Carl pushes through the screen door and eases it closed. He turns and brakes to a halt when he spies the body.

Zeke approaches and says in a whisper, "They need to be gone before the kids get up."

Carl nods, his head still wrapped in the sling.

He takes Carl by the elbow and propels him past the body, where they huddle close together.

"I'm open to suggestions," Zeke says.

Carl pantomimes a digging motion.

"Digging a grave big enough for three bodies will take us most of the day."

Carl shrugs. "I'm new to all this, Zeke," he manages to say.

"I hate like hell to disrespect the dead, even if I'm the one who did the killing. But we need a speedier solution. I'm thinking of tying them together and using Murphy to drag them as far away as possible."

"Whatever," Carl mumbles, not meeting Zeke's eye. It comes out "wha-evuh."

"Look at me, Carl."

Carl slowly looks up to meet Zeke's stare.

"I need you to be okay with this because I can't do it alone."

Carl nods, but then he's overcome by an intense anger, thinking about what might have happened. "Fuck 'em." It comes out "fa 'em."

Zeke says no more as they head toward the barn. He slips the bit into Murphy's mouth and throws on the saddle blanket. Carl tosses on the saddle and Zeke cinches it tight. They scour the barn for available rope and find enough to do the job. Zeke leads Murphy from the barn and stops near the two men he killed. The horse balks at the coppery scent of the blood that has soaked into the earth. Zeke strokes the horse's withers and whispers softly to him. He hands the reins to Carl and rolls the two dead men together.

Carl does his best not to look, but he does. He sees two unrecognizable faces. He whips the sling from his head and vomits onto the grass.

"Coyotes," Zeke says. He lashes the ankles together

and ties the rope off on the saddle horn. He takes the reins and leads Murphy over to the third man. Zeke quickly lashes the ringleader to his sons.

With a cluck of his tongue and a gentle pull of the reins, Murphy lurches forward. The three men are heavy and the horse strains to get the three bodies moving. Zeke leads him around the barn and he tells Carl to run ahead and open the gate so that the horse won't have to stop. Murphy drags the bodies down the ridge and through the grove of oak trees at a slow walk until they arrive at another fence.

Zeke stops and looks back toward the house. "See if you can find a gate, Carl. We need to move them as far as we can."

Carl walks along the fence line, searching. Midway down he finds an old barbed wire gate held up by wooden poles. He unties the baling wire holding the near post and pulls the gate open. Zeke restarts the horse.

They traverse another hill and at the bottom Zeke spots a thicket of persimmon bushes and steers Murphy that way. At the brush line he has to tug on the reins to get the horse to step through the brush. When they're deep enough in, Zeke halts the horse and unties the rope from the saddle horn.

Carl makes a coiling motion with his hands. "Rope?"

"Leave it." He goads Murphy back through the thick brush and they begin the return journey to the house. Carl turns to glance back, but Zeke walks steadily forward.

They spend four more days at Summer's home. Zeke bagged a deer on the third day and they feasted for a third night, another night where everyone went to bed with full stomachs. On the fifth morning, Zeke's up early to prepare the horses for travel. No doubt his parents are beside themselves with worry. The only way they'll know the rest of their family is safe is by Zeke and the rest showing up at their door.

His emotions are all over the place. Summer and he experienced some very tender, exquisite moments—moments Zeke hasn't had in his life in a long, long time. Maybe never. He continues to beg Summer to come with them, but her fear of abandoning her daughter is insurmountable. With sadness, he finishes saddling and leads all three horses up to the house.

Carl is doing much better, and Emma and Noah are excited to see their grandma and grandpa. Ruth steps out on the porch and offers Zeke a hug of encouragement. He hands her Murphy's reins and steps into the house.

Tears are drifting down Summer's face, matching the ones falling from his own eyes.

"We can leave a note and I promise we'll come back down here as soon as the power is back on," he says.

She tiptoes up to kiss him. "A piece of Aubrey is here, Zeke. I would wake up every day wondering if she and my father had made it home. That's not fair to you."

"I don't care about fair. If I thought Carl and Ruth could find their way to the truck I'd stay here in a heartbeat."

"Just make sure they make it home, Zeke. They need to be safe." She wraps her arms around him and he encircles his around her. "Come back if you can?"

Zeke nods and backhands the tears from his cheek. They stand like that for as long as possible. He leans down and the two share one last tender kiss. He removes the locket from around his neck and carefully withdraws the small picture of Amelia. He tucks the picture into his front pocket and slips the chain and locket over Summer's head. With no further words, he breaks away and makes his way out to the porch. Still leaking tears, he shuffles across the gravel drive and slips his foot into the stirrup, pulling himself aboard Murphy. With foolish anger he wheels the horse around and walks him out to the road. He looks back to make sure everyone is following, and catches sight of Summer standing on the porch. His heart breaks a little more as he nudges Murphy down the road.

Zeke is sullen as they ride throughout the day. The sun is out, the sky is a brilliant blue, but he takes no notice. He's confined to his misery. They stop for short breaks along the way, and he finds more of the little streams, this time with water, for the horses to drink from. In his self-imposed anger, he sets a fairly brisk pace and they make it to where the truck is parked as darkness begins replacing the light.

With Ruth's help, Zeke gets the horses unsaddled and loaded into the trailer. The kids are in the backseat with their father and Ruth takes the seat in front. Zeke retrieves the keys from where he had hidden them and rams them in the ignition. Before he can turn the key to start the engine, Ruth reaches over and puts a hand on his arm.

"Go back to her, Zeke," she says in a soft voice.

He sighs and leans back in the seat.

"We can get home from here, Zeke. You've done your part by rescuing us from Dallas. You've done enough."

He turns to face his sister.

"Go rescue yourself, Zeke."

He opens the truck door and walks to the back of the trailer. Ruth helps him separate Murphy from the other horses and also helps him resaddle him. Before he mounts up, Zeke gives his sister a long hug. Damn if they're both not crying, him for the second time today.

"Tell Mom and Dad that I love them and I'll see them soon. And tell the kids to take good care of Lexi," he says as he pulls onto Murphy's back. Zeke gives him a nudge with his heels and turns to wave bye to Ruth and Carl, Emma and Noah. They disappear into the darkness of night.

Three Years Later

CHAPTER 86

London Heathrow Airport

The relationship between Captain Steve Henderson and copilot Cheryl Wilson had soured after working so well to land their injured plane without serious injury to any of the passengers. The strain of being stranded in a foreign country so far from home finally took its toll. They had stayed together long enough to reach London, but parted shortly after. Now, in a cruel twist of fate, Captain Henderson and newly appointed captain Cheryl Wilson are scheduled to fly one of the first flights back to the United States.

After the power was restored, the pilots were forced to attend a monthlong immersion in flight simulation along with refresher courses in the classroom. Once completed, the flight crews spent some time flying the empty aircraft after each plane had undergone a very thorough inspection. The two had encountered each other during the training sessions, but never with enough time to rehash the old hurts. But today they're going to be confined in the small cockpit for at least nine hours.

Captain Henderson arrives early and threads his way through the growing crowds, down the Jetway, and into the cockpit. Three years since he had last sat in the cockpit of a plane that was going to be carrying live human beings. His last flight was one he hopes to put out of his mind forever.

He turns when he feels someone step aboard and sees Cheryl Wilson removing her hat. She steps into the cockpit and takes the right-hand seat.

"Good morning, Captain," she says in a chilly voice.

"Good morning to you, Captain."

"How long until we push back?"

"We'll start loading in the next ten minutes. We're scheduled to spin the engines in thirty."

"Good," Captain Cheryl Wilson replies as she reaches for the preflight checklist in the side pocket of the chair.

"Do you want to talk about it?" Captain Henderson says.

"About what?"

"Never mind," he says, already counting the hours down until they can once more separate.

CHAPTER 87

The Oval Office

Due to the national crisis and after some constitutional wrangling, President Paul Harris is five and a half years into his four-year term. Without electricity any thoughts of having an election were snuffed out. The next presidential election is scheduled for next year, but President Harris has already announced he would not seek reelection. Three years of the worst struggle the world has ever known have taken their toll.

He strides into the Oval Office, where the bright rays of the sun again paint shadows on the handmade carpet. One of his first acts, after the power returned, was to have the heavy steel panels hauled out of the office and shipped off to a scrapyard. Chief of Staff Scott Alexander is following a short distance behind and arrives at the desk as the President takes his seat.

"Paul, are you sure you don't want to run for another term? Hell, the campaign would be a cakewalk for you," he says as he sits in the chair flanking the desk.

"Scott, how many times do I have to say no? I'm tired and I just want to go home with my wife, maybe do a little fishing, spend some time on the golf course. My time in the White House has felt like two decades. One and a half is enough for me." He quickly changes the subject. "What do we have today?"

"FEMA Director Donald Carter should be here momentarily. The new Iranian ambassador has requested a meeting for this afternoon," Scott replies while looking over the schedule book.

"Put him off for a day or two until I can get up to speed on what's happening over there. General Safani still in charge?"

"Last time I heard, and that was yesterday. So far he has resisted all provocations to allow another supreme leader to take charge."

"I guess that makes him our friend, doesn't it."

The intercom buzzes. "Mr. President, Director Carter is here."

"Send him in, please." The President stands from behind the desk and meets him halfway across the room. "Let's sit over here, Don," he says, waving to the sofas.

They each take a seat on opposite sides of the coffee table. "Coffee, if you want it," he says, pointing at the table. "Scott, come on over here and join us."

Scott ambles over and takes a seat at the far end of the sofa.

The President pours coffee for all three. "Okay, Don, where are we on restoration?"

"About ninety percent of the country is back to full power. I don't know what you said to the South Koreans, but they're a godsend. The other ten percent will be restored soon, probably within the month. Some high-line issues, I believe. Something you would expect after three years of nonuse."

"Don, you did a fantastic job on everything."

"Thank you, sir. It's been a team effort, but we still have a ways to go."

President Harris leans back, coffee cup in hand. "What about communications?"

"If you haven't noticed, we are being treated to some incredible light shows in the night sky as all the dead satellites fall from their orbits. The landline phone system is up and functioning almost nationwide, but cellular service is probably at least two years away. NASA is working around the clock to launch replacement satellites, but it's an arduous process. There are several private space companies that are also working to launch all types of satellites: communication, weather, and even broadcast television."

"Frankly, I hope the restoration of the cellular networks takes longer," President Harris says. "Do you know how nice it is to pass someone in the hall who actually says hello, rather than ignore your existence, busily thumbing through their smartphones? It's refreshing."

"I agree, sir. We're actually enjoying live conversations with our children instead of the constant text messages. But at some point we'll need to reestablish service—cell phones are too big a part of our daily lives."

"How long before I can watch ESPN, Don?" Alexander says.

Both President Harris and Director Carter chuckle at his comment. "I know. It's like when we were kids," the President says, "back when we had only two or three channels to watch."

The FEMA director takes a sip of coffee. "My children can't understand how anyone could have survived without cable television. But, to answer your question, Scott, soon, I hope. The National Football League is hoping to resume play as soon as possible but I can't imagine they would do it without satellite television. All of the networks are spending through the nose to speed up the satellite-building process."

President Harris leans forward and places his coffee

cup on the table. "On a more serious note, Don, are all the water and sewage facilities up and operating?"

"Yes, sir. That was priority one, and I'm glad to say we accomplished it quickly."

"Don, you've earned yourself a long vacation," the President says as he stands from the sofa. He shakes Don's hand again and walks him to the door.

As he turns to go back to his desk, Scott says, "Paul, what if I find you a running mate that will take some of—"

The President stops in his tracks and gives his chief of staff an angry glare.

Chapter 88

The home of Dr. Samuel Blake

The power in Boulder is slowly returning, but it's intermittent at best. Numerous power lines were downed over the three-year period, the heavy snow collapsing poles all over the city, including the larger transmission lines that bisect the Rocky Mountains. The Space Weather Prediction Center is still mothballed because with no satellites in orbit there is little to do, but there are discussions about a reopening sometime in the future.

The ringing of the telephone interrupts the romantic dinner that Sam and a very pregnant Kaylee Connor are enjoying. "Let it go to voice mail," Kaylee says.

"Are you kidding? The damn thing hasn't worked for three years and you want me to let it go to voice mail?" He stands from the table and races across the kitchen to answer.

"Hello?" He listens, then says, "Yes, she's sitting here with me."

Kaylee arches her brow and stands, wobbling into the kitchen.

Sam slowly hands her the phone. "The New York City

Police Department." He stands next to Kaylee, one arm wrapped around her as she listens.

Tears begin to leak from her beautiful eyes, and Sam knows his fears have been realized. They had failed to connect with Kaylee's parents after numerous attempts.

Kaylee, now openly sobbing, hands the phone to Sam and turns away. Sam takes a moment to write down the contact information of the caller before joining Kaylee, curled up on the sofa.

"What happened?" he says gently.

She wipes the tears from her face and Sam allows her time to compose herself.

Kaylee sniffles and reaches her hand out, grasping Sam's hand as if it were a lifeline. "In the process of reopening the hospitals in New York"—she pauses to wipe away more tears—"they found the remains of my parents in one of the abandoned medical buildings."

Sam slides closer to her and wraps her in his arms.

"They found my father's wallet among the remains." She pauses again and turns to stare at the darkness lurking beyond the windows. "My dad had one of my business cards in his wallet. They've been trying to track me down for the last couple of days."

"I'm very sorry," Sam says, pulling her closer.

Kaylee, still sobbing, turns angry. "My God, they died all alone in some godforsaken place."

Sam reaches up to wipe the tears from her cheek.

"They've been . . ." She turns her gaze to the flames dancing in the fireplace. "They've been dead for a long time," she whispers.

"I'm so sorry, Kaylee."

"No wonder they didn't answer their phone."

Sam holds her and rocks her until all of the tears have dried.

Sometime later Kaylee reaches down and rubs her hand over her belly. “Can we name the child after one of my parents?” she asks.

“Of course. I think that would be a good way to honor their memory.”

They sit on the sofa holding each other as their dinner grows cold and the fire in the fireplace burns to ashes.

CHAPTER 89

The Peterson home

It's a beautiful spring day when Zeke leads Aubrey outside to Summer's car. She and Summer's father arrived back home almost a month ago, but the last month has been a period of adjustment for everyone. More so for Aubrey, who had to adjust to Zeke being in her mother's life.

The schools remain closed because a sufficient number of teachers can't be found to staff them all. He's taking advantage of the opportunity by taking Summer and Aubrey to meet his family, the first time Zeke will have seen them in over three years. They have talked on the telephone but they have yet to meet his new family.

After buckling Aubrey in, he puts her suitcase in the trunk and turns to help Summer, her arms loaded down with a car seat and their two-year-old son. Jacob is a beautiful redheaded little boy, full of rambunctious energy and always on the go. He already has Summer's father wrapped around his little finger. Aubrey wasn't sure what to make of her new brother when she first arrived home. When she left, her mother was in the ending stages of divorce. Just in the past week Aubrey's gotten more comfortable with all the changes, actually taking time to play with Jacob on occasion.

It takes Zeke a while, but he finally gets the car seat buckled in. Although the power is slowly returning, it has taken a month of continuous around-the-clock work for road crews to remove the abandoned vehicles from the roadways. According to the local news, the only news they get, all of the cars are being towed to an immense field north of Dallas in case the owners ever want to reclaim them. His guess is they'll rot there while the insurance companies try to honor their policies by replacing them.

Summer hands him Jacob and it takes him even longer to get the toddler strapped into the damn contraption. Aubrey sighs, but reaches over to help. Summer walks back to her father and gives him an extra-long hug. She breaks the embrace and gives him a peck on the cheek before turning and skipping to the car.

They're happy. Extremely happy.

She climbs in and buckles her seat belt. Zeke starts the car as she brushes her curly red mop from her face and slips on her sunglasses. He puts the car in gear and eases down the gravel drive. She reaches her hand over, interlaces her fingers with his, and graces him with the most beautiful smile he's ever seen.

GREAT BOOKS, GREAT SAVINGS!

When You Visit Our Website:

www.kensingtonbooks.com

You Can Save Money Off The Retail Price Of Any Book You Purchase!

- **All Your Favorite Kensington Authors**
- **New Releases & Timeless Classics**
- **Overnight Shipping Available**
- **eBooks Available For Many Titles**
- **All Major Credit Cards Accepted**

Visit Us Today To Start Saving!

www.kensingtonbooks.com

All Orders Are Subject To Availability.
Shipping and Handling Charges Apply.
Offers and Prices Subject To Change Without Notice.

Tim Washburn graduated from the University of Oklahoma with a BA in Journalism and currently lives in Edmond, Oklahoma.

UPC
0 32097 00999 4
03653

NOTHING CAN PREPARE YOU...

It strikes without warning. A massive geomagnetic solar storm that destroys every power grid in the northern hemisphere. North America is without lights, electricity, phones, and navigation systems. In one week, the human race is flung back to the Dark Ages.

NOTHING CAN SAVE YOU...

In Boulder, Colorado, weather technicians watch in horror as civilization collapses around them. Planes are falling out of the skies. Cars are dead. Pandemonium and terror grip the Northern Hemisphere. As nuclear reactors across North America face inevitable meltdowns, the U.S. President remains powerless in a heavily guarded White House. From London to Boston to Anchorage, there is no food, no water, no hope. It's every man for himself...and it will only get worse.

SURVIVAL IS EVERYTHING.

Only one man—army veteran Zeke Marshall—is prepared to handle a nightmare like this. But when he tries to reunite with his family in Dallas—across a lawless terrain as deadly as any battlefield—he discovers there are worse things in life than war. And there are terrible and unthinkable things he'll have to do to survive...

"WASHBURN BRINGS US A FRESH VOICE AND A NEW KIND OF TERROR."—Marc Cameron, bestselling author of *National Security* and *Day Zero*

"LIKE A NUCLEAR REACTOR, THIS STORY HEATS UP FAST! THE PAGES FLY BY...AND THE UNEXPECTED IS WAITING AROUND THE NEXT CORNER."
—Anderson Harp, author of *Retribution* and *Born of War*

Visit us at www.kensingtonbooks.com

ISBN-13: 978-0-7860-3653-0
ISBN-10: 0-7860-3653-2

PINNACLE
U.S.$9.99
CAN $10.99
PRINTED IN U.S.A.